OF STARS • BOOK ONE

A
SHIFTING
OF
STARS

KATHY
KIMBRAY

PRAISE FOR A SHIFTING OF STARS

"A thrilling adventure in a lushly imagined world—Kathy Kimbray is an exciting new voice in fantasy!"

—Kara Thomas, author of The Darkest Corners,
Little Monsters and The Cheerleaders

"With its lyrical prose, romance, and passionate storytelling, readers are sure to fall in love with A Shifting of Stars and be left eager for more."

—Mindee Arnett, author of Avalon,
The Arkwell Academy series, and Onyx and Ivory

"Poignant, exciting, and smart, A Shifting of Stars contains an intricately sewn world full of intrigue that will leave readers hungry for what happens next."

—Sarah Harian, author of Eight Will Fall and
The Chaos Theory series

FOR MATT

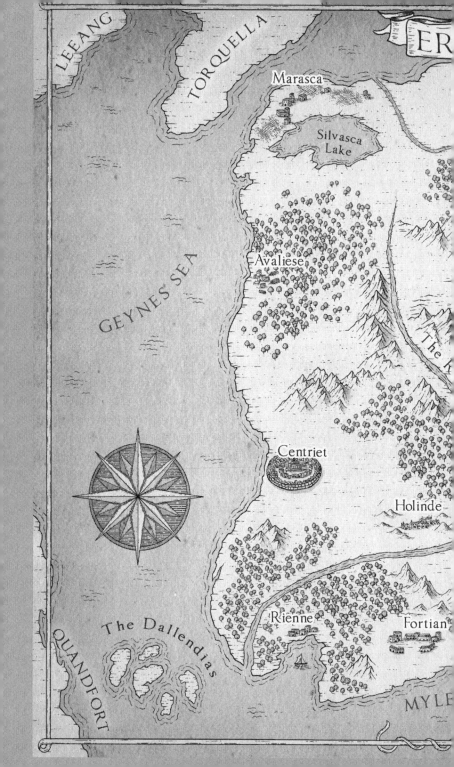

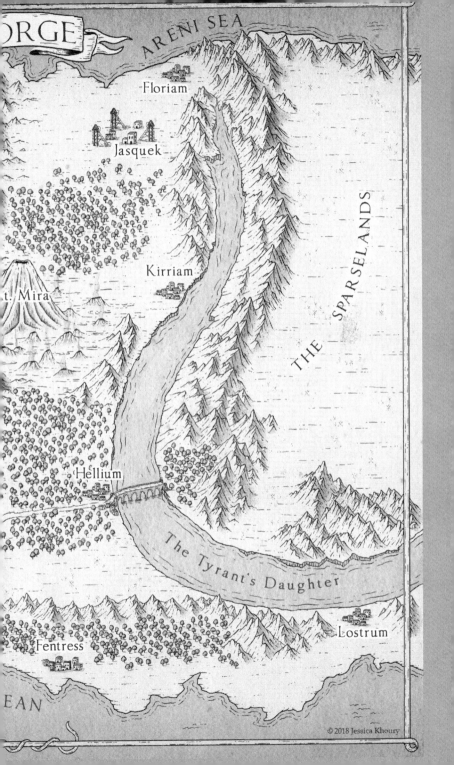

CHAPTER ONE

I SHOULD NOT BE HERE. I'M FOREIGN TO THIS VILLAGE OF BROKEN rooftops and dull stone walls. I brush my fingers over a pillar. Its coldness burns my skin, makes me pause.

Go home.

The words sing loud like a taunt as moonlight slithers across my shoulders. The parchment digs like thorns in my palm. I imagine its shape, every fiber and ink blot.

Something moves near my feet and I jump. It's just a rat, one of hordes from the city. They've grown bolder during these past few seasons, always darting out of alleys and running by arches, desperate—like us—to fill their bellies.

As it squeaks away, nails tapping in rhythm, I inspect the darkened street before me. Lamplight glows from a crooked post, but the shadows are still and the windows are empty. A leaf-strewn house looms in the distance, enticing me over the cobblestone ground. That house is the reason I've ventured so late into this weary part of town. Beside me, buildings cringe with moss. Walkways glisten with dirty puddles. Teetering balconies slouch from walls with garments strung between casements like cobwebs.

But that smell.

I halt to sniff the air. It wafts from the dwelling ahead of me. It winds from beneath its splintered panes—the pungent scent of broth and ale.

I wish it were stew.

Saliva brims on my tongue at the thought of meat cooked with spices and oils. The last time venison passed my lips, my mother was alive, my father smiled, and the future stretched before us, unending. Those were the days of Emperor Komran, a king who lived and bled for his people. I barely remember the white of his beard or how he limped through the fields during harvest. And it's the same with my mother. I'm losing her, too. The curve of her cheek. The shade of her tresses. When she died, we set her afloat in the Geynes, and I sat on the bank with my toes in the water, not wanting to break that connection to her.

It's a year tonight.

My chest starts to cave, but I fight and I fight to be still, to not cry. At least the dead are not hungry, not in turmoil. They do not see what Centriet has become.

I urge my feet toward the house. Komran would never have driven me here. When he reigned, our streets were routinely swept, and fountains dotted the well-kept pavements.

And medicine was—

A loose stone clacks. Forgetting my thoughts, I dart to an alcove. Since Komran's son became our emperor, soldiers lurk where you'd least expect them.

In the dark, I steady my breaths, in and out. Not that I'm breaking any laws—that I know of. I listen to the night: crickets chirping, a soft breeze, and the whinny of a horse that's so indistinct, perhaps it's from Sledloe, the next village over.

I wait longer, just to be safe. Many of the soldiers are kind, though not all. Father says they've been granted more powers, but that we won't know what it means for a while.

I hate not knowing. Just like tonight. I hate not knowing what awaits in the house. When the street remains silent, I rejoin the road, but my ankles wobble when I try to walk.

So I jog.

It soothes my jangled nerves, and I reach the house, breathless and flushed. Planks board the four square windows; rust from the nails seeps into the woodgrain. The stones are all different sizes and shapes, charred by the remnants of a long-ago fire. Ivy clings to the rutted surface, its end pieces curling like ribbon from the door.

You should leave, Meadow.

But I raise my fist. All I need to do is knock. I've already abandoned my stonebrick at dusk without letting Father know where I have gone. The loss of my mother hits me anew—the pain a reminder of why I have come here. That I've come to move on, to at last let her go. Even though I'm not sure what that means anymore.

Or if I can.

"Are you here for the Gathering?"

The question shatters the bracing air. Someone's behind me and I spin to face him, shrouding myself with my long dark hair. But I'm wrong. There are two. One's tall and strapping. The other is smaller in every way. As they chance another step, I notice that they're young—about my age, seventeen.

"Why I'm here is not your concern," I say.

"We do beg your pardon," the smaller boy says. He has a scar on his brow like a cutlass. And another on his forearm, dark as molasses. He gestures to the vacant street behind him. "Have you ever visited Yahres before?"

"Yes," I say, though my words are false. It's safer to make them believe I'm a local.

"And your name?" asks the boy, but I shake my head at the same time his companion lets out a grunt.

"Don't bother," he snaps. "We leave tomorrow."

The smaller boy nods, looking slightly embarrassed.

"We watched you for a bit," he tells me.

"And what did you see?" I ask.

He smiles. One of his teeth is chipped. "We assumed you'd turn back many times."

My pulse quickens at their presumption, especially since it's mostly true. The slums of Yahres are outside the walls. My home lies inside in the village of Maytown. In Maytown we're warned to always tread wisely in places like Yahres, Florian, and Sledloe. Perhaps that's why I'd appeared so unsure. Yet neither of the pair looks remarkably dangerous.

"You proved us wrong," the boy continues.

"No hard feelings," I say.

He laughs. "Come inside with us."

He holds out a hand, but I back away.

"Forgive me," he says, withdrawing swiftly, color blotching his cheeks. "We lodge with the man who hosts these gatherings . . . and I noticed you had a parchment to read."

"You saw?" I jolt, clutching it tightly, blood surging through my legs and arms. Since Mother's passing, it happens quite often. My heart beats fast, and I need to run.

"You don't have to read it," he says.

I swallow.

"Although you can if you want to, of course. Unless you didn't come here for the Gathering?"

"I doubt she's here for anything else."

It's much too hard to read his expression, but the taller boy speaks with a dash of disdain. He sidesteps his friend with two no-nonsense strides.

"You don't know my business," I say.

"Oh, please." He comes in close, reaching past me, and the scent of leather and steel is intense. It reminds me of sitting in my father's workroom when he's mending quivers for the elder archers. The boy raps on the door with his knuckles. Three times, then nothing. The way we're supposed to. "Of course you're here for the Gathering," he says, as metal grinds and a peephole opens.

My need to bolt escalates.

"Get in. You're the last," says the face inside. The

cumbersome timber shifts outward before us. It breaks the leaves and they flutter in spirals.

"After you," the tall boy says.

The parchment feels like a stone in my hand. It dawns on me how stifled this is—this narrow black corridor, deep in the kingdom.

I brush the still-dangling leaves to one side. The passageway stretches a good twenty paces. I could perish in there and no one would find me.

"Are you waiting for something?"

"No," I say.

Ignoring the boy, I stoop to enter, trying to focus my thoughts on the brickwork. The blocks have eroded from years of scuffing. They smell like lichen and tarnished copper. Light spills through the distant doorframe, and our guide clears his throat to urge us on. I double my pace, though the boys hang back. The weight of their presence behind me is strong.

The end of the hall yields a wider room, filled with scattered tables and benches. People loiter, holding dishes and goblets. They're facing a box that's been chiseled from sandbrick.

No one comments on my arrival. I wonder from where these people hail. Some could be fish-bearing merchants from the docks. Others—farmers, blacksmiths, and scribes. I press my back to the rough wall, comforted by the cool surface. I sneak a glance at the two boys who have just emerged from the gloomy hallway. I've never seen them before tonight. Not at market, not hunting in the neighboring woods. The smaller one folds himself against a pillar, his brown hair falling across his forehead. He unfastens a satchel from across his torso and drops it to the floor by his boots. The taller one sits on the edge of a table, the lamplight skittering off his blond head. They request two plates, and I'm instantly jealous when they're given two bowls of steaming broth. I'm about to ask for my own dish, when a man steps onto the sandbrick cube. His brows hang low and his mouth is tight, but he spreads his arms to include us all.

I do a swift head count. There's forty of us here.

"Welcome," he says. "I am Freedom Jove."

A gentle murmur sweeps the room. Of course "Freedom Jove" is not his name. But this night is not about who we are when the sun shines upon us, exposed to the world.

Freedom Jove blesses the soup. He blesses the heavily watered ale. As he does, I notice paper and hessian stuck to the windows like ill-fitting drapes.

"It is pleasing to see so many new faces." Freedom's pupils flash like gems. His intensity doesn't complement the gray hair that points up and out in all directions. He clasps his hands and the knuckles whiten. The pressure causes his wrists to shake. "I welcome you all to the Gathering of Wordsmiths. A place for stories, for poetry, for expression . . ."

Squeezing my parchment, I glance at the ceiling where lanterns swing from hooks and chain ropes. I scarcely recall what I wrote about Mother. I'd scribbled free-form in the colorless moonlight. I hadn't imagined I'd come here tonight, even though my friend Anai said that I should. She said that expressing my grief would be best—that somehow speaking to a cottage full of strangers would lift the veil, would start me anew.

I should have told her to jump in the Geynes; but it's too late now to scuttle for the door. Besides, I need to release my sorrow. To reclaim my spirit. To make things better. Since losing Mother, I've barely slept, never mind being able to rise with the sun. I've missed so many days at the markets that my father has often picked up my slack, working longer than he should to bring in more coin.

And it has to stop. He shouldn't have to do that. It should be me who looks after him.

Out front, Jove holds up an open palm. "Please lend your ears to our first orator."

The smaller boy.

No one applauds. They stand and wait, slurping their soup.

The boy removes a scroll from his satchel as if he has done this one hundred times. As he weaves his way to the sandbrick platform, I'm handed a bowl of cabbage broth. I join in the slurping, but still watch the boy, curious to know what he'll talk about.

Hopefully something trivial.

Trivial might calm my racing heart. I blow on my soup, but when I glance sideways, the taller boy glares with a gaze of blue frost.

My cheeks burn. He doesn't speak, but his eyes narrow, so I turn to the sandbrick. Becoming a target in Yahres is foolish in the middle of the night, as a girl without escort.

The smaller boy unrolls his parchment. He clears his throat, wets his lower lip. For an instant my hopes for the trivial depart. Perhaps he has substance I've not yet detected.

"I call this piece: 'Endless Love,'" he says.

Maybe not.

He slowly begins. It's a tale of two children who've grown up together. They frolic in the river, hold hands, and watch sunsets, before eventually marrying at the age of nineteen.

And when he's finished telling the story, the applause rebounds from the unvarnished rafters. From his smile, you'd swear he'd just won a joust.

It's what I feared about this gathering.

No one wants to hear about sadness. People don't care for the sorrow of strangers. They long for a future that's haloed by roses. To believe in the beauty of sunsets and lovers.

That escape down the hallway is suddenly attractive, but I battle against the urge—and win. I did, after all, come to Yahres for a reason.

Freedom points in my direction. "Young lady, have you prepared a piece?"

I'm caught mid-slurp, but manage a nod. I feel the eyes of the boys on my back as I put down my bowl with a too-hard thud. Smoothing my tunic, I think of Anai. She told me that no one would judge or make fun. Her cousin Caric used to frequent these gatherings before he took work sorting fish on the wharves.

With that in mind, I pick a path to the sandbrick, nimbly twisting between silhouettes. Jove helps me onto the platform, and I unwrap my scribbled-on parchment, eyes down. I draw in air to read my tribute.

"I call this piece 'In Grief,'" I say.

My eyes pass over the words I've written: *I still miss my mother every day.*

And I do. I *do*. But how do I say this? I suck in a breath to calm myself. In my head, I read the words again: *She was sick last year and we couldn't save her.*

My body shakes.

We couldn't save her.

Hot tears form, but I wipe them away. It's not the truth—not in its entirety. It conjures the image of a far-gone woman, whose death was a clear-cut, unavoidable fate. And I don't want to speak to this room full of people and dishonor her memory by letting them think that. It wasn't her time to be plucked from existence. It wasn't her moment to be taken from me. And all of a sudden, I want them to *know*. I want them to know the truth—the real truth. The pain I've never uttered in public because it wasn't the safe thing to do.

Folding the parchment, I look at the faces, pale against the black of the old battered stonework.

"I call this piece 'The Choice,'" I correct, not sure what I'm saying—or why I can't stop it. "It's about a woman whose name was Pearl. She was a mother who lived in a city. This city was tainted by an unjust ruler, who thought it was nothing to thieve people's money and invest it in blood sports for his own private pleasure." I pause, noting the sudden chill, noting that people have put down their bowls. Forty staring bodies now feel like thousands. Yet the silence is worse. It makes the room grow.

"Pearl grew very sick," I rush on. "One moment, she was

healthy. The next, she was not. Yet there was nothing her family could do. Her fever heightened. It consumed her body."

The tall blond boy slides off the table. Three paces and he's standing in the shadows by the wall.

The voice in my head sings out in alarm: *Stop, Meadow. Stop!*

Yet I do it.

For *her*.

"Imported zyphene could have saved Pearl's life." I stand up straighter, even though my voice trembles. "Yet the herbs had not been imported by the ruler because he'd squandered the money already. He squandered it building his useless arenas. Arenas to house the deaths of his foes. He paraded them like animals, locked them inside and relished in the sand turning red beneath their heels."

Gladiator matches. They're our new emperor's favorite. Pitting the weak against stronger opponents.

"When Pearl passed away," I tell the Gathering, "her family sank into deep depression."

The blond boy still watches me. I can see the whites of his eyes in the shade.

"They had no power," I continue. "But they had a choice— one that needed to be made."

I remember my mother's final days, how she squeezed my wrist and smiled through her pain. The beads of sweat rolled past her ears, soaking her nightdress, the reed bed, and linen. We fed her yarrow from the fields by the river, but the grittiness made her cough through the night.

"Meadow," she told me. "Look after your father."

And then, she was gone.

Forty-five years erased.

Blown from this world to the other side.

"The choice Pearl's family made was simple." I bite back the panic that tenses my tongue. "They decided to reject the ruler's blood sports by opting never to sit in the stands. At first, their neighbors thought they were senseless. Tournaments promised free food and drink. And broth made not only from offcuts and entrails, but mountains of beef, glazed chicken, and fish . . . and bountiful vegetables from every season."

Nobody speaks or moves or breathes, but I must say the rest while I'm here, while I can.

"The choice to boycott is ours," I say. "It's *yours*."

My bitterness hangs in the room.

The silence gapes, and I get it. I do. These storytelling nights are supposed to be fiction. A gathering of people with creative souls. Not this. Not me standing up here, loudly decrying the will of our emperor.

I dip my crown, forcing a breath, then disembark from the edge of the sandbrick. The lack of applause rings in my ears.

Freedom Jove is quick to stand up. "My apologies . . . Our next orator—"

"With respect, please allow me to volunteer." A man with a black beard raises his arm and Jove moves aside.

"By all means, my friend."

Jove scurries away from the stage, his shoulders heaving up and down, up and down. No one looks as I wander past tables, desperate to feel some support . . . from *anyone*. Even the blond boy pretends I have vanished. So does his friend with the tousled brown hair. Dread consumes me as I slink to the hallway. I've made a mistake. I shouldn't have done this.

Instead, I should have—

"Wait, don't leave!"

The words slap my back and I halt, mid-step.

"Your story of Pearl has inspired my tale. Please do not vacate this gathering just yet."

Quaking, I turn to stare at the speaker. It's the black-bearded man who is perched on the sandbrick.

"My piece is called 'Unjust Ruler,'" he says. "And thanks to you, I can finally share it."

"You can't!" says Jove.

"I can," says the man, holding him off with a pointed finger. Though his eyes are misty, relief floods through me. "If it bothers you, do not stay," he says.

Jove backs up but doesn't leave, while the man reassumes his rigid stance. Part of me understands Jove's objections. The will to be safe. To pull your neck in. But after a while, the resentment ignites. A little spark grows and cannot be snuffed. As I look to the man, I see it within him. The same need as I had is now springing forth.

His story begins with a tyrannical leader who came to power after Emperor Komran. Thoughts fail me, words even more so, as his yarn unfurls, so similar to mine. His is a tale of a wife lost in childbirth because the healer in his hamlet was ill. His is the tale of a child without medicine, who cried until, at last, she lay still. My heart breaks to know what he's been through, to know that his life once burst with color.

"The choice to boycott the Tournament is yours!" He bellows my message with startling vigor.

I nestle my spine against the wall, scanning the features of the watching crowd. As the man continues, it begins to happen. Small nods here and there. Lips bitten. Eyes wide. On the strength of this, the man rallies—and it's then I hear another sound in the mix. It takes me a moment to decipher its origin.

Not inside, but outside.

Then *inside*.

I freeze.

It's the scraping of something like wood against stone, like some great mass being dragged across pavement. A slight puff of air follows behind it, and then it's the pounding: *One, two. One, two.*

Footsteps?

I jolt at the realization.

FOOTSTEPS IN THE HALL!

"Stop talking!" I yell, but the man does not hear me. I'm next to the corridor, too far from them all.

He continues to speak in his rich, lilting voice, growing grander and louder and full of deep passion.

"Stop!" I scream, but the audience cheers. They've come alive at the very worst moment.

A silver-tipped arrow shoots past my head. It slices the chest of the black-bearded man. With an awful stillness, he blinks like a cod as blood soaks his clothes, trails down to the ground.

People shriek as the soldiers appear, pouring from the hall like spiders. Their weapons glint in the muted light. Swords and machetes and daggers, raised skyward. They secure the room, spreading up and down aisles, immune to the black-bearded man's final pleas. Their gray-and-red uniforms reveal their allegiance to the emperor of Erraforge: Ladislas.

A towering archer steps from the hallway. His sleeves are marred by sweat stains and dust. He lowers the bow beside his hip, adjusting the quiver across his shoulders. Beside him stands a slender youth with black hair offset by angular features. His entitled posture smothers the chamber, although he is scarcely older than me.

Prince Malthe.

Ladislas's firstborn. A breastplate crushes his grubby white tunic.

"How sad," he says, "that my company of men should perceive a disturbance on our return from Rienne." His brown boots beat the stones in displeasure as he surveys the surrounds with a thin, curled lip. "So we dismount our horses, and what do we hear? A room full of citizens from Erraforge, no less, spouting poisonous accusations against the Tyjans!"

We fall to our knees, our foreheads to the cobbles, to show our respect to the emperor's son.

"Which of you owns this establishment?" he asks.

No one answers.

"Who owns it?" he barks.

"I do, Your Highness." It's Freedom Jove.

"Cut out his heart then," Prince Malthe orders.

"No, please! Let me explain! Despite what you heard, we gather in peace!" My head snaps up to see Freedom Jove waving his arms to ward off the soldiers. His cheeks match the ashen shade of his hair. "We only tell stories and poetry, I promise!"

Malthe quirks his brow. "You *only* tell stories? Yet they're stories of treason to insult my father? Poems to paint him as Centriet's fool? Is that why you gather when the sun has departed?"

"No!" wails Jove.

"See what happens to traitors?" Malthe flings his arm at the man on the sandbrick. He's slumped, headfirst, in a pool of red. The tip of the arrow has sheared through his backbone.

"It was her!" yells Jove. "She is the traitor!"

I scrunch the parchment in a ball. Breathe out.

"It was her who spoke of treason this night. *She* is the one you should see about."

"And who is *she*?" Prince Malthe combs the room. If he locates my scribblings, I may appear guilty. I curl my body into the darkness—one leg, then the other, no sudden movements—like a fawn eluding a huntsman's blade.

"There! She's there! At the corridor's entrance!"

My heart explodes inside my chest. I'm not ready to join my mother just yet, not ready to tell her I died without cause. As Malthe's features slide to meet mine, I drop the wad of parchment behind me. I'm sure it sounds like a plate hitting tiles, but Malthe's attention never strays from my face. He tilts his head as if I'm a statue and he is an artist who's wielding a clay knife. He inches closer to where I'm crouching, his lips parted, black pupils aglow. "The old man is a snitch, I see." He addresses me with a strange, crooked smile.

"He's just frightened," I say. "We all are. Look what you've done to that innocent man."

There isn't a sound from the people, nor the soldiers, yet the temperature drops as Malthe's face darkens.

"I heard what he said about my father. Surely you would not call that innocence?"

He doesn't want to hear my opinion. What he wants, I'm sure, is for me to concur. Which I won't. Ever. What I witnessed was murder.

"What did you claim this girl said before?" Malthe turns to glare at Jove.

"Your Highness, she said to boycott the Tournament."

"I didn't!" I lie.

"She did, Your Highness. She was the one who started it all—"

"Stop." Prince Malthe drags in a breath, his expression enough to shift mountains, slay wolves. As he tucks a black curl behind his ear, I pray my parchment will not be unearthed.

I loathe the emperor for letting her die. Did I write it or think it? I cannot be certain.

With a sigh, Malthe rolls his eyes to the rafters. "Gyzen," he says. "Secure this filth."

Filth.

Me.

My wrists are manacled, the steel grip cold and heavy and strong. My ankles weep from the weight of the chains. Do they really think I'd be able to run?

"My name is Meadow!" I yell. "Meadow Sircha! Please tell my father what's happened to me!" But none of the people on the floor meet my gaze. Who I am—and my story—means nothing to them.

"And him. This weasel. Take him, too."

Jove howls as they bind his hands.

And the last thing I see as we're marched down the hall is the blond boy carefully bending in the dark and retrieving my parchment.

After that, we're gone.

CHAPTER TWO

WE MAKE A HAUNTING PROCESSION. A DOZEN STEEDS. TWO prisoners in chains. The velvet night wraps around us, and yet we're seen. I hear the gulps.

It's not the people from inside the cottage. It's villagers gathered on the cobbles like ghouls. The whites of their eyeballs glint in the moonlight, tracking our movement along the road.

The farther we snake through the laneways of Yahres, the scanter the silent crowd becomes. These people are free, but they earn no coin; and so they squat wherever they can. As we bypass their homes, tucked deep in the alcoves, the atmosphere curdles with the stench of old milk. Even breathing through my mouth does little, and it dawns on me what a state I was in when I ran through these streets with my yellowed parchment—oblivious to their sullied conditions.

But now . . .

I shiver in the chilly wind, as brown straw dances across the pavement. Of course none of that matters now. Now that I'm caught. And by Malthe, of all people. He rides at the front, his chest sticking out, like he's slaughtered a pirate and conquered a fortress. I strain to see pieces of Komran within him—the kindness, the humor, the care for his subjects. All that seeps from Malthe's handsome features are the twisted bits of his father, Ladislas. Ladislas, too, is nothing like Komran, as though somewhere down their line a mistake had been made.

We veer right along the next street, joining onto a wider road. The walls of Centriet tower beside us, built to protect our homes from outsiders.

Malthe extends a hand to the brickwork. "Hail my father for the fortifications!"

His soldiers beat gloved fists to their chests. "Hail Ladislas, Protector of the Kingdom!"

I knot my fingers in my lap, squeezing tight, until the blood has fled my knuckles. It's all I can do to muzzle the terror that zigzags like lightning under my skin. Their chants make not the slightest sense, as Ladislas didn't erect the walls. They've stood for centuries, enclosing our capital, possibly made by the very first Tyjans. But soldiers aren't meant to defy their sovereigns, and Malthe's men are proving no different. Which worries me greatly. For what will they do if their prince instructs them to cut me down?

As the village of Yahres sinks behind us, we enter a stretch of rubble and dirt. Citizens tend not to camp in the open, lest they be spotted by a Tyjan patrol. As the horses lug their hooves through the pebbles, I notice supply bags hanging from their saddles. Malthe rides ahead through an arch at the perimeter, where cobblestones rise in a gleaming pathway.

My spirits sink as we enter Sledloe, as lanterns bathe our trail in gold. On either side of the fractured pavement are makeshift tents of canvas and poles. There's shouting, too, and the crack of a whip, which I pray to Obellis is hitting a sandbrick. But a shriek erupts from inside a building, and a terrified woman begs for forgiveness.

I shudder.

Sledloe. The labor village. Filled with those who have broken the law. These are the people who work in the fields, disfiguring their hands building structures and roads. Even now some are working, ash coating their faces, as they tend the fires that blaze in the grates. Men in blue robes tip their hats to Prince Malthe. *Rigorates,* they're called. The overseers.

My breath returns as we ride out of Sledloe, although my nerves refuse to settle.

"Where will you take us, Highness?" I whimper, my voice so low I'm surprised when he turns.

"You will be kept in the Nothrick Prison until a date is set for your trial."

"But—"

"Hold her tongue," says Malthe. "If she speaks again, so help me—"

"Yes, sire." The soldier I ride with pinches my armpit. It hurts so much, but I swallow my scream. The Nothrick Prison is past my village, old and decrepit, like the cottage we came from. It's used to house petty thieves and adulterers until they're shipped to Sledloe or Jasquek. The main jail, Karacholl, resides in the south. I'm thankful Malthe isn't taking us there.

But a *trial*.

I cannot meet Jove's eyes, although I doubt he'd be happy to see me. As it is, I'm appalled at my lack of restraint. To speak such words was foolishness. My insides tug at the thought of my father, who'll awaken tomorrow to see I'm gone. He'll scour the whole of our village, I know it. He'll stay up all night just in case I come home.

"Please . . ." I don't speak to anyone, really. Not to the oaf that maneuvers my horse. Not to Malthe. Panicked tears sting my eyes like sulfur as we enter the ring of northern townships.

My village is here.

Centriet is a circle. Like a living cross section of an ancient tree. The palace of the emperor lies in the middle, fringed by Lake Lirye and the army barracks. Next come the districts of noble lodgings—apartments so fine, they boast silk rugs and curtains. And so spreads the city, round and round, out and out. The farther from the center, the less influence one wields.

And here in Maytown, just within the walls, we wield so little that it hardly seems just. We're fortunate in other ways,

I suppose, with access to fire and houses of stonebrick. Not to mention the freedom to *be*. We may not have meat or wine or good fruit. But if I compare our lives to Sledloe's, our withered wheat crops do not seem so unpleasant.

"Where are the people?" Malthe shifts in his saddle, and my gaze connects with the empty streets. We're several roads from my father's stonebrick. Even if I screamed, he would not hear me.

I fidget, unsure. It is awfully quiet. As far as I know, there's no curfew, no feast. I half expect candles to ignite in windows, but no movement follows, nor the smatter of whispers. It's been like this only once before. Once, not long after Komran passed on.

Up ahead a figure darts out of an alley. It's a boy, no older than ten or eleven.

"You!" Malthe kicks his horse to a trot, almost collecting the boy underfoot. The skinny kid stiffens like a calf that's been branded, dropping a handful of shriveled nuts.

"Master Lotte said I could take them, I swear!"

"We don't care about your pitiful nuts." The oaf who steers my horse guffaws, as we constrict the boy in a tightknit circle.

"Where is everyone?" Malthe demands.

The boy's lips mash in a taut line. His gaze flickers to the nearest stonebricks, squashed so close their thatched roofs touch.

"In the houses?" Malthe asks, wrinkling his nose. They're oversize blocks with crudely cut doors. In the lamplight, their outlines mar the landscape—in rows upon rows upon black, sprawling rows.

The people might be hiding, I realize, careful not to stir on their reed-covered floors. I spot movement in two separate windows, and yet all of Maytown could not be concealed.

Something's up.

"Do you have a tongue?" Malthe drags a needlelike blade from its sheath. He holds the metal to the milky moonlight, reflecting the whiteness in the boy's trembling face.

"I didn't do anything!" The boy starts to cry, and it dawns on me: *I know this kid.* Not well—there are thousands who live in the villages—but I've seen his dirt-smeared face at the market.

As if he hears the thoughts in my head, the boy blinks once and takes me in. And his tears turn to squealing when he glimpses my chains.

"Farrow," says Malthe. "Do what you will."

"With pleasure." The oaf slides off my horse and deftly strikes the boy in the jaw. The squealing stops as the boy's body crumples.

"Now," says Malthe. "Where are the people?"

A simple question, yet the boy doesn't answer. He covers his ears with shaking hands.

Malthe gently replaces his sword. "Farrow?"

The oaf raises his boot.

"Stop it!" I yell as the tip connects. Over and over. At his shins. In his ribcage. "He's afraid, can't you see? That's why he says nothing! He's only a child. Leave him be!"

"Gyzen!" Malthe waves another man forward, and I understand that they've done this before. It's normal for them, this ordered violence. Be the victims young or old . . . They do not care.

Gyzen kneels in front of the boy. He lifts his head, pats a palm to his cheek. I'm startled by the gentle touch of his fingers, especially when I notice the faded quiver.

Gyzen shot the black-bearded man in the cottage.

He props the boy up, whispers softly in his ear.

"Where is everyone in Maytown?" he asks.

"Gone." The boy weeps. "They've gone . . . to the arena."

Farrow leads me by the chain, up stone steps to a vantage point. Gyzen does the same with Jove, who has not spoken since leaving the cottage. Although it's dark, it's easy to see that the stands are bursting with people from the villages. Their raucous chatter fills the arena, and the reek of fish guts makes me heave.

"Sit."

I'm shoved on a cold rock bench beside two women in beaded dresses. Their crushed lilac perfume eclipses the fish bones, but they raise their kohl-drawn eyebrows at me. Jove's to my left, still mute and pale. Still wringing his hands like they're dripping with liquid. The soldiers stay close, but their shoulders have dropped, and they back-slap each other, making wisecracks and cheer.

Torches border the arena floor in one huge loop of flickering flames. Half-naked servants drag rakes through the sand until the surface is soft and level. We stare down from our carved stone tiers, stacked up and out, stretching high to the clouds. An arena of beauty, most people say.

If you overlook what happens inside.

I scan the crowd for someone familiar. Perhaps my best friend, Anai, may be present. But the night is a blur of bodies and movement. I do not see her among the fray.

"Jove," I say.

His glazed eyes lift.

"I didn't want this. If I'd known—"

"You knew." He spits the words like pomegranate seeds. "And none who are captured are ever found innocent. We're not coming back from this, don't you see?"

I do see. It comes together, fast and frightening and all at once. Our stop at the arena is only a detour, thanks to Prince Malthe's wretched bloodlust.

"I'm sorry," I say, but he says no more, and I feel the hate radiate from his skin. I can't help hating myself even more.

"Traitor!" yells the crowd.

I start and look up.

A lone man has entered the ring. The strawberry-colored doors of the cells slam behind him. In the blaze from the torches, he stares at the people, then turns his attention to the starlit sky. He's already bleeding from a wound to his bicep, and his elbow shakes when he lifts his shoulders. Angry, raised scars wind around his torso, patterning the skin like an exotic animal.

I do not know this man on the sand, and yet his presence ruptures my soul. The women beside me jump to their feet, joining the chorus of condemnation. A volley of fish guts rains down on him as he's pelted with slimy tails and fins. Dirt is flung, along with kelp sludge. And waste collected from people's latrines.

I wipe my eyes with my tunic sleeve, the weighty chain links clinking in protest. The man's body is sticky with filth when the strawberry doors crack open again.

Another man appears in the arena. He's twice as tall as the convicted traitor. And unlike the traitor, he's fitted with armor—a breastplate and thigh guards, a helmet and chain mail. He also carries a lustrous sword and his other arm bears a metal shield. An emblem of Ladislas adorns the front—the red and gray hawk with its wingspan cast wide.

Is Ladislas here? He *must* be here. Our emperor would have sanctioned this evil. He's known to love the drama of the evening. The backdrop of darkness with the foreground of bloodshed. While Malthe and his men are transfixed by the spectacle, I hobble to my feet with an almighty breath. I can barely walk in these hideous manacles, so I jump to the rail and peer over the ledge.

There. He's there. Two rows below. Front and center to this brutal display. A royal marquee obscures his figure, but soldiers stand guard, so he must be inside.

The shouts from the crowd intensify as a branch is hurled into the ring. But it's not just a branch, it's the condemned man's weapon. It's all he will have to fight off the soldier.

The soldier juts his sword at the branch, but the man doesn't lower his face from the sky. His lips still move, but his eyes are closed. To block it all out? To feign it's not true? I jostle to keep my place by the rail, but Farrow is ready and hauls me backward. I'm flung at the seat, landing heavy on my tailbone, knocking the women, who barely notice.

The roar of the crowd grows louder still, as the soldier raises his sword and bellows. I wish I could run from this wretched place, steal a boat from the docks and sail free across the Geynes.

But I can't.

Instead, I grit my teeth and watch the soldier appeal to the emperor. The people are quiet, awaiting a command.

As if there's doubt what the order will be.

"Death!"

The man won't pick up the branch, so the soldier lifts it. Tosses it aside. This is the part that squeezes my innards. It always has—this horrible *game*. The soldier's been trained in the emperor's ludela—gladiator school. I can tell by his stance. Cocky but alert, and bracing for combat—even when he holds the upper hand. He circles the man, his sword at the ready, but the man doesn't snap, doesn't change his position. Not that he's being sly. Quite the opposite. He's telling the crowd—the world—that he's done.

The soldier swings, and I can't look away as the blade connects with the man's injured shoulder. The metal slides smoothly through muscle and flesh. The arm comes off and the man topples over.

I gag as the crowd finds their feet again, as the man convulses like a broken insect. The soldier kicks sand in the man's gaping mouth. A final insult as he fades from the living. I struggle to watch his last few moments. How the red soaks the sand, makes a pool with rough edges. How the head is sawn like meat from the body to present to the emperor in a sign of respect.

But I do.

And as the cheers reach their apex, I retch on the stone between my feet. No one notices me wipe my lips and pray to Obellis it won't happen to me.

When I raise my eyes, Farrow blocks my view.

"Time to leave now," he says.

Another soldier grabs Jove by the collar, and we're dragged down the yawning hole of stone steps, once more en route to where I don't want to go.

I'm surprised to see Gyzen standing with the horses. Did he miss the traitor's execution?

"He died well," Farrow says.

Gyzen mounts his steed. Says nothing.

When we're all assembled, one person is absent. *Malthe.* Yet his soldiers seem far from concerned. A few moments later, he strides across the cobbles, a sheen of sweat coating his forehead.

"We ride for the prison."

"Wait!" I choke, struggling to be seen from behind Farrow's frame. He pushes me backward onto the saddle, clipping my shoulder, and I flinch with pain. "I didn't speak ill of the emperor, Your Highness. And neither did Jove. We would not do that."

Unmoved, the prince climbs into the stirrups. His mouth is set as he lifts the reins.

"Please, Your Highness!" The words fly out—and I know I'm begging, but I have to try. "Emperor Ladislas is a remarkable sovereign. I would never say otherwise—"

"And yet, you did." Malthe glances at the empty road, his eyes as black as woodland beetles. "Maybe I've been too lenient," he muses.

"Sire, you have taken her freedom already." Gyzen steers his horse beside Malthe's, but the prince is quick to brush him aside.

"You mentioned you had a father," he says, his pupils shifting over to me.

My stomach clenches, and Malthe frowns.

"Perhaps he deserves a visit from us?"

"No," I whisper.

"The Rigorates tell me that Sledloe could do with a few more convicts." His teeth flash between his lips, like a hunter taunting its kill before striking. "They're recruiting over the next few days. Maybe they should stop in your father's village?"

My throat goes dry. I suspect "recruitment" means arresting people for false offenses.

"Please don't do that to him," I plead. "He's a good man."

"So is the emperor. But if you hurt my father with words, it's only fair that I hurt yours back." Malthe raises one of his brows, then slaps the reins, and his horse walks on.

"Your Highness!" I yell, but he does not stop. He does not even turn around. The thought of my father on his knees in the street is too much to bear, and I stifle a sob. He's all I have left, and I need to protect him. I promised my mother, and I can't bear to fail her.

"If you're clever," says Gyzen, staring straight ahead, "you'll come to the Nothrick without a fight."

"And let Prince Malthe arrest my father?"

"He will not do that," Gyzen says. "His Highness can sometimes make overwrought threats. They are not recruiting any more men. But if you should wait with patience in the cells, this all may be sorted. Do you understand?"

I don't understand, but Jove comes to life.

"Thank you," he repeats, again and again. He glares at me, but my head is still swimming with all that has happened in the cottage, in the ring.

"Good," says Gyzen. "Then let us away."

And I feel like the girl on the sandbrick's been crushed. And I'm back to that child whose mother fell ill. Who cowered in the dimness, helpless and lost.

CHAPTER THREE

I T'S BEEN TWO DAYS AND THREE NIGHTS. I KNOW THIS BECAUSE OF the iron-barred window. It faces east across the ludela, spilling sunlight into my cramped stone cell. When I balance on my toes and press my fingers to the pane, I'm better able to discern my bearings. Of the three large buildings that form the prison, I'm locked in the center, tucked high beneath the turrets.

I sit on the stones, my knees to my chest, scraping my nails along the grout. No one has told me about my trial, and I haven't glimpsed Jove since the very first night. Each day a soldier unbolts the door and pushes a food tray across the floor. Well, it's not really food, it's something unsavory, like woodchips combined with animal fur. Apart from that, I've had no human contact. Just spiders who dangle from cracks in the ceiling. The words Gyzen spoke lose their power in here—his belief this mess would pass without incident. Perhaps he said it to make us come quietly. Perhaps I was foolish to trust without dispute. Perhaps my trial has happened already, and I will face judgement and don't even know it.

And my father.

I close my eyes, digging my thumb pads into my forehead. I try not to think too deeply about him, lest my mind wanders to the darkest of places. Instead, I reflect on his soft brown stare and warm coarse skin speckled with age. I picture him sitting up late in our stonebrick, attempting to piece together my movements.

Where did I go? What did I say? How could I possibly have vanished without reason? It aches to think of the pain in his heart—that he might now believe that my ending has come. He'd never blamed the emperor for my mother. Not once. Even as she lay close to death. Obellis, he believed, was the one who chose fates. And I pray with all the strength of my being that he'll be kept safe until my return.

A shout from the window straightens my spine, and I push to my feet, glad of distraction. Gripping the bars, I hoist myself up. I last only moments before slipping down. I try again and this time I'm successful. I spy the dusty fields of the ludela. Men in loincloths stand in rows, listening to the speech of their teacher, their Quill.

I drop back to the floor of the cell. The Quill's voice cuts the salty air. He commands that the men pair up with an equal and race each other across the soil. From my limited knowledge of the ludela's training, I know the men are not allowed sandals. And the fields are littered with rocks and branches and shards of metal from broken weapons.

It must slice their soles into strips, and I'm doubtful the Quills would possess healing herbs. But these men will die in the arena someday. I suppose, in comparison, the training's not dreadful.

The instant the thought takes shape, I frown. How could I think that? *Of course* it is bad. But for the few who have come to earn coin, these men do not stay in the ludela by choice. Some were picked up from towns in the south. Others captured west of the flowing Tyrant's Daughter. A few men are thieves who must pay their debts in order to secure their families' futures. Scarce would choose to sleep on concrete, bear gashes by day and fall before a crowd. The image of the man in the arena bursts forth. I close my eyes and he's there in the darkness.

"Girl," he says.

I know this is false. I know this is me making tales in my head.

But he says it again, more insistent this time.

"Girl!"

I jolt.

"Wake up. You've been summoned."

A hazy face appears before me, bobbing in the air, very near to my nose. I blink slowly and his features sharpen. It's a soldier, but it's a soldier that I do not know.

My grimy hands fly to my head. I check my skin to feel it's intact. The lurching hole in my stomach widens and I wonder how long I have been out.

"Get up."

I barely register his voice, for I'm straining to hear the Quill outside. Relief gushes through me when his yelling begins, ordering the men to pick up their knives. I wasn't dreaming. I had been awake. The men running barefoot, the spiders, all true. The open cell door looks like a mirage, so I gnaw on my lip—and it *hurts*.

This is real.

The soldier in my cell kneels beside me. His breath smells of smoke and days-old cheese. As I touch my fingers against my eyelids, he leans in close to pull me up. I push him off with the heels of my hands, but my palms connect with his powerful grip. He bends my arms back so I yelp, then he lets them go with a growl of remorse.

"Sorry," he says, under his breath, though he doesn't stop dragging me up off the floor. My head doesn't reach the top of his shoulder. He could lift me up with a single paw. "Come along with me now."

After long isolation, the pulse of my heart beats strong in my chest. It's that same frantic pounding that's rendered me dizzy ever since Mother sailed away on her crypt.

"We must not delay." His blue eyes dart. The door to freedom flares with light. It looks like a path to fresh air and brightness, except that it must lead to Malthe and my trial.

I root my feet, which is terribly hard when my limbs are

shaking from nervous vigor. The soldier sighs as I study his face. He's older than I thought. Perhaps in his fifties.

"Look, what I meant is . . ." His anger deflates, replaced with an almost worried demeanor. He tries again. "Come now. Please. We must be hasty in leaving this place."

My breath's a cottony wheeze of air, but the panic is gently replaced by agreement. Outside my cell, the corridor's empty. Candles mantle the moss-etched walls.

"Where are we going?" I ask the soldier, unsure if I truly desire an answer. There are places much worse than the Nothrick Prison. Places without windows and food trays and sunlight.

"Someone wants you," the soldier says.

"Someone wants *me*?"

"Yes, they do."

"So I'm not to have a trial?"

"By my honor, you ask a lot of questions for a silly girl."

Such words would normally fan my ire, but low on strength, I let it slide. After all he's a soldier who works in the prison. He probably came from a village like mine.

"Who wants to see me?"

We come to a staircase that spirals down to another dim corridor. Voices rise from the space below, begging for food and thimbles of water.

I still my feet. "Who wants to see me?"

"You're in no position to makes demands." The soldier curls his knuckles in my back, and I stumble down the first few steps.

"Is it Gyzen?"

The soldier pauses. His mouth contorts, but doesn't form words. He clearly knows of whom I speak, yet he scratches his stubble and flicks me on.

My mind races as I ascend to the landing. Drops of moisture *plink-plink* on my shoulder. If Gyzen has come, then maybe it's over. Maybe I will be free to go. And then another thought muscles in. It could be my father who waits outside. Someone from the cottage might have told him what happened. He may even have brought Anai. A smile forms as I think of my friend with her long eyelashes and too-wide grin. She'd press me for days about my ordeal. Well, as long as Symon wasn't present. My feet move faster, my hunger forgotten, until I'm stopped by a timber door.

"Fortune is with you," the soldier says, fitting the lock with a rusted key.

When the board moves aside, the sunshine clouts me with an incomparable feeling of warmth. I shuffle three paces over the threshold, marveling how I have missed it this much.

But as my eyes adjust to the color, I start to remember that awful night. It was dark when they hauled me up these stairs, leaving Jove on the horse with the other soldiers. It scared me then, but now in the daylight, the terror dissolves like sunlit dew. The sandbrick walls, although tall, menace less. The wire above them rattles in the breeze, flimsy and harmless like twine on a rod. Trees shoot through the paved courtyard, their roots upsetting the neat, tanned surface. Behind me the noise from the ludela continues. The grunting of exertion and the clashing of blades.

The soldier stalks past, checking the surrounds, and I shield my eyes.

"Where are you going?"

He rounds a corner, and I blow out a breath, suddenly aware of my filthy tunic. The hem is torn and the skirt is stained with whatever black foulness littered my cell. But there isn't a gate within the vicinity, so I pick up my skirt and follow his lead. An unmanned tower watches me pass, its stilt legs coiled with prickly leaves. I scan the four surrounding walls, but they're smooth and solid, despite their age.

"Hurry, girl!" the soldier calls.

I increase my speed around the bend.

Waiting in the shade of an oak is a carriage with four white wheels and a chestnut stallion.

Without a doubt, it belongs to the palace. Only the emperor

could afford such extravagance. The body is enclosed by a gray crafted hood that is plastered in swirls of flamboyant gemstones. A battle mural shines on the door, intricately detailed and varnished with gloss. Red drapes hang from behind the windows, and the perch and the footboard are coated with gold.

"If you wish to leave," the soldier says, "you must get in."

I stifle a splutter. "Why would I do that? It is . . . forbidden."

"To ride in a carriage is not an offense."

"It's a *Tyjan* carriage." I choke the words. It looks out of place in this barren terrain.

"The alternate is going back to your cell."

I fold my arms. "Who summoned me?"

The soldier glances sideways at the carriage, and it dawns on me it's the first time I've met him. The soldier who delivered my inedible food trays was a man with a red beard and large double chin. This man is older with craggy skin and white streaks running in lines through his hair. His mouth is drawn like he can't escape sadness—or maybe it's duty—though I really don't care.

"Make your choice," the soldier says.

"But I can't . . ."

"Do you honestly wish to stay here?"

Of course I don't, but the ominous unknown has always been my biggest fear.

"You'll never get a trial," says the soldier.

"What do you mean?"

"That's not why he brought you."

I shake my head, not understanding.

"The prince," says the soldier. "If you stay, he will hurt you."

It could be a lie; it could be the truth, but the expression he wears sends chills through my bones. An image of the black-bearded man assaults me, entwined with the vision of the traitor in the ring.

"He'll come back a few weeks from now. You'll be frailer then from lack of food—"

"And where are you planning to take me?" I ask. "Not to him?"

"No," says the soldier.

"Then where?"

"Somewhere secure," he says.

"Why?"

The soldier nods at the carriage. "I promise you only that this is your chance. Take it before it is no longer there."

I stare at him and he doesn't look away, but there's empathy lurking beneath his lashes.

"I will go with you," I concede with a sigh, for the choice is made. I cannot stay here. Quickly, the coachman springs from the box seat and opens the door as though I'm a duchess. The interior smells like carnations and lemons with a hint of a third scent that seems quite expensive.

Diamonds? I'm too shaky to recall if diamonds even have a smell. But no, it's the whiff of sparkling wine—a delicacy I witnessed once long ago. I was at the local markets with my mother when a noble lady sauntered by with her son. She drank from a chalice that fizzled with liquid. *White wine,* said my mother, *takes years to be made.*

And so I sit in the dazzling carriage, smelling white wine in my unclean tunic. The coachman clicks the carriage door shut, and I fold back the drapes to stare out the glass. The soldier removes his gray and red jacket. He waits for the coachman to climb into place. He jogs across the pavement to a break in the sandbrick, where steel bars stand in for the thick, rocky slabs.

With a heave from the soldier, the bars slide aside, allowing us access to the road beyond. The carriage bumps through the gate like a vessel, emerging in the noble marketplace: *Junoven.* People swarm the narrow streets, carrying purses and grapefruit and elaborate maps. No one gawks at the carriage as we pass. In Junoven, they're used to this level of wealth.

I press my nose to the rear window with just enough time to see the gate shut.

And with just enough time to see the soldier toss the jacket and speed off between the stalls without looking back.

I'm at a loss about the soldier—or if he was even a soldier at all. A handle gleams, gold like a dress ring, and I tug on it, but the door doesn't budge. I bang on the hood to alert the coachman, but he makes no sign he hears my call. The windows, perhaps. I could smash out the glass. But with what? I rummage beneath the seats.

Nothing. No, there's nothing there, except silk cushions and a mat for the floor. I grip the drapes, smoothing them flat, sucking in air and kicking my foot. But without boots, my strike is awkward, causing me to groan in pain. Upon inspection, I realize why. The glass is thicker than two of my fingers.

Panting hard, I sit up straight and bat the drapes with the tasseled cord. I attempt to guess our likely end point: a hidden apartment in the middle of the city? Maybe it's someone from the Gathering who calls. Or perhaps it's Jove, who may already be freed. And yet I doubt he would care to save me, so I cling to the hope that it's Gyzen who's summoned.

It doesn't take long for the scenery to alter from bustling markets to palatial estates. As we spiral past sprawling white-bricked villas, I can't help thinking how much things have changed. Hundreds of years ago, Centriet was a warzone, crammed with dozens of aggressive clans. They roamed the land, hunting and stealing, fighting each other for treasure and wives. Until Erratide, the strongest warlord, united the clans as the kingdom of Erraforge. He beheaded each of his staunchest rivals in public squares to the beat of percussion. Prisoners built the newly formed capital. Centriet, it was called, the center of the world. Erratide appointed himself to the throne and erected his palace at the city's core.

Emperor Ladislas is part of his bloodline, the nobles the relations of his most loyal subjects. And right now, as mansions fly by, it's clear our emperor still nurtures those nobles. Fountains stream with turquoise water. Dogs chase birds beneath luscious green canopies. Polished statues peek from ferns, their faces carved from burnished marble.

I haven't visited the noble district since Emperor Ladislas came into power. His army postings monitor entry. Good reason is needed to enter the region.

It wasn't like this when Komran reigned.

There were nobles, of course. And soldiers. And the free. There were even those who fought in the arena, but their matches were fewer—and overwhelmingly fair. I don't think Komran truly enjoyed them. He certainly didn't cheer like his son. And he'd never have sanctioned an impromptu killing in the middle of the night to put down a traitor.

The carriage halts with a massive thud, and I lunge at the window for a better view. We've arrived at the center of Centriet City—to many, the center of Erraforge itself.

I crane my neck. The palace looms like a private village of connected buildings. The gable rooftops glitter with silver. Meandering balconies curve around corners. Rows of pillars adorn the exterior, casting the outer halls in shadows. Four towers shoot from behind the facade, their long trunks smattered with obsidian flecks.

It's clear where Ladislas's coin is invested.

Some say the flecks are fragments of onyx. Others claim they were mined from volcanoes and smuggled in vessels that crisscross the Geynes. Combined with the handsome pewter-framed casements, they boast of the mammoth wealth of the Tyjans.

The coachman taps the carriage. "Ah, miss? I'm going to have to ask for your silence."

My silence?

He's lifted a small metal cover, revealing a hole the size of a button. His voice wafts inside like a nervous child's over the stamping noise of the horse hooves.

"May I have it?" he presses.

"But where are we going?"

Shimmering Lake Lirye surrounds the palace. The structure sits on an island in the lake, linked to the shore by a long glossy bridge.

I change my question.

"Am I to be pardoned?"

"Pardoned?" His tone is hurried. "Ah . . . *Yes.*"

"I don't believe—"

"Say nothing," he says.

"But—"

"They are waving us across. Now *quiet!*" He drops the cover but part of it catches, and I hear him curse under his breath.

I lean in closer. "Will they ask me questions?"

"Not if you are mute," he says.

As we slowly roll across the planks, the water's surface sparkles with light. The lily pads pop against the blue like moss-covered fingers stretching out through an ocean. I shrink against the slippery pillows as the carriage stops for the second time. My skeleton threatens to rip from my tunic, leap in the lake, and sink to the bottom.

"Good day, Pelletier."

"Good day, Captain."

I bend as far as I can, staying hidden. The coachman nods at one of the soldiers who blocks the road with his large square shoulders.

"Just bringing a girl to help in the kitchens." He slaps the carriage. "To cook for the Tournament."

I tense at the sight of the soldier's coat, hoping he didn't attend the Gathering. He wanders closer and peeks in the glass. His eyes are sharp, yet they pass me over.

"Make certain she cooks roasted chicken, you hear?"

"I'll pass on the message," says the coachman.

"Very good."

He waves us on with a flick of his wrist and we pass beneath the ornate barbican. At the end of the bridge the coachman steers left, bypassing a series of butterfly aviaries. I let out the breath that had swelled in my chest. Am I really here to cook for the Tournament? I picture the soup on the hearth in my stonebrick. Thin and tasteless and deficient of chicken.

We thud on to the rear of the palace, past the stables, through a thicket of willows. The Gardens of Erratide rise before us, attached to the palace but curbed by dark walls. The air is heavy with jasmine and mint, and little spinning fruit seeds twirl in the breeze. We brush by spruce trees with colored lanterns and grand oval ponds overflowing with goldfish. My hunger widens as I think of Maytown with its sand-ridden soil and giant mangled weeds. These manicured lawns sparkle with health as though they're fed meals by Ladislas's servants.

And they probably are.

There are wildflowers, too. Pastures of petals, all manner of hues. How can the emperor visit the arena—watch people perish—and return to this beauty?

The flowers thin out the farther we go, and the well-trimmed grass becomes patchy and sparse. The heavy carriage wheels bounce over loose stones before eventually stopping at the castle's back door.

It's a plain door. Like the one to my stonebrick. I'm surprised by its texture—the roughness, the burn marks. An old tattered cord hangs down from an awning, attached to a bell that's turned emerald with limescale.

The servant's entrance.

The coachman dismounts, brushing dirt and hair from his well-pressed suit. He's young, I realize, and thin like a ferret. He moves like one, too, scuttling quickly up the path, before clanging the bell with three solid tugs.

I try the handle to the carriage—*still locked*. I don't want to be here, although I'm intrigued. The coachman jams his hands in his pockets, blowing out breaths, rocking back on his heels. A woman in a white cap appears at the entrance, nods to the coachman and glances at the carriage. I clutch at the furnishings, futilely hoping that somehow they've mistaken me for someone else.

The coachman unclicks the carriage door.

"You're Meadow Sircha?" the woman asks.

"How do you know my—"

"It's her," says the coachman.

"Excellent, excellent. Please come along."

I step gingerly onto the pathway, avoiding the thistles which mar the grass. Dandelions cast white needles in the air, while sloshing noises rise from behind the walls.

The woman glares at the waiting coachman. "Did Errol manage to—?"

"On his way," he replies.

"And no one—"

"All went to plan," he assures her, and her wrinkled face relaxes.

"Go on, then," she says.

The coachman grins and tips his hat, bounds onto the perch, and the carriage rolls away. I'm left with the woman, who eyes my tunic as though she's an eagle and I am her prey.

"Why am I here?"

The woman takes my arm with even more force than the soldier in the prison. She pushes me through the door and shuts it.

"It was I who summoned you," she says.

"You did?" My mind's in a whirl. "But why?" I'm certain I've never seen this woman in my life.

"Her Highness's maid has gone," says the woman. "And you are to be—"

"Her *servant*?"

"For a time."

We enter a courtyard that bustles with activity. Men and women scatter carrying linens, carrying bowls. Hanging ropes flutter with dripping clothing. Girls stir cauldrons that bubble with soap suds. I notice the woman is wearing an apron that matches the white of her braided hair.

"I'm from Maytown," I say. "I'm not a servant."

"Is that why you sat in the walls of that prison?"

I swallow. How could she know about that? "My father didn't know where I was. How could you?"

"I serve Her Highness, just as you will. When you've served the Tyjans as long as I have, you learn how to listen, how to smile, how to notice." She leads me past a row of women, dipping sheets in basins over corrugated boards. As they scratch the stains from the fabric they chatter in the mellow undertones of the southern lands.

"Errol, that soldier who released me from the prison—"

"Shhh! Never mention his name, do you hear?" We come to the end of the rectangular plot, where ferns poke out from gaps in the mortar. The woman pulls me behind a column that curls in the early style of the warlords. She's quiet for a moment and her upper lip quivers as she twists a band of iron on her finger. "He was only doing what I asked," she says.

"You weren't supposed to release me," I say. From the shift of her gaze, I have spoken the truth. "That soldier was not a soldier at all. And me being here? As a servant? This is folly."

"It is not folly."

"Then let me leave."

She squashes her fingers in a ball, breathing hard. "Do you know what they'd do if they found you out there? Wandering about on the emperor's grounds?"

"I'll wait until nightfall," I say.

"No, you won't. There are more patrols in the evening, child. Why do you think we brought you in daylight? It's less suspicious."

"Why do you care?"

The woman smooths her apron with a sigh, a tired smile tinging her weathered features. It occurs to me that this is the smile, the one that she spoke of—the one she has learned. Something about it reaches inside to a part of my being that makes me feel guilty. She has, after all, salvaged me from the prison and done so with risk to her own personal welfare.

"I than you," I say, but her smile quickly fades.

"For now you must steer clear of Prince Malthe. He would not expect your presence in the palace, but if he found out . . ." Her voice dips low.

"If he found out . . . ?"

"We'd all be in trouble."

The wind kicks up, rustling the ferns. She turns sideways to break our gaze, but something about the movement is wrong.

"You said you summoned me," I say.

"Yes."

"But you're also a servant to the emperor. How did you manage to order a carriage and have a man pretend to be one of his soldiers?"

Her brows knit, hardening like glass. She's a lion, this woman. I see that now. She reminds me of old Mrs. Pensie in Maytown who raised four boys when her husband died.

"It's not your place to ask," she tells me.

"It *is* my place."

"Well, I cannot answer."

My jaw tightens. "Of course you can tell me. If you don't, I'll do it. I'll find the emperor."

Redness creeps up her neck to her chin, as she considers how to interpret my threat. I'm certain she wishes she'd left me in the cell.

But then she laughs. "And what would you tell him?"

"What would I tell him? I'd tell him that . . ." I stop, confused. She's right, of course. Would I really tell him I escaped from his prison? And now I am here? And this woman won't talk? If my words were paper, they'd flutter and tear; such is their uselessness on my tongue.

"We shall only *pretend* you're a servant," she assures me. "We'll keep it a secret. No one else needs to know."

"But—" Frustration spills from my pores, surely eclipsing my foul-smelling clothes. That she orchestrated my release, I am grateful. But to act as a servant? It makes me fume. It isn't because I don't like servants, it's because I shouldn't be playing pretend. I should be traveling the road back to Maytown, back to my stonebrick, back to my father.

"You must be hungry at least," says the woman, shifting her eyes to a large stone arch. "I'll take you into the kitchens for supper. Welsha's prepared a big pot of broth."

The mention of food throws me off balance, but I plant my heels, unwilling to leave. If we join other servants, my fate will be sealed. I cannot allow her to sweep me aside.

But it's clear she already wields the broom.

"We shall talk more later," she says.

"Why not now?"

She nods at some girls milling by the entrance. "It's suppertime for all of us, child." Removing her cap, she pats down her hair. "And as the Grande—the Head of the Women—of course I must be present at mealtimes." She mops the sweat from under her nose with a force that tells me her stance won't be altered.

I turn to stare at the door. It's locked.

"Be thankful you are here," she says. "Life could have been a whole lot worse if you'd chosen not to enter that carriage."

A flock of birds glides above us, their feathers thrashing like scarves in a gale. Their shadows skim the cracked tile floor, soar up the walls, and flutter beyond.

"We'll talk after supper." The woman backs away, and I watch her feet tap a path to the archway.

"Wait," I say.

She pauses. "What is it?"

"How did you know I'd been captured?" I ask.

"Ah." She answers without even thinking, her voice and her step never missing a beat. "I serve Emperor Ladislas, as do we all. And I told you I've learned how to listen and notice."

CHAPTER FOUR

THE SERVANTS AND I SQUEEZE SHOULDER TO SHOULDER AROUND the enormous hardwood table. It's thirty bodies—young and timeworn, fair and tanned, tall and petite. The grit on my skin turns to mud in the heat. My tunic clings to my aching torso. I dig a finger into my eyebrow, but it doesn't relieve the mounting pressure.

I should have run.

I know that now. In the grounds of the prison. Outside the palace. I eye the key on the woman's neck chain—metal that unlocks my pathway to freedom. She slowly moves to the head of the table, folding her arms across her chest. At once, the chatter melts to silence.

"We have a new arrival," she says.

I should have run.

They gawk at me, as though her words grant instant permission. I wring my hands under the table, tapping my toes on the dry stone flooring. Some of them smile. Others stare blankly. One even ventures the tiniest grimace. They're each dressed nicer than the servants to the nobles in their white linen clothing and sturdy brown sandals.

"Is she to be a Lissette?" asks a woman, who looks to be in her third decade. She thins her eyes at me. "I'm Tallesa. And I pray you're not replacing Lilly."

"I don't know who—"

Tallesa snorts.

"Enough," says the woman, clearing her throat. "Nothing has been decided yet. This is Mollie."

Mollie?

"Oh, really." Tallesa twists an ash-blonde curl, just one of the many pinned tight to her scalp. "And where in the kingdom do you hail from, Mollie?"

"Sledloe," I say.

"Oh, Freya. Come on." Tallesa turns to the woman. "*Sledloe?* Since when does Sledloe scum work here?"

"Go and bring in the food, Tallesa."

"But Carliss's about to—"

"Do it now." Freya waits, and I'm poised for a battle, but Tallesa nods and leaves the room. The moment the shutters bang behind her, Freya looks around. "Any more questions?"

No one speaks.

"Good," she says.

Tallesa emerges from the door with a pot. She thumps it in the center of the table and lifts the lid so steam swirls out.

"The Lissettes can serve themselves," she says. "And so can the Lissons." She sneers at some boys.

"You will mind your manners," says Freya as Tallesa shrugs and backs away.

"Here, I'll do it." A young girl stands. Her eyes are a rich, dark brown like my mother's. With a strained smile, she ladles the broth into the bowls and slides them toward us.

"Quinn's a Lissette," says the woman beside me, tilting her head at the serving girl. "Lowest standing in the villas of the Tyjans. Tallesa's a Midla. One step above."

"Good to know." I accept my broth. It burns my fingers through the bowl. I take a sip. No meat, just cabbage.

"Were you wrongly accused?" the woman prods.

I stare at her. "I beg your pardon?"

"It's just that you look so desperately sad." Her tired face softens. "I'm sorry to pry. If you'd rather not say . . ."

"I'd rather not say." I hunch my shoulders, hoping for distance, but the old woman pats my arm and smiles.

"We all have pasts we'd like to forget. And I've heard life in Sledloe is terribly hard." She raises a brow in a knowing manner, as though she and I share some sort of bond. I wonder for a moment if she could be trusted—if perhaps she could help me escape back to Maytown. But the answer presents itself almost at once. "You are blessed to be here now," she says. "I've encountered prisoners from Sledloe before. And I've seen their pain with my own two eyes."

I should have run.

My insides twist at how easily she believes I am truly from Sledloe.

"How did your fortunes change?" she presses, sucking the broth through a gap in her teeth.

"Uh . . ." I don't even know why I said it. *Sledloe.* Of all the nooks in the kingdom! Freya wanted my identity kept secret, but surely I could have named somewhere more appealing. Most are aware of Sledloe's reputation of whippings and shanties and meals in the dirt. The prisoners that live there are seldom kept healthy and few are released into household work.

"Well?" The woman prods me again, so I shove in another spoonful of cabbage. I should have claimed I was a servant from Venti or that I toiled for a merchant in Junoven.

"Well . . ." I say.

The woman leans forward. I can practically feel her wetting her lips.

And so I'm abrupt. "I shall not divulge. I've only just met you, after all."

"Stop questioning her, Victoria," says Quinn, the Lissette who's finished serving the soup. From her tone and the way Victoria chuckles, I deduce both women are of the same level. "I'm sorry about that," Quinn says to me. "By the look of your clothes, you've been though sufficient. But if you need help in any way . . ."

"Ask someone else," Victoria quips.

They both erupt in high-pitched giggles, and I find the corners of my mouth growing taut.

Quinn rolls her eyes at Victoria. "Can you believe this one is seventy-four years young?"

No, I can't, to be perfectly honest. Seventy-four is a ripe old age. It's twenty-nine more years than my mother, which is not a good thought, so I push it away.

"The Tyjans are not unkind?" I ask.

"They are wise and fair," say both women. Their faultless unison makes me shudder, and yet from what I've seen, it's true. These servants seem to be treated well. Food. Garments. Camaraderie between them. Not like some in the noble households.

"And who is Lilly?" I ask.

"Oh." Quinn motions that they should not say, but Victoria shrugs.

"We might as well tell her. She was the Grande Personale to the princess, but she disappeared and no one knows why."

I stir my cabbage in a big clumpy mess.

"Perhaps she fled," the old woman muses.

"If she did, the soldiers would have found her," says Quinn. "The Tyjans would punish such unlawful behavior."

I dig my fingers in the back of my neck.

"Are you ill?" asks Quinn.

I shake my head. But something has suddenly dawned on me that got lost in the flurry of leaving the Nothrick. "Please excuse me," I say.

"Of course."

I swing my legs over the bench and rise. I pass through the kitchen, back to the courtyard, the nausea swirling deep in my middle.

Outside, the sky is a brilliant orange, heralding the end of another day. I walk until I'm suitably sheltered, back in the alcove, surrounded by ferns.

I breathe.

I fled. *I* fled from the prison. I have done an unlawful thing. I may have been kept under false accusations, but it would not matter in the eyes of the emperor. And though the prince may not visit the prison for many weeks as the soldier explained, how had I forgotten the guards? They're going to discover that I have escaped. And when they do, I cannot be here, hiding within the walls of the palace. I need to return to my father at once. And we'll need to hide—well clear of the city.

Treading in circles, I ponder my choices. I could leave the Tyjan palace tonight. I break the journey down into steps. First out the door. Then through the gardens. A sprint along the bridge to the adjacent streets. After that, I'd hike through the districts, gradually working my way to the outskirts. Then through the dusty fields and the villages. Past the arena and markets.

Then *home.*

Even in theory it doesn't sound simple but my pores are twitching, demanding a plan. With the noise from the kitchens echoing behind me, I march quickly to the battered-up door. On this side, it's taller and wider. The palings have splintered, yet they're hammered in firm. A spherical lock is wedged in the timber, sunken and rusted like it's never been opened.

My fingers brush the jagged keyhole. Had I really presumed an escape would be simple? I'd still need to steal the key from Freya and evade the soldiers who lined the bridge. And if I was caught . . . My hands grow clammy. I don't want to think what the prince might do. Releasing the metal, I shuffle backward, the courtyard tilting like the deck of a boat.

But I can't stay here. I won't stay here. No matter how decent they seem in the palace. There's only one thing left to do. And I do not care if it's not the right moment—if perhaps Freya thinks

I am being ungrateful. I look to the sunset and say a quick prayer to Obellis, yes, and to anyone else. Then I turn from the courtyard and enter the kitchens with a sharp swell of courage I barely recognize.

She's speaking to Tallesa. Or rather, Tallesa is shouting at her. They stand outside the dining space with hands on hips, cheeks burning with color.

It's odd. In Maytown, I'd wait all day, not wanting my presence to interrupt. Tonight I take the opposite approach.

"Freya, I need to tell you something."

"*Excuse* me?" Tallesa's eyes widen. "Can you not see that the Grande is busy?" Her pitch brings servants from inside the kitchen. Quinn is one. I don't know the others.

"She promised me before supper," I say.

"Wait your turn," Tallesa snaps.

"No."

She shakes a finger at my nose. "Do you think you're above me, Mistress Mollie from Sledloe?"

And there—it's like she's shattered the spell that gave me strength to act assured. I *have* interjected when I should have been patient. Perhaps I *am* the one in the wrong.

But it's too late now.

"It's fine," says Freya.

"What?" says Tallesa, as though she's been struck.

"Mollie's quite right. I did give my word. Besides, as I've told you, she's not replacing Lilly."

Freya clears the watchers from the hallway, instructing them each to begin their night chores. Even Tallesa must leave us alone and return to the kitchen to scrub pots and dishes. She's escorted by one of the elder women.

"Shall we?" asks Freya.

I nod.

She leads me along a candlelit corridor, opens a door, and leads me inside.

I'm still shaking.

"Sit down, my child."

I decline her offer, propping up against the wall. I remember what Father advised for panic: *Observe your surrounds. Name objects in detail.*

A cupboard.

A pallet.

A table and washcloth.

A rug on the floor that's woolen and coarse.

"Did you tremble like that in Yahres?" asks Freya. "When you told all those people in the cottage your story?"

I stare. How could she know all the details? But when I ask, she shakes her head.

"Not many others would dare speak their minds. Now what did you want to tell me?" she asks.

Paper boxes adorn the shelves and plain white tunics hang from bronze hooks. Sandals row the floor in pairs, their soles and laces knotted from leather. Through the door, I hear the clink of dishes and straw bristles scraping across the tiles. I feel the vibration of hurried feet, and the truth of staying here hits me hard.

"I cannot pretend I'm a servant," I say. "The prince will soon learn that I have escaped." I hate how shrill and unsteady I sound, but this is important and it needs to be said. "When the guards find out, they'll raise the alarm. Soldiers will be sent to bring me back. I need to go home. I need to go now. My father and I could leave tonight."

Freya takes me in for a moment. "Where would you go?"

"I do not know."

She removes her cap and plops it on her knees, plucking stray hairs from the bristly material. "So you don't have a plan."

"This is my plan. I need to go home and see my father."

"You can't," she says.

"I don't understand."

"You can't see your father just yet," she replies.

I pause, transferring my weight between legs, hating how Freya is allowed to decide. "Why not?"

"Because for you to be safe, the guards must say that you have died." There's an eerie lilt to her confident tone. One that reeks of secrets and danger. I realize she's waited for this moment to tell me. Behind closed doors, not out in the courtyard.

"The guards will know the truth," I say.

"The guards who know are taken care of." Freya glances quickly at the door, pulls her stool closer, and drops her voice. "It's amazing what extra rations will do. A few days and they'll report you have passed. They'll pretend to have taken your corpse to the Geynes. Your cell will be swept and your memory erased."

"But Prince Malthe—"

"Will think you are dead." Freya shrugs with a careless grimace. "It will stop him from going back to your cell—and taking you into his part of the palace."

"But he said a trial."

"There won't be a trial. The emperor would not waste the time, nor the coin. And the prince would never tell him about you. He keeps his prisoners away from his father."

"You've done this before," I say, perplexed. "You've rescued people from the Nothrick Prison."

She doesn't jump to refute my prediction; instead, she slants her head to one side. "Yes, I have rescued girls," she admits. "Girls imprisoned by men for nothing. It's why you must stay hidden with us until the prison guards do their part."

The strength I saw in Freya before is magnified in the muted light. If she was discovered, they'd ship her to Sledloe. Or straight to the mines. Or somewhere worse.

"If you speak a word, I'll deny my involvement."

"I won't say anything to anyone," I promise.

"Then you'll stay?" she asks. "For a few more days?"

"But I feel like I'm letting him down," I answer.

"Who?"

"My father."

She leans forward. "How are you letting him down?" she asks.

I look to the wall, examining the lines, counting the number of flecks in each sandbrick. "The anguish he'd feel, I know it's my fault."

"Why?"

"Because." My eyes prick with tears. "If I hadn't spoken that night at the Gathering, he wouldn't be wondering if I am dead."

"So don't be dead." Freya stands up. She tosses one of the tunics at me. The fabric smells like soap and liniment, like the days I used to help Mother with washing. "Remain with us for a little longer. We know what we're doing. You'll go back alive." Her strength is contagious as she moves to the door. "The worst is over. You must trust me on that."

I do.

"So, you'll stay?" she asks. It isn't a question, though it poses as one.

I nod.

She exhales what I think is relief.

"Then go and be a servant," she says.

CHAPTER FIVE

TIME MOVES DIFFERENTLY INSIDE THE PALACE. HOURS SWEEP BY in nods and curtseys. I barely have a moment to rest my hands, let alone pause to think of my father. Instead I learn the structured reality of life inside the princess's villa. An existence of being cut off from the city, keeping food on the table and dust from the parlors.

On the second day, I'm in the kitchens when Welsha, the head cook, receives an order. A skinless cow is lifted through the doorway over the shoulders of three heaving boys. And then come the chickens—newly killed, feathers plucked. Followed by the pails of still-flipping trout. Marvelous creations grow tall on the benches, dripping in butter and sprinkled with herbs.

"For the Tournament?" I ask the assistant cook, Carliss. My eyes almost cross at the scent of meat. The Tyjans own private paddocks near the barracks and fund a fleet of seven to trawl the reef. Their vegetables, too, are grown in houses with netting that protects the crops from the sun. I'd always known that the Tyjans dined well, but the variety and quantity renders me stunned.

Carliss slaps a fish on the board. It's so fresh, its tail still twitches. "Definitely for the Tournament," she says. "You know how those Tyjans need to eat."

"*You* don't need to eat," says Amalia. She's Carliss's twin, but taller and fairer. She wheels in a barrow piled high with grain. "If you do, you won't fit into your apron."

It's a low blow. Carliss is slender, but I have seen her sampling the spoils of the kitchen. I would, too, if I worked there all day.

Anyone would.

"Don't be so rude." Carliss pauses to glare at Amalia, as a blaze of red blooms on her skin. She tears off the fish head and scoops out its entrails, tossing the pieces in a pot by the window. With a huff Welsha bustles between them, muttering something about blood being thick. Her shoulders have rounded from years of bending and a hump has formed at the base of her neck. She's less friendly to me than the others, as if old age has taught her suspicion.

Amalia sets the barrow by the pantry. "I'm not being rude. I'm just being honest."

"Then stop being honest." Carliss's jaw clenches. She slides her knife tip into the fish. I'd often thought it would be nice to have a sister—to grow up beside, to share secrets and dreams. I didn't factor in how nasty they could be. And *twins*. I'd imagined they'd be extra close. But as Amalia shoots me a triumphant look, she lets it slip that Carliss is in love.

Welsha pours liquid into a basin. "There will be no boys," she tells them both.

"There certainly won't," Amalia jibes. "With Carliss being such a gluttonous pig."

"Enough!" snaps Welsha.

"Well, she is," says Amalia. "She'd even eat suet if you left it unguarded. It isn't right that she takes extra rations when the rest of us try to do what's expected."

And that does it. To Amalia's delight, Carliss bursts into tears and runs. I don't know where she's heading to cry, though I don't wish to remain in the kitchen with her twin.

I walk out back. No one's about. The cauldrons are drying in the middle day sun. It's strange how familiar the area is, despite not being here that long. The door leading into the pastures tempts, but I turn my back without even looking. Not that I'd leave. For true to her word, Freya sent Errol back to the prison. Errol, of course, was the soldier who'd saved me. The soldier who wasn't a soldier at all. He promised the guards were taken care of and that I'd be freed in a few more days.

"Carliss?" I call. "Are you out here, Carliss?"

Either she isn't—or she's good at hiding.

I open my fingers. Sitting on my palm is a chunk of mutton I'd plucked from the kitchen. I savor the rich, luscious smell of the meat, wishing that I could bottle and keep it. Most of the servants are inside the palace, sweeping the parquets and polishing bannisters. A few have gone by carriage to Junoven to purchase additional supplies for the Tyjans. Freya says my job is to clean— the counters, the basins, the washboards and curtains. It feels wicked to stand outside, cradling a morsel of food I don't own. But I've nearly forgotten the texture of sheep, so I cram the mutton in my mouth and chew.

It's so good. After weak broths and brews, using my teeth feels like a sin. With each bite, the juices grow richer.

But then the door to the pastures creaks open.

I almost choke.

A girl creeps inside, carefully peering over her shoulder. Yellow hair whips against her cheekbones as she drags the hefty board closed behind her. A shapeless dress conceals her form, though she's young and slim and her face is pretty. A smatter of freckles dust her nose and her brows look flawless, as if they've been painted. She holds her body differently, too, like an invisible string tugs her forehead to the sky. It's the posture of a Tyjan, not of a servant; and it suddenly dawns on me who this is.

The emperor's daughter, Princess Kalliope.

The younger sister of Prince Malthe. The mutton turns to pulp on my tongue, and I splutter and cough, which makes her turn.

Her features harden, not unlike Malthe's. Her bright green eyes search my face. I drop my gaze to the ground at once, remembering Freya's cautionary tale. I'm not supposed to be seen by the Tyjans. I'm to stay in the servant quarters, tucked out of sight. But why is the princess sneaking in through the courtyard? Surely this isn't her traditional entrance.

Her footsteps scarcely brush the cobbles and she's gone through the kitchens, up the stairs to her world. I swallow the meat that was stuck to my teeth. It's such a waste—all the flavor is gone.

"Mollie?"

Carliss.

She emerges from a column, the tears dried up and brushed from her cheeks. She doesn't acknowledge the princess at all.

"Did you follow me out here?" she asks.

"I . . . *Yes.*" Still shaken from seeing the princess, I rest my arm against the pillar. It's impossible Kalliope would know who I am and relay the message onto her brother.

But still . . .

"You look just awful," says Carliss, which is quite a claim from the girl who'd been sobbing.

"I just came to see if you were all right."

"Did the Grande ask you to misuse her time?"

I blink, shocked by Carliss's terseness. I'd assumed she'd need a hug and consoling. But she scrunches her nose and I realize she's right. Servants are supposed to be working, not talking.

I turn.

"Wait. I'm sorry," says Carliss, grabbing my forearm to spin me around. She's discarded her apron on the mottled stones, but the stink of seafare is still awfully strong. She dips her hands in a skinny trough, scraping the redness from under her nails. "No one has followed me out here before." Her voice weeps with awe that someone should care.

"Is Amalia like that a lot?" I ask.

Carliss groans. "All the time." Her weary expression melts in the sunshine as she flings her hands to help them dry.

"Who is this boy?"

Her dark eyes narrow, yet I think deep down she was hoping I'd ask. She checks the courtyard, then cocks her head and I follow her lead to a fence, past the cauldrons. We sit out of sight behind a crestwood where the shadows of leaves paint shapes on our skin. That we're resting out here makes me slightly uneasy, but Carliss shrugs, seeming less than concerned.

"What Freya doesn't know won't hurt her," she says.

So I guess our Grande knows nothing of the boy.

"Can you keep a secret?" Carliss asks me, as the soft breeze ripples her thick amber hair.

I'm inclined to immediately tell her *no*. I harbor enough secrets to last a lifetime. But I did ask the question and Carliss seems to trust me, and I need a distraction as I wait to go home. Besides, it's nice to be friendly with someone and to chat about boys seems welcome and benign. I fiddle with a weed that's grown between roots. "I can keep your secret," I say.

She smiles. "Have you ever been in love before, Mollie?" She drums her nails against the pavement.

I shake my head. I feel a little silly. I'm very inexperienced in that department.

"It's a magical feeling."

I muffle a laugh, before noticing the seriousness etched on her face. She isn't being dramatic at all.

She leans in closer. "We meet every day."

"Oh," I say, because I'm lost for words, and I'm puzzled as to why this news is a secret. I've heard that servants are allowed to have lovers, as long as it doesn't interfere with their duties. I run through the boys that work for Kalliope. The Lissons are too young, but there might be some Midlons. I can't yet connect their names to their faces, as they move about swiftly and I don't tend to watch them. "Who is it?" I ask.

Carliss breathes out, then cranes her neck around the tree trunk. Obviously satisfied that no one is spying, she turns back to me. "You swear you won't tell?"

"I swear."

"All right." She rubs her palms, two lines appearing in the middle of her forehead. "He doesn't live in the palace," she says. "He lives in a village at the edge of the city." She's looking at me and I'm looking at her. At first I don't grasp what she's trying to tell me.

Until I do.

"Carliss!"

"Shhh!" She squashes a finger to her lips, eyes frantic.

I can't breathe. It feels like she's punched me. It feels like she's tricked me into hearing her tale. How could she do this with reckless abandon? Does she not know the laws? Or she just doesn't care?

"A villager," I say, and she nods.

"He is. He tells me so much about life in the kingdom."

"You know it's forbidden—"

"I know," she says.

"But the punishment, Carliss . . . Surely you've heard it?"

Royal servants are not permitted to have relations with people outside of the palace. It's deemed treason for there's too much scope for secrets to leak about the Tyjans. In Komran's day, offenders were whipped, but Ladislas amended those laws last year. Now if caught, both parties are detained with an identical limb being carved from their bodies. It's happened already in Septown and Maytown. Just thinking about it makes me queasy. I don't know how quickly these things are discovered, but they always are, and they never end well.

"It's fine," says Carliss.

"Does Amalia know?" Amalia obviously knows there's a boy.

"She thinks he's a servant," Carliss tells me. "She thinks it's Pelletier, one of the coachmen. And besides . . ." She pulls at a lock of hair. "We haven't done anything more than just kiss. So it's all right, Mollie. You don't need to fret. I won't be arrested anytime soon."

She doesn't believe in the punishment rumors. If she did she'd never disobey the law. I think the decree is unjust and cruel, but opinions don't count if you're found to be guilty. I hate that she's telling me this with her soul, expecting that I will wholly support her.

"How long have you known him?" I ask.

She glows. "Almost a week."

"Just a *week*?"

"Well, four days." Carliss throws up her hands. "Who's to judge me? I've never felt like this before now."

My heart sinks. She's invested in this. Trying to dissuade her would just spark the flame.

"We meet in the tower between South and East Gates." She can't hide the tinge of pride in her voice. I picture the inner section of the palace with its lawns and corridors and meandering masonry. Even under a cover of darkness, eyes could be watching from windows and galleries. I'm amazed by her boldness, but Anai always told me that people do foolish things when in love.

If *love* can appear after four short days.

Footsteps patter on the cobbles near the arch. I breathe out slowly, listening hard, watching as Carliss does the same. It's a pair of Lisson boys who've returned from the stables. They're rinsing their hands, complaining of the smell. One of them notices Carliss's apron. At once, they quiet and trot into the villa.

"I wonder," says Carliss, after they're gone, "if you'd do me a favor now that we're friends?" Her smile has become both dreamy and euphoric—like she's waited forever to ask this of someone. I guess her request before she speaks it, but my palms still sweat as she fashions the words. "When I meet my lover, could you be our lookout? I'm frightened that someone will discover our secret."

Of course they will. How could they not? I shake my head before she can finish.

Carliss crumples at my refusal. "*Please*, Mollie!"

"I can't," I say.

I can't risk getting in trouble right now, not when I'm closer to my father than ever. I feel awful—like I'm not a good friend—but what if Prince Malthe was to find me out there? Not only would it be my life in peril, but it would be Freya's, and Errol's, and Pelletier's.

"You think I'm a fool for doing this," says Carliss. "But you said it yourself. You've never been in love."

"I'm sorry," I say—because I am—"but, Carliss . . . *please* rethink what you're doing."

"You don't have to be my lookout," she answers, "but you don't get to tell me what I should or shouldn't do."

"But I've heard of a woman who was caught," I tell her. "She was a servant and her lover was not. They were sent to the Karacholl. Their legs were severed."

"It's nonsense," says Carliss.

"It's the truth!"

"Oh, Mollie."

It's hard to tell if she truly believes that the stories of the emperor's punishments are false. She *wants* to believe that her liaison is safe.

"Let's speak of something else," she says.

But I stand up, brushing my tunic, and tell her I think we should linger no longer. If the princess mentions she saw us at rest, we may be stripped of our nightly rations. Beyond that, I don't wish to stay here and listen to more of Carliss's rashness.

"We should go back to the kitchens," I say. "Your sister must be gone by now."

In the end, Carliss remains outdoors, citing the need to unpeg the linens. It's not her job, but I don't try to stop her. If she wants some alone time, now is the moment. Freya has likely followed Kalliope. Until she returns, our movements aren't watched. I shuffle through the courtyard, gnawing on my lip, filled with the memories of the woman in Maytown who'd returned to her family, shivering and howling, as she crawled to her stonebrick with her leg scythed off.

Her name was Yvette. She'd died that winter. Her thigh turned black and erupted with sores. Each evening the healers scraped her dead flesh with daggers and brought irons from the blacksmith, but the wound wouldn't seal. Hoping to drive the image from my brain, I march up the path, crossing under the trees. Carliss doesn't realize what danger she's in. Even in the night, the soldiers patrol. And if she's been meeting her lover in the tower, it means she's been leaving the safety of our villa. And we're only supposed to move around in the carriage and slip out the back exit. Never through the front. I still don't quite understand the reason. At first I thought it was a rule just for me. But none of the servants who work for the princess seem to bypass the columns in the foyer hall.

I wipe my sandals on a mat near the door, then walk through the empty dining space. Save for the table where I'd first eaten supper, the room is bare, the high ceilings grimy. As I sweep a damp cloth over the counter, I remember what became of Yvette's great love. When his parents had learned what happened to him, they called the healer, but his stump turned septic. Later, his body was found in the ocean, crabs yanking and feeding on his dappled cheek. He was still conscious, so goes the tale, and I cannot comprehend how four little days could make Carliss shirk the laws of the kingdom, however painful and unfair they may seem.

I finish cleaning the last bits of muck when Tallesa emerges from a door in the hall. In an instant all thoughts of Carliss dissolve as our eyes meet, as her lips arc down. I've managed to avoid her since meeting with Freya by pasting my back to the walls like a spy. Now I'm frozen in the empty room, without the means to conjure a retreat.

But she leaves the space between us wide.

"Tallesa," I say.

"Good morning, Mollie." She speaks my name like I sleep in the stables and I should be grateful we breathe the same air. She's carrying silverware in a large container. I've seen the plates and bowls upstairs. She thumps them on the wooden table, hauls out a bench, and plonks down.

My calf throbs. I'm holding it tight, watching as Tallesa polishes a fork. I walk quickly to the kitchen shutters.

"You're not from Sledloe," she says.

I halt.

As I turn, her eyes are black like ravens whose beaks pierce through my flimsy cover.

"You're a liar," she says. "That part is certain. You don't belong in the palace with us."

CHAPTER SIX

TALLESA'S RIGHT—*I DON'T BELONG*—BUT I WON'T LET HER grow more suspicious of me. On my second night in the servant quarters, I spend it in front of the kitchen washbowl. My nails soften in the lukewarm water and my fingertips resemble dried summer fruit. Patchy grease stains smear my tunic—a product of overcooked lard and gristle dried to the base of Welsha's pans.

I'm a Lissette. That's what Freya tells me. It doesn't make Tallesa sneer at me less. Instead she trains her pupils to the horizon whenever our paths intersect in the halls. The hours pass like rain-filled days. My bones crack and ache from kneeling on tiles. On occasion, I'm permitted upstairs to the salons to sweep leaves and mud from the marble landings. While I'm there I scan the doorways, always at the ready to scurry downstairs. When I ask Freya if Malthe might see me, she tells me he cannot enter the villa.

"It belongs to Princess Kalliope," she says, as though I should have known all along. "It would be the most offensive gesture if he were to stroll inside this building."

My presence here makes a lot more sense, but I'm wary of how the days roll together. It seems less and less like my leave is important, judging by Freya's quickening footfalls.

On my third day, I wake to shouting, echoing through the villa's stone walls. I wriggle to a stand and pull on my tunic, blinking the sleep from my half-focused eyes. It's dim in the room I share with Quinn, so I fling back the hessian that leads to the corridor. As I pad along, the voices grow sharper, rising and falling through the kitchen archway.

"We need to work swiftly."

I slip inside and try to blend in with the other servants. Everyone's gathered by the center bench—Lissettes, Lissons, Midlas, and Midlons. Between remarks about weapons and gladiators, they're cramming their mouths with strips of damper. I tear off a piece and gobble it down, but the flour's old and it tastes like ashes.

"You're late," says Tallesa, and it takes me a moment before I realize she's addressing me.

"I didn't hear—"

Her attention flits. "With the Grande touring the site of the Tournament, she has left me in charge of the villa's schedule."

The servants keep chewing, as if this is normal. And perhaps it is. Tallesa *seems* like a leader. As a tendril escapes from one of her pins, the blonde curl bounces against her temple.

"Guests of the Tournament are arriving this evening." Tallesa nods to confirm any doubt. "The princess will be welcoming her cousins and aunts, and a few of the women from Leeang and Torquella."

My ears prick up at the mention of Leeang, the island home where my mother grew up.

"We need to make certain the chambers are spotless. If the women have complaints, they will moan to their husbands." Tallesa rattles off a few more instructions, mostly concerning how she is in charge. The group breaks apart and vacates the kitchen, so I follow the Lissettes.

"Where do we start?"

"Here, come with me." Quinn gives a wry smile, which causes the tension to thaw from my shoulders. With our arms full of cloth, we ascend the first staircase, counting the fifteenth door to our left. She presses a key into a lock and the giant panels creak, opening inward. A staleness protrudes from within the chamber, and I wrinkle my nose as we step inside.

It's so dark. I can just make out that the furniture's sheathed by layers of canvas. Quinn draws the heavy curtains aside and a shock of sunlight blisters the carpet. An enormous bed squats near the window, piled with pillows and enclosed by a canopy. I search for a spot to place the linens, but the surfaces swim with cushions of dust.

"This room is one of the worst," Quinn declares, tugging the covering off a chaise. I balance the sheets on the fabric underneath.

"Why was it locked?"

"Too many memories." Quinn dumps her cloths on top of mine. "This whole floor belonged to Princess Astrid. You've heard of her, surely?"

"Yes, of course."

"She lived in this wing with her mother, Queen Ryell."

Astrid and Ryell. The names chill my skin. To think that I'm standing in their section of the palace! Queen Ryell was Komran's much younger second wife. It was said forty years separated their ages. Komran had entered his seventh decade when Ryell gave birth to their daughter, Astrid. The child was the same age as Princess Kalliope.

"This was her chamber?" I ask.

"No." Quinn angles her head to the door. "Her chamber was farther along the hall. We're not to open it—Her Highness's orders—though I think the command comes from Emperor Ladislas."

It must have been strange for Emperor Ladislas to have a half sister the same age as his daughter. The girls might have played together in the gardens and fought over toys and breakfasts and attention. I wonder if Astrid was more like her brother or if she had Komran's goodness within her.

"You do recall what happened?" asks Quinn, her brown eyes sliding from my face to the floor.

I nod. Astrid died as a child. At seven, she plunged into a bouldered ravine. Though ten years have passed, I remember the flags that adorned the streets—dyed black for mourning. After her death, Ryell took a knife and sliced her own throat while the palace slept. Her body was discovered by her Grande Personale, and her funeral pyre choked the skies with smoke, which hovered above the palace for days.

"The tale hurts my heart." Quinn turns to the window to knock webs and dirt from the corners of the pane. I stand beside her, gazing down, watching from above for the first time. The palace consists of an assortment of buildings. They each face inward, surrounding a square. The grass is tidy and clipped very short, dotted with cobbles and a few stray trees.

"I was like you," Quinn says softly. "There was so much to take in."

The area could house a regiment of hundreds and still there'd be space to shift about freely. I watch some soldiers meander through the square, dropping in and out of the sandbrick structures. Other people, too, shuffle about, carrying florets of greens and baskets of linen. I presume they are servants and yet I'm not certain, as they do not resemble those in our villa. These people seem closer to the prisoners found in Sledloe with their somnolent footsteps and mangled hair.

"They serve the prince and the emperor," says Quinn, before the question can burst from my lips.

"They look . . ."

"World-weary," Quinn suggests, although I'd been thinking of something less pleasant. My father once took me out to the docks where a warden's boat crouched in the weed-twisted shallows. It was said the ship had run off course and languished for weeks in the swamps of the southlands. By the time the men alighted from the deck, it was like the life in their eyes had been snuffed. These servants in the square have the matching gaunt faces, though their bodies slog on like a whip's at their backs.

We withdraw from the window and work in silence, cleaning insects and filth from knobs in the fittings. I consider why Freya keeps us in the villa—not only me, but the other servants, too. Is she frightened we could be mistreated out there if the prince or the emperor witnessed our health? I've noticed when Lissettes ferry messages and supplies, they use tattered shawls to obscure their faces.

"We're luckier than the other servants," I say.

"Very blessed," Quinn agrees.

"We have a lot of freedom in here," I continue, hoping for her to explain it to me. As we strip the bed and replace the sheets, I wait for an answer, but it does not come. She's nothing like Carliss—all floaty and romantic. "Why are we treated better?" I ask.

Quinn doesn't pause. "We're treated the same."

"Quinn!"

"We are. They have meals and white tunics. I am sure they sleep on pallets, as we do. And they'd have the same duties of cooking and cleaning."

I press my fingers against the padding, smoothing the wrinkles out of the linen. I imagine the demands of Prince Malthe in his villa—and what he'd do if a servant fell short. All I see are his pupils in the moonlight, shining with wrath as he stormed the Gathering. Unless he has someone in the palace to check him, I cannot believe we'd be treated the same.

"Have you talked to those servants?"

"It's not allowed." Quinn fluffs the pillows with unnecessary force.

"So how do you know what their lives are like?"

"It isn't our right to gossip," she says. She clears her throat a little too loudly, and I sense that I'm nudging her into a corner. Her chin grows firm as she tucks in the blanket, the muscles in her upper arms shaking with effort.

But she knows what I mean. Of course she does. She's been here for years; I've been here for days. She must have witnessed their unequal treatment. But then she's managed to keep herself safe, so who am I to question what she does to survive?

I let it be.

"Who will stay in this chamber?"

"I do not know. It is up to the princess. Though perhaps the ladies will choose themselves based on the order in which they arrive."

And with that, Quinn excuses herself, explaining she needs to bring up a pail. I do not ask if she wants my assistance. She likely requires a reprieve from my questions. When I'm standing in the chamber, alone with my thoughts, I take another moment to examine its expanse. It could easily house a family from Maytown. Or perhaps two families. It's such a waste.

With Quinn gone and nothing to do, I find myself drifting again to the window. There's commotion in the square below. Soldiers have gathered at the mouth of a tower, milling about, in a puzzling order. I can't make out what they're doing or saying, but I count nineteen men, clothed in red jackets. They're regarding something beyond my view. Something inside the tower entrance.

I wait. Near the tower a soldier whirls around, stepping backward into the square. The others join him in two straight lines, leaving a thin strip of grass down the center. I brace myself for the sight of the emperor. In fact, I'm ready to dive for the carpet. But I'm lulled by the shadow that forms on the stones, how the shape of the head and body come together, and a silhouette follows, the figure tripping forward.

I gasp.

It's *Jove.*

His feet are bare and his arms are stained with rust-colored grime. His hair is wild like it was in the cottage. It's the last thing familiar about him now. Chains drip from his withered wrists and pin his ankles unnaturally together. Behind him other men spill from the stronghold, stumbling and howling like condemned beggars, shielding their eyes from the overhead glare.

A soldier grips the back of Jove's tunic, hauling him up and shoving him on. The gap between the two lines shrinks as the soldiers compel the prisoners along. I can't comprehend why they're here in the palace. Aside from Jove, there are seven other men. Most have beards that stick out like brushes, and many have eyelids that keep lolling shut until they are struck by an alert soldier's boot.

"They're spares," Quinn says.

I turn. "Spares?" She must have deliberately masked her return.

She scrunches her nose, shrugging in distaste. "I know they've done evil to be held in the Karacholl, but no one deserves to die in the Tournament."

At first, her words are mere jagged pieces. *Karacholl. The Tournament. Deserve to die.* They do not fit together in my head. Is she even seeing the same scene as I?

Instead of responding, I observe the soldiers, looking much closer at Jove's ripped clothes. Only I was secured in the Nothrick Prison. That night on the horses, the prince kept Jove. I'd conceived he was taken to another cell, but I'd never guessed he'd been moved to the Karacholl. But now it makes sense what Quinn is saying. Jove was imprisoned with the kingdom's worst convicts—sealed underground to be used as a spectacle.

"A life sacrificed for entertainment," I whisper, the ghastly truth of his future apparent.

"I tell myself that they deserve this end. In a way it is how they atone for their sins." Quinn touches her forehead to the glass, then turns from the window. "We don't need to watch."

But it's my fault. I've caused this for Jove. I was selfish to speak of my grief at the Gathering.

"Where do they take them?" A foolish part in me wishes to break the chains from his wrists.

"There are cells in the basement next to the storehouse."

"Where is that?"

"Right down the end." Quinn points to the square's far side where a grand tower sprouts from deep in the lawn. Nestled by the structure is a low-lying opening with a lamplit path leading deep below ground.

I force myself to abandon the window, to follow Quinn's guidance and to pick up the pail. As I scrub and mop, my anxious mind teeters, swallowing the guilt that claws at my neck.

The Tournament begins in five days. The Lissettes have been air-drying banners and flags. The Midlons have brought in berries and nuts that are washed and packed in round cane baskets. It means that Jove has four days at most of being kept in the basement beside the tower. They'd likely transport the spares last of all, before chaining them up in the arena cavities. But if somehow—*somehow*—I could clear Jove's name. To make them see that he's not a criminal. If the other prisoners are indeed from the Karacholl, they must have done worse deeds than Jove?

Surely.

But maybe they haven't. It's a scary thought, but who knows who accused each one of their crimes? Prince Malthe doesn't check before locking men up. Neither would the emperor. So how could one tell?

Quinn takes three strides toward the door. "The Grande and Errol have returned," she says. The swishing of bodies echo through the cloisters, and Quinn's features tighten. "We need to hurry."

She means hurry to finish our chores, but my initial thought is not about cleaning. Instead I wonder, could Freya speak to Kalliope? She may not be as close as a Grande Personale, but she's allowed in her chambers and the princess would trust her. The only hindrance is the princess herself. Rumors abound that Kalliope is frivolous. Even in Maytown, villagers claim that her favorite discussions are of brooches and face rouge.

Yet I'm determined to try.

I know Quinn won't like it, so I bypass her quickly and traverse the soft landing. Freya's voice wafts up from the foyer, mingled with Errol's guttural, clipped tone. They seem to be deep in conversation about something that makes the Grande stutter. Her voice is so low and so hurried and patchy that she does not notice me standing above them.

"I can't comprehend it," Errol says.

Freya hisses something I cannot make out. The next time Errol is fainter of voice, but I do catch the one name he utters:

"Prince Malthe."

A dizziness almost knocks me sideways.

"Hush!" Freya pinches her husband's arm. She peers through the chamber for loitering servants before pushing him swiftly behind a pillar. As the click of their footfalls halt in the alcove, they chatter in earnest for a protracted stretch. With their murmurs increasingly hard to decipher, I creep down the staircase, my breath coming fast. Behind me Quinn hisses to come back at once, but I ignore her warning and strengthen my pace. As I reach the lower level, I pause, the pounding of my thoughts like a mallet in my head.

From this distance, their words are much clearer.

"You know we cannot risk it," says Freya. "We cannot predict what he will do next."

"I should have been more careful," says Errol.

Freya sighs, long and slow; her timbre is gentle, even forgiving. "You weren't to know he'd go back there so fast."

But Errol is downcast. "What must we do?"

"I don't know."

They talk on it longer, and I can't seem to still my restless hands. They're speaking of Malthe . . . *going back somewhere?*

". . . but you must cease visiting the Nothrick," says Freya.

I nearly choke as she mentions the prison. *The Nothrick.* Has Malthe returned to the jail? Have the guards already explained I have perished? Has the prince moved on and I can go home? But no, if that were the case, then why? Why would Freya and Errol be worried? And all of a sudden, their words snap together, and the meaning of what they're saying unravels.

In horror, I storm the pillar to confront them. "Are you saying Prince Malthe is aware I've escaped?"

They both gasp to see me before them, tussling to bring their composures to heel. But it's too late. In their surprise, I've seen their expressions, uncovered and truthful. And although they scramble to refute my question, in the end, they can't, and they both remain silent.

"How did he learn that I'd escaped?" My glare bounds from one to the other.

Freya clamps her hand on my wrist and pulls me farther into the hollow. "A prisoner heard you leaving," she whispers.

"Do they know Errol helped me?"

She shakes her head. "And he didn't spy the carriage, either, as his cell faces outward toward the sea."

A big relief for them, no doubt. On the other hand, it doesn't help me. But I nod, trying to keep a clear head, trying to absorb what this news truly means. "I suppose the prince is furious," I say.

"No," says Freya, but Errol jabs her side.

"He is," he admits, "but you're safe in here. There is no need for you to be alarmed."

His eyes dart, and my pulse thrums faster. That cannot be the end of the story. Malthe knows, yet I remain safe? I'm to proceed as if things are normal? From what I've learned of the prince thus far, he would be desperate to settle the score. He wouldn't remove his boots and eat berries, pretending that we had never crossed paths.

"Isn't he planning to track me down?"

"At first he was. But now . . . *no*." Errol and Freya exchange rapid glances like they're peeling off layers but concealing the core.

"Why has he stopped?"

Errol breathes out. "We managed to get in the prince's head. A soldier told him you'd fled across the Geynes. And fortunately, the prince believed him."

Gyzen. It must have been Gyzen who did that.

"And after that, he abandoned the hunt. As the sea is vast with many horizons, he deemed it too treacherous to mount a pursuit."

Freya nods to confirm the tale, and I suppose this should be welcome news. To know that the prince won't be searching for me. To know that Freya and Errol are secure. But a portion of Errol's neck has flushed.

"But . . . ?" I ask.

"That's all," Freya says. I can tell she's listening for prying ears. Perchance even hoping that some will appear. "We should get back to our chores," she continues.

But something about this still seems off. Again, I remember Prince Malthe's demeanor. He wasn't someone who could let things go, who could let a girl who insulted the emperor sail off in a boat—completely free. Especially one who'd escaped the Nothrick. The prince would never forget that offense. A blade for a blade. I recall his promise: *But if you hurt my father with words, it's only fair that I hurt yours back.*

My jaw tenses.

I'll hurt yours back.

"He may arrest my father as payback," I realize. If he can't take his rage out on me, he'll go elsewhere.

"He won't," says Freya, a mite too quickly.

But no—*I feel it*—and I do not believe her. I do not believe in her nonsense anymore. I trusted her words on my first night here, but it's a mistake I will not make twice.

"I have to go home and warn him," I say.

"I think, perhaps, you are overreacting." Freya glances at Errol again, but he's looking everywhere, except at me. Smoothing the pockets of her tunic, she sighs, patting my forearm with a knowing smile. "I doubt the prince would pursue your father. We know how he works. You have to trust us." But though her convictions may have swayed me before, this time I silently kick them aside. It's clear she wants me to stay in the palace, tucked out of sight and under her thumb. If I am caught, they are caught also. And to her, of course, their protection is paramount.

"For a few more days." Her smile extends wider.

"For a few more days." I nod. "I can do that." I have no intention of prolonging my visit, but I let her relax as she sidesteps the pillar.

"Which Lissettes were you working with?" she asks, as though nothing I've mentioned matters at all.

"Quinn," I say.

"Just Quinn?"

"Yes."

"Did she see you come down here just now?"

"She did."

"Then I want you to go to the kitchen. Fetch a pail of water and take it upstairs."

So apparently fetching a bucketful of water is supposed to be the reason I spoke with the Grande. The same fire sparks in my belly that interrupted Tallesa on my first night here. But this time, it blazes taller. Burns like the husks that are lit beneath cauldrons.

"Well, go," says Freya, and I force my own smile, biting my lip to disguise what I'm plotting.

Carliss is in the kitchen with Welsha when I snoop in the corners for a bucket to fill. On a stone by the firewood sits a wooden pail used by Lissons to carry in kindling. I empty the twigs into one ordered mound and slink past the bench, my eyes on the windows. The courtyard outside hums with Midlas and Midlons, and

I'm not about to saunter past Tallesa in order to fill my container at the well.

I'll take a dry bucket.

Welsha glowers at me as she boils eggs and corn for the princess's lunch. "You shouldn't be in here."

I steady my voice. "Are there any old lemons to use in our cleaning?"

Welsha squints with her big gray eyes, causing the rest of her face to prune. "We've some in storage," she says. "Who wants them?"

"The Grande," I say. "I can get them?"

"I'll do it."

As Welsha waddles into the larder, I quickly pull Carliss aside with a head flick. She dries her hands on her tattered apron, her left brow rising like a crescent moon.

My heart thunders.

"What's the matter?" asks Carliss.

"Where do you meet your lover?" I ask.

She's slow to reply. "Between South and East Gates . . . ?"

"I want to be your lookout," I tell her.

The instant the words are free in the air, my blood pounds at what this will mean. *I'm going to leave the palace tonight. My father and I will have to flee.*

"What made you change your mind?" asks Carliss.

I cannot tell her the truth. "Love."

"Well, it *is* worth all of the gold in the kingdom."

And the smile overtakes her entire face.

CHAPTER SEVEN

THE ROOSTERS IN THE EMPEROR'S FARM HAVEN'T YET CROWED when Carliss tugs my tunic sleeve. Against the wall in a rumple of hessian, Quinn breathes in and out in rhythm. Gulping my fear I manage a nod, and Carliss gives me the thumbs-up sign. She's already dressed and her hair is tied, and she smells like mint and lavender drops.

I do not bother checking my reflection in the shard of mirror glued to the bricks. I already know my black hair's tangled. Seeing my fraught complexion won't help. I throw back the textile and slowly stand. Carliss points beyond the arch. As she disappears, I stretch my shoulders, then follow her into the gloomy hall.

"Come on," she whispers, grabbing my arm, pulling me through the kitchens in joy. She reminds me of Anai when we were children, pretending that we would run away. Anai lived next door to my stonebrick before she moved to a larger apartment. We'd plot our passage on boats across the Geynes, dreaming of living in huts on the islands. Once we got as far as the pigsty before the pair of us lost our nerves. We'd spun on our heels and fled back home before our parents could uncover our quest.

Carliss's brown eyes flitter like stars and the action reminds me of Anai even more. Last season, Anai met a boy called Symon and kept meeting him every day in the paddocks. Love seemed to drive her a little bit wild and Carliss is definitely on the same course. She tows me past the base of a staircase, the second of three which scale the walls.

So far everything is going to plan. Well, Carliss's plan. My plan isn't solid. I can't predict what awaits us outside. All I know is that this is my chance to escape the villa and return to my father. Waiting here longer with Freya is pointless. Her *a few more days* may never pass. I consider sharing my scheme with Carliss, but I'm too afraid she might press for answers.

"Ready, Mollie?" She squeezes my hand.

Right now I know our exact location. I've dusted these busts, swabbed these mosaics, and swept dry loam from between these crevices. We're in the foyer where I'd confronted Freya—a large, open space the size of a horse field. The ceiling glares from its incredible height with its paintings of chariots and clouds and goddesses. Beyond this room is the atrium, and Carliss leads me toward it now. The center houses a bathing pool, rippling with water and dusted with petals. During banquets the women soak here, eating grapes and figs and toasting from goblets. We hurry through the chamber to another that is darker and flanked by an indoor emerald forest. Trees shoot from holes in the floor in custom-made circles, sawn to fit trunks.

"This way," says Carliss.

"Wait!" I hiss. There's movement in the shadows beyond.

We lunge behind the closest tree, the bark scratching against my bare skin. A soldier lurks near the far wall, chewing on something that resembles dried apricots. I wasn't aware that soldiers came in here, but I guess he's not in the inner sanctum. He leans languidly against a pillar, just one of the many that pepper the villa.

"Do we have to go past him?" I whisper.

"No. Fortune smiles. There's another way."

We backtrack silently through the atrium with Carliss directing me toward a side door. On the other side is a room swathed with moonlight. Crisscross patterns adorn the terrazzo. Carliss pastes her body to a column and I do the same.

The pathway is clear.

We're at the entrance to Kalliope's villa. Beyond the pillars, steps descend. Once our soles hit the grass beneath, we'll be in the square that I viewed from the window.

I drag in air. If we're caught outside, we'll be bolted in stocks for defying curfew. Except if we're found by Malthe, of course; and my stomach knots at what he would do. Beside me, Carliss stares straight ahead. She points to the tower that looms in the distance. It's black and hulking like a sentry on night watch, the tip blanched by the glittering moon.

"That's where I meet him," she says, all breathless, like she's sprinted from one end of a village to the other. I glance sideways at her profile. Is this love? My father would have done the same for my mother.

Pain stabs me.

"Let's go," I say, not wanting to think on it too long. I need my mind blazing like a furnace if I'm going to do this. "Are you ready to run?"

Carliss nods like I've somehow bolstered her, and then we're dashing full tilt down the stairs. My hair streams back and the damp earth squelches, but no one shouts and tells us to halt.

We pull up in front of the tower. A little to the right lies the entrance to the cells. Despite my arms being riddled with goose-flesh, a patch of sweat has formed by my temple. I half expect a soldier to appear, but the only movement is Carliss's fingers. As she fumbles with the padlock that swings from the tower, I turn to inspect the basement opening.

Poor Jove.

My guilt rises to know that he's locked in a windowless cell. The passage slopes down, lit by torches, illuminating the scuffed rock walls. I wish I had the strength to do something—or the means to do something that could make a difference. But it would be foolish to divert from the plan, so I tug on my waistband to settle my breathing.

"Oi, Sylvan! Is it almost daybreak?"

I freeze at the man's voice. Hazy, but real. It wafts from within the yawning passage, upsetting the quiet of the palace square.

"It should be changeover soon," says another.

"Who's replacing us?"

"Levicus and Rendon."

"Drank too much ale," the first voice says. "I need to go piss."

"Don't take too long."

As his soles scrape grit, he starts to whistle and I pivot on the spot, almost smacking into Carliss.

"Mollie?" Her voice is sharp and confused, but there isn't the time to explain what I heard.

"There's a soldier coming!"

Carliss doesn't move. Her face is a mishmash of contour and shade. I cannot tell if she believes me or not.

"Where is the soldier?"

"Coming up from the basement!"

I grip her arm, yanking it roughly. I don't care if I pull too hard. She doesn't object—in fact she starts sprinting, streaking ahead, so she must understand. She reaches the side of the tower first. She heaves the door and a space appears. I turn sideways and squeeze inside with Carliss behind me, closing the gap. In the dark, I quickly lose track of the moments as they seep together, blending like paint. I strain to hear the soldier outside—but all that comes back is the rustle of branches, swept back and forth in the southerly breeze.

I'm not sure when it's safe to exhale. I leave it as long as I possibly can.

"I don't think he saw," Carliss says finally. She flicks her fringe and it tickles my brow.

I believe she's right. If the soldier had spied us, he would have been knocking on the tower by now.

"Why were you near the basement?" asks Carliss.

"I heard a noise."

"Well, that was too close."

She's not wrong. I'm beginning to wonder if perhaps this entire plan is unwise. But the moment I do, I think of my father—and how I cannot afford not to try.

"You stay here," says Carliss.

"What? Where are you going?"

"Where do you think?"

"I'm not staying here without you!" I hiss. "If you're going upstairs, then I'm coming, too."

I'm sure if the tower was light enough, I'd witness Carliss's frown of displeasure. But I won't remain in the bowels of a stairwell. My escape lies above, outside in the darkness.

"That soldier could still be out there," she says. "Which is why, as my lookout, you need to stay here. I will return when my lover has left."

"Carliss!"

"Don't follow," she tells me.

"Carliss!"

Her shadow darts up the stone spiral and I give chase, although I can't see. I haven't gone far when I come to a landing where a sliver of night spills through a small crack. With my arms outstretched, I trace the panel. The crack is the rim where the door's ajar. When I jam my face to the hole, I can see her running to a boy in the dappled moonlight.

I wince at the thought that someone might spot them, although I'm reminded that they've done this before. But how has this boy evaded security? Could he be friendly with one of the soldiers? They're so close, their bodies have merged, and I roll my eyes at the low giggling sounds. As I wait, I regard the landscape behind them. How the earth is raised on this side of the tower at the same height as the bridge to the mainland.

This must be the road to freedom. And Carliss's boy . . . I could ask him to guide me. It's the only way. The smartest choice. But it seems the pair of them stand there for years. As the moments tick by, my patience falters, the blood draining south of my cheeks. The dusk is still gathered tightly around them, but it won't last forever.

"Carliss!" I hiss.

Their silhouettes detach.

"Who is that?" he asks.

"The sun will soon be up," I warn. I notice that Carliss draws the boy closer, but he presses against her and steps away.

"Who are you?" he snaps, and I'm about to tell him that I need his help, but then he stops. Laughter echoes through the bushes behind him, laced with voices that are deep and gruff.

Soldiers.

The boy springs back. *"Go!"* He starts to run. "I'll head them off!"

"Wait!"

But he's brisk like a practiced bandit. The darkness swallows his form in one gulp, and the noise of the men heightens around us.

"Move!" Carliss appears beside me, and she drags me backward into the tower. She closes the door with a gentle thud, and I swear I can hear her thrashing pulse.

Though it could be mine.

"Come on," she says. Her palm is hot as she grabs my hand. I don't want to go, but we sprint to the bottom, faint light spilling through the upper casements. The fuzzy blackness is stirring outside, and my chance is rapidly slipping from grasp. Carliss lays her fingers on the handle, but when the door opens, she lets out a shriek.

On instinct, I shuffle back up the stairs as Carliss is pulled through the door to the square. There's someone outside, and I hear Carliss pleading, though the pitch of her voice is muffled in the updraft. The purple shade of night lifts farther and a shadow moves, veneering the door. From outside I hear Carliss yell that she's sorry, that she's young, that she was trying to be efficient, that she wants to go back to complete her chores.

"I'm alone," she says.

I blink. It's a warning. I've been dithering so long that my mind is in tatters. But she's letting me know that I can't remain here. Her assailant may enter and I need to make haste. I turn and jog up the stairs once more, gritting my teeth in a bid to calm down. Thank goodness Carliss does not know my secrets in case she'll be forced by the soldiers to spill them. I'm watching the windows as I round each loop. I'm almost to the landing when an outline appears. I pause, but the figure descends without halting. His body knocks against me.

"Carliss?" he says.

"No," I whisper. It's her lover from the gate. "But we have to go up. Someone else is downstairs."

"We cannot," he grunts.

"You'll be caught—"

"As will you. Don't speak for a moment, they're outside behind me." He holds up his arm to still my tongue, and we stand in the silence, listening to the night. I wish I could make out the curve of his features to determine whether to trust him or not.

And then I hear it. The drumming of footsteps. The door flies open on the landing above us. Into the tower steps a band of three? Four? I cannot discern the true numbers.

"Keep going down!" the boy grunts at me, and I turn without thinking and skid down the steps. His breath is controlled as he matches my strides. The voices above us are definitely soldiers.

I need to repeat that the square isn't safe, but it's much too chancy to utter the words. When we hit the bottom, I'm panting hard, though the soldiers above show no hint they've heard us. Metal is sheathed and jokes are exchanged in that boorish manner becoming of drunkards.

"Ah, Farrow, you brute," quips one man in glee.

Farrow. The name strikes fear in my chest.

I rest my ear against the door. I cannot hear Carliss or her captor outside. I roll the timber to the left just a hair and murky half-light floods into the stairwell. The luminance paints a stripe on the brickwork. I grit my teeth, but the soldiers keep talking. The space is too small to squash ourselves though, but if the gap widens, they're going to notice.

We only have moments left to spare before the sun bathes the palace in yellow. And with Farrow above me, my choices constrict. I push the door farther.

"Wait," says the boy.

"We have to go." It's our best chance to hide. At least in the square we'll be sheltered by trees. Yes, they are sparse and, yes, there are few, but it's better than lingering as game in the tower. I don't wait for him to protest my decision—or even agree. I heave the board. From my limited view, I cannot spot Carliss.

But the boy reaches out and grabs my shoulder.

"It's you," he says, and the way the words form, an unwanted chill trickles over my skin. I know that voice. From somewhere, I know it. But not from my village. From someplace foreign.

Before I step into the square, I turn to look at him in the light. And my mouth drops open when I see the blond hair and the cold expression.

It's the boy from the Gathering.

CHAPTER EIGHT

IS GRIP NUMBS MY FINGERS AS WE SHOOT LIKE RABBITS INTO the square. The air is thick and gray like dishwater, though the edge of buildings are beginning to sharpen. So many questions pile in my head about what he's doing inside the palace. But I dare not speak as we dive for an oak tree, winding our bodies around the trunk.

We're three strides from the holding cells. Close to fifty from Kalliope's villa. With the darkness lifting, we need to find shelter. Something more lasting than the rear of a tree. I wish we could race to the protection of my quarters, but the soldiers have spilled from the tower behind us. Farrow's shoulders rise and fall, his breathing ragged like the grunt of a boar.

He knows we're out here.

His head is angled, the untidy whiskers snagging his collar. With the gait of a wolf, he observes the surrounds for signs of servants who have broken curfew. I don't recognize the other two men. Their stomachs bulge, straining their jackets. They split up quickly and canvas the perimeter, measured and observant, like hunting jackals.

My insides clench. What if they find us? I turn to the boy, who surveys the expanse. His attention is drawn beneath the eaves to a skinny smatter of dull cobblestones.

There's movement in the fragile light.

The boy inhales, and so do I. Concealed in the shadows, their skirts billowing, are Carliss and Freya, their features like glass. It must have been Freya at the base of the tower who'd dragged Carliss into the square. Perhaps she noticed our empty pallets or perhaps she trailed our steps through the kitchens. Regardless, she's trapped with Carliss now. They've pressed their spines into the wall. But with tunics so pale and soft in the night, in less than a heartbeat, Farrow has spied them.

I cringe. Farrow's chortle is low and triumphant, as if he lives for moments like these. Freya links arms with Carliss and runs, their bare feet slapping against the pathway. Even a Grande can be fastened in stocks and pelted with moldy filth from the gutter. Carliss is nimbler, so she reaches the villa, but a soldier appears from between the columns.

"We can't go back to my quarters," I whisper. "We need to get back to the tower."

"No." The boy grabs my wrist, jerking my arm. I tug it back, which makes him groan. I get the feeling he'd have enough strength to dislocate it if he desired.

"Why not?" I snap.

"Why do you think? The possibility's high that there could be others."

There could be others.

My lips part, but I can't find the words to refute his logic. He must know the patterns of the soldiers by heart. He'd have to know them to sneak in the palace. We wait in silence, my chest heavy, as Farrow and his men close in on the women. I want to do something—*anything, really*—but what is the use if I'm snatched by them, too?

My vision catches on a small alcove with its entrance hidden by a drooping willow. Years of playing in Maytown with Anai meant slinking between stonebricks to evade her cousin. Now it's me who tugs at the boy, tilting my head at the veiled space. It's only a few steps from the edge of the oak. We could easily make it without being noticed. The boy nods back and we don't bother counting. We dart together, skidding into the darkness. The leaves graze our necks like spidery fingers, and I realize it's a passage between two buildings.

From our new nook, I spin to see Freya, shielding Carliss and pushing her ahead. She directs her to rouse the rest of our quarters and to summon the princess to come to the courtyard. Carliss dashes up the steps to safety, dodging the apricot-eating soldier with ease. It renders the Grande alone on the pavement.

"Come here, old woman!" calls one of the soldiers.

Contemplating a distraction of sorts, I twist a twig off one of the branches. The boy's hand tightens on mine. He knows what I'm thinking, but I jerk away. If I lob the stick into the cloisters, the soldiers may pause and Freya can flee.

"She's the princess's Grande," a second soldier cautions.

"Not at this hour she's not," says the first.

Freya pitches her shoulders back and takes three strides toward the villa. I ready myself to toss the stick, but the boy's hand slides to my upper arm.

"Wait," he whispers.

Freya keeps walking. Her chins juts out as she stares in a line. I don't think they'd hurt her just before dawn, but if they did, I'm unsure who would mark them. With all my strength, I hurl the stick. It bounces off a trellis and falls, unheard. The boy makes a choking sound in his throat that's a mixture of relief and wanting to kill me.

I don't blame him, but I drop to my haunches and sweep the terrain for a rock or some clay. Sand and earth push under my nails. There's nothing larger than crumbling shale.

Another figure emerges from the tower. Even in the dimness, his grand height stands out. He isn't carrying a bow on his shoulder, but the hide of a quiver sits crooked to his backbone. The boy beside me breathes in and I'm curious if he recalls Gyzen, too. He'd surely remember the black-bearded man tumble from the stonebrick with an arrow through his torso.

Gyzen's arrow.

The sun is rising, tingeing the ground with a buttery glow. When the soldiers glimpse Gyzen, they hastily part, and Freya glides past, her stoic face sallow. I cannot see Malthe, but Gyzen's very presence makes me worried that the prince is not far behind. And when a farther two soldiers detach from the landscape, it's clear any path to the tower is futile.

The wind picks up and I glance skyward, straining to see through the swaying foliage. Pieces of navy burst through the gaps. Not long now and our cover will dissolve.

My gaze flicks sideways. To our right is a shed that houses grain for the Tyjan kitchens. According to Freya, the shed remains locked to prevent hungry servants from pilfering rations. On our left is a wall, but it's curved and strong. There aren't enough hollows to get a good footing. Moreover, we cannot scale a tall building with the sun about to burst from the heavens. The entrance to the building faces the square. It's possibly crawling with soldiers, too. I swivel to the boy, hoping for ideas, but his outline has vanished from under the willow.

"Search the grounds."

I wheel around.

Malthe. It's *Malthe.* My whole body tenses.

"Your Highness, there is no need," says Gyzen.

"The grounds, soldier. Search them for me."

With excruciating slowness, I shrink back. Thank goodness the grass is damp and quiet. As the image of Gyzen slips farther from view, the boy grabs my hand and pulls me inside.

Inside?

I muffle a kneejerk yelp. He's dragged me into a small, stuffy room. A whiff of mildew hangs in the air, but the stillness tells me that we are alone. The boy drives a wooden board shut behind us. Without any light, the space seems to narrow. I stretch my arms and my hands brush objects—sculptures, cabinets, boxes, and fence posts—or at least that's what I think they are. When enough time passes, the blackness wanes and my eyesight adjusts. We're in a storeroom. Outlines of portrait frames, statues, and worktables nestle together in disorderly mountains.

We must have entered the side of the building, likely through a door used solely by servants. I can feel the boy's eyes on me as our intakes of air combine in the silence. I step back, but my body hits stone. Gently, the boy taps a finger to his lips. I listen for voices in the alley outside, but it seems the soldiers have bypassed the willow, hopefully heading to the bridge or the stables.

It doesn't make my shoulders less rigid.

"I remember you from Yahres," I say.

The boy twists past an ornate copper urn, joining me in the cramped space.

"Who are you?" I ask.

"Vogel Lashler."

I'm startled he parts with his name so quickly. He runs a hand through his mussed up hair, the blond strands glistening as if they are wet.

"And you?" he asks.

"Meadow Sircha." It feels good to speak the truth.

But he nods as if he thought I'd say more, and when I don't, he turns away. His attention fixes on the way we came in, then darts to the ceiling, then the corners, and walls.

"Have you found something?" I ask.

"Maybe." He points to a second door set in the bricks. The wood is thick and marred by abrasions, like someone has tried to kick it in. He jams his ear to the splintered surface, then jabs the handle, but it doesn't budge.

"We should probably stay in here," I say.

He tries again to rotate the knob. His upper arm tightens as he thrusts with his weight, the lean muscle straining against the steel.

"Vogel."

He releases the handle. "Do you think the old woman will talk?" he asks.

"Freya? No, I don't think she would. But what about Carliss?" He shakes his head.

"How did you get in here?" I ask.

"I swam across Lake Lirye," he answers. In the murky shade, his eyes are blue torches, alight with emotion I cannot decipher.

"You *swam?*"

"Yes. There was so much weed." A little half smile plays on his lips. It almost seems like a sense of humor. Or a hint of it. But it slips away.

Moving forward, I consider our options. We could run outside or lay low. Running outside is definitely more risky, as Malthe may post his men in the square. Nevertheless, when the palace wakes up, the grass will flood with Lissettes and Lissons. We might be able to blend in with the crowd and jostle a path to Kalliope's villa. But then, of course, come the problems if we make it. I am a servant who lives in the palace. The others may assume we are secret lovers. And no doubt Tallesa would rat me out.

"Where is your friend from the Gathering?" I ask.

"Casper's still at the cottage," says Vogel.

"Does he know you're here?"

"Well, he thinks I'm a fool, so I wouldn't be counting on him coming to save me."

Smart friend. He's probably asleep on a cozy straw cot with the casement ajar. I think of my father in his reed bed in Maytown and curse myself that I'm now in this bind.

"So I guess we're staying here awhile," I say.

Vogel shuffles backward and sits on the ground. He's wearing the clothes he did when I met him—boots, black breeches, a loose cotton shirt—yet he's not the same as before.

It's jarring.

I slide beside him. Not because I want to, but because there is space. His legs reach far across the stones, butting against a wooden rail.

"How did you meet Carliss?" I ask.

Ever so slightly, his shoulders stiffen. "At the market," he says, and I'm somewhat surprised that he divulges so promptly without any prodding.

"But I thought you and Casper were leaving the city?"

"We were," he says, "but then with Jove . . ."

"I'm sorry," I say, but he waves it aside, and for some odd reason it makes me feel worse. "I know where he is," I add.

"So do I. Locked in the basement. Carliss told me."

"Did she tell you he's slated to fight in the Tournament as one of the emperor's unfortunate spares?"

"No, she didn't." Vogel shifts, the shadows enhancing the line of his jaw. His shirt sleeve grazes the tip of my elbow and something on the fabric catches my eye. I glance at it strangely, perplexed by the brightness. It haloes the length of his arm in light. I'm still attempting to piece it together when Vogel drops low, his chest to the stone.

I blink.

"Get down," Vogel says.

The brightness expands, flooding the room. I gaze at the yellow, still a bit awestruck, as voices rise at the mouth of the chamber. Vogel swipes me deftly in the ankle. Two soldiers have rolled the board aside. I duck, pasting my cheek beside his, as the sunlight creeps over the brickwork behind us. I feel his shallow breath on my neck. The soldiers trudge in, grumbling about breakfast. They quip that the Tyjans should save them some bread since they're doing their bidding finding old battered stocks.

My ears burn.

Old battered stocks.

So Malthe must be planning to punish Freya. The soldiers lift pottery and heave hefty slats with the care of two bulls in the emperor's glasshouse. Sweat forms in the soft curve where my lower arm folds against my bicep. Dirt from the floor turns muddy on my palms and something with feelers slides over my fingers.

I grimace.

Their search stretches on, until finally the soldiers crow in relief. I grit my teeth as they unhinge the stocks to check that the beam on the top swivels cleanly.

"Farrow swears there are two," says one.

"Let's get this out there first," says the other. The wheels creak and grind as the apparatus rolls, the vibration rattling the less sturdy furniture.

The moment they're gone, Vogel hums to life.

"What is it?" I ask.

"In front of us. Look." He's up on his knees, his hand on two planks that are balanced across a coarse stilted frame. The panels connect with three level holes, the middle one sculpted much larger than the others. A corroded padlock dangles from the timber, offset by the gleam of two mottled hinges.

The second set of stocks.

We're hunkered behind them. Scanning the room, I can't see another. Either we must find a new spot to hide or bolt from the storeroom before they come back.

I jump to my feet and Vogel's at my heels, combing through the piles for another sheltered space. The soldiers have demolished most of the stacks. Boxes and basins are scattered like rubbish, obstructing the paths between still-intact towers. It's like trying to hide in a tree when the cold has plucked the leaves from its branches.

"We have to go now," he says.

"I know." I drag in a mouthful of air and exhale.

The soldiers have left the door ajar. A shard of light bleeds through the gap.

"Wait," says Vogel. "Do you hear that?"

"Yes." My heart over-beats in familiar rhythm. Two voices disconnect from the bustle of sloshing buckets and scuffling sandals. *The soldiers' voices.* Loud and abrupt. A few strides at most and they'll be upon us. Panting, we stumble away from the entrance, looking this way and that and finding nothing. We slide behind a mound of junk that's as tall as an armchair but a lot more unstable. From the floor, I check the rafters and walls, and it's then I notice a rectangular patch. It's fitted in the stone behind a statue, its full size obscured by damaged sandbrick.

I nudge Vogel. He sees it, too. He hauls the statue out of the way. It's a hole that's crudely covered with hessian, tacked along the top but not at the base. Raising the hessian, I peer behind into a tunnel the breadth of a wood stove. The stench of decay worms outward like smoke.

"Go," growls Vogel.

"But—"

"Go."

I fall on my hands and knees at the entrance. The world pauses—or maybe it's me. I'm reminded of the corridor in Jove's cottage. I'm reminded of the dread that swept up my insides, telling me not to move. To turn back. But once again, I ignore that feeling—and go. Spiderwebs stick to my face. Their tackiness strains against my lips, and with clawed fingers I bat them away. I keep my arms extended in front, my head to the side, knees scrambling fast. The smell gets stronger—like something is rotting. Then Vogel's behind me and my heartbeat increases.

We crawl and crawl and do not stop until we're deep inside the walls. After a while, other noises fade and all I can hear is my own rapid breath. I'm not frightened of insects or rodents, but I hate not knowing where the tunnel ends. I loathe the inky blackness around me, how it seems to inflate with every bend.

And then, like magic mixed with good fortune, shimmering light-rays spark in the distance. The speckles strengthen into tiny orbs. Like a dazed moth, I propel toward them. My palms collide with a metal barrier. It flies out and clatters on the stones. I suck back a wheeze, but no one starts shouting, so I wriggle forward and squirm through the hole.

I've come out through the back of a grate. Around me, the

room sits empty and silent. It's much smaller than my quarters in the villa, with its four gray walls and tall cupboards squashed against them. Plump glass jars line the shelves, brimming with red and amber liquids. Flames throb from oxidized lanterns, casting eerie slender figures on the pitted plaster.

Vogel inches from the hole behind me. His dirt-smeared face must mirror my own. With a frown, he inspects the cluttered benches and the razor-sharp implements hanging from hooks.

Medical supplies?

I breathe in. The rancid smell is definitely stronger. A door lies open beyond the last cupboard and I tiptoe toward it and peek through the arch. It opens into the belly of the tower—an uncluttered space, the size of a ballroom. The ceiling curves upward into a bell and the windows are masked by roof-to-floor curtains.

And it's empty. Well, except for some tables that cram a far corner like dimly lit islands. Is it someone's residence? A laboratory, perhaps? An area to meet under cover of darkness? I tread slowly, but Vogel whisks past me, as if not knowing is too much to bear. The muted candlelight skims his back, catching on cobwebs that speckle his shoulders.

I squint. He reaches the benches quickly and peers down at them, one by one. There are four in a row. Four rows in total: lined precisely, the same width apart. I keep walking at a sluggish pace, an odd unease pressing into my skin. Vogel has stopped and is standing quite still. His lips are parted, his shoulders slumped forward.

Something is wrong. I walk faster. A queasy sensation sprouts in my stomach. Coldness grows at the base of my neck, the tingling migrating down to my fingers.

And then, all at once, Vogel exhales. The sound of it makes me stop where I am. He blinks once and shakes his head. He means not to look, but it's too late. My eyes drop to the benches around him. They're fashioned from steel and highly polished. A narrow trough surrounds each table with a liquid blackness lining the bases. The closer I get, the more I can see. The more I can smell and comprehend.

And I realize the liquid isn't black.

It's dark *red*.

And clotted like sludge.

I pull away. There are leather restraints, the straps looped tight and hanging like vines. I glimpse the limbs. The elbows and hands. The thighs and rib cages flat to the iron. The shapes come together in frightening swiftness. The familiar shapes I had somehow missed. And the truth of it knocks the air from my lungs when I grasp that I'm gazing at sixteen corpses.

I heave and it's a jarring rasp, shattering the quiet until the bodies come to life. Until I fathom they were never dead. These bodies—these people—were always alive. They've been kept breathing in this harrowing chamber, forced to endure these horrid wounds. Our presence has brought them back to awareness, and their breaths turn to cries, turn to shrieks, turn to wails, until surely nobody who tethered them down could expect to sleep soundly ever again.

When I rise, Vogel walks stiffly toward me, his blue eyes drained of any clear thought. He doesn't need to say it—we need to leave. And we can't take them with us. He's checked that already.

I close my eyes to push down the bile. None could walk with their severed legs. The only one in here with intact lower limbs has deep red gashes that have sliced off her calves. She was pregnant, too. Her belly is stretched, but whatever the life in her womb, it's now gone. Her skin is wrinkled like a peach in the sunlight that's been left for seasons.

"Please," she croaks.

I stare helplessly at her figure. She seems like a nightmare clinging to life.

"We have to help them," says Vogel softly.

I nod furiously, but I don't know how.

He picks up an instrument off a tray on a table. The silver flashes in the darkened room.

"No," I say.

"They're in pain," he says in a hollow voice that sounds like nothing.

He goes to the woman with the stretched stomach. She has no tears, no fear, nothing left. As Vogel approaches her body from behind, I see deep cuts across her torso.

And the stitches.

I fight the vomit once more. She's been slashed and mended so many times. Her left side concaves and I realize why. They've taken ribs and set them in jars.

Her death is quick. Vogel makes sure. He moves to a man with three missing limbs. He blesses them each as he ends their suffering. A few moments later, the room is silent.

I'm numb.

"We need to leave," Vogel says, and I nod again, but the movement feels distant. I've seen death before—my mother, other villagers, starving animals, the man in the arena. And even though their sufferings were huge, it does not compare to the plight of these people. How long have they been strapped to these benches? How many times have their bodies been opened?

I barrel back to the room with the tunnel. When I get there, I crouch in a ball by the grate. Were they traitors? Were they couples like Carliss and Vogel? Or men, like Jove, who'd committed no crimes?

Vogel stays longer in the tower by himself. His weight thuds in circles as he breathes in and out. I cannot imagine the pain he must feel to know he'd just ended so many lives. I hope he can see what he did was a kindness. Those people may have lived for weeks, maybe more. As his footsteps halt, I resolve to tell him—to let him know that it wasn't his fault.

His outline appears at the door, and I stand. His eyes are

heavy, like he's seen the world burn. "I left the knife . . ." He points to a trough. "I should . . . bring it with us . . ."

"Don't worry," I say.

He places an arm against the wall, steadying his legs that threaten to fold.

"You're braver than most," I start to say, but the noise of a bolt unlatching stops me.

Vogel's breath hitches. "Go back to the storeroom." He pushes me toward the grate. A mob of voices leak through the wood, and he swings around to reenter the tower.

"No, Vogel!" I clutch his arm.

"When I stall them, Meadow, make sure you get out."

"You must come, too!"

He shakes his head. "Be certain to tell Casper what happened, all right?"

"Vogel!"

"Swear it."

But before I can, the far door opens, and my chest presses in. Are they soldiers, servants or someone else? I keep myself hidden beside a cupboard, desperate to peep, and frustrated I can't. A cool draft blows in through the gap as Vogel marches to the middle of the floor. Footsteps glide from the door to greet him.

"So there is someone in here," Prince Malthe says calmly.

I struggle to keep my panic contained as Vogel raises his voice so I'll hear it. "I should have assumed you would own this chamber." He's telling me to flee. I can feel his composure.

"How did you breach the tower?" asks Malthe.

"I came through the window," Vogel answers.

"The glass is sealed," Malthe responds. He's surrounded by a bevy of trusted guards. I hear them filing into the room, checking under benches and pushing back curtains. Are they not repulsed by the bodies at all? Or do they fear showing any sign of loathing?

I creep to the tunnel and climb inside it, lifting the grate and clicking it in.

"You seem familiar to me," Malthe continues.

"Your Highness?" says a soldier.

He sighs. "What is it?"

There's a lengthy pause and I freeze in place, stifling the quaking that's flooded my gut.

"Your subjects . . ." says the soldier.

"What about them?"

"Well, Your Highness . . . they appear to be dead."

Malthe tone darkens. "What do you mean?" I picture him leaning over the corpses, dissecting their cuts with his tarry eyes. "You killed them?" I presume he asks this of Vogel.

"It was you who killed them," Vogel replies.

There's a longer pause, and the only sound is the tap of Malthe's bootheels, languid but exact. They come to a halt, and despite my concealment, I can almost feel the heat of his breath. "How else does one learn of the human condition if one does not try to seek it out?"

"So you forced this upon them," Vogel spits.

"They were nothing but criminals from the realm," says Malthe.

My stomach roils as I remember when Errol warned me to leave the Nothrick Prison. He said if I stayed, Prince Malthe would hurt me. I could have been one of them, lashed to a workbench.

The tap of boots resumes again.

"You did not come through the window," says Malthe. "But you came from somewhere, and I mean to find out, even if it means that we linger all morning."

He's not bluffing. He tells his men to search high and low for anything suspicious. And suspicious would be a tunnel in the wall, joining their chamber to a crowded storeroom. I scuffle backward, trying to be soundless, cringing each time my toes scrape the rock. The light through the grooves still flickers like embers, no matter how far I wriggle back.

"What shall we do with the boy?" asks a soldier.

"He'll join the spares in the Tournament," says Malthe.

"I will not fight for you," Vogel vows.

"No one expects you to fight," Malthe replies. Snickers from the soldiers trickle through the room as the men carry out their prince's orders.

I'm almost halfway between the rooms when there's scratching on the other side of the grate.

"There's something . . ." A soldier kneels on the stone. For an instant, I'm plunged into unnerving darkness.

I toss out the notion of quietly retreating. If he pulls off the grate, he'll see my face. I crawl back clumsily, hitting my hips, the muck underneath me sloshing like sand.

"Your Highness!" calls the soldier.

I'm panting hard, trying to rebuff the need for air. The light comes back, then disappears. His fingernails tap against the metal.

I feel a rush of breeze behind me. Stretching my legs, I tip the hessian. At the other end, the grate pops off, and I slam my face into the ground.

I wait.

"There's someone in there!" he yells, and it's no use pretending. Not anymore. With a head start, I could sprint through the square and perhaps disappear before they can catch me. Blocking their yelling, I slide through the hessian, skirting by the wedges of the scattered sandbrick. The board's still ajar, but the stocks have been moved.

"It's a girl!" someone hollers from inside the tunnel.

My head spinning, I stumble for the exit, the sunlight ferocious as I hit the outdoors. Then I turn and run toward the willow, my sandals punching into the lawn.

CHAPTER NINE

THE LANDSCAPE FLIES BY IN COLORS AND SHAPES. THERE'S swirling noise, but I can't make it out. It thrums from within the walls of the square, but it's distant and hollow and eclipsed by my breath. I squeeze my eyelids, but it makes no difference to the calamity of movement fluttering nearby. I repeat to myself that the villa is my safe house. That no matter what happens, I must get inside.

As I round the tower at the end of the grass, my body smacks into something hard. It drives the precious little air from my throat, and when I struggle for it back, I gulp in alarm. Two large hands encircle my shoulders, holding me at length as I drag in the wind. A dark face lowers from its height to meet mine. The brown eyes sharpen. Then the stubble on his chin.

It's Gyzen. *Gyzen.* I try to say his name, but I splutter the letters and cannot finish. The yellow sunlight drenches his head, and I feel my legs sink forward into his.

"Help me," I say.

"Get up," he snaps back, and my forehead creases as he lets me go. I teeter for a moment, the world at an angle.

"They're going to find me!"

"They have found you already." He steps to the side and the square expands. The blurry images clear and connect. My eyes roll around to the staring crowd. It's a mass of servants and soldiers and guests.

My hopes dive. They are gathered by the stocks watching Freya and Carliss, who balance on a platform. They've all come out to witness their punishment. Even the ladies have buckets of offcuts.

From the tower entrance spit Malthe and his soldiers. Vogel, though, is not among them. The tears spring to my eyes. Have they hurt him? Have they strapped him to a bench in that hideous workroom? The soldiers see me as I see them, but we're all imprisoned by the eyes of the people. Perhaps if it was a normal day, Prince Malthe would arrest me, the watchers be damned. But today is not like other days. Most of the people are noble guests. They have traveled from Leeang and Torquella and the north, and Centriet is on show—and Prince Malthe knows it.

"What do I do?" I ask Gyzen, but his answer is to take a farther step away. Malthe and his soldiers are less than ten paces, but they do not inch closer, so I turn my head. I shake out my hair to shield my face, praying that Malthe has not truly seen me. A murmuring skirts between heads in the crowd like they're eager for something exciting to happen. They're scattered in a curve in front of the stocks, the women in their dresses, the men in their day suits. My gaze travels slowly up to the platform where Freya and Carliss are outfitted in beige. Their braids are matted and their feet are bare, their faces crimson from the unwanted showcase. Carliss glances my way. Freya doesn't. I'm filled with remorse that we've done this to her.

And then, it seems, Malthe changes his mind. He commands his soldiers to arrest me at once. None of them move, and neither do I, as if we're not certain his request should be followed.

"Take her," says Malthe, his voice louder.

I'm hemmed in, but I look up at Gyzen. I don't know what I expect him to do, but he clamps his hands on my shoulders and holds.

"Gyzen!"

His grip tightens. His features lock like they did in the cottage.

I wriggle like a lizard, but I cannot escape him; yet I still have a mouth and there are ears that can hear me.

"Malthe is a murderer!" I scream. "He experiments on people inside his tower!"

Someone laughs. A woman on a white stool.

"He cuts them!" I holler. "While they're still alive!"

"Be quiet," says Gyzen, as soldiers advance, fencing me into a smaller ring. He removes his hands and leaves the circle, allowing the prince to advance to the front.

It's only then that I notice the figure seated under a parasol. His hair is black and his beard is pale gray, and his eyebrows bush with a mix of both shades. A cape swamps his thickset frame, clasped below his drooping chin. Beneath it, a tunic stretches over his pants, black and scarlet with flecks of gold stitching. He beckons to a boy, who must be a Midlon, and a white-clad servant leans in dutifully. The emperor whispers instructions intently, never removing his eyes from the platform.

The servant takes a route around the people, swerving to stop in front of Gyzen. He's terribly short and Gyzen needs to bend, but he relays the message and Gyzen nods.

The guests turn back to the women on the stage, sniggering as soldiers swing open the stocks. Freya and Carliss move into them willingly, then the beams are lowered and the timber is padlocked. It's like a performance, though it seems abhorrent that their punishment reaps so much interest from nobles. Among the crowd, there are even young children, whose eyes widen, not understanding, when their parents applaud and hurl rotten fruit.

"Girl, come with me." It's Gyzen again. He parts the soldiers with a flick of his head. I glance discretely at Malthe and the soldiers. Their eyes taper, but I do as he commands. I'm expecting the prince to shadow our footsteps, but he stays in the square as we follow a pathway. We slide out of view, and then I realize—he's ferrying me toward the emperor's villa.

"You have to let me go," I plead.

Gyzen says nothing.

"You must."

His eyes glaze.

"Why bother helping me escape from the Nothrick if you're planning to let me die anyway?"

He reels on me, his arm raised, the whites of his eyeballs speckled with red. His voice comes out low and brusque. "How dare you accuse me of such an act!"

"Did you not—"

"I did *not*."

But his urgency confirms it. Why else would his anger bubble like broth? And there's something else. A twitch of his eye. Even when he lowers his arm, it won't stop.

"I would never reveal that you helped," I say.

"A fool you are, girl." He turns back to the path. "And no one would ever believe you," he tells me. "Not after that outlandish display." He pulls a jagged key from his jerkin and unlocks a door, shoving me through it. It isn't the emperor's villa. It's a room. A holding room with a bench and no windows.

"Sit down," says Gyzen.

"Why am I here?"

"Sit down."

"No." I fold my arms.

Gyzen places a palm on my shoulder and pushes me roughly onto the bench. "The emperor wants an audience," he says.

"Why would he want that?"

"I do not know. All that's certain is you weren't supposed to do this. I knew it was unsound to rescue you."

"You know what Malthe does to the prisoners," I say.

He doesn't answer.

"I saw them," I spit. "He tortures them. He cuts them like cattle. Takes out their ribs while they're still alive." I hesitate to mention Vogel.

"Give nothing away," Gyzen says. He slams the door and latches it closed. And I sit in the darkness, awaiting my summons.

Without the sun, I cannot judge time, but according to my hunger, it's late in the day. My lower body twists like a wrung strip of cloth, and I wish I was home with my father in Maytown. I think of how we'd rise in the morning. Him before dawn. Me after sunrise. My father would brew a tall mug of herb tea and slowly sip it, sitting outside our stonebrick. He'd watch as the village came to life around him. He'd coax me to join him, but I preferred the indoors. I'd drink my brew and stare through the window, trying not to think of my mother and failing that task in extraordinary ways.

I fail even now. I look at the door, and the grain in the wood makes me think of her jewel box. Which makes me wonder where it is now. Did my father keep it? Did he tuck it away? One thought about her connects to the next. My mother's jewel box was brought from Leeang. She refused to speak of her life on the islands, and I never pressed, so I'll never know anything. It washes a wave of pain across me that I cannot talk to her now that she's gone. And the thought that she's gone lashes me coldly, reminding me again, like it has so many times, that I'll never hear her voice again or see her face or be wrapped in her arms.

The tears come and stream down my cheeks. I haven't had a moment like this since last autumn. I did at first—in fact I had many—but they wore me away, eroded me down, until tears did not come as frequently as before. But these sudden memories have sharp edges that saw inside me where I thought I was healing. I end up gulping like I did in the square, my shoulders heaving, my fingers shaking. I don't have a cloth to dry my face, so I let the moisture drip down my tunic. It feels good, like cleaning a canker, and I do not care how much my eyes crinkle, how red my face blotches or how much my nose runs.

And then, it's gone. The feeling wanes. The hole in my chest fills up with the present. In an instant, my mind is back in the room. There's a click in the keyhole and the door opens.

It's a soldier I have never seen before, and from his vacant expression, he has never seen me. He's younger than Gyzen and wider than Farrow, and the creases between his eyebrows are deep. He jabs me with the end of a baton.

"Get up."

I stand and follow him out. We hug the brickwork and skirt the square. The sun has dipped from its height in the sky.

I hate that he doesn't speak to me. It's as though he's been warned I am blemished goods. We stop at the edge of a patterned carpet that unravels into a darkened hall. Soldiers stand at the entry arch and are stationed along the extended aisle. Warm orange candlelight brushes the columns. They frame my path like elegant trees. At the end of the runner is a flight of steps, leading up to the foot of a throne. The soldier nods and his boots snap together, letting me know that I am alone.

Feeling stronger since shedding my tears, I enter the hall with my shoulders back. Torches flicker in urns on the landing, casting their glare in front of the emperor. He resembles a statue without any features, like blessed Obellis in Maytown's plaza. His spine is as stiff as cedar arrow and his hands are balled in a wad on his lap.

I keep walking. The soldiers are frozen, their eyes trained to the opposite walls. Even so, I feel the attention, their breathing hitching with each of my footsteps. At the base of the stairs, I still my feet, a dull pain forming behind my eyes. I'm unsure if etiquette dictates I must bow. Then again, I'm feeling suddenly defiant.

"Come closer, girl." The emperor beckons.

I climb the steps to the lowest landing. He squints through eyes surrounded by wrinkles, his black-gray brows sinking into his skin folds. There's nothing particularly overwhelming about him. In fact he resembles many men from my village. He's even replaced his boots with sandals and has taken off his bulky rings.

"You spoke about my son," he says.

The mention of Malthe makes my legs unsteady. There's movement to my left that isn't the soldiers, and the prince emerges from a shadowy wing. His hair is combed, his boots have been shined, and he wears a strange lopsided expression. To his right is Kalliope, and she scampers swiftly, as if touching the carpet will give her hives. She glances at me without looking closely, then leans on the arm of her father's throne. I pray she won't remember our meeting in the courtyard, and she yawns loudly and tosses her head.

"My son, child," the emperor repeats.

"His Majesty asked you a question, girl." A man drifts in from the opposite wing. He's bald in the center with a rim of white hair and an upturned nose like a human turtle.

The first thought that enters my head: *The emperor did not ask me a question.* Yet debating semantics would likely prove fruitless, especially in the presence of three of the Tyjans.

"Prince Malthe held victims in his tower," I say.

"You dare!" says the man, cutting me off. He hobbles toward me, his chest caved in, as though I had poked him square through the heart. With each step, he winces a bit, as the impact of stone travels up to his knees. "You said this in front of *nobility*, servant. In His Majesty's home. Do you not understand?"

Ladislas raises his palm at that, sweeps it to the side, and the man whisks away. "You called my son a murderer," he says, his lips firm, his eyes fixed on me.

I can still feel how the air changed when the bodies came alive on the tables. I can still hear the desperate shrieks and the sickening ache when Malthe cornered Vogel. "He tortures people. He ties them to benches. They're still alive when he cuts them open—"

"You filthy liar!" Malthe lunges down the staircase, his mouth twisting as he jerks back his forearm.

My vision goes black. When I open my eyes, there are stipples of light dancing around me. Touching a finger to my lip, I draw blood.

"In the name of Obellis, you're a fool," says the emperor.

A soldier grips Malthe, holding him back. His knuckles are red.

"Why would she say this?" Ladislas glares at his son.

"She's a liar!" Malthe juts a crooked finger my way. "She was in the slums spewing treasonous words, telling people in the kingdom to boycott the Tournament. She would say anything to save her own hide."

"If she's from the slums, then why is she here?"

Malthe falters, and Ladislas sighs.

"And what were you doing in the slums, my boy? Making sure the streets were safe for children? Or whoring in the taverns with my seal across your breast?"

Malthe's cheeks flood with pigment, matching how red my chin must be. "That was the night we returned from Rienne."

"One of your worst failures yet," says the emperor.

As Malthe fumes, unwilling to counter, I realize this is my best chance. I have to expose who the prince truly is and pray that the emperor is not the same. I muster all my remaining courage. "He tortured a pregnant girl," I say. "And he kidnapped an innocent boy, Your Grace. He'll hack him to pieces—or worse. I know it."

"Lies," spits Malthe. "You can check my quarters. I would never defile my residence like that."

He's moved the bodies out of the tower. That must be why he dangles the carrot. I look across to Princess Kalliope, wondering why she says not a word. But she's nowhere in sight. Did she slip out quietly when her brother slogged a girl in the jaw? The turtle-nosed servant has also departed.

"Girl, I believe you," the emperor says.

Malthe and I stare at him.

Stunned.

"Father—"

"I'm tired of your embarrassments," he says.

Malthe squirms. I can see the sweat beading like dewdrops above his brow. A ridiculous hope seeds in my chest that maybe, just maybe, he'll be locked in a cell and I'll be permitted to return to my stonebrick.

"It's absurd that after all these years, you still think I'll fall for your blatant untruths." Ladislas taps the curve of the armrest. "Leave us," he says to the remaining soldiers. They do not ask for further instructions. They turn and march to the end of the hall. I attempt to follow, but Malthe stamps his boot, bellowing that I am required to stay.

I look to Emperor Ladislas. He dips his chin and raises it again. I plant my feet, heart trembling through my breastbone, suddenly drained of confidence again.

When it's just us three, Ladislas narrows his eyes. "Who was the pregnant girl?" he asks. When Malthe doesn't answer, he slams his fist with so much force it resounds through the carpet.

"I do not know her name," Malthe admits.

Ladislas grunts. "What did she do?"

"She had relations outside of the palace."

"And the man?" asks the emperor.

"Gone," says Malthe.

Ladislas nestles his chin on his hands, fingers swiping at his large fleshy nose. I watch his gray eyes climb the walls, tossing around the truth in his head. I wonder how it feels to know that your blood has committed these sins without shame.

"I do not want people to know," he says finally.

"Yes, Father."

"Promise," he says.

"I promise, Father." Malthe's tone relaxes.

"How can that be your response?" I say. "Your son is torturing people, Your Grace. *Torturing them.* They had been there for days!" I don't know where the nerve in me comes from. To address the emperor like this is treason. But I can't scrub the images of death from my memory. And I think of my mother, sweating on her reed bed, and I curse the Tyjans all over again.

"Where are the bodies?" asks Ladislas.

"Taken care of," says Malthe, almost proudly.

"And the men who have seen what you've done?" asks the emperor.

"Are trustworthy, Father. Of this I made certain."

My hatred grows. It spreads so wide at the callous nature of these men with crowns. In rooms like this, they choose our fates. They sit behind walls with their legion of soldiers, dictating who should live or die. And good people are crushed like ants—for pleasure or boredom or because they don't care.

We mean nothing.

We are nothing.

"Father, there is the matter of the girl?"

"Ah, yes." The emperor nods, steepling his fingers against his thin lips. After a moment, he glances at me with the hate that should be reserved for his son. "I hope you'll understand," he says.

My pulse pounds. His face is like granite.

Then he rises from his throne and strolls from the hallway, calling to Malthe. "Get rid of her."

CHAPTER TEN

WITH FARROW FALLING IN STEP BEHIND US, MALTHE GUIDES me back to the tower. I holler for help in the fresh night air, but the buildings and walkways stand mute and unmoving. Once the prince's villa surrounds me, saliva lodges in my throat like cotton. My legs shake. I tug at Malthe's arms, until Farrow darts forward to hold me still.

They drag me back to the room with the tables, but when we arrive, the tables aren't there. Except for one. The red sludge is gone and the leather restraints are hidden from view.

Malthe was ready. He'd cleared the space in case his father inspected the tower. Despite my fear, my bloodstream boils at how swiftly he could dispose of the bodies.

"Lay her on the table," says Malthe.

I drive my nails into Farrow's neck. I wriggle and kick, but his grip only tightens. He slams me backward onto the metal and my breath comes out, swirling above, and I struggle and heave to draw it back in.

And that's all the time they need. As I wheeze, the restraints bite into my flesh. Four of them bind my ankles and wrists, two across my body and one to my forehead.

My entire body fills with ice.

"I thought you had escaped," says Malthe. "I heard you'd sailed across the Geynes, yet here you are. Somewhat alive."

I want to run. Need to run. But I can barely rattle the leather binds. When my lungs expand, I scream again, the agony sweeping like a scythe through the darkness.

Malthe waits for me to finish. "That fool in the cottage in Yahres," he says. "The one with the big black bushy beard. I heard what he said about my father, blaming him for the death of his wife as though somehow—magically—we could have prevented it."

I gulp in breaths so I don't pass out, perplexed by his words at the same time. Of all the despicable acts he's sanctioned, he still can't get past what was said at the Gathering?

"That oaf should have traveled to the Sparselands," says Farrow, "if magic was what he truly craved."

But people who venture east of the kingdom and into the Sparselands never come back.

Everyone knows this.

Farrow knows this.

Though I doubt it is magic that makes people vanish. According to my father, the Sparselands are dangerous. Filled with all manner of unsavory nomads.

But they're not magicians.

Farrow moves aside, and I wish I could thrust my knee in his face.

"Is that what you think about Tyjans?" Malthe presses. "That we're obliged to save you, no matter the cost?"

I swallow as he leans his face close to mine. In another world, he could have been handsome. But I cannot blot out his cruel eyes. "I don't know," I say.

"You don't *know*?"

"I don't know."

"Well, could I have prevented the death of that woman?" He challenges me with a curled lip. I don't understand why he wants my opinion. I'm nothing to him. I am grit beneath his heel. I wish my expression alone could defy him, but he traces his finger down my ear, unperturbed. As he touches my cheek, I suppress a shiver, and the reality sinks in that I cannot move, that my life is his, so I must watch my words.

"You did not kill that man's wife," I say.

"If anything, I am helping," agrees Malthe. "I serve this kingdom each time I draw breath. I visit Rienne to bring food to our city. I negotiate. I toil. Yet ungratefulness prevails."

"I'm sorry," I say, even though I am not.

Malthe takes something from his thigh and inspects it. "Your apologies are unnecessary," he says, shining the object against his sleeve. He presses the tool into my arm. It doesn't hurt, but I feel the shape. It's long and flat. The side of a blade. "It is your turn now to serve the kingdom," he says.

My courage has never been more absent. I can't calm my mind. I want to so badly. I wish I could string together my words and tell him how much his family has hurt me. But it's like I've forgotten how to speak and think. I've definitely forgotten how to strategize. And in horror I realize that if Malthe was to ask, I would spill any secrets, large or small, in order to leave the tower alive.

Malthe strokes the metal up and down on my flesh. "I'm a good person, you know," he whispers.

"It was wrong of that man to blame you," I stammer, in case it is what he yearns to hear. The words taste bitter, but I do not care.

"Such a good person," Malthe repeats. He taps the blade in a rhythm on my bicep like he's recalling a song. *One, two, three. One, two, three.*

He steps back and the chamber goes quiet. All I can do is wait in dread. But then, I remember: *I have a voice.* It's the only weapon I possess in this room. So I scream again. I scream and scream. It roars in my ears, making them burn. My words oscillate between pleas for help and long painful cries to raise the alarm.

By the time my throat cracks, he's behind me once more, stuffing a wad of cloth in my mouth. It tastes like grease.

"If they heard you," says Malthe, "they will sooner pretend that they did not."

It's not grease. It's something else. My vision wobbles and my eyes sink and rise. I'm scared what will happen if I fall asleep, but the heaviness descends, pulling me under, the candlelight beating like butterfly wings.

Only Malthe's voice keeps me awake. Every word rings crisp and clear in my head.

"You were wrong to speak ill of me to my father. You're a loathsome weakling to cause such offense."

I squint at him. His eyes become four, but his voice remains low and perfectly serene.

"I remember what you said in the cottage," he tells me. "You said that your name was Meadow Sircha. And I know your father lives in Maytown, Meadow. And he lives all alone. Which is very interesting."

I struggle to grunt that it isn't true, but it's mixed with my thoughts of *what will he do?* Tears leak from the corners of my eyes as he gently tugs the cloth from my mouth.

"Yes?" he says.

"You're wrong about my father. He died last year from the wilting sickness."

"I don't think he did."

"He did. I swear it." But my eyes are closing, sealing me in here.

And the last thing I hear before I black out is Malthe telling Farrow to send a patrol to Maytown. And I wail, clawing against my restraints, as he tenderly whispers, "Say farewell to your father."

Water hits my face. For a beautiful moment, I am renewed. I stick out my tongue to soak up the moisture only to be smacked with another blast. It flies up my nose and I gurgle and cough. With my arms still pinned, I can't wipe my eyes. And then the memories come streaming back.

Vogel.

Malthe.

My father.

The bodies.

And now me, the newest victim.

I open my mouth and shout at the ceiling, yelling so hard my cheeks vibrate. A coarse hand covers my lips and I tussle to bite the fleshy palm. He growls, whipping his hand away. I smell iron and taste sweat. I attempt to release my forehead from the leather, rotating my neck from left to right.

It doesn't work. I wriggle back and a face appears in the space above me. I can only make out the silhouette, but the jaw is slender and a shock of hair is coiled in a knot on the top of his crown. It's impossible to decipher the expression he bears, but when he shifts, the light hits his collar. His lips are chapped and his eyes are wide. And then I see the white servant tunic, encasing his shoulders like a loose sack of grain.

"Untie me," I plead. My voice sounds calm, and I curse myself for trying to bite him.

But he doesn't answer. Instead he exhales and pinches my eyelid between his thumb and forefinger. He lifts it in the direction of my forehead. He peers at my pupil with his soft green eyes. Eyes that seem to know I'm a person, but are keenly striving to pretend otherwise.

"Please," I say, but he shuffles from view. Metal instruments jostle on a bench. He picks them up, lays them down, walks in circles and mutters to himself in phrases I cannot comprehend.

I don't know how to make him listen. At least Malthe and Farrow don't appear to be present. But the prince's promise lingers beside me. That he knows of my father. That he's going to hurt him.

I call out to the man. "Who are you?"

Again, he ignores me.

"Please, what is your name?"

I hear him put even more space between us. It sounds like he's moved to the room with the grate.

"I don't want to die," I call after him. "Please. I saw the people in here . . ." I swallow, not wanting to dwell on the images. "Please! What are you going to do?"

The servant doesn't answer and I'm forced to wait for what seems like the stretch between dawn and dusk. I wonder whether he has slipped from the tower, but then his footsteps pound the stones. I tilt my head, but I cannot see him, though I know he's there from his subtle rasps. His hands clasp the base of my jaw, wrenching it smartly into position.

"Wait—"

He yanks my lips apart and drizzles something into my mouth. The drop tastes salty. It begins small and spreads like spice across my tongue. A dulling sensation oozes outward, burrowing deep inside my veins. And then it happens. I cannot move. My lungs still work and I can think, but I'm frozen in place, unable to cry.

Paralyzed.

He reaches forward, lifting my eyelids so my sight goes fuzzy. This time both lids stay wedged open without him having to hold them up. Apparently satisfied that the potion is working, he edges farther around the table. He paws through a selection of instruments—hooks, forks, spiral drills, and pointed knives with unwieldly handles.

By this stage, I am a mess. Is this what befell the other victims? He angles a blade this way and that, deciding how best to slice my skin. And something inside me dies right then to know my story will end like this. I strain to yell or to kick or to anything, but my body is corpselike and all I can do is lie on my back as my mind shrieks.

Get away from me!

He comes in closer. Warm air escapes his lips. He examines me like a rare piece of meat that shouldn't be spoiled by a hasty nick. If my eyes would move, I'd jam them shut. At least I wouldn't have to watch him assault me. At least I could playact that I was asleep and slowly and peacefully drift from my body.

But I can't.

And then his wrist descends, the pointed silver tip drawing near to my face. I brace myself for the moment of impact, praying the potion will keep pain at bay.

Please, Obellis.

I can't even cry.

But then—without warning—he drops the blade. It clatters into the trough beside me, and he crosses the stones and begins to retch, heaving from the pits of his stomach.

A kernel of hope sprouts within me.

"I must," says the servant, repeating it over. I hear him sag against the wall, hammering his fists against the furrows. "Lord Obellis, forgive me," he whispers.

But there isn't sufficient forgiveness in the world.

Moments pass, and he still hasn't moved.

So I wait.

And wait.

And wait some more.

I cannot guess how much time's dripped away, but slowly my lips begin to tingle. I need more time. If he stays by the wall . . . My tongue prickles and my chin starts to twitch. When my eyelashes flutter, I pray to Obellis, begging him to speed up the process. But nothing else happens, so I try to be patient despite the thoughts that loop in my head.

Farrow.

Maytown.

The patrol.

Malthe's threat.

I try to wriggle my shoulders. They shift. I send a purposeful message to my fingers, urging them to follow suit. My thumb wags, and I inwardly cheer. A warm feeling builds in my palms. It coats the skin of both my hands, casting ripples of sensation up to my elbows.

I can do this. I know I can. I flip my arm so the fingers hang down. My nails scratch the metal trough, my grip closing on something solid.

The blade.

I poke it beneath the leather. The bind snaps with a gentle twang. I reach to free my other wrist, then slash the straps at my head and my hipbones.

As I sit up, the chamber spins. I swivel to observe the cupboard-filled room. The servant's shadow sprawls up the brickwork, his shoulders quaking as if he is weeping. I shake out my arms, reaching down to my ankles, releasing my feet so they stretch and crack. As I drag them over the edge of the table, my calves spasm with the influx of blood.

I need to move. With my palm to the trough, I lower my soles onto the ground. Despite the tingles, my legs remain sturdy, and I tiptoe across the rutted stones.

The servant fails to hear me coming. He's like I imagined—squashed up against a door. When he sees my shadow, his chin jerks up, and I lunge with the blade, jutting out at his throat.

"Please," he says, his voice frail. Instinctively, I lessen the pressure.

"You're one of Malthe's servants?" I demand.

"Yes."

"What were you going to do to me?"

"What His Highness, the prince, told me to do." The servant flinches, as I push the blade harder.

"You were going to kill me," I say.

"Not exactly."

"Then what? Torture me? Take out my organs?"

The servant gulps. "It is the prince," he says. "He intends to solve a particular problem. He wants to know the workings of sight. He tries to cure people's vision."

I shudder. "You were going to cut out my *eye*?"

"The prince wanted it, not me. I would never desire something like that—"

"But you came at me with a knife in your hand! You paralyzed me with your wicked potion!" I should ram the blade into his voice box. Even then it would not equate to his evil. "I saw what you did to those people in here. They were screaming and in pain. A woman was pregnant—"

"No! No! I didn't. I *couldn't*." The servant's eyes refill with tears.

"You're a liar!"

"No!" He shakes his head. "I did not do it! Believe me, please!" He sinks back, his palms raised, and I almost—densely—feel sorry for him.

"You didn't?"

"No! You see what I'm like. My stomach, girl. I don't have a strong one."

It's the last thing I expect him to say, and not something I'd have thought would move my heart. But all of a sudden, my breathing heightens, my composure dissolving into shallow sobs.

"You believe me, then?" the servant asks, though I do not remove the blade from his neck. I swipe at my face.

"Who did it?" I ask.

"A servant named Reynard. One of the Midlons."

"Why did he do it?"

The servant tips my knee. "Will you cast your weapon aside?"

"I will not."

He gnaws on his lower lip. "I'm not dangerous. If anything, servant girl, I am a coward."

It may be true, but I still don't trust him, despite the aura of defeat in his pupils. I press with more force. "Finish your story. I want you to tell me what happened with Reynard."

Candlelight skims the servant's long lashes and he nods,

sloping his head to one side. "The prince made Reynard do terrible things. Such *inhuman* things." He points to the tower. "It's exactly what you witnessed yourself: the cutting, the stitching, the testing, the torture. With each return, Reynard's face became different. A little more grieved and a little more weary until it seemed he was no longer there."

The servant's facade is much the same. Gaunt and ashen with a sunken mouth. It seems he's scarcely older than me, yet sorrow has scored deep ravines on his surface. I pull the knife away from his throat. "Where is Reynard now?" I ask.

"Dead." The servant looks down at his palms.

"Do you know who killed him?"

"Yes, it was Malthe." The way he utters the prince's name, it's as if he's dared not say it before. "Reynard didn't want to torture people. The poor soul could no longer sleep. He began to see their faces in his dreams, but when he told the prince, he was strapped to a table. They brought me in and I saw what they did. They told me I needed to take Reynard's place." The servant tugs at hair by his ear. A patch of bald skin shines underneath. "Malthe promised that if I refused, he'd make me useful by other means. And after I saw what they did to Reynard . . . I knew the decision was already made. And when Reynard begged for a merciful death, I stumbled with it. I was too afraid."

His face crumples, and I'm lost for words.

"I should have stood by my fellow servant." Blue lines bulge at his temples, and I realize now that he is the one who sees dead faces when his eyes are closed.

"What is your name?" I ask.

He pauses, as though amazed that I should inquire. "I'm Orian."

"And you're a Midlon?"

"Yes."

"I'm a Lissette from the princess's villa." I question whether I should tell him my true name, but decide to keep the nom de plume. Just in case. "My name is Mollie, and we both need to get out of here."

His eyes brim with so many questions, but he does not refuse, so I stand up. "There was another boy in here before. He was about my age. Blond hair. Quite tall."

"They took him to the cells," says Orian.

I curse at the news under my breath. Risking a visit to the basement is folly with soldiers posted all over the grounds.

"Did you know him?" asks Orian.

"A little," I say, helping him rise to his shaky feet. He's a good deal slighter than he looked in the tower.

"You said you lived in the princess's villa?"

I nod.

"You must know the coachman, Pelletier."

"Yes, I do."

"And how is he?"

"He's fine," I say, and Orian smiles.

"Finally, Mollie. Some good news for me."

I wonder how they know each other. Servants from different villas don't mingle. But before I can ask, there's a shuffle of movement. Not in the tower, but somewhere outside. I glance at the grate. It's been sealed with plaster to ensure no one crawls through the tunnel again.

"Not that way," Orian says. "I know of a far better route through this building."

"You do?" I scour his features. Can I trust him? He could easily take me straight to Prince Malthe.

But Orian guesses my fears at once. "His Highness would have my head," he says.

I presume he means that Malthe would blame him, whether or not my escape was his fault.

"We will leave this grim place together," he says, and although I don't know where his loyalties lie, at this point, I have no better choice.

CHAPTER ELEVEN

WHEN ORIAN OPENS THE BOLTED DOOR, A WINDOW GREETS us on the other side. Bright sunlight hits the chamber, and I realize I've lost all sense of time.

"How long have I been in there?" I ask.

"A day," says Orian.

"A day?" My mind brims with thoughts of Farrow. Could he have located my father already?

I answer my own question: *No.* Surely he would have rested last night. And he'd no doubt have stayed for today's morning meal. I cannot imagine him passing that up. In fact, the patrol may be just setting off, trying to determine the best route to Maytown. With any luck, they'll lose their bearings, especially when confronted with so many stonebricks.

With a nod to myself, I enter the hallway, suppressing the growing fear for my father. I'm reminded he takes long walks in the woodlands and he's very aware of the world around him. If he heard hoof beats or spied Malthe's men, he'd slide behind a tree and merge with the bark. Or I hope he would. Though I suppose it depends if he thinks the soldiers bring news of his daughter.

"Mollie?"

"Yes?"

"Are you with me or not?" Orian raises an unkempt brow. The faintest flush tinges his cheeks, which makes him appear suddenly alive.

"Of course I'm with you." I glance around. The hall is narrow and void of people. It's curved at the top with multicolored rocks, and a thin fraying carpet runs across the stone floor. Grunting with effort, Orian drags the door closed, his skinny ankles peeking from under his hem. I rush to help, but he brushes me aside, accustomed to struggling without assistance.

"Are you hungry?" he asks.

"A little," I say, and a knowing expression crosses his face. From his build, he hasn't eaten well for many years. Perhaps his whole life.

"Take these," he says.

"I can't."

"No, please." He drops seeds on my palm. They're clammy with moisture and blackened from age. "I nabbed them from the kitchen this morning."

"You should have them."

"It's my way to say sorry." He twirls the thin hair above his ear, the long silver streaks mingled in with his bun. I'm still convinced that he's near to my age, but up close like this, he appears so much older. Seeds in Malthe's villa would be hard to come by and Orian requires them more than me. I press them into his hands with a frown.

"Will you hold them awhile?"

"Of course," he says.

He drops the seeds into his pocket, and I trail him to the corridor's end. Dome-shaped casements puncture the bricks as the passageway swells to an airy room. Outside, greenery obscures the glass, keeping the interior concealed from the square. Despite the space, there's no sign of movement, so we scurry across the unswept tiles.

"This way." Orian skirts a pillar that flakes with paint from another era. With his eyes flicking this way and that, he urges me into a small musty room. Handwoven baskets mottle the floor. Some are plump. Others lined with mold. He plunges his arm into hamper and unearths a snowy cotton shawl. It's old and battered with numerous stains, but I wrap it around me, no questions asked. It reeks of spores and abandoned places, but next to the tower, the smell is divine.

Orian regards my disguise thoughtfully, then nods his approval, and we shuffle through the door. He must be aware of the stark contrast between Malthe's servants and those of the princess. My heart twinges. How luckless for him when a villa nearby offers so much advantage. But he says not a word as we cut through more rooms and climb endless stairwells before arriving at a foyer.

"Head down and slump your shoulders," says Orian.

I picture the servants from the guestroom window. They trudged through the square like malnourished horses under the weight of buckets and laundry. As my shoulders sink forward, bodies plod around me—barefoot and smothered with dirt smears and ash. Unlike within the princess's residence, there are no exchanged greetings, no chatter, no smiles. Fatigue and fright permeate the room. No one stops Orian and asks who I am. As we walk, I smell meat roasting on the fire and the unmistakable whiff of baking dough. My mouth waters. It's not fair that Orian's treat should be perished seeds. I'm trying to recall what we have in our villa when Orian shoves me behind a rail.

I land heavily.

"Not a peek," he grunts.

Now the room is unnervingly quiet. Footsteps echo through the wide-open space, then come to a halt in the middle of the tiles.

"Excuse me, servants," says a measured voice.

I remember the nuance of his tone. *Gyzen.* And the pain catches in the back of my throat, for if Gyzen is here, then no one in the patrol has the strength to save my father from Farrow.

Not that Gyzen does a lot of saving.

"Is the prince in his quarters just now?" he asks.

"Yes, Forte," says a female servant.

"Has he been there long?"

"No, Forte."

I'm surprised to hear her address him like that. Forte is a term to revere the soldiers. It was phased out when Komran took power, as he desired less divide between the royals and the citizens.

Gyzen says nothing about the name. He thumps his boots, and the woman rushes on. Her voice shakes. "His Highness has company. Forgive me, Forte, but I do not believe he would wish a disturbance unless it is urgent."

"Is it a girl?" asks Gyzen sharply.

The woman clears her throat. "I believe so."

"What did she look like?"

She hesitates.

"I asked a question," Gyzen repeats. "Do not make me ask it again."

The woman's voice is so tiny and scattered, she must think she's making a grave mistake. "Uh, Forte, his guest was red-haired and tall. An older woman with a blue silk robe."

Air whistles through Gyzen's teeth. "Lady Claudia," he says. "The prince's aunt?"

"Yes."

"I see." He sounds relieved. "Very well, Lissette. I thank you for your candor."

With that, Gyzen sweeps through the villa, as if he has somewhere more pressing to be. It makes me wonder why he inquired. Did he ask for my sake or for his own curiosity? I'm not sure why I think he cares. He delivered me into the mouth of the lion. But he helped me escape from the Nothrick Prison. Surely that has to count for something.

Orian jabs the small of my back and I raise the knife from under my shawl.

"Do not be ridiculous," he admonishes. "Put it away and follow me."

With our gazes averted, we slink from the rail. The servants have resumed their silent work. None of them bristle in any way to suggest they knew we were hiding from Gyzen. We come to a row of thick white pillars that lead into the palace square. *The way out.* I tug forward, scooting through the columns and into the sunshine.

"Mollie! Wait!"

I slow my steps, as soon as I realize I'm in full view. A few servants trample across the grass, so I pull the shawl tighter and drop my shoulders. It's such a struggle to move like a snail with so much energy coursing through me. I suspect almost dying on the table is the cause—this compulsion to flee Malthe's villa entirely.

I'm walking in the direction of Kalliope's quarters when I notice Carliss clamped in the stocks. She's been cast away from the main platform. Apparently nobles love pristine gardens, so the apparatus rests behind a tree, purposely kept out of sight of their casements. She's too far from the villa to be given food and drink, but she's not far enough to avoid the humiliation. The remnants of vegetable peelings and fish entrails stick to her clothing and hair, and her legs are heavy with the weight of standing, too tired to flinch and kick at the hungry insects that make trails across her shins.

Freya is nowhere in sight.

I feel sick. This is the punishment for breaking curfew? A whole day and night bent into an unnatural shape? As I approach, the sun skids off Carliss's open lips. Her bloated tongue pokes out and she moans in horrible rasps. I wish I had a goblet of water to pour into her dry mouth, but I tell myself to keep my body hunched and my sandals trundling across the earth. I cannot stop. I cannot give away my identity. I cannot be found by Malthe again.

And yet . . .

There's a garden a little way in front of Carliss, notched into the space between two walls. Although it hasn't stormed recently, the surface of a large broken urn glistens with the sheen of rain-water. It's full of small swimming creatures that I've seen turn into frogs.

I shouldn't help her.

I mustn't.

It would be reckless of me to draw attention to myself.

And yet, this is Carliss. This is the girl who warned me not to come out of the tower. This is the girl who endures a punishment that might have been forced upon me.

And she is my friend.

With a quick glance over my shoulder, I spy Orian leaving Malthe's villa. He'll take a moment to catch up, so I stride to the garden and lift the urn, balancing the clay piece on one palm and keeping my shawl secured with the other. Behind me, Orian's footfalls speed up. He's not even halfway across the lawn and I can practically feel his fingers digging into my ribcage, dragging me away from Carliss. I walk faster. I'm nearly beside her when a shadow falls over me, and I drop the urn in surprise, the water splashing my toes.

Attention drawn.

"Do you want to be found?" Freya snarls. "Carliss will survive her punishment. You needn't be concerned."

Shocked to see the Grande looking so healthy and clean, my tongue loosens along with my shawl. "But she needs water."

"What she needs is to learn her lesson, which you obviously have not. Now get inside before you are seen." Freya trots up the stairs, beckoning me into the safety of the foyer. At the same time, Orian reaches my side and yanks the shawl over my forehead, cursing under his breath.

We follow Freya into the villa. She takes a sharp turn through a back corridor, avoiding most of the servants. The only one who sees us is Quinn, who doesn't stop staring at me and my filthy tunic. She goes to step forward, but Freya swerves and tells her to go to the kitchen and assist Amalia and Welsha since Carliss is otherwise engaged. Still gaping at me, Quinn retreats.

"Where are we going?" I ask.

"Outside," says Freya matter-of-factly.

We reach the arch and pass under the branches into the courtyard. As Orian hurriedly fills her in, Freya glares, her mouth pinched.

"The time has come for you to leave." She swipes the chain from around her neck and presses the key into the padlock. "Stay here," she says.

"Thank you, Freya," says Orian.

I reel around. "You know her name?"

Orian doesn't answer, which I suppose is an answer in itself. The door slams and we're left standing on the cobbles like two people who don't belong together. With the sudden halt in our escape, the rustle of the breeze through the overhead leaves seems to magnify the quiet.

"Your villa is nice," says Orian after a while.

I blow out an anxious breath. "Yes, I suppose it is."

We endure the discomfort for a few more beats until Orian presents his seeds again. "Do you want one now?"

Of course I don't, but I pluck one anyway, sighing at the sheer absurdity of the last few moments and how swiftly relationships can change.

"How do you know Freya?" I ask.

"I used to be a Lisson in here," says Orian.

I don't even try to hide my astonishment. "You were moved from Kalliope's villa?"

He nods. "It was supposed to be Pelletier, but I volunteered myself." His eyes slide to the sun as if the memory is a painful one.

"I'm sorry, Orian."

His fingers creep up the back of his neck, finding their way to another bald patch toward the rear of his scalp. "It amazes me that you apologize to the servant who would have stripped you of your vision had he possessed a stronger stomach."

The bleak irony isn't lost on me, either, though thankfully, Freya chooses that instant to reappear. The apples of her cheeks are pink and a large cane basket hangs from the crook of her arm. "Come, Mollie," she says, squashing her back against the door to hold it open.

"Orian is coming, too," I say.

"Well, of course he is," she huffs, as though I am the most ignorant girl in the kingdom. "He certainly isn't staying here. Not after he has witnessed me helping you flee from the palace!"

Orian juts his chin at the opening, and his meaning sinks in: *Hurry along.* Three steps later and we're through the door, finally outside the courtyard walls. Emotion wells in my chest. Seated on the patchy grass is a small village of stables. They're surrounded by mounds of golden hay and paddocks fenced in by sandbrick and malleable wire. Orian could have ploughed this land before he was sent to live with Prince Malthe. He leans toward the settlement, adjusting and readjusting the knot on the top of his head like a horse waiting to bolt.

"Let him know we're ready," Freya says.

"Yes, Grande."

Orian disappears inside the stables. Eventually the gates open on one of the large structures and a Tyjan carriage rolls out with no jewels, no golden casing, and no elaborate murals painted on the hood. Pelletier and Orian are sitting up front. They steer the horses to a halt in front of Freya and me.

I don't need to be convinced like I did at the Nothrick Prison. I seize the door and fling it open, the hinges creaking in dissent. Pelletier jumps from the front of the carriage and comes around to help me in. As he does so, Orian moves beside him. Their hands touch and for the briefest moment I think I see them pause to look at each other shyly. Pelletier clears his throat, his cheeks turning a deep shade of red, and Orian's eyes dart to me as he makes a show of lifting up the pillows and blankets on the seat, instructing me to lie on the floor of the carriage next to him. The

final step is to place a sheet of fine cloth over our heads. Pelletier
does this, whispering that everything will be all right—although I
get the distinct impression that he does not direct the comment
at me. Finally, Freya climbs onto the seat with her huge basket.
With the door closed and Pelletier settled at the front again, the
carriage rolls away.

I keep my lips closed and my breathing to a minimum. The
knife is cold against my skin. Each time the wheels bump, I imagine what would happen if the soldiers stopped us on the bridge
and demanded to search the carriage.

But they do not.

They speak briefly to Pelletier and Freya, and I hear though
the small hole in the hood that Freya is embarking on a market
trip to Junoven because the new noble guests have requested
items that are not already stored in the Tyjan kitchens. The soldiers groan. They even make unflattering comments about the
arrogance of some guests who are too fussy to eat our fare. And
we start rolling again almost immediately. Possibly because no
one has yet discovered that I am missing from the tower room
and possibly because the soldiers are more concerned with vehi-
cles coming in than going out.

It's surreal to be leaving the Tyjan palace. Part of me knows I
should be ecstatic, and yet I can't find the joy in it. All I know for
certain is that my breath stays locked in my chest until we have
crossed Lake Lirye and it doesn't puff out again until we are traveling through the surrounding noble neighborhoods.

Toward freedom.

I know the precise moment we leave the noble district. The beautiful smoothness of the wheels falls away and we're tossed from
side to side by loose stones. My head pounds. I try to ignore it
at first, but the more I do, the harder it thrums. It dawns on me

that all I have eaten in the past day are Orian's sticky seeds. As the carriage bumps on, the pain becomes so unbearable that I sit up swiftly, knocking the pillows and sheets from my back.

Freya whacks me in the ear. "Get down! We're not there yet."

But I'm going to be ill unless I can get outside in the fresh air. Scrambling to my feet, I hook my hand into the carriage door, but it will not open from the inside. Frantic, I bang my fist against the hood and yell through the small hole to Pelletier to let me out.

He pulls the horses over by the side of the road. When the door opens, I sink out onto the dirt track, heaving deeply.

"We must keep moving," I hear Freya tell Pelletier. "After we take her to Portia, I need to get to Junoven to pick up supplies, else the palace soldiers will become suspicious."

"Who is Portia?" With the smell of grass and soil, the pounding begins to ease. I blink and look around. I recognize this wooded area, with its stony stream that meanders through the Bezzlay Forest toward my village. We're close to Jantown, a couple villages north of Maytown. If I run, I could reach my stone-brick before the morning sun passes the quarter point in the sky.

"Portia is someone who can take care of you," says Freya, not bothering to swab the irritation from her tone. "The prince will send out his soldiers once he knows you have escaped. Portia lives at the edge of the kingdom, far from your village. The prince will not find you there and, with time, he will forget about his anger toward you and we can move you back to Maytown." Freya reaches down to pull me up, but I don't take her hands.

"The prince already sent a patrol to arrest my father. I'm not hiding out at the edge of the kingdom. I have to make sure he's safe."

"He will be safe."

"How do you know that?"

She digs her toe into the earth. "We need to go."

I thin my eyes at her, loathed to be dismissed. There's no way I'm climbing back in the carriage if she's just going to ferret me away to another useless location. I feel like screaming, *We're not in the palace anymore. You're not my Grande.* Then again, she never really was my Grande, though sometimes she makes it easy to forget.

I stand up and turn around.

"Where do you think you're going?" she demands.

"Back to Maytown."

"But you cannot be *seen.*" Exasperation drips from every syllable. "You know how crucial this is. It was part of our discussion from the beginning. It puts all of us in peril if you act selfishly."

I swipe at a winged ant, glancing along the narrow rise. Trees with splatterings of amber juice on their trunks line the edge of the road like a fence. "You had me convinced that my father wasn't in immediate danger when you first rescued me from the prison."

"Meadow—"

I shake my head. "I'm sorry, but he's my family, Freya. If Errol was in trouble, you'd do anything in your power to make sure he was protected."

"If we are seen by anyone out here, Errol may well be in a lot more trouble that you can imagine," she snaps back.

She's right about that.

And I hate that she's right.

"Might I suggest sending Errol to Maytown?" Pelletier rests his freckled arm against the open carriage door. His attempt at a wide stance seems farcical until it becomes apparent that he's shielding my figure from the road.

"I am not putting my husband's life on the line," says Freya.

Pelletier shoots her a meaningful glance.

"Though perhaps I *could* send him," she corrects herself, upon realizing his intent to placate me, which, of course, does little to convince me that my father's life would be safe in their hands.

"Leave me here instead," I say, trying to offer them both a better solution. "You've already risked so much for someone you don't know. I can find my way home. I will keep a low profile and stay out of harm's way. I know my way around the villages. I'll get my father out, and we'll hunker down somewhere. The prince will never find us."

"We cannot leave you on the side of the road," says Freya.

"But I need to go home."

"Well, it's not possible," she says. "Not anymore. If you had stayed quietly in the villa as I had told you to do, then we could have taken you home without any problems. But you had to listen to Carliss and break curfew and let Prince Malthe see you. For your own protection, you must stay with Portia until this matter is resolved." Her voice is crisper than the linen in the Tyjan cupboards, though there is an edge to it that betrays the truth. She does not do this because she cares about me. Again, it is to save her own skin. No doubt the prince will send his soldiers out to find me. He will want to know who rescued me from the Nothrick Prison. He will want to know who released me from the tower room and aided my journey across Lake Lirye.

"I will remain well hidden," I repeat.

"Is that so?" Freya steps closer, her sigh causing my lashes to flutter. "And if you are apprehended?" Her nostrils flare, reminding me of an old sow I once saw at harvest.

"I will not be," I promise.

"But if you are, how do we know that you will not incriminate us to save your own hide?"

I look toward the carriage. Pelletier now leans his hip against the metal, his body halfway inside the door. He's in deep conversation with Orian, who is still fully concealed beneath the satin and velvet. Although no one appears to be watching the road, Orian knows his fate if anyone reports his whereabouts to the prince. I wonder how Freya and Pelletier would react if they knew the true extent of Malthe's depravity. And then I wonder, what if they do?

"I would never incriminate you," I tell Freya, and the old woman balks, scratching her head in aggravation.

"To think!" she says.

"To think what?" I ask.

"Nothing." She clenches her jaw as if she is at war with herself and the only thing left to do is shout or grimace. Luckily for me, she chooses the latter; but it's clear she won't be changing her mind and letting me flit back to my village anytime soon.

"I appreciate all you have done for me," I say. Even though I mean it, the timing makes my gratitude sound contrived.

"We saved your life," says Freya.

"And I will always be grateful."

"Well, show us some of that supreme gratefulness now and stop being so difficult." Freya spins and signals to Pelletier to move up front and ready the horses for departure. "We still have a fair journey ahead of us to get to the safe house, you know . . ."

But I don't know—*and I'll never know*—because that's when I make my move. And I'm not sure if her face drains of color or if it explodes with red or if she picks up my dropped knife in disgust. I'm not even sure if she sends Pelletier after me or if she bundles herself into the carriage with a racing heart and continues on to Portia with Orian.

Because by the time Freya turns around to tell me to get into the carriage, I am already flying through the Bezzlay Forest, following the stream to Maytown.

CHAPTER TWELVE

MY VILLAGE LOOKS THE SAME. IT SHOULDN'T SURPRISE ME. It's not like my absence from Maytown would have been keenly felt by anyone except my father and Anai. I slip from the edge of the wood, where the grass gives way to poorly cobbled streets, and inhale the familiar scent of chimney smoke and dust. The streets are jammed with citizens, crouching outside their stonebricks, digging in clay-ridden gardens and hanging sodden cloths over slouched knots of rope. As the wind picks up, my dark hair lifts, mingling with dirt and dry pieces of straw that gust up from serrated cracks in the sewer ditches.

I stifle a sneeze and sprint into the chaos of labor and movement. I'm fairly confident Freya and the carriage are not on my tail. Pelletier could never maneuver the wheels through the tightly packed trees, and I'm doubtful he'd know the shortcut past the parched pond in Bezzlay. A flicker of guilt for running off and causing them anguish singes my skin, but the anticipation of a reunion with my father knocks the thought from my head.

My father.

Despite the throng of villagers, warmth pools in my chest. He has to be here. He has to be all right. Surely I would feel an ache in my gut if something had gone awry. I find myself making deals with Obellis—Obellis who is supposed to bring good fortune to all who believe in his wisdom. *If you assist my father in eluding Malthe's patrol, I will bring fresh flowers to your statue during harvest, I will assist the elder archers by retrieving their arrows from the farthest pines, and I will finally accept that my mother's death was all part of your divine plan . . .*

But if my father is safe, where would we hide? I contemplate this as a horde of children race by. My father's old mentor, Nish, lives in Septown. He once taught me to decorate arrows with vivid jettybird fletchlings. I'm sure Nish would be delighted if we showed up at his door, as his wife and grandchild died last year from the same wilting sickness that stole my mother. He and my father often spend long afternoons drinking sweet brew and reminiscing about their wives. But I don't like visiting Nish. Sure, he's kind and all, but whenever he subdues his sorrow with a smile, I think of how different our lives might have been if Komran was still alive. Which makes me sad.

A hacking cough behind a latrine drape jolts me to awareness, and I pick up speed along the road, hugging the barrier posts and obscuring my face with cloth. Fortunately, it's relatively simple to blend in. More than the usual amount of people clog the path, which I suspect is due to the upcoming tournament. When the thatched roof and gray stamped walls of my stonebrick come into view, my knees sag with relief. Scanning the greater area for uniforms and horses, I see none. There are no villagers looking nervously at me, either. And with a tentative mix of joy and trepidation, I bolt faster than I did through the woodlands, pushing open the entrance board and calling out, "Father! Father!"

It smells so familiar—earthy and dry with a weak scent of basil. With my hand still clutching the rectangular board, I peer into the open room. Everything is in its place. Our chipped pot sits on a plank of wood, a pail beside it is full of undisturbed well water, and our reed beds lie untouched in their same two spots against the walls.

But my father is not here.

My heart sinks. I close the door behind me and race to our possession baskets. Tearing off the woven lids, I discover they are still filled with our most treasured objects. Mine have calf-skin parchments, quills, a couple old books and a small tapestry my mother sewed of a flowering rose. My father's has his uncle's brew cup, a leather quiver from his childhood hunting supplies, and my mother's cotton kerchief.

I scour the rest of the room. Our herb garland still rests beneath an upturned dish. Our coin case is hidden from view behind a blanket hamper. Even my father's clothing remains stacked in a rumpled pile beside mine.

Could Farrow have been here already? It's hard to know. The scared part in me screams that my father has been taken. The rational part in me remembers Farrow's brutality and cannot imagine he would have arrested my father without destroying some of our belongings in the process.

I dash outside. Our neighbors, the Landry boys, lounge in a tight ring on the sandy soil, carving tree stumps with rusted daggers. Before they notice my presence, I slink behind a potted melonai plant, its curled leaves brushing my neck. It's likely Malthe isn't aware I've escaped yet, but I don't want anyone falling at the patrol's feet in the hope of a reward, staunchly proclaiming that I was prowling around my stonebrick.

I head back inside and pace in circles by the window. Where could my father be? There's a small chance he has gone into the woods by himself. He did that many times during my mother's illness to regain his composure. He always came back with fresh root vegetables and renewed patience. I tell myself that he has likely done the same this time, but I cannot breathe easily until I know for sure.

So that's where I'll go.

After changing into a plain knee-length dress that binds at the hip, I place a shawl over my head to hide my face. Sneaking into the street, I pick my way along the crumbly gutter until the stonebricks diminish and the dry fields connect to a mass of tangled shrubs and vine-choked trees.

I know this place well. Although there are a few woodland areas near Maytown, this is the closest to our home. I spend the rest of the morning methodically raking the terrain, on alert for clues of his footsteps, watching for snuffed fires or piles of shriveled leaves or shallow holes made by the wide end of a branch.

But I find none.

And for all my prayers to Obellis that my father would be sitting among the greenery, waiting patiently for my arrival, they go unanswered.

And I have to face the truth.

He's not here, either.

Hot air brushes my cheeks as I hurtle down the street. *How long before Malthe realizes I've escaped? Will he come after me?* And then the most disturbing thought: *Has he already captured my father?* Past the last of the small sandbricks rise the larger apartments. These buildings have two cube-shaped boxes stacked on top of each other with a rickety ladder connecting the ground to the second floor. I creep to the left and follow an alley to the final apartment beside a yellow field. Horses, cows, and goats used to graze in the tall grass until an insect-borne disease brought big patches of dust to the surface and the animals were slaughtered to make broths to feed hungry children. Darting to the front of the battered building, I tap on a timber paling that crisscrosses the window hole.

"Anai?"

I try to keep my voice down.

"Anai?"

There's tense scrambling. I step back from the entrance board, shielding my eyes, staring up at the second floor casement. Footsteps pound the interior ladder, followed by light toes scuffling toward the door.

"Meadow? Is that you?" Anai flings the wood aside and squeals. Not a small squeal like when you're presented with a meal of syrup on toasted flour, but a squeal that should be reserved for big occasions like matrimonies and days of birth. I cringe, trying to shush her, but her cheeks pull so far to the sides that she's all grin. "Where have you been? You never came back from Yahres that night and I wondered what had happened to you!"

She hugs me and I hug her back, attempting to explain that I need to stay hidden. But a moment later, there's movement behind her. Symon, the boy she used to meet every day in the fields, emerges, smiling broadly. A little too broadly.

"Good day, Marlow," he says.

My belly scrunches. Even though that's not my name, I don't want anyone besides Anai knowing I'm in Maytown. I pull the shawl tighter around me as Anai touches his lower arm.

"It's *Meadow*," she says uneasily.

"*Meadow*. That's what I said." Symon gives Anai a half-hearted side-squeeze and pushes past me into the street. I catch the whiff of drink on his breath, but he doesn't acknowledge me any more than he already has, which has always been his way. I bite my lip. Maybe he won't remember this meeting, though I wouldn't put it past him if soldiers inquired, jingling purses of coin. "I will see you at the Tournament," he says, winking slyly at Anai.

"Perhaps." To her credit, Anai doesn't return his smile. I can tell by her rigid stance that she's none too pleased by his misplaced manners.

"Never mind about it then." Symon lingers for a moment, holding her gaze with his piercing eyes. Then he jumps onto the dirt path and gallops across the open field with a barely there shrug.

"Sorry about that." Anai watches him go. Symon's short and solid with thick arms and a mop of unruly brown hair. I'm not sure why Anai likes him so much, although she did once proclaim he was an astonishing kisser. Perhaps kissing is everything when you are courting. Then again, since I have no experience in the matter, I usually refrain from prying.

"Is everything all right?"

"Oh, yes. Everything's well." Anai forces another smile, adjusting her dress with peculiar intensity. "Symon's applying for soldier training next season, and his family doesn't exactly approve. I think that's why he's been so out of sorts."

Yet if I remember correctly, he wasn't applying to be a soldier when I last saw him, or the time before that, or the time before that.

But I let it go.

"Yes. So anyway, it's been a difficult time." Anai keeps her eyes on Symon, right up until the moment he lopes through a dense row of trees. "Ever since he met the Jungshed boys at the tavern, it's been all about training and weapons and knocking back the most cups of ale. He's happier though. I'm not disputing that. It's just that sometimes . . . I don't know . . . sometimes I wish he'd pay more attention to me." She rests a hand on her hip, seemingly transfixed by the yellow field. I don't know what to say. Of course I care and I want to listen, but she takes off again with another story. This one is about Symon's mother, who blames Anai for her son's interest in the army.

I suddenly feel like the most inconsequential speck in the village, and part of me wonders whether my best friend is even aware that I was missing. Then again, she did squeal when I arrived, so she obviously knew that I was somewhere other than Maytown.

"I'm sorry to hear it's been difficult," I say.

"Thanks, Meadow." Anai takes my arm and leads me inside. The lower level of her stonebrick is made up of one square room, about the size of my entire home. A golden hue leaks through the east-facing window, and I'm reminded of the many mornings I used to spend here with Anai and her grandmother. "I just finished boiling an enormous pot of broth." She strides across a plaited rug. "Did you know that Symon was able to bring down a rabbit in the forest? He had to take the spoils to his family, mind you, but he managed to bring me some of the leftover entrails, and I surely didn't waste them . . ."

"Good for you."

She hesitates, but carries on without addressing my comment. "I haven't eaten rabbit for seasons, you know. I've forgotten how it tastes to be honest."

Pressure builds inside my throat as I realize she hasn't been worried about me. I thought she would've camped by my stone-brick—day and night—to find out what happened. And yet she blathers on about rabbit and Symon and how hectic her life has been. And yes, she may have asked where I was, but not in the sense that she wanted to know.

"What's wrong?" she asks.

And she still doesn't get it.

"Nothing." I'm scared if I say, I might scream. Everything pushes hard against my windpipe, pounding the back of my closed lips.

"I have until late afternoon," she says, "before I have to work at the markets." She observes me closely. "So feel free to stay. I do not need to leave in a hurry." With her long auburn hair and cornflower eyes, she's always struck me as a rare beauty. But since last year, a chasm has grown. Her with Symon and me with my mother. And I wish it didn't exist at this moment. I need her now. I need her to care.

"I'm in trouble," I say, and I feel the emotion welling inside me, threatening to spill.

"Trouble?" She seems thrown by that.

I nod.

"I thought . . ." she trails off. She takes a breath, stubbing her toe, knotting her fingers in front of her stomach. "Is that why you've been away?"

"Yes."

"Do you wish to talk about it now?" She says it slowly, like she might offend.

"Of *course*! I've been waiting for you to care!" My voice booms through the enclosed space, and Anai swallows, tugging her sleeve. "I'm sorry," I say. "I didn't mean it like that."

"Is it something bad?" she asks.

"It is."

"Tell me."

And now, it's me that wavers. Unsure where to start. Unsure *how* to start. In the end, I realize there's only one way.

"I was arrested by Prince Malthe."

"*What?*" Anai's mouth drops open. "Why? Are you all right?"

"I'm fine," I say. But then, my mouth wobbles and twists, and all my composure drains away. I cover my eyes as the tears stream down, pooling over the back of my knuckles. And I cry and cry for all that has happened. And for all that awaits if I don't find my father.

"Meadow." Anai rushes to hug me, but it's different to the one she gave me outside. It's the hug I needed in the prison and the palace. It's the one that helps to dry my eyes.

When we pull apart, she leads me to the table and we sit across from each other, staring through a bouquet of dried river flowers—dusky reds and pinks that are now closer in shade to the bark from an oak. She folds her slender hands, resting her chin atop her thumbs. Her blue eyes grow round with concern as she waits for me to calm down.

"Do you need another moment?" she asks.

I shake my head.

"Then tell me the rest."

"You must swear to keep it a secret," I say.

"I swear it, Meadow."

"Even from Symon."

"Symon?" She balks at the very thought, as though making

her swear is a joke. "I promise I'll keep it a secret from Symon. Not that he's ever interested in discussing affairs of the kingdom that he deems gossipmongering. And you know me. I would never tell any members of my family."

That, I know, is true. Anai does not get along with her mother, and her father is at sea on a treddek, sweeping the reefs for fish and shelled delicacies to be brought back to the noble markets. The only person she holds dear is her grandmother, but the old woman lost the ability to speak two seasons ago and lives with a distant relative at the edge of the settlement.

"All right."

I begin with my speech at Jove's cottage. I tell her of the black-bearded man. The soldiers entering. Blood on the stone-brick. Jove and I getting manacled and lifted onto saddles. I progress to the injured man being slaughtered in the arena, to being held in the Nothrick Prison for three days, to pretending to be a servant in Kalliope's villa, to almost having my eye removed by a servant in Prince Malthe's tower, to the prince's deadly threat against my father. Anai's features move with my story. Every so often, she grabs my hand and inclines her forehead, clearly devastated by all the new information.

"You poor soul," she says, when I've finally finished recounting my carriage ride through the streets and running on foot through the woods to Maytown. "I had no idea what you were going through all this time. I mean, your father did come and see me at first—and ask me if I knew where you were—and we looked for you in all the spots that we thought you'd be, but I just really thought in my heart of hearts that . . . that . . ."

"That what?"

She shrugs, and her smile turns watery. "I thought you were sad, I guess. I mean, obviously, I knew you were sad. That's why I suggested going to the Gathering in the first place. But I think I just assumed that you needed some alone time and you would be back when you were ready to be found." And there it is. That strain in her pitch. The thickness in her throat. That wedge that's been present in our conversations ever since my mother's death. "And now I feel just awful, of course. You have to know that."

"Anai, stop." The words come out more abruptly than I mean them to, so I gnaw my lip, attempting not to frown. I project back over the last four seasons. From the moment my mother passed to the Afterworld, I know I've been a different person.

"I should have tried harder to find you," she says.

"No—"

"Yes! You've been through so much."

But it's not her fault any more than it's mine. There were countless times I'd disappeared into the woods to clear my head, to grieve on my own. So, of course, she'd assumed I'd done the same thing after the Gathering.

"Don't think on it," I say.

"But I will."

"Please don't."

She blinks, as if my words are fragments she cannot slot together. "I'm glad you're safe," she says at last.

"Thanks, Anai."

"And for what it's worth, I'm truly sorry." Her eyes glass and she looks away. Her pain punches me in the gut. She's never been one for showing emotions, so I reach out slowly and squeeze her wrist.

"When was the last time you saw my father?" I try to divert the conversation.

Wiping her eyes, Anai rises from the stool and unhooks a ladle from a nail beside the window. "I cannot be certain. Early this morning?" She pours the thin broth into two large bowls and carries them to the table, looking relieved by the topic change. "You checked your stonebrick?" she asks as she stirs her mostly cabbage-stuffed fare.

"Yes."

She lifts the spoon to her lips, blowing on it. "Well, I haven't heard any news about a patrol in Maytown today. I guess that's something."

"No one heard anything about me, either," I remind her.

"I suppose that's true, but your father did mention something about a young boy from the outskirts being roughed up by a group of soldiers on the night of the Gathering."

A tart taste forms in my mouth, recalling the heaviness of Farrow's boots. "Did the boy make it?"

"Yes, he did. He's back at Lessons. Doing well." She slurps her broth. "But my point is that we'd know if there'd been a patrol. The village was near deserted the night the boy was set upon. If a patrol rode to your stonebrick in the middle of the day to grab your father, everyone would know about it from here to Septown. Especially by now."

"You're probably right."

Anai points at my bowl. "Eating will make you feel better."

She's probably right about that, too. I pick up a spoon and take a sip. Sharing meals in Maytown is a huge gesture of friendship, especially a meal with a hint of rabbit. "Thank you," I say. "I also checked the woodlands near our home. But I want to search a few more places. Like Sledloe, for instance."

"Sounds wise." Anai taps her sandals on the rug, and I notice how white her face has become. "You realize I'm coming with you," she says.

I open my mouth, but she flings her hand.

"I know what I'm getting into," she says, taking another mouthful of broth. "But if you can endure all that you did, then the least I can do is to help you with this."

My father is not in the corner tavern. He's not at the silversmiths. Nor by the stables. Anai and I stride quickly about, like pickpockets keeping to the shadows and nooks. Finally, after middle day, we exit the city beneath the arch. We tread the docks and inspect the shoreline before hurrying along the path to the slums.

By the time Sledloe appears in the distance, my hope for my father is beginning to wane. Granted, it would be easier to locate him if we asked around and showed our faces, but we have to make do with cunning routes and subtle glances if we are to remain safe. At least there's no sign of Malthe's patrol—which leads me to believe that the prince only intended to view Orian's completed work. And the queasy feeling returns with flourish, imagining what Orian's final work would have been.

Pushing the thought from my head, I concentrate on the street. Sledloe during daylight is deserted. Which makes sense. The prisoners would be dispatched to multiple locations for labor, many at the arena to transport sand, scrub the audience seats, and assemble marquees for the Tyjans. Even so, I curse that we've walked all this way to a phantom village. A few Rigorates sit at benches playing games on unrolled parchments, but that is it. The yeasty smell of ale lingers between the canvas and a stack of worn boots are piled in a line so the men can wriggle their calloused toes in the warm air.

My father is nowhere to be seen, thank Obellis, but it doesn't rule out an arrest. Anai and I slip through Sledloe and out the other side, not stopping until we're sheltered by the dilapidated stone buildings of Yahres.

"I didn't see him," she confirms.

"Neither did I."

She looks over her shoulder. "Should we turn back and try the other woodland areas inside the walls?"

I shake my head. "I'll do that when you go to the markets."

As we creep a little farther, I take in our surroundings. The unlit lanterns and the broken ruins transport me back to that fateful night.

"I shouldn't have suggested the Gathering," says Anai, reading my mind. "It feels frightening to be here now, never mind when the darkness descends. And you only had yourself." Her stomach grumbles, loud and strident, and she taps a palm to her dress. "That reminds me," she says. "I know it's probably not safe for you to go to the Tournament tomorrow, but Symon told me the Tyjans are cooking chicken, pork, fish, and even turkey for the spectators." Her eyes light up with longing. "Did you see any of that in the palace?"

I nod, and she groans.

"Would you go just for the food?" she asks. "And not watch the matches?"

"I don't think so."

"We could go together and stay hidden."

"I thought you were going with Symon?"

She sighs. "He'll be there. Drinking with boys from the tavern."

I sigh, too. The notion of being anywhere near the arena coils my insides. And not just because I'm worried about being caught. As it is, I have condemned two lives. There's Jove, for one. The poor man is shackled underground, waiting to die. And then there's Vogel. I think back to before I entered the cottage, recalling how Vogel said he was leaving Centriet the next day. Now that he's locked up—presumably with Jove and the other spares—the regret of my decision to speak out at the Gathering weighs heavily upon me. And then I remember his companion. *Casper*, Vogel had called him. He doesn't even know that Vogel has been taken by Prince Malthe. For all I know, Casper is still in the cottage a few lanes away anticipating Vogel's return. He may not even go to the Tournament. He may always wonder what became of his friend.

And Vogel had asked one thing of me.

One thing that I would be cruel not to do.

"Anai?" I ask.

She's trying to catch my eye, possibly because my gaze had drifted through the streets to the direction of Jove's cottage. "Yes?"

"There is something I must attend to while we're in Yahres."

"And what is that?"

I purse my lips. "I need to find someone."

Anai and I huddle together, our sandals beating against the pavement. We've already garnered the attention of three beggars, who stretch their cupped hands, pleading for coin we do not have. With sunshine on our necks, we scuttle faster, gagging at the brown waste that seeps from behind a row of broken pillars. By the time we arrive outside Jove's cottage, the street is bare and silent, yet I'm almost certain the cracked walls have eyes.

"Are you sure this is the place?" asks Anai. "Because if it's not, I am quite all right with that. In fact, I would happily go to the market and begin my labor early."

"It's the place," I say, feeling somewhat less assured than I had on that very first night. I rap on the timber. The hanging vines sway in the warm breeze, but no one comes to the door.

Anai wanders to the planked up windows and tries to peer through. "They're covered from the inside," she says.

I grab the handle and pull it, but nothing happens. I hear a clicking sound and turn, only to be greeted by a bird on the eaves, cocking its feathery head at me.

"Let's go around the back," I say.

Anai is already on the move, having discovered a stepping stone path. The cottage is squeezed next to a high sandbrick wall that must have once belonged to a residence beside it, though all that remains is moss-caked rubble. The wall looks like it could collapse at any moment, so we suck in our stomachs and scamper along until Anai points to a window with loose boards. I come up beside her. We grab the timber at the same time, and a shower of borer grains falls off, coating our lower legs in lumber dust.

"Ugh." Anai lets out the daintiest sneeze, and we pause in

unison, lest the noise alert anyone in the house. When no one shows up, we spring to life. We pull again, and this time the paling breaks off. Grabbing the one beneath it, we keep pulling until there is enough space to climb through.

I go first. Usually Anai is the bold one, but she hangs back and I feel a surge of pride to be the trailblazer. When I'm in, I swing around and help her through. She looks a little annoyed that she is not as nimble as me.

"There could be beggars in here," she says.

I nod, although it depends whether Casper has been present to keep them away. Despite the dark interior, light slivers seep through the foundations, sufficient to guide us along the corridor to the room with the sandbrick platform.

"I cannot believe you visited this place on your own," says Anai, and again I feel slightly accomplished, although the memories of what happened in here make my eyebrow twitch. Thankfully, no sign of the soldiers remains and all traces of blood have been scrubbed from the cobbles.

"Casper?" I call.

"Casper!" yells Anai.

We leave the big room and investigate the chambers that branch off from the main corridor. Some are empty. One is filled with cauldrons and discolored farming equipment. Another makes us halt.

Anai jogs to the window and rips two holes in the paper, letting light pour in. We're confronted with ceiling-to-floor cupboards crammed with parchments and old leather-bound books.

"A library?" Anai asks.

"I do not know." I pick a few parchments off the shelves and unroll them, scanning the hastily scribbled text. Names and dates. Villages and family members. "They're records," I say, scrunching my nose in confusion. "Birth and death records for all the people in this ward of the kingdom."

"Odd." Anai slides out the door, then darts up the corridor, her footsteps erratic. When she returns, her cheeks are flushed. "There are more rooms exactly like this," she says.

So that's Jove's occupation.

"But why would birth and death records be kept in this part of town?" I wonder.

Anai nods to a map on the wall. "It looks like he doesn't keep them for the whole kingdom." Nailed crudely to a brick is Centriet in its large circle, split into zones by inked lines. It seems Jove only manages the birth and death records for a small selection of villages, including Yahres, Sledloe, Septown, and Maytown. And I suppose appropriate residences are difficult to come by in this part of town.

Since little else can be gleaned from the parchment chamber, we proceed down the hall. We come to a small room with a low pallet and a desk dotted with candles. It must be Jove's personal space. The candles have been burned to pasty white puddles and unbound papers are weighed down by smooth river stones. Leaving Anai to investigate, I withdraw to the corridor, hoping to uncover the quarters of Casper and Vogel.

It's simpler than I'd anticipated—the next room along. Two reed beds, separated by a large shelf in the middle of the floor, and the distinct odor of the outdoors give it away.

I creep inside. It's easy to decipher which side of the room belongs to which boy. Vogel's has bows, quivers, leather jerkins, and hunting knives. Casper's is filled with tomes and quills—not unlike the contents of my own possession basket. I glance at the shared desk. Half-rolled parchments curl on the surface like treasure maps. The parchments are a mix of faded and freshly scribed records, so perhaps Jove's job also entails making copies of the population's birth and death information. I do recall Casper mentioning that he and Vogel boarded with Jove. If they didn't have coin, they may have worked for him in exchange.

Trailing my hand across the desk, I traverse the room, combing for additional clues that might reveal Casper's location. I unearth books, clothes, and satchels. Then, a cane hamper, partially concealed beneath a rodent-nibbled blanket. Intrigued, I lift the lid, and there's more parchment inside.

"What is that?" Anai asks, coming up behind me.

I pull it out, slipping the cord from the end. The writing is relatively new—I can tell by the vibrancy of the ink. But that's where my comprehension stalls, for the sinews are patterned with all kinds of symbols—ticks and crosses, numbers and shapes—and references to a particular year and season that I can't quite understand.

"Some sort of research?" I say.

"Strange," says Anai.

"Really strange." I push it back in the hamper and replace the lid. "Maybe I should write him a letter so he knows what happened to his friend?"

"Good idea." Anai looks carefully at Vogel's hunting equipment as I scribble on a parchment. "Was he handsome?" she asks.

I pause mid-word. "What do you mean?"

"This boy," she says, gesturing at the bows and knives. "The dangerous ones are always the most attractive, aren't they?"

I think of Vogel sitting in the storeroom, how the shadows made his ice-blue eyes crackle in the dark. "I guess."

"What do you mean *you guess*? You met him twice, didn't you?"

"I did."

"Well?"

"Well, nothing." I place the letter on the table and walk to the door, not wanting to think about Vogel and what will happen to him in the ring. "Come on."

"Fine."

Anai and I head back to the window. We climb out and scoop up the boards, replacing them so they balance in the frame, giving the semblance of protection.

Then we leave Yahres. We quickstep through Sledloe. We

linger at the shore of the Geynes Sea, watching the treddeks jolt on the waves. It's only when we're wandering toward the city that I realize I don't have a place to stay.

"With me, of course," Anai says, the instant my question hovers in the breeze. She links our arms, the decision made. "It's too dangerous to stay in your stonebrick alone."

I begin to protest that *I* am dangerous. If she's found with me, she'll inherit my trouble.

But her eyes are fierce. "We'll take rugs to the tool hut. No one will think to find you there."

Since I have the afternoon to wait while Anai sells wares at the citizen market, I take the opportunity to circle back to my stonebrick.

My father is still missing.

Deflated, I lean my head against the door. With each new place he ceases to be, I can't help thinking that, perhaps, I am too late. Perhaps he is already toiling at the arena with the other Sledloe prisoners. And if he is, he's out of reach. At least for now. Tournament preparations are in full swing and perimeters have been erected to keep the public well clear.

Sighing, I leave my stonebrick and take a left through the main square. Bright banners with red-and-white flags thump in the wind. They're strung from arches, looped through fence posts, and stretched between the thatched rooves of several stonebricks. Little wonder the village swims with bodies. Everyone from here to Marasca has returned to Centriet for the Tournament. I stop at the base of Obellis's statue. He stands atop a coiled serpent, his sandaled foot rammed behind the snake's head. He's in his human form—a young man with graceful limbs, shoulder-length curls, and heavy eyebrows. I hope he's in a mood to answer my prayers. Then again, as I glimpse the overcrowded tents in the outer lanes, my confidence dives. I start walking again, head lowered, trying to block out the bone-thin patients with their familiar rattling coughs.

Finally, I arrive at the yellow fields bordering the woods near Anai's apartment. This stretch of forest was planted by our ancestors—great, tall maples and birches lodged so snugly that their canopies intertwine. Inside it, one can feel truly free. That's what draws my father here, I'm sure of it. Picking a path through the shrubs, I try to sense the memory of him in the leaves.

But I can't.

In fact, the main memory that fills this part of the forest is the memory of when my mother was ill. Or maybe that's because it follows me everywhere, that feeling.

I call out to my father. I wander and call, wander and call, to all the special places in this section of the wilderness that we know—the twin boulders cloaked with springy moss, the large fallen tree with its roots splayed out, and the old hollow that is full of ants and flying beetles.

He is nowhere.

At long last, I come to a grand tree in the clearing. This is my tree. The branches shoot outward and upward and I haul myself into the naturally made platform, hugging the bark with my arms, my legs dangling over the boughs, too high for anyone to see if they walked beneath me. This was where I used to come by myself whenever my mother was having one of her rare good sleeps. Although I could have stayed in my reed bed listening to her ragged breathing all day and night, I worried that if I shifted in the wrong direction, I could scrape the floor and wake her up. So I came out here. I sat in the middle of trees and flowers and let my head fill with all sorts of awful thoughts about the future and all sorts of terrifying thoughts about how I would cope when she was gone.

Suddenly remembering, I push to my feet and examine a patch of the smooth trunk with my etchings in it: *Stay awake.* I remember writing it with a stick, digging into the timber until the sticky sap oozed out. I wrote it on the day the village healer told my father and me that there was no hope for her now. I think I'd always known that to be true, ever since she coughed so much that the blood dripped from her lips, but I realized then that I had to keep my eyes open and clear until she died so that I didn't miss any more of her life.

As I sit back down, I run those words over in my head. *Stay awake.* They were words that meant something to me, but really, what did they mean to my mother? What did she crave the most in the end? *To not be alone. To be with those she recognized.* And it would likely be the same for Vogel. But if I cannot find his friend Casper and no one goes to the Tournament tomorrow that knows him, he will die in the ring, forlorn and abandoned, with no one of familiarity to bear witness.

And so will Jove.

I drop from the tree. A precarious thought is taking shape. It's a thought that's been prodding at the back of my skull, perchance since Anai and I were in Sledloe.

Maybe I *should* go to the Tournament. And not just to bear witness for Vogel and Jove. Of course, I feel the pull of guilt, knowing they're spares because of me. But beyond that I need to know . . . I need to know that my father's not there. I need to know that he hasn't been taken. Which he probably hasn't—and I pray that he hasn't—but if I don't go, then the chance may be gone. Not all prisoners remain in Sledloe. After, they may be sent to the mines. And if my father is one such prisoner, he could disappear and I'd never know.

I rake it over as I pace back and forth. It's a dangerous idea. I know that well. But then I think of a life without Father, when I had this chance to find out, to be sure. I cannot recoil and pass this up, so I make a deal with myself right then.

If my father hasn't returned by tomorrow . . .

I will go to the Tournament to find him.

CHAPTER THIRTEEN

UT IT'S LIKE A CURSE. ANOTHER MORNING OF SEARCHING PASSES, and yet my father remains absent. Anai and I stop by my stonebrick for one last check before the Tournament. When I close the entrance board and rejoin Anai on the road, tears whisper under my eyelashes. The empty room no longer smells earthy and dry. It smells like a windy tunnel, where old memories are easily swept away.

Anai slips her arm around my shoulders.

"Are you sure you want to do this?" she asks.

I nod before I lose my nerve. Today, I'm swathed by another shawl. I hunch to disguise my regular stance. "I have to know that he's not a prisoner."

"I could look for you—"

I shake my head. It has to be me.

"He's lucky," she says. "To have someone like you that cares so much."

"For all the good it will do him," I say.

I struggle to push my worries aside as we arrive in the arena's outer grounds. The usual barren nothingness has been transformed into a whirl of color and pageantry. Every conceivable style of tent patterns the soil—wide and narrow, circular and squared, some even complemented by furniture, wagons and glossy horses. Flags fly from the apexes, proudly announcing their inhabitants as Erraforgian, Leeangi, or Torquellese. The cloying scent of meat hangs in the air, combined with a spicy aroma of ale, which has managed to put everyone in a good mood, it seems. There is impromptu singing and dancing and children roleplaying with sticks, pretending to be gladiators fighting to the death. My stomach turns over. I think of the man who died in the arena, given only a branch as a weapon, and it takes all my willpower not to wrench the sticks from the children and break the wood beneath my heel.

"This way, Meadow." Anai yanks me toward the arena where a dozen lines of spectators wind from a dozen different entrance stairwells. I'm sure she's concerned we'll be seen. When I told her last night I planned to attend the matches, she tried to talk me out of it, but I insisted. She keeps one eye on me now as we join the shortest snake of people. The line moves slowly, which allows me to check the on-duty soldiers. They're not familiar, thank goodness, and they're happily tossing back cups of mead. When we get to the head of the queue, the swarm of people fans out. They shove their way past the soldiers, and Anai and I gladly follow suit, sliding into the stands, unseen.

Thousands cram the space inside. The noise hurts my ears. It pulses, pounds, relentless as a storm, ricocheting off the benches and pillars. Now I'm among the masses, however, I'm less concerned that I will be found.

"Anai!" yells someone.

She freezes beside me. "It's Symon," she hisses.

"ANAI! UP HERE!"

She waves to him, but her eyes are panicked. "We need to stay together," she says.

"I'll come," I say.

"Are you certain?"

"I'm certain. It will be easier to hide in a group."

I follow her to a stone slab, where Symon sits with boys from our village. They're donned in matching red-and-white tunics, clinking mugs and stamping their feet.

"You took your time, didn't you?" As Symon wraps his arm around Anai's neck, he casts an irritated glance in my direction.

"Anything of note happened yet?" asks Anai.

He ignores the question. "Why were you not here earlier?"

"No reason," says Anai, and it warms my heart to know that she's not about to share with him that we lingered outside my stonebrick for my father. Again. "Did you manage to get any food?" she asks, as the crowd grows restless, more people streaming in beneath the archways.

"They're not giving it out until after the matches," says Symon.

"Oh."

"Which you would have known if you had been here when you were supposed to." He stares at her, unblinking, like a hawk trying to intimidate a sparrow.

"I apologize," says Anai.

"You do, do you?"

"Yes."

One of the boys to Symon's right thumps him on the back and he swivels around to accept another mug of ale.

"We can sit somewhere else," I tell Anai.

"It's no bother," she says.

"Are you sure?"

"Just leave it alone." She turns back to Symon, tugging his sleeve, and part of me wonders if things would be different if only I'd been more present last year. Not that Anai would have gone to her friend with no courting experience for love advice. My eyes fall to the rows of people below us. A teenage boy with black hair twists in his seat. He stares at me, and I look away.

I let my gaze travel to the opposite side of the arena. The royal box is empty. A luminous red sun cloth arcs above the emperor's gold-plated throne. Silk cushions and a satin foot stool have been placed beside it with special care. On either side of the throne are two grand chairs, just as elaborate as his, but with varied color schemes. One is silver and blue. The other, sea green and deep purple. These must be reserved for King Rolyo of Leeang and High Sovereign Zementa of Torquella, as the hues match their flags. Aside from the three important seats, there are many more brilliant, although less extravagant, placings. No doubt to be filled with the noble men and women who saw me arrested in the palace square.

Without warning, the strawberry-colored doors open in the ring. The crowd erupts in cheers, even though it is premature to celebrate when the stands are still filling up. A flock of prisoners creep onto the hard-packed sand. They have rakes and wide eyes and unmarked tunics knotted at the waist. Scanning their faces, I'm relieved to note that none are my father, although these men and women look freckled and leathery, as if they have spent their best years under the glare of the middle day sun. A trio of Rigorates, dressed in fine blue apparel, appear along the bottom of the stands. They instruct the prisoners to spread out and to keep their mouths sealed. The prisoners move apart reluctantly, as if staying back-to-back in a circle will protect them from being knifed in the spine. They begin to rake in long slow movements, pupils darting and knees wobbling, until their overseers bellow to move at a less embarrassing pace.

I weave my fingers together like I'm holding my own hand. A gaggle of nobles enter the arena from a private entrance, making a show of sitting properly, throwing back their shoulders and fluffing out their shimmering dresses and cloaks. Once they are seated, the Tyjan family and two well-dressed men arrive beneath wide black parasols, held by servants, who have to move jerkily in time with their footsteps. Malthe and Kalliope take their seats in the less extravagant chairs. The two well-dressed men sit beside the emperor. King Rolyo is an imposing figure with ink-colored eyes and biceps the size of a man's head. The High Sovereign Zementa is tall and reedy with nervous hands and a scraggly beard that badly needs a trim. Seeing Prince Malthe for the first time since the tower makes my palms perspire, so I shield my identity by turning side-on so he'll only see the distant dot of a shrouded profile, if any of it at all.

The Rigorates eventually deem the arena fully raked. At the periphery of the ring are potted plants with vines that crawl all the way to the first row of seats. The prisoners slip into the small alcoves between the pots, one hand clasping their rake and the other pasted to their hip. The leaves sprout beside them like emerald waterfalls, the uppermost stalks entwining the copper rail like thread.

"This is going to be the best Tournament yet!" yells Symon, and the people around us stand and shout, pumping their fists to the sky as though they have won the right to eat full meaty meals for the rest of the year. As if infected by the same hysteria, other sections of the audience join in the cheering. It's a sea of noise and hardened eyes and a thirst for something that I have never quite been able to grasp. Clearly they haven't learned anything since the traitor's execution—or perhaps it's me who stumbles, unable to view the Tournament as anything but thinly veiled murder.

"Worthy day, Centriet!"

The bald man I'd encountered in the emperor's throne room rises to his feet, his wrinkled arms spread wide. He's separated from the royal box, but that doesn't seem to dampen his spirits.

"Welcome to the Training Rounds!" he booms. "How fortunate we are to behold this time-honored tradition. Gladiators from the three competing kingdoms—Erraforge, Leeang, and Torquella—will each be afforded a practice match to hone their skills and to test their weapons!"

If I'd thought the cheering was loud before, now it's scaled to fierce new summits. The stands explode, the crowd like children, yelling words they do not understand.

"And beyond that . . ." The bald man smiles, rotating his head to drink in the atmosphere. "The Emperor Ladislas wishes to make it abundantly clear that any who step into the ring this day are obliged to entertain *you*, the people!"

Another roar rips from the audience, as the man dips into a sycophantic bow. Everyone knows the meaning of *entertainment*. Blood must be spilled. Limbs cast off. Grown men reduced to begging for their lives. It suddenly feels all too real, and I ponder if I've made a dreadful mistake. I'd promised never to watch such depravity.

"Bring forth the first matchup!" the bald man cries.

At the west of the arena, facing into the sun, a huge banner sags over a pole. At the nod of a Rigorate, two prisoners wind the end handles and an enormous parchment unravels, spilling down the side of the sandbrick like an oversize scroll. Another pair of prisoners catch the base. They twist it around a second rod, securing it in place with a hook. The sign reads: *Training Round #1—Elyor Vass (Leeang) vs. The Masked Marauder.*

The noise dissolves to gentle chatter as drums begin to pound. In the middle of the ring strides a lanky man with intricate body art swirling down his arms in the shape of shrunken skeleton bones. He wears a tan skirt made from cow hide and dark brown sandals that crisscross his legs, tying above his knees. His weapon of choice is a slender sword that hangs delicately by his thigh. His blue-black hair falls below his ears, tucked neatly and all the same length, parted down the center like a crow's feather and slicked with fat. This must be Elyor. He's unclothed from the waist up. Servants have smothered his torso in grease, and the shine from the sun is immense.

A contingent of Leeangi visitors vault from their seats, waving blue flags with silver stars. A growl tumbles from Elyor's lips. He strikes a fist to his oily chest, leaving a bright red slash across his heart.

When the crowd quiets, the strawberry-colored doors open again. A figure lurches from the shadows as though he's been body-slammed by a wild dog. He hits the sand, landing awkwardly, and there's a sickening crack as his wrist bends sideways.

The reaction from the crowd is to gasp. Finally a reaction that matches my own.

When the man stands, swaying on shaky legs, the gasping switches to laughter. The "Marauder" wears a ridiculous mask that is visible for the first time. Constructed from thick porcelain, it is molded in the likeness of a hog. The protruding snout has been sculpted with finger-size nostrils, balanced by two rosy cheeks. With a broken wrist and an absurd headpiece, the man can hardly walk, let alone fight. He's clearly a spare, and judging by the cuts and bruises on his legs, he may have been held in the Karacholl for a long time before this moment. He has a little more fight in him than the executed man with the branch, and he's been gifted a tiny silver dagger. He lifts it with his good hand, slicing messy Xs in the air, though I doubt he can see properly through the narrow eye slits.

"Training Round number one!" shouts the bald man. "With Emperor Ladislas, King Rolyo and High Sovereign Zementa as our witnesses . . . Gentlemen, please begin!"

My ribs clench. *Gentlemen.* Why speak so ceremoniously of a spare who has been ferried here to die? The spare stops slashing and takes a step back. Elyor glides sideways, thumb on his hilt, a confident sneer twisting his mouth. They're unevenly matched in every way. Elyor is a giant. The spare is the size of a stunted adolescent. I mutter under my breath, "Come on. Come *on*," but the spare's knees buckle as he nurses his wrist, and I wonder for how long he'd been locked underground, his back stooped like an ailing elder's.

Too long.

The spare halts, unable to detect his opponent's position. He slashes again, striking at nothing. Elyor laughs and throws back his head.

I don't want this to happen to Vogel.

The spare strikes the air again and again. He strikes until he is so exhausted that he bends at the middle, palm to his knee, trying not to collapse in the sand.

It's the perfect set up for Elyor. Every so often he leans in to nick the spare with the tip of his sword. It's quick, like he's making art. Lines of red pour from the wounds and the crowd dies down, watching—almost entranced—by the precision of each stroke. It doesn't take long for the spare to topple and the audience descends into their jeering true selves. All eyes fly to Emperor Ladislas to determine whether the spare should be dealt the final death blow, but Ladislas waves off the attention and selects a plum from a gold-plated fruit bowl.

"Not worth his consideration," says Symon gleefully. Beside him, Anai has fallen silent. How must she feel knowing that the one she kisses at night revels in the pain of others? Although, that would describe most of the crowd.

I'm also curious what will happen if Ladislas becomes bored. I draw in breath, realizing I'm squeezing my hands so tightly that there's sweat beneath my nails.

The Leeangi contingent yell to their gladiator to be more vicious. Elyor pretends not to hear, but the corded muscles of his neck flame pink. He swings his sword, shattering the porcelain, ripping a layer of skin from the spare's face. The man lets out a strangled cry, burying his jawbone in the sand, his good arm flailing beside his ear, as if not knowing where to rest it.

The flags flap faster.

"Get up," says Elyor.

At once, the spare kicks onto his back. His cheek has peeled away from his face. He gurgles something that sounds like defeat.

I breathe out. I'm going to be ill. The sour taste of acid swells in my mouth.

"I said *get up*." Elyor lifts the sword, driving it into the spare's flank. The man moans, and it's all but over. As he writhes like a squid, Elyor pauses. His gaze flickers up to Emperor Ladislas, who wrinkles his nose and chews on his plum, shrugging as if the fruit isn't ripe. "You worthless coward." Elyor clouts the spare, and it occurs to me that he will be in just as much trouble if the emperor is not entertained.

But then . . .

The emperor nods once at Elyor and mouths the word *death*. The Leeangi bows to Ladislas in relief. He sinks the blade through the spare's temple, and the audience blares to life once more. But the blow to his head makes me think of Vogel being forced to kill the people in the tower. Innocent people. Just like the spare. And again, I choke back the rising bile.

"Are you quite well?" Anai squeezes my hand. Symon catches my eye and his pupils flare with disgust at my *frailty*. I ignore him.

"That was sickening," I say, but I don't think she can hear me over the stomping and clapping. In truth, I don't think I can hear myself.

I try to remember why I came to the Tournament. Aside from my father, to bear witness for Vogel and Jove. But this match only proves that it's not enough. Bearing witness for strangers is equally important. They had families and homes, histories and dreams. They surely didn't think as they sat at their Lessons that they'd grow up to die without honor in the ring. So as the prisoners scoop the spare onto a board, I whisper a prayer under my breath, sad that I'll never know his true name.

And it continues like this all morning. The rolling banner reveals gladiators from one of the three competing kingdoms—Erraforge, Leeang, or Torquella—and they are paired with an ill-equipped spare who has been given a ludicrous name and a humiliating costume. All the spares fall. Encouraged by the boredom of Ladislas, the gladiators hack through the trembling men, dismembering their opponents in the most gut-wrenching fashions. The sand turns red and clumpy. The prisoners are forced to use shovels and pails to remove the mud-like substance from the center of the floor.

I've lost count of my prayers when the banner drops for

what seems like the hundredth time. It reveals the next match: *Bourdais Allett (Torquella) vs. The Fool.*

Bourdais is shorter than many of the other gladiators we've seen so far. In fact, he looks about my height. Like many of the men from Torquella, Bourdais has a long mustache that hangs from his lip like frayed rope. He wears a loincloth that is already stained with fluid and sand. He carries an ax and a terrifying expression. His eyes are so wide and fierce that even his eye color—green—can be determined from our seat halfway up the stands. He lopes around the ring on his bandy legs, swishing the ax to his left and right.

"Where is my opponent?" he hollers.

The Fool is pushed from the strawberry doors. A little withered man with his face painted like a king's jester and his gray hair matted and sticking out like an animal caught in a thunderstorm.

Jove.

He's been given a long skinny pole. As if that will protect him from Bourdais. And Bourdais charges at once. Jove squeals and dodges to the left, but the ax swipes him in the ribs. Jove breathes in heavily. He looks to the crowd for a brief moment until Bourdais snarls and Jove is forced to run again. But he's clearly injured and exhausted and perhaps he's thinking of the traitor in the ring who gave up. Perhaps he's thinking he, too, should lay down his life without fighting anymore.

My heart squeezes. Jove scoots to the side—again, too late—and this time Bourdais thwacks his shoulder. Jove shrieks in pain, holding up his other arm, his palm raised like one might do in the middle of a game to surrender.

"Stop," he pants. "Stop, please. I can't keep running. I can't." Tears pour from his eyes and the crowd boos as his sobs grow stronger.

Bourdais looks to Emperor Ladislas, his eyes shining because he knows that this kind of wretchedness is usually well-favored in matches. Emperor Ladislas gives his consent almost immediately and Bourdais slams his ax into Jove's skull.

The record keeper falls.

I'm crying as the servants carry him out. I'm shaking and praying. Cursing myself. Cursing the Tyjans. And it's at this point I realize that I cannot sit here and watch Vogel be killed by a gladiator in the same barbaric and excruciating manner. I know I made the promise in the forest tree, but the thought of it makes me faint, so I stand up to move out of the stands.

"Where are you going?" asks Anai.

"I need to leave. I can't . . ."

She grips my hand, and I'm looking in the direction of the rolling banner when it drops to declare the next round.

Vogel Lashler (Erraforge) vs. Old Man Time

And when the strawberry doors open this time, two figures are shoved into the spotlight instead of one. And I scream.

It's Vogel, a gladiator, representing Erraforge.

And my father is the spare.

CHAPTER FOURTEEN

I'M TOO SHOCKED TO MOVE. ANAI'S HAND TUGS ME DOWN AND I land heavily on the stone bench. My vision tunnels until all I can see are the two lone figures standing side by side.

My father wears a robe that scrapes the ground, and he holds a wooden staff. Pasted to his face are curly white ringlets. Perhaps this is their sick humor to make him appear like an old man. Underneath the garb, I see the truth of who he is. I see the composure in his posture. It is not defeat like that of the executed traitor. It is not fear like that of Jove. It is not desperation like the first servant who fell at the hands of Elyor. My father cannot hide his pride, his spirit, his strength. Sometimes I fear that I don't have enough of him in me.

"Meadow, that's . . ." For the first time, Anai comprehends the magnitude of what is happening. Symon is on his feet with the rest of the bloodthirsty animals, but she pulls roughly away from him and slides beside me, her eyes wide with horror. "We should have . . ." She cannot finish, but I understand how she struggles for words because she knows deep down like I do that nothing we could have done would have prevented this moment, save for me going back in time and never speaking openly at the Gathering. She doesn't need to say the other part: my father will not survive. Vogel is the epitome of gladiator. He wears a leather skirt and sandals. Thick hide straps cross his muscled shoulders and he carries a gleaming sword.

He's godlike.

Dangerous.

Tanned and athletic, as though all he does is train and hunt.

And I do not understand. Was Vogel one of them all along? With his chest oiled like Elyor, he certainly looks the part. But why would he have hidden with me in the storage room in the tower? Why would he have killed those people to save them from their suffering if he was in league with the prince all this time?

My questions are almost answered when neither my father nor Vogel make any sort of movement. Instead they glare at the stands. Two men against the crowd. And the crowd decides it will roar louder, perhaps believing that the gladiator does this for show. Their thousand strong voices knot together, the cacophony bringing forth a sole bellow—demanding blood. And still my father and Vogel stand firm, until I can bear it no longer.

Amid the noise, I jump up and bolt down the steps to the rail. I need to get closer if this is the end. The thought of being caught by the emperor or Malthe makes not the slightest bit of difference, as long as my father is able to see me. I throw my arms in the air to gain his attention, but his head does not rotate. His brown eyes stare at the tent where Ladislas sits. And suddenly the people join in my arm-flailing so that the whole stadium swirls with madness and I am swallowed by their mirth.

A familiar hand lands on mine. I turn and it's Anai. She's paler in the face that I've ever seen her—the color of wheat after it's been threshed by a machete. I'm frightened she's about to keel over, but she rests her body against the rough sandbrick and swallows her fear. Probably for my benefit.

"I'm trying to think of a way to get him out," she says. "That gladiator looks too strong." She glances at the banner and spies Vogel's name again. Her lips move, running the sound of it through her teeth. "Vogel? The boy you said was in the palace? The one who lived in Yahres—"

"He was boarding there," I correct. My heart rises to my throat. I don't know what to do, either.

But then, neither it seems does Ladislas. The emperor raises a single paw. At once, the screaming crowd falls silent. Even the mothers hush their infants. We all know what happens to those who defy the emperor in a public forum. It involves being carted away by soldiers and not being heard from ever again.

Ladislas beckons a Rigorate, who has been busy instructing prisoners. The blue-clad man rushes so quickly to the emperor's side that he stumbles in his cream-colored sandals. No one laughs. I watch the soldiers, surveying the aisles for signs of insolence. Upon regaining his footing, the Rigorate bends in front of Ladislas. He nods, listening intently, then nods again. Straightening his spine, the Rigorate steps toward the rail.

I hold my breath. The Rigorate pauses, digging his fingers into the copper. He drops his eyes to Vogel and my father. "You *will* commence the match!" he orders.

"I will not," says Vogel.

"I will not," says my father.

"His Majesty commands it," the Rigorate bellows. "To refuse the order is treason to the kingdom. What say both of you to that?"

"What say both of us?" There's a tense stare-down between Vogel and the Rigorate, before Vogel makes a grand show of raising the sword high above his head and tossing it aside.

I exhale.

My father grabs the springy ends of his pasted-on beard. He tugs down and a stringy white substance comes off with the ringlets, stretching out like melted goat's cheese. He flings the mess of hair and glue in the grains by his feet and drops the end of the staff on top, mashing the humiliation into the ground until nothing is left.

I close my eyes as the audience gapes. Tears spike my eyes.

Ladislas motions forcefully to the Rigorate and the arena remains soundless, unsure what will happen next. The Rigorate stoops low to the emperor again, listens, then climbs the stairs beside the royal box, making a beeline for a loitering soldier. It only takes an instant before I recognize the dark skin beneath the soldier's jerkin and the quiver pressed against his upper back. After a small exchange, the Rigorate yells, "Death to them both!" and Gyzen raises his bow in an unhurried manner, aims, and shoots an arrow into the ring.

The whole scene brightens in front of me, so much I can barely discern what unfolds. It's a dream within a dream. The silver-tipped projectile tears through the air and buries itself in my father's torso. His staff falls and then he collapses. Vogel moves swiftly to shield his body. And it feels like hands are slapping against me, hitting my face, my chest, my arms. I push myself against the onslaught, thrashing and shouting—and yet there is nothing. I cannot feel anything because it's not real. It cannot be real.

Because that would mean . . .

I heave and my body convulses. I'm screaming into the wind. I'm screaming at no one and at everyone but no one hears me except for Anai. She grips my shoulders, tears streaming down her cheeks. Suddenly I'm lost in her bright eyes. Her movements seem to slow and I know inside that she's trying to tell me something important but I can't quite make it out over the thunderous tumult around us.

"What?" I half scream, half cry at her.

"He's not dead!" she yells back.

I spin and gaze down into the arena, straining to see when my eyes will not focus. I suck in air to calm myself. I do what my father always advised and concentrate on the little details. Pot plants. Prisoners. Fallen rakes. The banner. Then I see what she's talking about. My father lies on his back in the sand, Vogel pressing a cloth to the wound.

"Anai, he's . . ."

"No, he's not." He looks so lifeless, but Anai is adamant. "He was pierced through the side," she says, imitating on herself. "He isn't dead."

"How?" I ask.

"The soldier?" She frowns, and it takes me a moment to understand. She's saying that Gyzen missed his target.

"On purpose?" I ask.

"What does it matter?"

The bald man is on his feet, leaning over the sandbrick barrier. "Kill him, gladiator!" he shouts with venom. "Kill him swiftly. End this now!"

Vogel lifts my father's hand, showing him how to hold the cloth. When my father nods, Vogel rises. He pulls a knife from a band at his ankle.

"I'd rather kill myself," he yells, "than kill an old man for your Tyjan thrills." His hand is bloody from my father's gash, the redness trickling onto the blade.

The emperor whispers in the bald man's ear.

"Wait," the bald man calls to Vogel.

Vogel stops.

"The emperor is confounded that you'd save a spare that you don't even know."

"Let him die!" shouts Malthe, and Ladislas glares until the prince shrinks back in his chair. The emperor says something else to the bald man, who relays the message to a Rigorate.

"Take the spare!" the Rigorate yells, and the prisoners sling my father on a strip of hessian. Six of them hold the edge of the cloth, carrying him through the strawberry doors.

"Let's go." Anai clinches her fingers with mine, trying to drag me away from the rail.

"Wait," I say.

"Come on!" she says. "We may find out where they're taking him!"

I'm scared to vacate the arena without learning Vogel's ultimate fate, but she's right. We'll need to leave immediately to discover where the wounded are headed.

"Now!" Anai yells.

As we turn to the exit, a shadow steps in front of us.

"Where are you running off to?" asks Symon.

"Nowhere," says Anai.

His face darkens. "*Nowhere?* Really? What does that mean?"

"It means, Symon, that we need to go." I'm so thankful that Anai is coherent because I feel like I've lost my bearings again.

But he claps his hand on her shoulder. "Wait. We were supposed to be spending our time here together."

"We can talk about this later," she says.

"And if I wish to talk now?"

"I will see you this evening." Anai jerks out of his grip, but Symon is fast. He grabs her hair. The beautiful curls twist in his knuckles, and Anai stumbles, her neck bumping back.

"We will talk *now*," he says.

"Get off her!" At once, Symon is Prince Malthe. He's Farrow and the bald man. He's Emperor Ladislas. He's anyone I've ever known in my life who's tried to hurt my mother or father. I shove my fingers under his chin with so much force he gags and falls sideways.

"Meadow!" cries Anai, but her hair swings free.

"You're shameful!" says Symon, clutching his collar. His breath stinks of watered-down ale, and he suddenly lurches on the cobbles and retches.

"Let's go!" I tug Anai by the sleeve.

"We'll be no longer courting!" Symon hollers.

Anai points to the closest exit, pretending she did not hear what he said.

Before we leave, I turn to the ring. Vogel is being escorted through the doors. Unharmed, it appears. At least for now.

We scoot past Symon as he squirms in his mess. His friends from the stands have come to his aid. And we tumble down the stairs, past the black-haired boy who'd looked at me before.

He continues to stare.

CHAPTER FIFTEEN

ANAI REFUSES TO TALK ABOUT SYMON. INSTEAD SHE SEIZES MY hand and we skim the outer perimeter of the arena, trying to locate an entrance into the underground tunnels. The lofty wall curves beside us, constructed from thousands of sandbrick pieces. The pieces are chiseled in perfect cubes and fitted together with melted ore. Since Anai doesn't speak, I don't speak, either. It's probably for the best because I think I might cry if I open my mouth. Either that or I'd tell Anai how tired I am of everything. Tired of the Tyjans. Tired of running. Tired of watching people die.

An uncomfortable quiet wraps around us as we bypass the alleys of empty tents. Stray soldiers roam the grounds. Older citizens, too frail to climb the steps into the arena, have drooped beside fence stakes, their eyes half-closed, awaiting the conclusion of the Training Rounds. We keep walking. We step over revelers, who wriggle on the dirt like dying roaches. And yet, at least, they are alive. Unlike Jove. Unlike the spares. And if we don't find him soon . . .

My father will join them.

"It was only a flesh wound," Anai assures me, breaking the silence by guessing my thoughts.

"A flesh wound can still turn septic," I say. "Especially if they pile him on top of the corpses." An image of bodies enters my head, defaced and soulless, their stories forgotten. I push it aside and keep my legs moving, reminding myself that my father's not dead.

After a while, Anai slows her feet. "Do you see an entrance?"

"No."

"Nor do I."

We've paced the entire border of the arena, patiently running our fingers over the exposed blocks, only to arrive back where we began. But I can't give up that easily. I *won't* give up that easily. When I start the loop for a second time, Anai jogs a little faster to catch up. I know what she's going to say, but I don't want to hear it. Just like I never wanted to hear her tell me to get out of my reed bed and go for a stroll in the sunshine after my mother had died.

"I need to be sure." I pull ahead. My chest constricts as I look back, but her expression is not what I envisaged. She's not trying to stop me. Instead she points at a metallic door that we somehow missed on our first rotation.

"Do you think it could be the way in?" She chews her lip, trying to stare and not to stare at the same time.

"Perhaps." I count six soldiers blocking the entrance, their fingers shining with chicken-bone grease. I draw Anai inside a tent. One of the soldiers looks like Farrow.

"Would he know you?" she asks, after I tell her.

"Yes, and he'd drag me back to the tower. But I think you're right. That must be the entrance. Unless it's another route into the stands?"

Anai leans around the tent poles, but we're too far off to get a good view. "I'm going to take a closer look." She ducks under my arm with a head toss, ruffling her hair and yanking her tunic. "How do I look?"

"Anai, you shouldn't . . ."

"I won't engage. There's no need to fret."

"You remember what I told you happened in the tower?"

"Yes," she says.

"So don't," I plead.

But she's gone from the tent, hiccupping softly, pretending to be drunk on a cupful of wine. All I can do is stay where I am, my figure sheathed by the heavy canvas. One or two soldiers turn from their food, but she trundles past, her footsteps ungainly. Though they don't know Anai and can't leave their posting, my worries compound and I dig at my knuckles.

It's like watching my childhood again. Anai, the brave. Meadow, the cautious. Except this time I've a right to be wary. When it comes to Farrow, I'm well versed. Anai feigns an interest in the clouds. She throws her head skyward, eyeing the door. The soldiers hover over a food tray, and she shuffles along to another empty tent that sits directly opposite the entrance.

My breathing returns to its regular rhythm. She'll stay there awhile and then come back. Pity she couldn't have shared her plan. It's a lot less dangerous than I'd first imagined.

I step back from the split in the fabric, pressing my fingers to the ridge by my nose. The murmur of a headache swells at my temples. I need to sit down.

"Meadow Sircha?"

I jolt at the unfamiliar voice that somehow seems to know my name. Retreating into the shadows of the tent, I'm stunned to discover a boy behind me. Short hair, the color of soot, and big eyes, like liquid honey. It's the boy from the stands who swiveled and stared. The one we passed on our way down the staircase.

I almost stumble into the walls. My nails scratch against the canvas.

"Who are you?" I ask.

"Ein," he says. He's dressed in gray like the men on the tred-deks. He's younger than me. Not a lot, but younger. His arms are thin and his skin shines with sweat. A crooked smile plays on his lips, as if he's aware of something I'm not.

"And what do you want?" It's all I can manage. Has he watched from afar this whole time? I inch closer to the billowing opening. I may be fatigued, but I can run.

"I heard you at the Gathering," he says, his voice dipping low to almost a whisper. He moves in closer. "That night in Yahres when the prince rode in and arrested you."

He takes another step, and I freeze. He slips his palm into mine and squeezes. It's a friendly gesture, but I pull away. The space in the tent seems to shrink even more.

"We're not allies," I say.

"We should be."

For one so young, his poise is astounding. He isn't even as tall as me, yet when he speaks I can't help but listen.

"You're not alone in your thoughts," he says. "There are others who feel the same as you do. People who do not believe in the Tyjans. Those who think there's a better solution."

"A group?" I say.

"I suppose it is."

"How many?"

"Our numbers are growing," says Ein. "If you want to learn more, you can meet us tonight. Below the forked tree in the Bezzlay Forest."

I know the tree. Ten paces from the pond, tucked behind a clump of overgrown thistles.

"And what is your better solution?" I ask.

"If you come this eve, you will find out." Black hair falls across his forehead. He lifts a hand, sweeping it aside. A tattoo circles his thumb like wire, spiraling up to the base of the nail. "So what say you?"

What say you.

Words the Rigorate spoke in the ring. And with them the smallness of the tent disperses, the memory of my father pushing in.

"I'm sorry. I can't."

His forehead wrinkles, which makes me feel like I may have upset him. For some reason, I don't doubt his motives. If I'd known of Ein and his group before the Gathering, perhaps

I would have held back from speaking, and perhaps my father would be in our stonebrick, vehemently refusing to acknowledge the Tournament, the way it always should have been.

"It's normal to be frightened," says Ein. "It's not in our nature to talk of these issues. But when I heard you speak of your mother, I saw something in you—a fire and goodness. Qualities, Meadow, that we have, too."

I open my mouth, but he shakes his head.

"Tonight. Bezzlay." His tone is sharp.

The flaps rustle, and Anai barges in. "It's definitely the entrance down to the tunnels, but we cannot get past them. We must wait it out."

I wheel around, but Ein has vanished.

"Did you hear what I said?" asks Anai.

"Yes." I ogle the spot where Ein had been standing. He must have crawled under the folds.

"I think you should sit," Anai says slowly. "You look as if you're about to collapse." She takes my hand and we sink to the rug, the surface beneath it gritty with pebbles. "You look like you've seen a specter," she says.

It feels like I've seen a specter if I'm truthful. I want to tell her of Ein and his group and the secret meeting in the Bezzlay Forest. But she's been through enough with Symon today, and I don't want to hit her with any more problems. And since I'm not going, there isn't the need. Though I could tell her later when all this has passed.

"I'll watch the soldiers if you need to rest." As she shifts, her blue eyes brim with concern. "If anything changes—and I mean anything—I'll wake you up."

"What about Symon?"

Anai frowns. "He'll be fine with his friends."

"I'm sorry about what happened."

"I know."

"I jabbed him in the throat . . ."

"Don't remind me." Her body stiffens, though her mouth curls slightly, and she slopes her chin so I won't see her smile. The knowledge that she isn't angry at me lifts a burden from atop my shoulders. Best not to press about Symon though. When she's ready and able, I know she will speak. The ceiling blurs and sharpens with the sunlight and my elbows crack as I stretch out my arms.

And that's when it strikes. The pure exhaustion.

I close my eyes.

And dream of nothing.

When I come to, the flood of everything—memories of the day, the sounds of the night and the smells of the banquet food—are too intense. I mash two fingers into my closed eyes until I feel the shape of eyeballs rolling around in the sockets. When I let go, silvery stars frolic in front of my face. Drum beats mix with high-pitched singing, and then I remember I'm outside the arena and my father is captured and he's been shot by an arrow—

I peer around the edge of the tent. There are even more soldiers standing with Farrow. Anai is nowhere in sight. Around me, full-bellied revelers dance in rings, and I roll to my feet, stifling a yawn, my eyes adjusting to their rapid movement.

Orange light pours from torches notched into the dirt. The flames create a series of warm paths, leading to clusters of white marquees. Within each marquee, servants spoon portions of meat and vegetables into people's hands. Soldiers and Rigorates stand guard to prevent the masses from becoming overly greedy, although it seems they are all too quick to dip their own fists into the serving cauldrons, claiming more than their fair share. Not that it surprises me.

With darkness cloaking the grounds, I step into the open. Gaggles of children whisk by with their tiny palms full of chicken.

Families perch on soil mounds, rivulets of meat juice streaming down their forearms as they bite into cuts of beef. There's so much joy and gratitude pulsing from person to person that the image of the deaths in the arena seem to plunge into a locked box and remain. For how could the Tournament truly be evil when it offers so much nourishment? And how could the Tyjans truly be wrong to spend the kingdom's coin on a new arena when it brings so much prosperity to the city?

But that's the lie. Even knowing what happened to my father, I'm tempted to slide into wonder about my surrounds. When I was a child, Komran sanctioned outdoor celebrations during harvest. And they were just like this. The same excitement. The same aromas. The same odd feeling that troubles did not exist until the sun came up. Of course back then, problems were meager. A leaking roof. A shriveled fern. I cast a fleeting glance at the entrance to the underground tunnels, forcing myself to dwell on the uglier truth of the present.

And that's when I see him.

Casper.

He's dawdling on the edge of a group of men, listening to a merchant spout tales between slurps from an overflowing goblet. We lock eyes. A shawl's draped over his dark hair, but he raises his chin in a sign to follow.

I cross the cobbles at a run, jostling through the ebbing crowd. When I pop out the other side, Casper's with me, grabbing my arm in a clawlike grip. He leads me into a deserted side street, dropping the shawl on the stones.

"I found your note," he says. "Thank you."

I nod. "Did you see what happened in the ring? They used Vogel as a gladiator against my father!"

"I heard," says Casper, his voice a little off-kilter. "I heard because . . . Vogel managed to escape."

"What?"

"Come with me."

I turn back to see if I can spy Anai. She'll be terribly worried if she returns to the tent and finds that I have disappeared. But Casper breaks through my hesitation with his urgency.

"Your father," he says, and I snap my neck around as quickly as possible.

"Is he all right?"

Casper throws up his hands and makes a noise in his throat like the news is both good and bad. It causes my heart to skid to a halt.

"Well, what?"

"They've already taken him," says Casper. "I came out here to see if I could find you because Vogel saw your father in a wagon with some of the other . . ." He stops abruptly, as if realizing the word he was about to use is not appropriate. "Uh . . . Vogel said that they were taking your father and the expired spares to the infirmary on the other side of the Tyrant's Daughter."

"The Tyrant's Daughter? *Why?*" A shiver courses through me. Aside from the news that my father is traveling with cadavers, the Tyrant's Daughter is a vast river that borders our kingdom like a wild, flowing fence. Across the blue expanse lies the Sparselands—a barren place of nomads and enigma. People are warned not to breach its threshold. Most who do never return.

"I'm not sure why," Casper admits. "But Vogel will know."

There's a knot in my chest. I recall Farrow speaking of the Sparselands—how he believed that magic existed in its landscape. Not that I believe in such magic. It's the folk in the Sparselands who concern me the most. Long ago, when Erraforge united, a few cunning warlords smuggled their people across the river to avoid execution. Tyjan army posts lie along the river to prevent such people from crossing back and forth.

"The infirmary is not in the Sparselands," says Casper. "It's across the river in an Erraforge safe zone."

"What does that mean? Are you saying he'll be safe?"

Casper wavers. "Of course not, no."

I picture my father bleeding and helpless, transported far from his village of birth. If he does pass, he can't pass in the outskirts. He has to die here with my hands holding his, under the roof of my mother's last breath.

"We can try and catch the wagon," says Casper.

"How long ago did it leave?" I ask.

He shrugs. "But it's true that the longer we linger, the farther ahead they will get from us."

I glance at the swarm of exuberant revelers. "I need to let my friend know where I am going."

He takes my hand. "There isn't time—"

"For what?" asks a voice.

We both turn.

"Did you think I would have missed you wandering off?" Anai stands behind us, hands by her hips. Her fingers drip with turkey juice. "And who is this?"

"Casper," I say.

"Oh, *Casper.*" Anai looks him up and down.

"This is my friend Anai," I explain.

"And where were you planning on taking her?" asks Anai.

"Vogel escaped from the tunnels," I say.

She stops, staggered. "How is that possible?"

"The exit to the tunnels comes up in the streets," he replies. "When they were transporting the bodies . . . and Meadow's father . . . Vogel sneaked out before they could close the gate. He popped some soldier in the jaw."

"And where is he now?" I ask.

"That's where we have to go before we leave," Casper says. "But, like I said, we have to go now if we want to grab him and pursue the wagon."

"Wait. You're going after the wagon?" Anai's eyes bulge at the news.

"They have my father," I retort. "They're taking him to an infirmary on the other side of the Tyrant's Daughter."

"Meadow," says Anai.

"I have to do this."

She grabs me by the arm and drags me out of Casper's earshot. "That's the Sparselands, isn't it? No one really knows what's out that far."

"Casper says there's a safe zone."

"A *safe* zone? Does such a place even exist?"

I do not know, but I have to try. He's my flesh and blood. My only family left. The thought of losing my father so soon after my mother—and due to the Tyjans again—is unbearable. Besides, does she really believe I could go home tonight and forget everything that has occurred?

"Do you trust him?" asks Anai, nodding at Casper, when she realizes that I have made up my mind.

"I don't know Casper well, but I trust Vogel from what I know of him," I say.

"So you don't know much about them at all," says Anai as Casper calls that we need to hurry up, as they will soon notice that Vogel is missing and send out soldiers to bring him in.

"I'm going to do this," I tell her.

Anai scrunches her nose and looks to the moon, muttering something under her breath that could be a prayer to Obellis or it could be a curse about being my best friend.

"Oh, fine," she says, her grasp like talons as we walk in Casper's direction. "But if you're going to do this, then I will be damned if I'm left behind."

CHAPTER SIXTEEN

ASPER GUIDES US ALONG A ROAD THAT'S SPLASHED WITH starlight and peppered with clefts. A ramp climbs out of a cavernous hole. It connects to a street running into an alley, then carves through the city to the Nothrick Prison.

"That's the tunnel from the arena," says Casper, tilting his head at the gaping pit. We give it a wide berth, taking a swift right and proceeding along a skinny lane where the stonebricks huddle so close together that a man could lean through a neighbor's window without vacating his own abode.

With the drumming and the laughter dying down behind us, the atmosphere takes on a hollow quality, almost like we're sealed under the surface of the sea. At the end of the narrow street, Casper taps his hand against his thigh in a *one-two-one-two* pattern, and a few moments later, Vogel's familiar form lopes from a cobwebbed alcove in one of the residences, scanning left and right as he sprints to join us.

He's still wearing his gladiator clothing, which makes him look quite forbidding in the darkness. Even though I've met him twice, I hold back, confused, not certain if the costume he wears is a truer reflection of who he is or whether it was the boy with the bow and arrows and annoyed expression from Jove's cottage all along. At least he is wearing a shirt. Vogel approaches me with equal caution. I think I could burst with the amount of questions I need him to answer, and yet I cannot think of where to start.

There's an awkward moment where we just stand there, running the words over in our heads, not allowing any of the thoughts to form on our tongues.

Fortunately or unfortunately, Anai fills the uncomfortable pause. She stretches her arm to grasp Vogel's wrist in greeting, but Vogel stiffens and does not reciprocate the gesture.

"Who are you?" he asks coldly.

"Anai Marcheller," she replies. "I am Meadow's best friend."

Vogel turns his eyes on me, and I can tell at once that he holds sympathy for what I saw in the ring between him and my father. It strikes me that he is cursed with a similar quandary to myself. He has questions to ask and answers to impart, but he holds them inside as I do.

"I told her about her father," Casper says to Vogel.

"How do you know they are taking him across the Tyrant's Daughter?" I ask.

Vogel touches a finger to the corner of his mouth. A little drop of dried blood has seeped from an injury. "That was their promise," he says. "Whether killed or wounded, once their time in the ring is up, all spares were to be transported to the infirmary."

The way he says the word *infirmary* makes me doubt it is a place to be healed.

"But is it really an infirmary?" I ask, not sure I want to know the answer in my heart of hearts. Well, especially if it is *not* an infirmary.

Vogel goes quiet. We share that horrid memory from Malthe's tower, and I sense the tightness in the air as he reflects upon it, too.

"It's not what we saw in the palace," he says gently, "but not exactly where you'd like to be taken if you are wounded, either. There are healers at the infirmary, yes, but the soldiers made it very clear that any survivors would not be patched up and sent home."

"Then what happens to them?" It doesn't make sense. Why would the emperor waste time and resources transporting injured spares out of the kingdom? We have healers in the villages. Perhaps they do not possess the knowledge of those under Tyjan employment, but who is my father to Ladislas? Certainly not someone worth saving.

Vogel shifts between his feet. "I believe they'll be taken to the Jasquek Mines."

His words pass through my chest, taking precious moments to absorb. Just like the Sparselands, people never return from the Jasquek Mines. Although there are many mine sites sprinkled throughout the kingdom, all offer the same fate—blackened lungs, destroyed vision, and hearing deadened by filth.

And that's if they survive.

"But we can prevent that from happening if we get to him first." Vogel recaptures my attention, and I blink, feeling the nudge of his gaze divert me from despair.

I press my lips together. "How long ago did the wagon leave?"

"A while," says Vogel. "The one with your father left before I got out of the tunnel. It would have been well on its way out of Centriet by the time I was free."

"So we need to hurry," says Casper, but Anai lunges forward and shoulders me back. I always used to like her playing the protective big sister, but this time, I step around her because it's my father and not hers, and I need to be the one to make the decisions.

"So you're going to take me to the infirmary?" I ask. "Both of you?"

"I can't very well stay in Centriet," says Vogel. "And neither should you. Your father said the soldiers who took him did so on behalf of the prince because you somehow escaped from the tower room."

I nod.

"But why would you take her there?" asks Anai. "From what she told *me*, you met her once outside the cottage in Yahres and then in the palace. Why not go off to Avaliese or Marasca in the north? Why risk going across the Tyrant's Daughter yourselves?"

Vogel exchanges a look with Casper.

"Why?" I ask.

"Because," says Casper. "We have been to the infirmary before."

"You have?"

Vogel nods to confirm what Casper has revealed. I wonder if it has something to do with why he was paraded out as a gladiator and not a spare. Before I can ask, Casper's eyes grow large.

"We need to go."

Behind us, footsteps clatter on the cobbles and boisterous voices skitter between the gloomy buildings. Two hazy figures appear on the rise. One of them whistles to alert the other, which can only mean one thing.

Soldiers.

"Go!" says Casper. "Now!"

The four of us take off. Thankfully, we only have to turn one bend and we're out of their line of sight. Casper speeds past my shoulder. He rounds a corner to the left that's streaked with veins of pasty moonlight, and by the time we're hidden by a second set of walls, I slow my feet, inhaling deeply, straining to hear if the soldiers have decided to pursue us farther.

The street is silent.

I glance at Vogel, standing beside me, not puffed in the slightest. "Casper said you struck a soldier in the jaw?"

He tips the corner of his mouth again. "I hit a Rigorate and ran when they opened the gate for one of the Quills." He doesn't sound proud to admit it. If anything, his voice is tinged with regret. And now I understand why Vogel must leave with haste. Striking a soldier is ill-advised, but striking a Rigorate is high treason, punishable by death.

"Do either of them know where they're going?" whispers Anai.

I'm not sure. As Casper inches along the gutter, he passes beneath an unlit lamp post eerily swathed with red and white ribbons and hooked like a cane. I think we're close to Kessler Row. I'm not greatly familiar with this area, but if we keep pushing forward, we should emerge near a strip of old taverns, likely deserted due to the free food and drink in the arena grounds.

It's deathly quiet. Signposts jut from above heavily bolted doors. Candles have been extinguished. No whiff of broth. Even the sense of being watched is lacking. I scrape my eyes over the rotted timber clinging to the tavern foundations, trying to locate a break in the wall where we might be able to squeeze our bodies. No such luck. Up ahead, a hefty log balances atop two rocks, forming a thick rail, and a soft whinnying disperses in the atmosphere. As we pull closer to the noise, horse silhouettes stand out against the blackened inns. There are only two, and they're small and bony. They must belong to a pacifist who has decided not to participate in the feast, or perhaps to a merchant who resides on the street.

"Can you ride?" asks Casper to Anai and me, and although I can—and quite well, thanks to my mother—it's obvious that the poor little beasts would never be able to withstand the weight of two bodies on their narrow backs.

"We're not riding those," I say. The nearer we get, the tinier they look, although I'm not sure Casper truly intended us to ride them out of the city like a band of vigilantes. I pat one of the horses on the nose. It breathes out, its whole face quivering with the attention, as if it hasn't had the pleasure of human kindness in quite some time.

"We will not catch up to your father on foot," says Anai.

"If we're lucky, we can trouble some travelers for transport along the way." Vogel looks at me. "Does this mean you take up our offer to travel with you to the infirmary?"

"We know a couple of the staff," Casper chimes in.

And I am sure it is the only way to find my father.

"Do we need supplies?" I ask. "How long will the journey take?"

"It's at least five days' ride," says Vogel, "and that's just to the river. We'll still need to cross it after that."

"Supplies?"

"We'll grab some from Jove's cottage on our way through Yahres," says Casper.

We each pause for a moment at hearing the name of the fallen man. Vogel swallows and wanders onward, turning the corner at the end of the block. I watch him go.

"So are you coming?" asks Casper, again more to me than to Anai, despite how she has seemingly attached herself to my hip.

"We're both coming," Anai predictably says, which is the last pledge I want her to make, despite how much she thinks she owes me.

I turn to her. "You don't have to do this. You have your mother and you have your labor. If you don't show up at the markets tomorrow, Miss Renata will give your rations to another. And this whole thing could be dangerous—"

"You think I care about that?" Anai shoves me in the arm. "I should have looked for you when you went missing before, instead of telling myself that you were safe. So don't ask me again. It's settled, all right?" She glares at Casper. "I'm in."

"Very well."

I sigh. It's no use trying to dissuade Anai, especially when she thinks she's making amends. Goodness knows how Symon will react. I only hope he doesn't explode when she returns to Maytown. Or worse—assist the soldiers in trying to find us while we're gone.

All of a sudden, a voice splits the air from a street at our rear.

"There they are!"

I seize Anai's wrist. I wonder how the soldiers would react if they knew that among this group is not only the escaped gladiator, but also the very girl that their prince desires to bind to his worktable.

Vogel comes jogging back. "I've found more horses," he says. "Ones that aren't so slight."

We follow him into the alley. True to his word, three sturdier creatures have been secured to a post. They stomp their hooves, observing us with interest, but despite our approach, their doe eyes remain calm. I feel awful about what we are planning, yet I know it is the only way we are ever going to catch the wagon.

Casper and Vogel each untie a horse. Anai and I run to the third. Behind us, the voices grow louder. Casper and Vogel swing onto their steeds. I jump onto mine and Anai mounts the back, wrapping her arms around my waist with so much strength that the life pushes from my ribs.

As we're choosing a route to take, a group of figures step into the alley from a side building.

"They've got our horses!" yells a panicked voice.

My eyes widen. I can just make him out in the half-light. It's Ein. When he notices it's me, he does a swift double take, but he reels in his surprise. My gaze travels to his companions. They look able and confident, and I realize that they are likely his gang of followers who are keen to change the kingdom.

"Meadow!" calls Ein.

"You know him?" yells Anai.

"The soldiers," I call to Ein. "That's why—"

Ein nods. "Ride to the place I spoke of before," he says. "Do you remember where I said?"

The forked tree.

He knows I remember, but the forked tree is in the opposite direction to where we must go, and although part of me wants to join him, I have to save my father.

"We will meet you there," he says.

"I can't," I say. "I'm so sorry." I squeeze my thighs and my horse gallops off, past Vogel and Casper, into the night.

"We need those horses!" yells one of Ein's friends.

As the soldiers enter the space, Vogel and Casper clap their reins and tear after me. As the hooves pound the cobbles, I twist back. Ein and his followers have disappeared from the alley and the last thing I see are the outlines of the soldiers, scurrying to catch up with us and realizing that they cannot.

We ride through Sledloe and arrive in Yahres to collect supplies from Jove's cottage. With the whisper of soldiers on our tail, Anai and I crouch below the eaves with the horses, while Vogel and Casper slip indoors through a side casement to gather whatever they think we will need. Every shadow is a moving soldier. Every puff of wind is a scout who has spied us. Every heartbeat is an added moment that my father is driven farther from Maytown.

"Who were those people in the street?" asks Anai.

"I don't really know," I tell her. "They heard me speak during the Gathering and asked if I'd meet to discuss the Tyjans."

"I thought I knew all about you," says Anai. "It's a bit humbling to find out that I actually don't know a thing." She observes the tiles, blowing out a stream of air.

"Is the discovery good or bad?" I ask.

"I'm not sure."

I feel the same. Ever since the Gathering, simplicity has softened and melted away. Well, at least for me. There's still a chance for Anai. I reach past her, unraveling the leather strap from her fingers. "You should go home. The soldiers don't yet know who you are."

"I told you," says Anai, her teeth clamping. "I am not leaving you. Especially not with these two." She snatches back the reins, causing the horse to jolt, and a large chunk of me is glad to hear the force in her tone because I'm not certain I would be comfortable traveling alone with a pair of boys. "And, of course, there's your father," she continues, and I nearly mist with tears because she does it first, knuckling the moisture from her face with a sniff.

"I don't want anything to happen to him, either. After what they did to him in the arena with that revolting costume . . . I just need to know that he's all right—that he's made it."

I rest my hand against her shoulder. "What will your mother think when you don't come home?"

Anai shrugs. "What she always thinks. Nothing."

"And Symon?"

"Symon can drown in the Geynes for all I care, but I'm fairly sure if he avoids that fate, he won't be sitting in his stonebrick pining for me."

Our conversation is cut short because Vogel and Casper choose that instant to spring from the cottage like a couple of thieves. Each carries a stuffed rucksack of provisions and Vogel has the added bulk of a bow and quiver. They fasten their equipment to the side of the horses with strings, transferring some of the waterskins into saddlebags, leaving Anai and me to ride together without any extra weight. Well, except for the waterskins they give us to share. I tuck those into our pouch and tighten the buckle.

"We're trusting you," I say to Vogel.

"Understood," he says. "But we know the way. Casper and I have traveled outside the city walls many times before, haven't we?"

"Too many times to count," says Casper.

"I'm not sure if that makes me feel better or worse for the suspicion," Anai whispers in my ear.

Nevertheless, we mount the horses and clop across the broken cobbles, roaring into the great big world beyond the confines of Centriet. It's frightening at first. The hairs ripple on my arms, and I think Anai feels the same way because I hear her inhale a huge breath when we clear the last of the village settlements and canter into the open paddocks.

The air smells different out here. Sweeter and dustier at the same time. There's no scent of ocean water. It's shrubs and tussocks that roll on forever through fallen twigs and diffusions of pines. The breeze on our faces is cool. I'm glad the boys know where they are going because it feels like I'm rushing into a swirl of endless night. I try to let go. I try to picture the wagon bouncing over the loose stones, my father staring at the infinite sky. I try to assure myself that, despite the arrow in his torso, he is holding on, clinging with both hands, refusing to allow the blackness to swallow him whole.

We stay off the road, instead riding beside it. When the moon shows its face, the cleared path shimmers, spooling like an unwound sash. Sawtoothed pebbles scatter and flip, little clouds of earth wafting up beneath our horse's hooves.

And we push on through the vast fields of nothingness.

Never looking back.

CHAPTER SEVENTEEN

WE RIDE ALL NIGHT. WE RIDE UNTIL THE WIND AND OUR faces combine and we cannot feel either. Eventually, the grass vanishes. The slightest blush of indigo breaks on the far horizon and I understand in alarm that we're about to greet a new day in the middle of a foreign land. My heart hammers as golden light creeps over the barren ground. It occurs to me how precarious this is—being out here, unprotected—even though we are a party of four. I'm stunned it didn't dawn on me last night. Or maybe it did. I can't remember because nothing about yesterday seemed real.

With the landscape appearing before us in startling color, Vogel, who is at the helm, slows his horse to a walk. He pulls farther from the road and Casper and I follow suit. The sunlight has revealed a winding stream set back behind a shock of top-heavy trees. Large red boulders mar the earth, interspersed with patches of weeds. I help Anai from the saddle. I lead our horse straight to the water and she steps boldly in, splashing and dunking her nose in the coolness. Upon watching me, Vogel and Casper guide their own horses to the edge. They slacken their grips on the reins, letting the horses choose where to stand. And when the morning haze lifts further, filling the air with sharpness and luster, we find ourselves frozen in place, studying one another in a peculiar square.

"So we made it," says Casper, raising his arms to the ruddy backdrop.

"It's a little early for celebrations," says Anai. "Where are we exactly?"

Casper sighs. He scratches the scar above his eyebrow, as if he can't comprehend why she is not in better spirits. "We're out of the city and heading to Holinde."

"Which is?"

"Holinde is the first village we'll pass through if we stay on this road," Vogel explains. "It's a remote mining settlement on the bank of the Ribbon."

Although I've never heard of Holinde, I'm familiar with the Ribbon. Akin to the Tyrant's Daughter, it winds across the dusty landscape like a blue snake. Except it's narrow, bulging with sharp stones, and usually only ankle-deep. But crossing the Ribbon would be the first sign of progress—the first true sign that we're headed in the right direction.

After watering the horses and tying them to solid trunks away from the view of the road, the four of us sit on a flat piece of rock that extends at an angle from the soil. At our backs, a cave peeks between two boulders. The boulders stick together like enormous eyeballs, surveying the red-tinted land.

"Everyone agreed we rest during daylight?" asks Casper. "That way we can stay out of sight in case any soldiers have been dispatched."

I'm so tired I think I would agree with any idea if it meant I didn't have to stay on the horse.

"I believe that means yes," says Casper, and since no one objects, he nods to himself, looking a lot more pleased than the situation warrants. Perhaps his thrill comes from the fact it was an easy decision, although by the drawn expressions on our faces, I'd sooner believe it's because we don't have the energy to disagree.

"Did you bring any food?" I ask.

Casper pulls out a small bundle of cloth. He unrolls the material and passes around a strip of squashed damper that tastes like grit. My throat is so dry I can barely choke it down, but I do. So does everyone else.

After that, we resolve to rest in groups of two, so that one pair can stay awake on watch duty while the other pair dozes. I'd assumed Anai and I would sleep first, but Anai and Casper head into the cave because Anai says she doesn't trust the boys not to ride off without us.

This leaves Vogel and me sitting on the rock. Since it's the first time we've been alone outside the palace walls, I find myself clamming up. Vogel is no longer wearing his gladiator garments. He must have changed in the cottage, and now he's shifted back to the boy I met in Yahres with his simple breeches and loose shirt. I much prefer this version of him. I think it's the version that holds the most truth, even if I still don't know much about him.

"Do we have a plan once we get to the infirmary?" I ask.

"No," he says.

"They're not likely to just let my father go because we ask them nicely."

Vogel takes a long swig from his water pouch. "The infirmary is situated near the river to service the four army postings along the bank. The staff have been stationed there by the Tyjans—many against their will. Imagine being stuck in the middle of nowhere. They'll be easy to bribe," he says with an air of confidence that seems irrational.

"But what do we have to offer them?" I ask.

"Maybe one of the horses," says Vogel, again not seeming too concerned. "It depends how hungry they are. I did bring a few precious items from the cottage. I've got some silver from my arrow tips and a hunting knife from my mother's side of the family that is over two hundred years old." He fishes the knife out of his rucksack. It has a beautiful ivory handle and a blade that has been rusted from centuries of slicing.

"Why would you do that for me?" I ask.

"Because your father is a decent man."

I scoff at his reasoning, even though he could be sincere. "You built that much of a kinship with him after only a day or two? You really expect me to believe that?"

"I don't expect you to believe it," he says. "But despite what you may think, it is the truth. He could have easily tried to slaughter me in the ring when he knew that I would not fight. For a spare to kill a gladiator would have been quite a coup, but he did not."

His gaze lingers a mite too long and I look away across the grass. Up until now, I've only met Vogel face-to-face in the dark. With the sunlight on his skin, he's a whole different person. The kind that causes my cheeks to get hot.

I chew on my lip. "So you were a gladiator," I say.

Vogel runs a hand through his hair. "Only after one of the Erraforgian gladiators injured himself on a spear. Unfortunately that meant there was an opening in the Tournament." He fidgets with the cap on his water, twisting the knob on and off. I suppose in one regard, it was bad luck for him to be used as a gladiator. In another, he avoided being used as a spare, which would have been a lot worse.

"Thank you for not killing my father," I say.

"Well, I'm not in the habit of killing senselessly for sport." Vogel tosses the pouch aside and leans backward, rotating his shoulder.

"How did you know Ladislas wouldn't kill you?" I ask.

"I didn't," he says.

"Oh." The weight of that sits heavy in the air. How did he manage to stand so tall with his life at the mercy of Ladislas? Unless he doesn't feel afraid. But that's not true. Everyone feels fear. Even Elyor flinched, frightened the emperor would order his death if he didn't put on a show. I breathe out. "I'm sorry about Jove. I know you were close to him and assisted him with his record keeping."

Vogel's features brace. "How do you know about that? Did Casper tell you?"

I shake my head. I explain how Anai and I went looking for Casper and Vogel nods in understanding.

"We didn't know him well, but he was always kind to us. He certainly didn't deserve to die, just as I'm sure none of the other spares did, either."

They certainly didn't. No one deserved that. Who were they anyway? Traitors to the kingdom—or men who'd somehow insulted the prince?

"You met my father in the tunnels," I say. "Before the matches."

"I did, yes." Vogel winces at the memory. "He said he'd been brought in by the soldiers because they couldn't find his daughter, Meadow. We sat together in the pits before going out. If anything, he comforted me more than I did him."

"That's my father," I say, feeling my chest cave in. "He's always had this strange ability to be calm in the face of terrible things." Yvette from my village comes to mind—the girl who'd had her leg sawn off by the Tyjans. My father visited her stonebrick with broth. He sat with Yvette when her mind swam with nightmares and talked her through them when all hope had left.

"He also mentioned your mother," says Vogel.

"Please don't talk about my mother."

I say it too quick and I think he notices, but he backs off and tries something else. "And who were those boys that stopped you as we took their horses?"

"Boys I met at the Tournament," I tell him, not really liking that topic, either.

"What did they want?"

I shrug. "Who knows?"

"The main one said that you'd agreed to meet him somewhere."

"I never agreed to do that," I counter. "I said it to make him leave me alone."

Vogel quirks a brow but doesn't press, although I'm doubtful he believes my story. But I'm not ready to share just yet. I still wonder whether I could reconcile with Ein and help his cause when I return to Centriet. I wonder whether he would ever forgive me about the horses.

I'm lost on how to change the subject, but Vogel doesn't hold it against me. He stands, stretching his arms above his crown. As his shirt lifts, I avert my gaze. I hear him maneuver across the slab, his shadow grazing my crossed legs. I ponder how he honed his physique. Perchance he's trained in the pastures with his family? Maybe his tutor took him outdoors to hunt?

I watch as he jumps off the edge of the rock and wanders through the surrounding brush. The horses cluster around him like puppies, nipping his pockets, hoping for apples. Whispering softly under his breath, he touches the chestnut mare on her nose. As her ears rotate, Vogel pauses, softly and carefully observing her coat.

I turn my head in the other direction, feeling the tussle of breeze through my hair. Everything except the road is visible. Vivid red soil beneath a cloudless sky. Trees the color of bleached bones. If my father knew where I was right now, he'd probably chortle and flash a grin. Not because I'm trying to save him, but because I'm doing something unexpected. Something unlike me. Something on a whim. Something I think he'd wished I would do after we said farewell to mother. Instead of me going the opposite way—retreating inside, shutting people out, refusing to acknowledge all it was I still had.

Later in the day, Anai and Casper wake from their slumber. They stumble out of the cave, rubbing their eyes, not appearing any more rested than they had when we dismounted from the horses. After a brief exchange of news—which is to say that nothing of note has happened in their absence—Casper swings his palm to the cave, inviting us to take their place.

Vogel and I climb up the edge of the rock. We haven't spoken since he asked about Ein. When it becomes clear that only one person can squeeze through the entrance at a time, Vogel stops at the opening and gestures for me to go first. I nod in thanks and drop to my hands and knees, wriggling into the space. Once on the inside, the cave widens and there is plenty of room to stretch out. Vogel moves in and crawls to the left, leaving an ample gap between us.

I've never slept beside a boy. Given everything from the past few days, I'm not sure why it terrifies me so much. But it does. I can just make out Vogel's outline in the dark. He's so tall, his feet almost touch the walls of entrance, and the quietness of his breathing heightens the silence.

I don't want to tell him to *have a good night*—or *pleasant dreams*, like my father always says. But it feels amiss not to say something.

"Vogel?" I whisper.

He stirs. "What is it?"

I gather air in chest and release. "I wanted to thank you."

"For what?"

"The tower."

He hesitates. "There's really no need."

"But I want to, Vogel. I truly mean it." More words form at the back of my throat, but I cannot lace them together with coherence. I want him to understand *why* I'm thankful—not only for stalling in front of the prince, but also for helping the victims when I couldn't. "You're a good person. I hope you know that."

Facing the ceiling, his profile tenses.

"Don't," he says.

"Don't *what*?"

"Say that."

"Don't say that I think you're a good person?"

He sighs. "Yes, I think it's strange." He doesn't sound humbled, he sounds like he's bothered. I wonder if it's guilt he feels about the people.

"It wasn't your fault in the tower—"

"I know." He groans, easing onto his side so I'm left with only the curve of his back. "It's not that at all."

"It's not?"

"No. But saying *you're a good person*. Who says that?"

Thank Obellis for the gloom, as my face must be pink. Does he think I'm trying to stroke his ego? Or worse, does he think I'm flirting with him?

"You don't know me and you don't know Casper." Something about his voice has altered. It's icy like it was when he first met Anai.

"I just meant—"

"Go to sleep," he says.

So I take it all back.

But I don't sleep well.

CHAPTER EIGHTEEN

I'M WOKEN BY THE JARRING PEAL OF LAUGHTER. SUNLIGHT STREAMS in through the cave entrance, so I know I haven't overslept. Across the other side of the chamber, Vogel's space is unoccupied. I coax my body out of the hole and slide down the edge of the rock into the fresh air. Vogel stands with the horses, while Casper and Anai are engaged in some sort of storytelling competition. There's a lot of eye watering and throwing back of hair, so I wonder if the stories are real or imagined.

"Good afternoon," says Anai.

"Hello."

It looks like Vogel has repacked the saddlebags so the rucksacks are lighter to carry. I don't give him a second glance. After our conversation in the cave, he doesn't deserve a greeting. Not if I can help it.

"We have some more damper," says Casper, opening a cloth and passing me a bit of the doughy bread.

"Thanks." I've transformed from not hungry to ravenous, but I'm also aware that the sun is sinking, so it's the perfect time to restart our journey. I motion to Anai. "How long has Vogel been awake?"

"Quite a while," she says. "Why?"

I tear off a morsel of bread, chewing furiously, not knowing how to answer. She slips me a sly wink—which is definitely not why I asked—and I shake my head, horrified by her assumption.

"Oh no, it's definitely not what you're thinking—"

"Sure."

"Well, you're very friendly with Casper," I say, trying to steer her in another direction.

I ready myself for her annoyance, but instead, she says, "I want him to trust me."

"Why?"

"You're not the only one who can be devious in the face of peril." She taps her nose, giving off the air of conspiracy, though a vein has hardened beside her temple. "From what you've told me, we've nothing to fear, but I'm not about to let my guard down with them. Not until I know for sure." Her pupils glimmer, not quite by accident, and she tucks a curl behind her ear. She seems to be waiting for my approval, so I give her a nod.

"It's a smart strategy."

"And you watch Vogel."

But she says it too loud and Vogel looks up, his eyes clashing with mine. I turn, pretending to be entranced by the shape of the boulders, but heat creeps up my neck, making it impossible to conceal that we'd been talking about him.

Fortunately, Casper intervenes by cutting a path in front of the horses. The paler mare carries less weight than the other two. "Do you really think that's a good idea?" He poses the question to Vogel with a smile, but his cheeks pull in. He's inwardly groaning.

"She's not up to heavy lifting," says Vogel. "Can't you see she's fatigued?"

"We're fatigued, too," says Casper with a chuckle, but Vogel responds to the comment by scowling.

"This horse has not long been brought from the wilderness. Look at her markings. She's wild. She's not built for the workload of the others."

I don't know a lot about wild horses, except they are known as wildock and they're exceedingly rare. The ones my mother taught me to ride were of the common ferlin breed, which were known to be strong runners who loved to stretch their legs by cantering around fields.

"We need her," says Casper. "She could carry more equipment and we'll ride two apiece on the ferlins."

Vogel drifts past him and carefully removes the remaining saddlebags from the wildock's back. The moment she can shake her shoulders, her ears flick forward and a ripple slides along her spine. Vogel rises slowly and backs away from the horse, and I can see what he means about her markings. It's a subtle difference, but she has tiny brown lines on her rump that are swept in different directions. She spins in a loop, almost at once. She does a quick scan of the four of us, then bends low, her hooves digging into the soil, stretching her knees until they crack. Vogel plucks the supplies from the grass and dumps them on the soil next to Casper's boots.

"Very mature," says Casper, rolling his eyes, but Vogel takes the reins of the wildock and walks her to the stream for one last drink.

Casper opens his mouth to say something, but decides against it. "Sorry," he mouths at Anai and me, but I wave the apology away. Recalling what Vogel said earlier about trading a horse for my father's life, I do not hold this against him. If anything, I am grateful he wants to keep the wild horse in pristine condition. It almost makes me forgive him for the way he spoke in the cave.

Almost.

When it's time to leave, I half expect Vogel to ask me to ride with him, but instead he calls to Anai, offering her a hand onto his ferlin. I'm surprised by the spasm of indignance that jolts within me, but I shake it off and turn to Casper, pretending not to notice as Anai climbs behind Vogel and clasps him around the middle.

Casper picks up the discarded supplies, strapping them into his saddlebag. "Sometimes," he mutters, glaring at Vogel.

"What?" I ask.

He shakes his head.

Darkness descends slowly and then all at once, as if Obellis relishes in throwing a veil over the sun before blowing it out in one puff. The moon drips white onto the powdered surface beside the grass. We clod over it, upsetting weeds and flattened stones that may have sat there, unmoving, since the last wet season. We haven't encountered so much as a fox. And certainly no people. Casper confirms if we keep following the curve of the road, the first settlement we'll stumble upon is the mining town of Holinde. Apparently once we arrive, we should steer clear of eye contact, needless conversation, and the many holes that blight the land. But I just want to get there. I'm ready for civilization and a sleeping nook that isn't crawling with nibbling earwigs.

The night drags on. Casper and I tug to the front, as the wildock horse needs constant variety between walking and trots, even when unburdened by the weight of supplies. Vogel and Anai have lapsed into silence. Earlier, I heard Anai inquire about Vogel's family and his archery equipment, but he replied in short monotone sentences that made Anai sigh deeply and shut down, twisting her head to the dusky fields, feigning indifference. Not that I wish to understand Vogel any more than I already do, but something's definitely changed in him.

"Apologies for my friend," says Casper.

His voice startles me, as if I've been caught out, even though Casper has no way of knowing I'd been thinking about Vogel. "There's no need to apologize."

"The horse issue?" Casper chuckles. "He can sometimes be a little dramatic without even realizing it."

I smile at his attempt to make me feel better. He clicks his tongue to make our horse jog faster, giving us space to chat by ourselves.

"It doesn't matter," I say.

"It does mean it'll take us longer to get there."

"But I can see why he's doing it," I say, and when Casper doesn't say anything for a while, I rush on, "so we'll have something to bargain with at the infirmary?"

"Oh, right. I suppose so." He doesn't sound convinced.

"You don't think it's a good idea?"

Casper turns to look at me over his shoulder. "I actually think it's a great idea, but I also don't believe the wildock horses are as fragile as he makes them out to be. I'm fairly certain they're just proficient in histrionics. We could get to your father a lot quicker if we used all three like we did last night."

I sigh. He's probably right. "So how do you and Vogel know each other?" As the question forms in its entirety, I'm surprised that I've never asked it before. But now that I see their differences of opinion, I wonder how it is that they came to be traveling together on the road.

"How do you think we know each other?" Casper asks.

I'm not irritated by the counter-question. Goodness knows we have time to banter back and forth.

"I thought you might be brothers or cousins," I say, remembering when I saw them at the cottage in Yahres. "But you look and move differently, so I'd say you're childhood friends."

"Nope."

"No?"

"We met as gladiators," he says.

Of all the explanations, I was not expecting that.

"Gladiators?"

"Well, not gladiators. We were initiatum. Gladiators-in-training in the ludela. I was there because my family owed a debt to keep their livestock and I was their only son. Vogel was in trouble with the law for stealing food and they chose to put him in the ludela instead of the prison because able-bodied youth are more valuable to the system that way."

Of course the emperor would see it like that.

"There's nothing like training to be a gladiator that makes you more scared for your life," Casper admits, shifting his weight back in the saddle. "I lost the bottom part of my front teeth in the first week, and I received slashes through probably every surface of my skin at some point during my time there. The scars from the stitching was worse. They like to clean you up quick in the ludela because there are always so many going in and out of the healing facility."

"And that's how you moved to the infirmary?" I ask.

"As a result," says Casper. "Leading up to graduation from being an initiatum, each student had to compete in a gladiator-style ring fight with real weapons. It's not supposed to be to the death, but it's brutal. The healing facility in the ludela is unable to accommodate all the injured men. This was not something we were aware of at the time. However, when I was badly wounded and Vogel was badly wounded and so were some others among us, the Quills transported us to the infirmary near the Tyrant's Daughter without so much as an explanation."

"That's awful," I say.

"It is. They made us go to sleep with crushed herbs, and when we woke up we were in the infirmary camp."

"And what was it like?" I ask, not entirely sure that I want to know, given the circumstances.

"They were under instructions to make us well again," says Casper. "But at any price."

"What does that mean?"

"It means," comes a loud voice from behind us—that obviously had been able to hear the entire conversation—"that you do not need to pry into our experiences, Meadow." As Vogel circles, still gripping the wildock's reins, Anai clings to him for dear life. "What are you doing?" he spits at Casper.

"Telling me what to expect at the infirmary," I say.

"Well, don't," Vogel says, still focused on Casper. "It is none of her business and you know it."

"It is everything to do with my business," I call after him as he trots around our horse again. "I should know what we are saving my father from."

Vogel glares at me.

"I think she's right," says Casper diplomatically.

"I see," says Vogel. "Well, go on then. Tell her your little story if you think it is for the best . . . If you think it will make her feel better to hear it."

I hear Anai talking to him under her breath as they ride onward. It sounds like she is trying to calm him down—and failing spectacularly.

"Sorry about that," says Casper again.

"You don't need to keep apologizing for him," I say, watching Vogel's shoulders sag ever so slightly in the distance. Something bad obviously happened in the infirmary that he does not want to share with someone he barely knows, and I can respect him for that, despite his ill-mannered approach. "Do you think he's all right?"

"Yes." Casper falls quiet for a moment. "Anyway, without getting into too many details, we finally managed to escape from the infirmary because we did not want to return to the life of gladiators."

"Aren't you afraid that the infirmary staff will recognize you and inform the palace?" I ask.

"A bit," says Casper. "Although I think Vogel is more afraid than I am. Perhaps we will hang back and let you and Anai do the bargaining."

That makes my stomach drop to my feet.

Up ahead, Vogel has steered his horse down an incline, so Casper turns our reins to catch up. We trot into a clearing with a narrow brook, thick reeds bordering the translucent water. The four of us fill our waterskins in silence. Anai jostles over to me to debrief, but before we can delve into anything too personal, we're back on the horses and riding again. By the time night bleeds into the morning, we're in another sheltered spot, off the road, pillowed by textured trees. We eat more damper and I slip off my sandals. My toes are gritty with mud and horse hair.

"How far is the Tyrant's Daughter from here?" Anai asks as Vogel lights a fire, constructing a small mound beneath it from sticks and dessicated undergrowth.

"Another three days' ride at least," says Casper.

We're reclined in a square again, facing inward with the crackling fire in the center. I glance at Vogel. He seems preoccupied with the dancing flames.

"Do we have enough food?" Anai asks.

"Of course we do," says Casper.

They lapse into their own conversation after that and I twist my hands in my lap. Vogel doesn't look at me. I try not to look at him either but decide that I might as well clear the air if we're going to be in each other's company for three more days.

"Sorry for asking too much about your time at the infirmary," I say, wriggling over to sit beside him. "If it makes you feel any better, Casper didn't really tell me anything about your experiences there."

"It doesn't make me feel any better," says Vogel coolly.

"Oh, all right." I hesitate, unsure if I should just cut my losses and vacate the conversation. In the end, I resolve to press on. "Casper said you were both initiatums at the ludela for a while before you went to the infirmary."

Vogel stares at me with his ice-blue eyes, as if he cannot believe my ill manners. "I said I didn't want to talk about it." But for the first time, he sighs and I contemplate what it means that he does. Maybe nothing. Maybe something huge. He turns his body away from mine, but not before a shadow falls over us and Casper materializes, warming his hands by the flames.

"Everything civil over here?" he asks, looking pointedly at Vogel. I glance at Anai. She's lying on her side with her eyes closed, her chest heaving up and down. When Vogel doesn't answer, Casper lets out an extended grunt. "He's not still annoyed by the horse, is he?"

"No," I say.

Vogel frowns at Casper.

"I'm just saying," protests Casper, raising his hands in a sign of innocence. "Rest well," he says to me, and shuffles back to the other side of the fire.

The next few days pass in a blur of light and dark. My eyes burn from sleeping in the blazing sun, and my lips chafe from the relentless cold that batters our faces as we gallop through the night.

In the early eve of what Casper assures me is our final ride before reaching Holinde, I splash my face with water. I've climbed a little way up a hillock, following a stream as it carves a path through rugged limestone slabs. As the liquid trickles into a pond, the surface ripples with semiopaque tadpoles. It reminds me of the murky water I tried to give Carliss in the palace. How long ago that seems now. How strange that I am traveling across the land with the boy she is in love with.

A while later, I slip carefully down the rise to join the others on the flat terrain. After skirting the last shrub, I halt. Anai, Vogel, and Casper stand, almost frozen, staring at each other. This is nothing new. The mixture of exhaustion, hunger, and unfamiliarity weighs on us all. Except, upon second glance, this is a different kind of frozen. This is the kind of frozen that makes my limbs tighten.

"So you just made the decision for all of us?" says Anai. It takes me a heartbeat before I realize she's glaring at Vogel.

I walk faster.

Casper snatches a dropped rucksack. Without saying a word, he straps the supplies to the rear of his ferlin saddle, lips squashed together in a rigid line. And that's when I notice there are only two horses. The wildock is nowhere to be seen. Its saddle and bridle are draped over the branch of a small tree, the leather and metal of the stirrups swinging from side to side in the dying light.

"You said we could trade that horse for Meadow's father,"

says Anai. She stops, as do they all, as if they can sense my presence.

"I had to," says Vogel, not addressing any of us in particular.

"What happened?" I ask.

"Vogel took it upon himself to release the wildock into the forest," says Anai.

The moment I glance at Vogel is the moment I know she has spoken the truth.

"Why?" I ask.

His voice is even. "Because it was the right thing to do."

I don't answer. I'm not sure how to. He looks earnest and defiant and conflicted all at once. It's an odd combination—and may not even be an accurate one. Nevertheless, my hope plummets. It feels like my father's chances have decreased by one thousand now that we don't have the wildock to trade.

"We should go," I say.

"But Meadow—" says Anai.

To keep my temper, I shake my head. Fury feels like the wrong emotion—because I love horses and I care for their welfare—yet at the same time I want to scream that we needed the wildock in order to bribe the infirmary staff, and an arrow tip or an ancient knife is barely the same thing, especially when a life is involved.

But I don't.

Instead, I turn my back to Vogel.

"Can we leave now?" I ask Casper.

Casper nods. Anai's face is a concoction of shock and confusion about what this all means, but she shows her support by heading over to Vogel and climbing onto his horse without any argument.

We ride and I simmer. My mind is still in a whirl. It must show in my breathing and body position because Casper suggests we hang farther back.

So we do.

We put a good amount of distance between us. Enough that Vogel must know my feelings. Enough that it will be awkward when we do stop. We remain in our two separate pairings until the sun departs and the moon appears, surrounded by flickering stars.

"It was a bad decision," Casper says to break the silence. "Wildocks may be moody, but they're supremely valuable in overwater markets."

I have no idea if that's true or not, although it's widely claimed that King Rolyo has a menagerie on Leeang with reptiles the size of fallen trees. I picture him puffing his chest, throwing vast sacks of coin at Erraforgian merchants in order to acquire our native horses. For that reason, I'm glad the wildock is free. And if the infirmary staff hoped to kill the wildock for its meat, then I'm glad it's free for that reason, too.

"I can't work him out," I say.

"Vogel?" Casper groans. "Nor can I. My best counsel is to let him rant. Then smile and nod and stay well away."

It's terrible advice, but it must work for Casper, and who knows how long they've traveled together?

"Do you fight much?" I ask him.

"No."

"As you're always so obliging?" I guess.

"That is right."

Poor Casper. That must be annoying, and my fury at Vogel flares once more. He should have asked to release the wildock. And since he did not, he should have been sorry. I think of his face—so calm and assured. And justified, like he did no wrong. But then I remember that it wasn't our horse, so how am I even allowed to be angry?

I suppose I'm not. I groan at the wind, feeling the fire in my belly disperse. Did Ein and his friends need these horses for labor? Had they raised them from foals? Were they planning to sell them? In my quest to save my father's life, have I ruined the lives of so many others?

"These horses should be returned," I say.

"What?" asks Casper.

"When we get back."

He doesn't bother answering me. He probably thinks I'm delirious. He slaps the reins and we catch up to Vogel and Anai, who have stalled on the crest of the track, observing the spread of dry plains fanned out before them.

Holinde. It's there in the distance, enclosed by a fence that's built in a giant square. No trees or crops grow on its surface. The area is a flimsy pockmarked shell with deep holes and mountains of dirt.

"The miners live underground," whispers Casper.

There are very few stonebricks. No farmland. No people. Slender paths run in loops between the mine shafts, and long skinny pipes poke up through the soil. To the west, the road to the infirmary winds on across the bridge of the low-lying Ribbon. At the northeast corner, beyond the fence, sits a barrier made from linked metal circles.

"What is that place?" Anai asks, before the words can exit my mouth.

The barrier extends like a prison wall, severing Holinde from the lip of a wood. I don't like the way the trees cinch together, their branches mingling with the leaves beside them. Not that it's different from the forest near my home, yet there's something forbidding about those shadows.

"That's the edge of the Sparselands," says Casper.

"The Sparselands? How is that possible?" I ask. "I thought the Sparselands didn't begin until we had crossed the Tyrant's Daughter?"

"You're right." Casper flicks his palm at the barrier. "But over time, the plants have thrown out their spores and spread across the land to the east, over a section of the river that splays into this part of the kingdom. The people of Holinde erected screens to keep it from spreading further. Every so often, they light fires and take axes to hack it back."

It's probably less frightening to see the trees in daylight. Even so, I'm glad that the road curves in the opposite direction.

"Is it true there's magic in the Sparselands?" asks Anai.

"Out here they call it the strangeness," says Casper.

The strangeness.

"But does it exist?" Anai turns her head, but Casper shrugs.

"So they say, but I've always said that the wisest of people choose not to find out."

We start moving again, clopping softly down the ridge, bending this way and that between tall piles of soil. By the time we pass, unchecked, beneath Holinde's rectangular entrance arch, my lungs have filled with dusty air.

"Where should we shelter?" Anai whispers.

There's the faintest clatter of faraway movement. The miners must be stirring underground, the noise carrying up through the crooked vent pipes. Which means they will hear our voices and footsteps unless we conceal ourselves in the fields. Which means we must slink across the expanse, avoiding the gauntlet of huge holes.

Casper urges our horse from the road, but she hesitates with a snort of resentment. I don't blame her, so I hoist my leg over and slide to the ground, taking her reins. Lamps are posted throughout the mine site, and I guide her into the flickering orange. A solid spot beckons. It's behind a triangular hill, sheltered from the center of the village, with sufficient space to stretch and sit and a battered stump to secure the horses.

"We'll take turns being on watch," says Casper.

No one disagrees with the plan.

"Did you bring any food except damper?" asks Anai.

"What's wrong with the damper?" Casper says with a wink.

"Nothing at all." She smiles at him, and even in the darkness, I feel him smile back. And though I don't want to, once we've wolfed down our meal, I offer to take my watch with Vogel.

Vogel doesn't look impressed, but I'm beginning to think it's his default expression. On the contrary, the other two brighten.

"Thanks," says Anai with the tiniest grin.

She and Casper settle down for first sleep, and I entertain the thought of speaking to Vogel. But my patience has drained and I don't want to fight, so we do not talk for the rest of the evening.

CHAPTER NINETEEN

WHEN I AWAKEN THE FOLLOWING MORNING, HOOVES ARE pounding into the soil. Beside me, Vogel curls into himself, his eyes closed, his breathing steady.

"I hate this wretched town," says a voice. "Loathe it. Always have. This bleeding dust ruins my breeches. Finds orifices I never knew I had."

There's a hefty thud as boots hit the ground.

Then a second.

And a third.

"Would they hide underground?" asks someone else.

"I mean to find out. You lot, stay here." A man who sounds suspiciously like Farrow kicks the dust and pebbles go flying. "Sweep this area, and when I get back, don't dare think to tell me you haven't found them."

Sweet Obellis. I tip Vogel's shoulder so he doesn't startle as he wakes from slumber. When he blinks and rolls, shielding his eyes, I manage to obscure his line of sight. I nod at the other side of the mound, where the soldiers maneuver between the mineshafts. Vogel scrambles next to me and we press our backs against the dirt.

Where are Casper and Anai? And the horses? I stifle a moan. *Have they escaped?* I somehow doubt they would ride off without us, leaving our fate to the Tyjan soldiers. My thoughts are confirmed when one of the men asks what to do with the extra horses.

Someone suggests they be tied to a fence post in the middle of the village so they don't get spooked.

After lengthy debate about the best kind of knots, the horses are moved, and Farrow returns.

"They're not underground," he's quick to report. "Which means they're either hiding like roaches or the traitorous fools have tumbled down a mine."

My fists clench. I hate his voice. I hate the thought of him inside my stonebrick. I wish I could shove *him* into a hole and listen to the scream as his spine broke on quartzite.

Vogel traces a finger by his chin. "I think we should make a run for it." As he tilts his head at the northeastern barrier, my murderous thoughts are replaced by panic.

He can't be suggesting we enter the Sparselands. Not after Casper's warnings last night. But he points this time, so there's no mistake.

"The soldiers won't breach the fence," he says.

"But it's dangerous, Vogel!"

"It's unknown," he says. "Which doesn't always mean dangerous."

I beg to differ. It's dangerous *and* unknown, which is so much worse. There's an abundance of reasons why this would be foolish, but I start with one. The most obvious first.

"What about Casper and Anai?"

He nods. "We'll try to spot them before we go."

"And the horses?"

"They're tied. We'll have to leave them."

"Our supplies?"

Vogel points to the pack at his ankle. "We have all we need for the journey in there." He twists his head around the dirt pile. "Come look," he says, after a moment, shifting aside and patting the earth.

I follow his gaze. There are six soldiers. Two are waiting with our horses at the entrance of the village. Four are spread out like hunting dogs. At present, their backs are to us, but they stand—facing the opening of a half-sunken building—almost in a line across the terrain. All of a sudden, I spot a pair of eyes. Beyond the soldiers. Peering tentatively from behind a red hill.

It's Casper.

"Do you see him?" asks Vogel. "On the other side?"

"I do, yes!"

Anai is beside Casper, thank goodness. They could turn and reach the bridge and slip into the brush beside the road without the soldiers noticing. Casper doesn't have his rucksack that I can see, but both of them hold water pouches and Casper stores the damper cloth in his pocket. If they keep going, they could reach the infirmary on foot. They could make it.

"Split up," says Farrow. "They're here somewhere."

But if Vogel and I linger too long, our chances are slight. Petrified of what awaits us if we're captured, I suck in air before turning to look at the shimmering barrier. "You're right. We have to run. There's no other way."

Vogel doesn't ask me if I'm sure. There's no time. With Casper's eyes trained on his, he signals to him that we're heading into the Sparselands. He points to the road to indicate that Casper and Anai should proceed without us and we will meet them as soon as the path is clear. Or at least that's what I think he's saying.

There's a short pause, but then Casper nods. He glances at Anai and her already-pale face loses the rest of its color. She locks eyes with me and all I can think to do is to blow her a kiss and pretend I'm certain this will work out fine. Finally, she turns her back and Casper takes her arm and guides her to the side of the road. They merge with the greenness and become silhouettes before slipping into the haze and then they're gone.

And it's our turn.

Vogel picks up the rucksack and slings it over his shoulders. He leaves his bow since it's large and unwieldly. We tiptoe nimbly from one tall hill to the next, inching closer to the fence, angling our shadows to fall on the ground where they cannot be seen. We zig and zag, and zig and zag, and I almost believe we're going to make it. I'm too frightened to check what the soldiers are doing. There's safety in not looking, I think. Like the only reason they would spot us is if their eyeballs were drawn to ours, so I paste mine to the path before me, concentrating only on the next mound.

"There!" yells one of the soldiers.

I freeze, which is possibly the worst reaction, albeit the most natural when the hunter has spied the prey.

"Come on!" Vogel yells. He thwacks my arm to jerk me from my reverie, and then we're dodging the holes as the soldiers give chase, their boots thundering behind us. I trip on a stone and almost slide into a mineshaft, but Vogel grabs my waist to prevent me from falling. My water pouch is not so lucky.

"Leave it!" shouts Vogel.

Not like I could climb down and retrieve it anyway. I regain my balance and surge ahead. The edge of the wood looms like a safe house. The barrier stands firm, but a tiny section has lifted at the base.

"Hurry, Meadow!"

Vogel tears the wire from the dirt and holds it up. I roll underneath, the pointy ends snagging my tunic. I try to take it from him on the other side, but it won't bend inward, so Vogel shakes his head, drops it with a snap and runs at the fence, climbing over it like a wild cat. Launching off the top, he lands on his feet beside me, just as the soldiers halt on the other side. There's five of them, dressed in Prince Malthe's colors, with Farrow in the center like a hideous spearhead.

"You're as good as dead in there," he says. "Just like your father."

My blood runs cold. His round cheeks shine as he fingers his pommel, his thick black eyebrows squashing together, daring me to form a retort.

"Don't engage," says Vogel under his breath, which is easy for him to say when they're not talking about his next of kin. He urges me behind a protective screen of trees, leaving Farrow and the soldiers pacing back and forth, unwilling to approach the fence, and with only the weaponry of using Obellis's name in vain.

"Sylvan and Xerys, wait here in case they come back out," I hear Farrow bark. "You vermin haven't escaped His Highness!" he bellows through the trees.

"Nice guy," Vogel mutters.

"The nicest," I say, my voice grim.

"Are you ready to do this?" asks Vogel.

"Ready?"

Turning from the barrier, Vogel begins to walk deeper into the Sparselands.

"Wait!" When he doesn't answer, I sprint in pursuit, catching him under the branch of an elm. "Where are you going?"

"Where do you think?" His eyes flash. "We have to keep moving." His gaze falls to his lower arm, where my fingers have wrapped around his wrist. My hand shakes.

"Sorry," I say. As I let him go, he slowly exhales.

"You know what they'll do if they catch us," he says. His voice is stonelike, but the edges are smooth.

Of course I know. I've been in the tower.

"Why don't we wait until they leave?"

"Because that will take too much time." Vogel nods in the direction of the mines. "Holinde will host them for as long as they wish it. It could be days—or even weeks. And we shouldn't dawdle within this place. Not if we can help it. Not even at the edge."

"So you've been through the Sparselands before?" I ask.

"No."

"You haven't?"

"Never," he admits. "I've traveled across the Tyrant's Daughter, but I've always done so via the road." The fear must be stitched through my features like thread, as the hardness dissolves—just slightly—from his eyes. "But for all the stories, it's likely superstition."

"The strangeness?"

"Yes." His voice grows quiet. His tone doesn't give me the utmost assurance. In fact, he sounds a tad uneasy.

"Even the soldiers are afraid," I say.

"But you want to rescue your father?"

"Of *course*."

He looks at me. "It's directly through the woods. It's a much shorter route than taking the road."

"Then why were you taking us the longer way if a trek through the Sparselands is so much quicker?"

Vogel hesitates, and it's in that moment with the sun on his face that I'm struck by a thought. I really wish he liked me more. Under the aloofness, under the frown, there's something about him I crave to know. But I toss the notion swiftly aside, as I drag my stare away from his jaw.

"It doesn't matter what our plans were," he says. "We have to make new ones, even if we don't want to."

Inhaling a breath, I know he's right. When it comes to my father, nothing should stop me. Not distance. Not soldiers. Not superstitious strangeness.

"Meadow?" he calls.

I'm already walking.

CHAPTER TWENTY

WE DON'T SEE ANYTHING REMOTELY MAGICAL FOR THE REST of the day. In fact, by the time we stop to rest for the night, I'm confused why Farrow and the soldiers were so afraid. There has been nothing out of the ordinary, except a few ebony birds with beady eyes that watch us from the uppermost branches of fir trees. And it's not like they watch us for very long. We're terribly uninteresting. All we do is weave through the undergrowth, keeping our attention to the sun to make sure we are hiking closer to the Tyrant's Daughter.

We only stop when we arrive in a peaceful clearing. The trees dwindle and the land is shaped like a cloud with little sprinkles of shrubs making the perimeter soft and curved. The fading light tinges the area in purple like a giant bruise, and I glimpse the sky, framed by the canopies, the pasty moon crisp against the growing darkness.

With my feet aching, I collapse on a log. Vogel sits beside me, which I hadn't expected, but he seems quite agitated about being in the Sparselands, despite his earlier claim that the strangeness could be hearsay. He unslings his rucksack and sets it on the grass. The straps leave patches of perspiration on his shirt. He unpacks a squashed roll of damper and breaks it in half to share, and I'm so famished that I cram it in my mouth, ignoring the expression that crosses his face—a mix of distaste, amazement, and something else I cannot decipher.

After a few moments of stretched-out awkwardness, I'm the first to speak. "Are we all right?" I ready myself for his unfriendly reply and am not disappointed.

Vogel's eyes grow small. He scoops his water pouch and lifts it to his lips without answering. I watch his throat swell and deflate as he swallows the liquid, wondering how it is possible that my father made an impact in such a short amount of time. When he's finished, he uses his sleeve to wipe his mouth, and I notice that his shirt is crusted with the red powder of the mines. "Why do you want us to be on good terms?" he asks.

"Are we not on good terms?"

His mouth tugs down.

"When I said you were a good person . . ." I raise my shoulders. "I didn't mean it." I'm quietly pleased by the indifference in my pitch, though Vogel shrugs with equal disinterest and props his head on top of his pack.

"You'll take first watch?" he asks.

"See? Not a good person at all," I grumble.

"At least I asked." He crumples on his side, crossing his arms over his chest.

I sigh, watching his eyes seal shut as he fades into immediate sleep. Without awareness, his jawbone untenses, his lips glide apart, and his long lashes flutter. I start to imagine who he is—beyond the ludela, and Yahres, and now. Does he have a family—a mother and father? Does he have a home, a place to recline, where his defenses wash away like the Geynes tide? With his features relaxed, it's easy to envisage. It's easy to believe he belongs somewhere else. But I'm frightened he will rouse and catch me gaping, so I tear my attention away from his face.

The silence of the clearing hurts my ears. It fills my head with a myriad of worries. Are Casper and Anai safe on the road? Did Farrow send soldiers to scout ahead and drag them back to Prince Malthe? And then there's us. As the light withdraws further, the woodlands plunge into suffocating shadow. And I repeat to myself that the strangeness isn't real, that our passage will be hasty, and before I can blink, we'll be standing on the shore by the Tyrant's Daughter.

The next day begins with the crow of a bird, the eating of more damper and a small mouthful of water. We desperately need to find another stream.

Once out of the clearing, we trample through a thicket of mulberry bushes. The ground clumps with bloodred juices and scattered waxen leaves the size of our palms. Dangling from branches are the plump black fruit, shining in the sunlight, waiting to be picked. But something about their ripeness seems odd. They gleam too perfectly, so we do not stop, and instead continue in the same direction, the blazing sun confirming our course.

It must be around middle day when the air changes. There's a chill to it, as though a ghost follows our movements, skimming its icy fingers across our bare shoulders. Vogel notices it, too. We both still our feet and glance up at the waving leaves. It's more silent than before—almost as if strips of material have been stuffed in our ears and we can no longer hear the branches creaking. We decide to keep walking. We quicken our steps, but the iciness pursues us as easily as the wind on our backs. The trees thicken. The low-lying branches knot together, obstructing our path like webs, so we divert to the side, sweeping our arms through the brushwood, then circle back to our original trail.

It is then that the sun blows out like a candle. All of a sudden, Vogel and I are standing in the middle of the forest, hemmed in on all sides, with no light around us. Vogel reaches out and grabs my hand. I clutch it tightly, glad and surprised. My heart hammers and the familiar wash of cold spreads like frost down my arms and legs.

"It must be the strangeness," says Vogel.

"I thought you said it didn't exist."

"I said it was superstition."

I shiver. "Honestly, Vogel. It's the same thing."

With his hand still twined with mine, we push on through the plants and rocks. As the sun peeks out from behind the clouds, a passage glistens between the trees. The light wavers, so we gather momentum, swishing through the grass to reach the end of the path. But once we arrive, the sun reignites, and we pull back into the cover of bushes.

There's another clearing.

But larger.

And neater.

Bathed in an unnatural, buttery glow.

It stretches much farther than my vision permits, hedged on the far side by a tall field of corn stalks, the crops planted in meticulous rows.

It doesn't seem real.

"Shall we turn back?"

Vogel chews on his lip. "No."

"What is this place?"

"I'm not sure."

"Is it part of the strangeness? Or might someone live here?"

And by that I mean many someones. It's large enough for a whole community. In fact, as my gaze sweeps over the expanse, a hamlet of rundown shacks sticks out with scattered tools and fat bales of hay discarded in clumps of wispy weeds.

"It could be a settlement, perhaps. One that belongs neither to the Sparselands nor to our kingdom." Vogel drops my hand, and the absence of him stings. "Are you all right?" he asks.

"Why do you ask?"

"You're breathing heavily."

"So are you."

He glares at me. As the air leaves his lips, it puffs out like a small gale. But I wave it off. "Never mind. Let's keep moving." I think I startle both of us by taking the first step into the clearing.

I'm expecting something bad to happen, but the landscape is calm, almost relaxing. The golden tint warms my skin, bringing puzzling relief to my aching calves.

Vogel joins me, pointing ahead. "I'm certain we'll need to pass through that cornfield."

The field extends like a leafy fence. There aren't any premade paths through the shoots, though a few bunched sections have not matured.

Thankfully, Vogel doesn't seem the least bit interested in scoping out the shelters before we go. He strides to the edge of the field where the towering stems rise like giant asparagus spears. Pushing aside the floppy leaves, he crunches over the cracked soil. I'm poised to follow behind when something catches my attention. I reel around to see two children disappearing between the stalks.

I grab Vogel's arm. "Did you see that? There are children here."

"Children? Are you sure?"

"I think so. They went in over there." I point at a row of swaying crops and Vogel regards them, his features pinched.

"We need to make haste."

I nod in agreement. Even among the plants, the hazy yellowness strangles the air and I have to keep reminding myself that this is a cornfield and I am awake. I twist my fingers into the back of Vogel's shirt. As we walk, the leaves scrape my shins and shoulders, flicking my eyelids and poking my hair. It doesn't take long and we're swallowed entirely, the clearing and hamlet dissolving behind us.

"Is this the strangeness?" I ask.

"I don't know. It feels like it might be," Vogel says.

Scared to be separated, I press further into his back. I've never been this close to him before. "How will we know when it is?" I ask.

"I've heard the strangeness can feel like the world is not right.

Like your feet and your arms are not controlled by your mind. Like everything around you is jumbled and wrong. And it can't be corrected, no matter how hard you try."

"That's how I feel now," I say.

"So do I." He reaches back to squeeze my wrist. "But the important thing is not to believe it's real. If we can just keep walking, even though the strangeness may hover around us, soon enough we will pass through it and be on our way to the Tyrant's Daughter."

It's not an easy task.

"Vogel?" I pause. It's then I hear the tinkle of laughter. Or two tinkles of it—both very different sounds. I immediately connect the laughter to the children and my blood freezes because something about the pitch of it makes me squirm.

"Keep walking," Vogel says. He reaches back with his other arm and wraps it around my shoulders, holding me to him.

The laughter stops after a while, but then come the harsh whispers, shearing through the noise of our footfalls.

"Where are you from?" they ask in childish voices, almost singsong in quality.

When my body trembles, Vogel holds me tighter, although I can sense the quiver in his arm.

"Do not ignore us!"

At once, Vogel halts. Two tiny figures block our path. They're the same children I saw entering the cornfield. Up close I see it's a little girl and a little boy with dark eyes and brown hair cut bluntly below the earlobes.

"Are you lost, travelers?" the boy implores.

"Do not engage with them," Vogel says.

"You look most weary," the girl continues. "Such a shame you have been ambling aimlessly all this time, and with such modest nourishment to tide you over."

It chills my bones to hear her speak, making me wonder if they have been watching us as we trekked through the forest.

"You are strong and able," the boy says, slanting his head to inspect Vogel. His dark eyes run up and down Vogel's form with particular interest.

"Surely not him," says the girl.

"Not for me," the boy replies. "But his hue is impeccable. A brilliant blue like the water in a frozen lake."

I have no clue what he is talking about, except perhaps to explain Vogel's eye color, but at hearing the words, Vogel slams into the children with his full weight, knocking them to the ground. As their legs go up in the air, he turns and grabs my arm. He drags me through the stalks, and I run wildly, feeling like I'm going to fall and simultaneously feeling like I can sense the children's hot rasps on my neck. Their laughter rings out behind us as Vogel's panting accelerates.

"He's perfect!" The boy's voice echoes in the distance.

"He must be acquired!" the girl titters back.

As we sprint, the stalks merge into each other and it seems the land is on repeat. A rustle of leaves begins at our heels. It sounds like a wild cat creeping through the leaves, hunting, urging itself to pounce. The noise grows louder. Nearer. More insistent. Heaviness seeps into my legs. And then I realize that the rustling is beside us, tracking our steps, and Vogel gasps.

"Meadow, you need to keep going. Get to the river. Find Casper at the army posting in Helliam."

He must feel them closing in—or perhaps he can gauge that my legs are slowing.

"Find Casper in Helliam," Vogel repeats. And then he hauls me in front of him.

"What are you doing?" I scream.

"Go!"

"Vogel, I can't—"

"Keep running to the river!"

The force of his yank, combined with my already-in-motion feet, sends me flying and I cannot stop. Vogel jogs behind for a few steps. For a moment I think that all is fine, that the children have left, that we're going to survive. The stalks die down and there's more space to tread. I pray that the blueness of the river will appear.

But then . . .

I hear Vogel scream.

I spin around, batting the corn. But I can't hear anything except my own wheezing and I suddenly realize that he's not behind me. That the rustling has gone.

And I'm all alone.

CHAPTER TWENTY-ONE

MY HEART LEAPS INTO MY CHEST AS I SCREAM HIS NAME. THE only answer I receive is empty whooshing and the call of a bird. The bird makes me blink, compelling my eyes to the azure sky. The yellowish tinge has dissipated, the stalks fading away by my hips and I find I'm standing at the end of the cornfield, listening to the pound of the Tyrant's Daughter.

I've made it.

But what transpired? It seems like Vogel was a dream in a dream and our journey through the Sparselands didn't occur. I shake my head. But it did. I know it did. The odd glow. The neglected sheds. The small children with cognizant eyes. All of it was real.

And yet . . .

I walk to the edge of the river. It appears so normal, so commonplace, all spray and gushing water. I swivel to the cornfield behind me, but for some reason, it's no longer there. I swipe a hand by my cheek. I seem to have stepped from a grove of mulberries, their fleshy fruit dripping from fragile twigs. But I'm sure I only just left the cornfield. Could it be I have wandered a greater distance than I imagined? Could it be that Vogel was taken a lot farther back than I thought?

The one thing that doesn't feel distant is Vogel yelling at me to keep running. Still the command ripples through me, as if my skin doesn't wish to let go. I kneel beside the Tyrant's Daughter and cup my hands in the cool liquid. I splash it over my face and neck, gulping mouthfuls to quench my baked throat. A gentle breeze tousles my hair, chilling the moisture that clings to my face. Then I rock on my haunches, staring up at the clouds, trying to piece together what's happened.

The strangeness. Did it kidnap Vogel? I'm still unsure what the strangeness is. I gather it's magic that's seeped from the Sparselands, spreading out here as the woodlands expanded. I recall the tales we'd been told by our tutors. Stories about the formation of our kingdom. When Erratide united the warring clans, a few belligerent warlords escaped. They smuggled their people across the river, even though to do so was dangerous. And they never returned. Could these children be the ghosts of the people who fled from Erratide's clutches?

I rub my eyes. Of course not. That happened hundreds of years ago. Besides, ghosts do not exist. Nor does magic. I stand up. If anything, they are children of thieves. Or children with nothing better to do. In the clearness of day, my mind unclutters.

I have to go back and find Vogel.

But how?

I spin around. I need to retrace my steps through the woodlands. Now that I know what lurks within, there should be no cause for it to alarm me. With the river to my back, I stretch my arms, willing myself to reenter the trees.

But I can't.

My body trembles. Not on the outside, but deep within.

"Come on, Meadow." I push out a breath. The air is clean and natural and bright. I chide myself for not being stronger. They were children. *Children.* Maybe seven or eight. They couldn't have been that frightening, could they? Did I let myself get carried away?

Perhaps.

And yet their voices were eerie. As if they hailed from another age.

I place one foot in front of the other.

I walk. And walk. Away from the river. I'm surprised by the ferns that lap at my ankles, riddled with dew and flopping like bluebells. I do not remember these ferns from before. I move faster, but the ferns only thicken. Why has the landscape altered so much? Where are the cornstalks? And where is Vogel?

Composing myself, I press on. The ferns melt away and hedges appear. The hedges are huge and trimmed in round balls. They definitely weren't in the Sparselands before. My teeth sink into my lower lip and my fists clamp into shaky orbs. The hedges vanish in a tendril of mist, and now my sandals are sloshing through swampland. I pull my legs through the growing water. It swills to my ankles, dense with weeds. I slash at the rising panic in my chest. I was wrong. I know it. Magic is real.

I open and close my eyes.

And again.

The swamplands evaporate into the earth. Ahead sprouts a forest of dark jade willows, their foliage hanging like strings of kelp. Vogel did warn me that no matter what happens, I need to keep walking, ignoring the strangeness. So I part the greenness and squeeze through the gap, curving my frame by the huddled trunks.

I stop.

I'm in another clearing. Not the one from before, as the lawn is mottled with brown and white. Shelters constructed from collaged fur pelts have been propped in the center by wooden posts. But the shelters are not what concern me the most.

As the willow has vanished, I crouch behind a shrub. Sitting in the open, his legs outstretched, in front of a row of people, is Vogel. His feet and hands are bound with twine. His eyes are shut, as if he is sleeping. How have they forced him into this state? Have they knocked him out, or is this . . . *the strangeness*?

I scramble to get a better view, but the shrub has extended to double its width. My mind racing, I count the people. There are thirty in total, and a range of ages, though nothing seems to unite the group. Fair. Tanned. Dark. Freckled. Different hair and body shapes. They glare at Vogel with the same expression, and I notice the boy and girl from the cornfield.

I shiver as an old man breaks from the queue, holding the arm of a pretty woman. She looks, perhaps, two decades old with honey-blonde curls and pointed features. She rests her hands on the old man's shoulders, and he sighs and presses his wrists together. With a wet smile, she ties them in place.

"Do not forget his feet," says the boy.

I quake at the sound of his high-pitched voice. As my heart flutters, his tiny grin widens.

The woman turns her attention to Vogel. Though seemingly awake, he's blank and unfocused. She quickly unlaces the cords of his shirt, resting a hand on his smooth chest. His breathing hastens, and I grip my hands, feeling the blood divest from my knuckles.

"Do you agree?" the woman asks.

Vogel's head doesn't move. "I do not."

She trails her thumb up to his earlobe. "It will be easier than the alternative," she says. She cradles his cheek.

"I do not," he repeats, appearing to muster all the strength he has left.

Beside him, the boy pulls a knife from a basket. As he moves to drag it across Vogel's throat, the little girl giggles and claps her hands.

"No!" I yell.

The boy stops, and all the attention slides to me. My gaze connects with Vogel's stare and at first it's like he does not see me.

"It's *you*," says the girl.

"Let him go. Please." I inch backward, which seems to amuse them. The others point to me and themselves.

"What about her?"

"What is her hue?"

The boy's smile widens again. He's missing some of his small front teeth. "Her color does not suit us," he says, buffing the blade against Vogel's sleeve.

"Go *now*." Vogel's voice is a husk. "The river," he chokes. "Find Casper and Anai."

I hadn't realized he could sense my presence, but I look at him now. "I won't leave you here."

"You have to." His eyes are hollow, the veins by his hairline bulging with effort. It doesn't go unnoticed by the boy, whose attention flickers from Vogel to me. The people behind him close their lips as he beckons me forward with a lily-white finger.

"What is your name, traveler?" he asks.

"Meadow," I whisper.

He smiles. "Meadow."

The dry lawn disappears at once, and daisies spring from under our feet. *A meadow.* "Do you like it?" he asks, as the little girl laughs and twirls in glee. When I don't answer, the girl's laughter stops, and she razors me with furious eyes.

"Please let him go . . ." I say again, but the boy has vanished from Vogel's side. Something scurries out the corner of my eye, then the coolness of metal prods into my back.

"Surprise!"

The girl starts clapping again as the boy jams the blade against my flesh. He looks at Vogel. "Have you changed your mind? Or must I cut her until you submit?"

In horror, I realize what I've let him discover. He can use me to get to Vogel.

"Well?"

"I agree with your terms," Vogel whimpers.

"You will do as we ask?" asks the boy.

"I . . . will."

"At last," says the boy to the watching group, handing the knife to a woman beside me. She holds it tight to the folds of my skin, her fingernails gripping like wintry chains. Vogel exhales, sagging forward and back. His limbs twitch with unnatural force. A bellow unleashes from deep in his stomach like a demon escaping an unfamiliar body.

"Don't hurt him!" I shout.

"Hush," says the woman.

Vogel calms and his limbs relax. The blankness departs and his eyes refocus. It seems the boy has withdrawn his magic.

"If I do it, you'll let her go?" Vogel asks. He sounds like himself, though his voice remains rattled.

"Of course we shall," the boy confirms. "She's of no use with the color she possesses. She is at liberty to stroll from these woodlands after you fulfill your promise to us."

Before I can ask what they want him to do, Vogel turns to look at me. "Meadow, listen." His eyes are icy, but for all the blueness, they're not unkind. They're the eyes he wore in the dark of the tower. Eyes that make me wish I knew him. His tone drops low. "Once you've found the river, head east toward the army posting."

"But—"

"You can do it," he says.

"But I won't. You're asking me to walk away!"

Vogel opens his mouth to answer, but the boy interrupts. "We must not delay."

"Wait!" I cry.

"Time is short."

"Tell me what you're making him do!"

The boy draws a circle in the air with his finger, and Vogel mouths at me to leave. He uses his feet to spin on the grass. He's face-to-face with the withered old man. "Begin," says the boy, but Vogel shakes his head.

"Release her first."

"Very well." The boy gestures to the woman at my heels, who removes the knife and steps away.

I'm free.

"Vogel?"

"Proceed," says the boy.

Vogel knots his fingers in his lap. He closes his eyes and his lips start to move, though I cannot untangle what he says beneath his breath. But whatever it is, it excites the people, who break from their rows, arms stretched to the sky. They bound up and down on the springy grass, their voices raised in grisly unison. The clearing becomes a cloud of bodies, a stream of chanting, yellow haze digging in.

Something's unfolding. I don't know what, but the old man and Vogel are deeply entranced. The ground shakes like a storm's overhead, like a crack has formed and it's splintering the land. Everything feels upside down. The joy in the air is misplaced and unsettling. I find myself spinning to take it all in—the forest, the yelling, the vapor, the stamping, and the woman beside with her catlike eyes, her bare toes squishing the bountiful daisies. She doesn't look at me—no one does—she's too consumed by the shouting and jumping. From moment to moment, she droops her eyelids, rotating her crown, her brown hair bouncing. My thoughts sharpen as metal flashes. The knife protrudes from her right hand. She lets it teeter like a loosely held quill—and it's then I know what I have to do.

I grab for it. Her lids shoot up, but I seize it on my first attempt. I sprint to the boy who stands behind Vogel, resolved to stop him, whatever it takes. The woman's yell careens through the crowd, but it ricochets through without finding an ear. Or so I think. Someone grips my arm, twisting it back so the knife goes flying.

It's the honey-blonde woman.

The jumping stops. I'm locked in place, scared to look up. But the people are not concerned by my presence. Their interest is fixed on the old man and Vogel. Even the honey-blonde woman lets go, as if she's forgotten what I'd planned with the knife.

"It is not working," the old man says.

"Do not cease!" the young boy shouts.

The people cluster in a half ring around them, but the old man and Vogel have halted their chanting. The clearing fills with an obvious quiet—the shelters receding into the soil, the grass sprouting, throwing spores to the breeze.

The honey-blonde woman skids across the lawn. She falls to her knees in front of the man. "What do you feel?"

His eyes well with tears. "I sense only emptiness. Infinite time."

"Try it again," the young boy says, but the old man refuses, his drawn face sallow. He extends his wrists in a gesture of defeat, and the honey-blonde woman reaches forward, unpicking his binds with her shaking fingers. Her cheeks shine with tears and redness, as if her faith has been ground by a pestle.

"Perchance one day," the man says gently, wiping beneath her eye with his thumb.

"Another failure," someone murmurs.

"Next time," says the boy.

"Will there be such a time?" The old man raises his ragged voice, and the boy shrinks behind his dark-colored fringe. The people turn their gazes from Vogel and wander past him as though he's a log. They follow the old man into the forest, arm in arm, their many heads bowed.

As the last of their figures dissolve from the clearing, the yellow light shudders and breaks apart.

I run to Vogel.

"What happened?" I ask.

He swallows, taking a moment to see me. "Whatever was supposed to occur . . . it didn't."

I slide the cords from his hands and feet. "And what was supposed to occur?"

"I don't know." With the binds dropped, Vogel scrambles to his knees. He wears an expression that looks different, almost humbled. "When I saw you come back . . ." he begins.

"You're welcome."

"No," he grunts. "I was so mad."

"And now?" I ask.

He shakes his head. "I'm still not happy."

"So you're back," I say. "And just as cheerful as you ever were." And before he can give me a withering look, I snatch his hand, and we collapse on the grass.

The sky above is blue and soaring. I could close my eyes and sleep forever. My eyelids drop, and it feels so simple. Life seems simple, here on the lawn. All my worries absorb in the soil. Lightness and silence gather like cushions. But then, the cool wind blusters my cheek, reminding me of my time near the river.

The army posting.

Casper and Anai.

My father.

The wagon.

We cannot stay.

"We need to keep moving." I force my eyes open, but Vogel has fallen asleep beside me. I nudge his side. "Come on, get up."

"I want to sleep," he protests.

"Not here." I tug at him while glancing about. The clearing is empty, but I do not trust it.

When his eyes refocus, neither does Vogel.

"Let's go," he agrees.

We roll to our toes. And we lope through the Sparselands in the direction of the river, desperate to leave the strangeness behind us.

CHAPTER TWENTY-TWO

OUR JOURNEY IS SLOWER THAN MY INITIAL RUN TO THE Tyrant's Daughter. Something is wrong with Vogel. Although he walks beside me with his eyes focused and his breathing rhythmic, he carries himself in a strange manner, as if his limbs are burdened by rocks.

"Can we pause a moment?" He stops, leaning his weight against a trunk, his cheeks the color of ripened beets.

"Of course. Do you want to sit down?" By the time the query has left my mouth, he's already sagged to the grass, panting heavily. I sit next to him, offering and withdrawing my hands, feeling useless. I'm not entirely sure that he would want my assistance, and yet I don't trust these woodlands, even though I was fortunate enough to pass through them before and emerge on the other side, unscathed. "What did they do to you back there?"

"I wish I knew." He clenches and opens his fingers until the knuckles crack. "How much farther is it? Did you get all the way to the river before?"

"Yes, it's not far." Although we'd still need to follow the water to find the bridge near the army posting. That could take a whole lot longer.

"I just need to rest my eyes," he says.

"Sure."

"I won't be long."

A moment later, he's asleep against the tree, his fists bunched, the curve of his forehead lathered in sweat. I reach to peel aside some rough bark, but my fingers slip and I brush his neck. With a nervous gasp, I wrench away. His body smells like scented oils. Warm blends of lemongrass and spearmint. The last reminder that the strangeness was real.

"Vogel?"

He doesn't stir. Instead, his head slides to my shoulder. Gently, I prop him against the trunk, only for him to droop again. So I let him stay. It does seem odd that a gladiator is brought to his knees with fatigue. And that he's relying on my shoulder for support—I'm rendered as rigid as an entrance board, my hands wringing in front of me.

What are we going to do? If Vogel is delirious, how are we going to make it to Helliam? And once we're in Helliam, what then? If the army posting is anything like Centriet, aid is not something given to outsiders. Well, not without the outsiders giving up something in return. Our only hope is that Casper and Anai have garnered more success on the road than we have. I lean my head against the tree. Although we are out of the yellow area, I don't trust being in the woodlands any longer than we have to be. Especially not as night falls.

"Vogel?"

His body trembles, and he slips from my shoulder onto the grass. I try to rouse him, and his eyelids flutter. I rest the back of my hand to his forehead like my mother did when I was a child. He's hot to the touch and sticky with moisture, the dampness extending up to his hair. I touch the fabric covering his back. It's soaked through, almost transparent, even darkening the grass where he lies.

My mind goes straight to the wilting sickness. It's probably not—there are many other reasons for fevers and lethargy—but the image of my mother still burns bright. On the nights when her sweats were most intense, my father and I took turns filling buckets, wiping her skin, dipping her feet, coaxing her to swallow as much water as she could. Perspiration was life leaching out. Water was life draining back in. That's what the village healer would quip. And that's what Vogel needs to survive. He needs water—he needs it swiftly—and I have none to give to him.

The obvious place to get water is the river. I scramble to my feet, but what can I do? I don't have a waterskin to carry the liquid. Our only chance is if Vogel walks, too.

"Can you hear me, Vogel?" I prod him again, and he groans through his clenched teeth. "You have to get up. We have a bit of a journey."

His groan transforms to a drawn out lament. "Go by yourself, and leave me be."

"You don't get a choice with this," I say. I worm my hands under his side, lifting him into a sitting position. Despite his moaning, he doesn't resist. If anything, he tries to help me.

Once he's seated, he's a little more lucid. "I see you're not going to listen to me."

"You don't listen to me," I answer.

"I suppose not."

"Can you stand?"

"I'll try."

I scoot around to grip his wrists, but he threads his fingers through mine, palm-to-palm. Even though he's likely delirious, a fluttery feeling invades my stomach. Ignoring it, I pull him up and although he's shaky, he's able to stand. His hair is pasted across his forehead, the droplets sliding by his ears to his chin.

"Here." I nestle beside him, tugging his arm over my shoulder. I notice he doesn't pull away, but he doesn't lean his full weight on me, either.

"You don't have to do this," he says.

"Yes, I do." We hobble like elders through the thin trees. All seems normal. No ferns, no mulberries, no large clipped hedges, no stifling swamplands or whispering willows that sway in the updraft. The bird is back, twittering above us, like it ushers drifters in and out of the foliage. "You were dreaming," I say to keep him awake.

"Dreaming about those strange people." He seems upset by the mention of them. Or perhaps the thought of what could have been.

"The old man said that something didn't work. What did he mean?"

"I don't know."

"You were chanting something."

"I don't remember."

"And the young boy talked about colors," I say.

Vogel lifts his arm from my shoulder. One step, and then two, and he swabs his brow. "All I remember is being crushed. Like a snake was wrapped around my windpipe." He stares ahead for the longest time, then begins to walk, his legs unsteady.

"That sounds scary," I say.

"It was." Vogel turns to look at me. Faint ridges appear at his temples.

"What is it?" I ask.

He shakes his head. His icy eyes comb my face, soft and swift, almost in apology. I cannot decipher what it means, except perhaps that his pain is raw. I won't gouge his wound any further. Whatever the strangeness was, it is over.

So I catch up and we walk together, our shadows elongating, overlapping on the lawn. And it doesn't take long for the trees to fall silent and the gush of the river to welcome me back.

Despite wanting to charge for Helliam, Vogel needs to rest awhile. I know he would press on if I asked, but the air is mild, so we sit on the bank. We drink water and scrub our faces. My stomach rumbles, but the river roars louder. The flush has dropped from Vogel's cheeks and now he's pale like he's never seen daylight.

I feel bad that he's even here.

"I'm sorry," I say.

"For what?" he asks.

I shrug. "For putting you in this position. That you had to go through what you did with the strangeness."

He winces. "No apology necessary."

"Apology withdrawn," I say.

But that seems to make him a bit more distressed, so I wriggle closer and nod at the water.

"You said you'd traveled out here before?"

"I've traveled a bit through the lands near Holinde." Vogel lets me sit beside him without tensing up or moving away. The lemongrass and spearmint have all but vanished, and with it the coldness he'd displayed in the cave. "When Casper and I escaped the infirmary, we stayed underground in a chamber for weeks."

It's perhaps the most he's revealed of his past.

"What was it like?"

He scrunches his nose. I ready myself for his mood to change, but it seems the strangeness has made him less distant.

"The miners were interesting folk," he says.

"How?"

"Most were former gladiators." He doesn't say more, and I don't want to push, but then he sighs and leans back. "I hated the ludela, you know. I should never have been an initiatum."

"Why not?"

He looks to the sky.

"You don't have to talk about it," I say. I'm expecting him to close up more. To tell me he's tired or it's not my concern. But he doesn't. Rather, he rubs his eyes, as though he's uncertain of quite how to answer.

"Casper said he sustained life-threatening injuries when he fought to become a gladiator," I say.

Vogel nods. "Most of us did, even if we won. Sometimes it was obvious that the Quills and the Rigorates had wagers about us." There's an edge to his voice, like he's cautious to tell me, but wants to test the waters. "And even as initiatums, it was gory entertainment to behold. It wasn't considered a match if blood wasn't spilled in excess."

"That's horrible," I say.

"It was inhumane." Vogel hesitates, and it seems he's going to tell me what happened to make him visit the infirmary, but he stops short of an explanation, his pupils focused on a distant tree. I get the feeling that ale would be a lot better for this conversation than river water. "But moving on from my story," he says, "that's not the only reason why the Tyjans need to be stopped, is it?"

I'm so shocked by the abrupt change of topic that my fingers slip as I restrap my sandals. "What do you mean?"

"I heard you at the Gathering talking about your mother's lack of medicine. I found your parchment, too. I read it over many times after that night and it made me angry. You see, that's what the Tyjans do, isn't it? They treat us as if we are nothing."

I don't know what to say. I haven't seen this side of Vogel. The thought of him reading my words on the parchment makes me feel a little exposed. "I didn't realize you felt so strongly about the lack of medicine," I say.

"I feel strongly about anything the Tyjans do that violates basic human rights," he answers.

"Since you saw what happened in the tower?" I ask. "Or since you were an initiatum?"

"Since the Tyjans stopped caring about their people," he says, and I'm so taken aback by his earnestness that I stifle a cough, again perplexed that I haven't witnessed him like this until now. "What about you?" he asks. "You seemed livid that night when I met you."

"I was," I admit. "But I wasn't planning on saying what I did. I just had all these thoughts in my head since my mother died and I didn't know how to get them out."

Vogel is quiet for a moment, and I worry that I've said too much.

"Sorry."

"You say that a lot," he says.

"I know. It's just a natural response."

And I loathe it.

"Anyway," he continues. "Do you still feel anger toward them now?"

"The Tyjans?" Of course I do. And here by the river, I realize my words can be freer, less careful. "I hate how they rule. I hate how their lives are opulent. I hate how they put themselves first. How they let us suffer with our food and our health. And after being in the palace and seeing what it's like up close." I exhale. "It's more unjust than I originally thought. I mean, look what happens when you speak your mind at a tiny cottage in the middle of the slums. Nothing important changes. It just means that your life and your loved ones' lives get irrevocably altered. And things are only going to get worse with Ladislas—and then with Malthe when the crown passes to him."

I stop. I cannot believe I've said so much. Pressing my palm to the ground, I shift, twisting my head to the Tyrant's Daughter.

"What if you could change it?" asks Vogel. "Would you do it?"

"Do what?"

"Make things better."

"I suppose. Wouldn't you?"

"Absolutely," he says. "I would do anything to bring them to justice and alter the course of our kingdom's history."

Fierce words. Dangerous words. Words that many are too scared to utter. And words that never come to fruition, despite the strength of conviction behind them. And yet as I look at Vogel now, I dare to have faith that *his* words mean more.

"How would you do it?" I ask.

He frowns. "By putting someone else on the throne."

"Who?"

He shrugs. "I don't yet know."

"But there's no one else, except Kalliope."

Vogel digs a finger in his elbow, testing for bruising along his arm. "I guess I just feel like you did in Yahres. I'm angry at being powerless, and I crave doing something to make a difference."

"There might be a way you could contribute," I say, suddenly thinking of Ein and his group.

"Oh?" says Vogel.

But I brush it aside, not wanting to take that path just yet.

The sun has been replaced by clouds, their undersides mingled with gray and black.

"How are you feeling?" I ask.

"Better." Vogel looks up at the gathering dark. His complexion reflects his surprising fervor. His glow has returned and his eyes are lively. "If we hurry, we can make it before the storm."

"Well, in that case," I say. "Why are we still talking?"

CHAPTER TWENTY-THREE

A S IT TURNS OUT, THE ARMY POSTING ON THE TYRANT'S Daughter called Helliam is home to a busy fishing village. Vogel and I arrive late in the afternoon when people are packing up their pails of sea life and either trotting toward makeshift houses or into one of the small battered taverns. I scan the signposts. Most of the names mean little to me, although there are smatterings of the word *inn*. Given our lack of coin, I'm doubtful we'll be greeted with vigor, but I have to try. We'll need all our wits at the infirmary. And having four walls to protect us from soldiers would no doubt make the night pass swiftly.

Regardless of his earlier profession of health, Vogel's lungs are slow to return to their full capacity. As I glance at him now, his shoulders rise and fall as though he's been in a joust—and he is the horse. The sky turned sour in the last part of our journey. The clouds are now so bleak, I'm sure small balls of ice will plummet within a matter of moments. A cool breeze has blown in across the water, causing bumps to appear on my skin, and the sand by the river kicks up, the spindly branches of lakeblossom trees bending against the force of the gusts.

I decide to enter the village alone to find a place to rest for the evening. Since the bridge has been closed, there's no way for us to cross the expanse. Vogel stays under a tree at the edge of the settlement. The area smells of fish tails and dried octopus meat, but I think both of us are just thrilled that we are no longer in the

Sparselands. Although the strangeness still seems like a distant dream, something inside me wonders whether my memories of the children and the changing environment will vanish altogether after a long night's sleep.

Every sinew in me hopes so.

I follow the road into Helliam, folding my arms in front of my chest. It's different from the docks outside Centriet's walls. There are no colorful sheets shielding market produce from the weather. There are no timber planks snaking into the water or boats tied to posts, bobbing on the waves. No, Helliam is much like the army in the sense of its décor. The walkway by the river is constructed from stone, broken in places by a few solid arches. The shelters are made from a hodgepodge of material—wood, metal, and fibrous board—and they stretch on behind the path in careful rows that are paved with sunken cobbles.

No one seems interested in the shivering girl wandering by herself in filthy garments. It means I can easily examine the shelters without concern for eyes on my back. The numerous dwellings—combined with clothes-washing facilities, tubs for people to bathe in and boats stacked on end—mean this is a village that may well shield Vogel and me from a soldier raid. After walking a while longer past chopped logs and mounds of foul-smelling dirt, I spy an inn tucked behind a series of paneled barrels. No one is about, so I press open the door and walk inside. An old man, who is shorter than me with his hunched back, gets up from his chair, wobbly with a cane. I hold up my hand, indicating that I will come to him.

"Do you have a room?" I ask.

"I don't have rooms."

When I look closer around me, it's the truth. The inn is separated into stalls by sheets that hang from piddly threads.

I reword the question. "Do you have space?"

"No space," he says, squinting through eyes that are almost sealed with crusted liquid.

"Do you have a stable?" I ask.

"What would I need a stable for? I have lived here for over seventy years. Why would I need a horse?"

I suppose he poses a good question, so I thank him for his time and let myself out the door. The dark skies shroud the atmosphere in shadow. A couple of fat raindrops plop on my head, so I lower my face and take off, running along the slippery lane. Crooked rooftops rise in the distance, similar in shape to the old man's inn. The farther I run, the more people I see squatting under lengths of soiled cloth. This must be the poorer section of the village, as families huddle, holding each other, trying to keep out of the storm. Some have bowls on the ground by their feet, collecting rainwater. They pay me no heed as I sweep by and enter the first of the metal-sheeted inns.

As soon as I'm inside, I cover my nose and mouth. There are many people spread across the floor, taking advantage of the wide-open space. In the center of the room, a woman stirs a cauldron that looks like one from Kalliope's villa. From within the pot drifts a pungent smell—one that I recognize almost at once. It smells like the herbs we boiled for my mother to stave off the wilting sickness. Glancing at the sleeping bodies, it dawns on me that they're flushed and sweating. Some have soaked through their clothing. Others are trembling in their sleep. Still others stare at the rafters, their lips moving, without sound coming out. I haven't walked into an inn. I've walked into a Helliam sickbay.

"May I help you?" asks the woman.

"No, I am fine, thank you," I say.

Her stirring stick is the size of a boat's paddle, but she has nonjudgmental eyes. She does not seek to know who I am, just wants to know what I'd ask of her.

"They're not contagious," she says. "I promise."

I want to get out of here and it shows. But what she doesn't understand is the truth of my fears: I'm afraid of becoming emotional. This feels too familiar, too close, too soon, too similar to my mother's last days. Even if my mother's last days happened over a year ago. Being here makes the wound fresh. It rips the bandage off, exposing the gash to the cold night air, and I'm back in that place where my heartbeat races, telling me to run away.

"Forgive me," I mumble. I wish I could eloquently explain what is rolling through my head, but the woman smiles, lowering her face to meet mine.

"There is no need to apologize," she says, and I think it is her kindness—this honest variety of maternal kindness—that nearly makes my tears spring over. I haven't felt this warmth in such a long time. I almost can't remember when it last stopped by. "Do you have a relative who is sick?" she asks me, and before I can think of anything else to do, I find myself nodding.

She shakes her head in empathy, making a clucking sound with her tongue. "I am truly sorry to hear that. What is your loved one's name?"

"Pearl," I choke out.

"Pearl." The woman leaves the stirrer in the cauldron and wipes her hands on her brown tunic. "Does she need a bed to rest?"

When I don't answer, the woman points to the bubbling pot. "It is a combination of valerian, lemon root, and chamomile," she says. "The aroma makes the sick relax, and a spoonful of the liquid sends them to sleep in an instant. If you bring your loved one here, dear, I can give her something to make her feel more comfortable. Does she have the wilting sickness?"

"She did," I say.

"I see." Again, there is no accusatory glimmer in the woman's brown eyes, even now that she knows the truth. "I am most sorry to hear of Pearl's passing, dear. May Obellis look after her sweet heart in the fields of the Afterworld."

"Thank you," I say.

"And be well yourself," says the woman, taking a knob of dough from a shelf and pressing it into my hands. A man coughs and she turns away from me, just in time. The flood of tears are threatening to fall and I shuffle for the door.

As I step into the street, a crack of lightning streaks above the village and the skies open. Sheets of rain pelt the cobbles. As the droplets hit my crown and stream down my cheeks, I raise my face to the clouds and let the tears bubble out of me. It feels ridiculous and overindulgent to cry like this over my mother again, especially given everything that has happened since the Gathering, but I can't help it. The faces in the sickbay remind me too much of her. Every time I saw their twisted bodies, my mother's strong figure vanished from memory, replaced by the gaunt outline that was only her for a short while, and yet felt so eternal.

I resume walking to the next shelter, hoping it will be an inn, when a blur of red forms in the distance, climbing the rise. With the torrenting rain, it takes a little while to piece together the jumbled shapes. But when I do, my knees lock.

It's the uniform of the emperor's soldiers.

Spinning on my heels, I march in the opposite direction, heading back to the tree where I'd left Vogel. The soldiers have not noticed me, and I do not wish to draw attention, but it is excruciating trying to walk slowly and get away from them at the same time. I slide between shelters and emerge in the laneway closest to the river; then I sprint as fast as I can to the tree where Vogel is sitting in a tight ball, trying to stay out of the rain.

"Did you find a place?" he asks.

"No," I say. "But the soldiers are here."

"Where?"

"Back there in the middle of the village. And I can't find an inn to take us for the night."

"It doesn't matter. I found something," he says.

"You did?"

"Yes." He nods at the river. "I watched the soldiers locking the gates. There's an alcove under that bridge where we can shelter."

"Are you sure?"

"No, but we'll be out of sight and out of the storm, and ready to cross in the morning."

With the rain pounding our backs and no other choice, we sprint toward the bridge. Droplets glance from the sandbrick structure, the rivulets streaming from its semicircle arches. Vogel and I slide down the rocks, slicking our feet with mud and moss. A substantial recess is hollowed in the brick, enough to block the pouring rain.

"That's it!" he yells.

"You go first." My teeth chatter, as he leads the way. He sloshes through a puddle and tumbles from view, swiping at cobwebs that curtain the entrance. I follow him. Once we're inside, we move away from the jagged opening. There isn't a lot of space, but at least the ground is dry and we're concealed from the wind and Farrow's soldiers.

"Are you all right?" Vogel asks.

"I'm fine," I say.

"You don't look fine." There's obviously sufficient light flooding in for him to see my tear-streaked face. "Are you worried about the soldiers?" he asks.

"No."

"They're not going to find us," he says.

"I'm not worried about them at the moment."

"You're not?"

"No."

"It's something else?"

"It's nothing, Vogel." I sidestep around him and retreat to the opening at the other end. My mouth twists in an awful shape, but I can't prevent the tears from leaking. I don't have anything to wipe my nose with, so I lift my tunic to use as a kerchief. Which is mortifying. I dab at my eyes and take a breath, inhaling the rain.

Vogel nudges my shoulder. "Here."

It's a square of cloth—damp and crumpled—but still a lot cleaner than my grubby clothes.

"I can't," I say.

"I insist," he says. "Nose-blowing on a tunic should be a crime."

Turning my head, I catch him staring, but for some reason, I don't mind. I pluck the square from his hands. "Thanks."

"Are you thinking about her?"

"Who?"

"Your mother."

I breathe out. "I am a little." I don't know why I admit it to him. Maybe it's because I don't know him well.

"You saw something in the village?" he guesses.

Another tear pops out of my eye. "A room full of people with the wilting sickness."

"Oh," he says. "Your mother had that?"

I nod.

"How long ago did she pass?"

As he crouches beside me, I swallow.

"A year."

I feel the need to strike off "and a bit," as it seems ridiculous that I'm still this emotional. I wait for his advice to come. That a year is a long time. That I should have moved on. That she would want me to be happy, so I should not dwell on what I can't change.

But he doesn't say it.

Instead, he just sits there. And it's not an awkward kind of sitting there where he's running words over in his head and squeezing his hands while he thinks about what to say that wouldn't offend. I mean, perhaps he is doing that in his mind and I don't know about it. If he is, he's doing an excellent job of making it look like he isn't. He just doesn't seem hurried. Or like he wants to jump in the river to get away from my blubbering.

Give it time, I suppose.

He pats the ground and I sit beside him.

"I feel better, don't worry." I hold out the handkerchief, but he shakes his head with a wry grin.

"Keep it, it's yours."

"Oh, of course." I take it back, folding the material in my palm. Thunder and lightning take turns in the sky. We watch the rain slap the earth, flooding the grass, forming pools in small holes. Then I remember what I have in my pocket, and I dig out the knob of blobby white dough.

"Do I want to know what that is?" asks Vogel.

"Dinner," I tell him.

"That's really not funny."

But I tear it down the middle with my nails and we eat as night descends on the village. It's another night without Anai and Casper. Another night without my father. I've lost count of how many nights it's been now, which makes me feel like the very worst daughter. But *soon*. We're nearly there. At the cusp. And I cannot wait for this to be over.

I glimpse Vogel through the dark. I suppose my fortunes have not been all bad. "Carliss will be wondering what happened to you." The instant the sentence leaves my lips, I wonder what made me bring her up.

Vogel keeps chewing. "She will, I suppose."

"She was taken with you."

He doesn't reply.

"Do you plan to go back and find her again?" I should stop the questions, yet I find that I can't.

"No."

"Why not?"

He looks away. "I wasn't entirely honest with her." He finishes the dough and stretches his arms, letting the rainwater splash his fingers.

"What do you mean?"

He shakes his hands, then wipes them on the thigh of his pants. "I guessed that Jove had been taken to the palace. That was why I befriended her."

It takes a moment to sink in.

"So you used Carliss to gain access?"

"I did not mean it to go so far. There wasn't anything romantic between us, but I let her think that perhaps in the future . . ." He sighs. "I shouldn't have done that, Meadow."

"You cared enough about Jove," I say.

"And look where that got him," he mutters, standing up.

"If it's anyone's fault, it's Malthe's," I say.

Vogel touches his hand to my shoulder, the warmth of his skin caressing my neck. My breath stops in the back of my throat, and I realize why I asked about Carliss.

"Thanks for dinner," he says with a smile.

I gaze at him though the shadows. "You're welcome."

He lingers beside me for a few beats more, and something passes between us. I feel it. He doesn't despise me, despite how he's acted, and I know I've never despised him, either. Such an odd realization to have in a storm, in a foreign place, concealed by a bridge.

"Sleep well," I say.

"And you, Meadow." Though his voice is soft, it cuts through the rain.

And my heart pounds in the strangest rhythm, as he walks to the other side of the alcove.

CHAPTER TWENTY-FOUR

VOGEL WAKES IN THE MIDDLE OF THE NIGHT. HIS BREATH becomes short, sharp and loud like he's choking on a peach seed, then he kicks out his arms and legs, banging them against the sandbrick wall. When I open my eyes, the light from the moon is shining through the rain. He's hunched in a ball, his chest heaving, but when I go to him, he shakes his head. Perhaps he thinks that after being a gladiator, having nightmares is terribly childish. I don't think he has anything to be ashamed about, but I wait in the darkness, following his wishes, and eventually his breathing slows.

He wakes up four more times. With each I grow a little less able to return to my own slumber, and by the time the sun floods the alcove, I feel like I haven't slept at all. But Vogel seems to have finally relaxed, so I leave him be and creep out from under the bridge, stretching my arms above my head, enjoying the sweet sensation of cracking my bones.

Checking that soldiers are nowhere in sight, I search for Casper and Anai. I trot along the edge of the sand to get a better view of the road leading into Helliam. It snakes through the trees and leads to the opposite end of the village. I hadn't managed to make it that far in the rain before I saw the soldiers. It's quite conceivable that Casper and Anai sheltered in an inn on the other side of the settlement. Hopefully that means they will make their way through the village to find Vogel and me.

And we will do the same.

I feel Vogel's presence behind me just as I'm about to turn around.

"I cannot see them out there," I say.

"The soldiers or Casper and Anai?"

"Both."

He rummages in his side pocket and pulls out something impossibly shiny. "Hungry?" he asks, raising his brow, knowing full well that I must be starving.

"You've had that all along?" I admonish.

"It wasn't much good to us in the Sparselands." He rests the coin on the back of his thumb and flips it over the rest of his knuckles.

We venture to find the closet tavern. Most of the village must still be resting as stray cats roam the deserted laneways. Fisher folk cluster by the water. Some sit on the edge of the bank, setting bucket-size traps in the reeds to catch shellfish, while others push skinny boats in the water and balance on the rims of their vessels with string nets and sharp eyes, searching for the movement of scales beneath the ripples.

Vogel and I choose the first tavern that looks to be open for morning meal. Inside, there are scattered sandbricks and a man behind a bench slopping fish bones into a black, flat-bottomed pot. He hasn't stoked a fire yet, so I suppose the soup is as cold as the river from whence the fish bones came. Vogel slides the coin across the counter, and the man slips it under his robe and ladles the thin soup into two earthen bowls.

We carry the bowls to a corner and slouch on the sandbrick seats. A plant with leaves like a fountain hides our faces from the entrance, and there's a window cut out of stone not three steps from where we are sitting, should we need a swift escape.

"What's the plan today?" I ask. "Eat and then go back to the bridge to wait for Casper and Anai?"

Vogel takes a slurp of his soup. "Casper knows to meet us there."

"If he doesn't show up, we should cross ourselves." I know that we'll have a greater chance of success at the infirmary with larger numbers—especially since Vogel still seems unsteady and exhausted—but I can't wait any longer to see if my father is all right.

"We should wait," Vogel says.

"I'm not waiting. They could have already crossed, thinking that we are already on our way."

Vogel wrinkles his nose, but it's an expression that means he won't press the argument. Goodness knows, he's probably aware that he won't come out the victor. I decide then and there that I am only going to wait for middle day at the very latest. After that, whether or not we find Casper and Anai, I am marching across that bridge and following the road to the infirmary.

"How are you feeling now?" I ask.

"Good," he says.

"That's a lie."

"You're right." Vogel wipes his red-rimmed eyes. "It's ridiculous. I can't sleep. I was never this bad. Not even after the tower."

I don't see how it's ridiculous, but I don't object to his words. "The strangeness really knocked you about. Can you imagine if those beings were to leave the woodlands and march into Centriet?"

"They won't," says Vogel.

"Why not? They could be quite a match for the Tyjans, except they would be scarier sovereigns."

Vogel frowns, and I curse myself for sounding so frivolous when they almost killed him.

"They lose their powers when they leave the Sparselands," he says. "When Casper and I stayed in Holinde, that's what the miners believed."

That news is definitely well received. With the power to transform the world around us, not even the soldiers would stand to defeat them.

I scoop up my spoon. "We should talk about strategy for once we get to the infirmary," I say.

Vogel rests an elbow on the sandbrick. "What would you like to know?" he asks.

I'm taken aback by his cooperative nature. I think I'd half expected him to revert to his old aloof self, but I'm ever thankful for the reprieve. "What does the infirmary look like?"

"Like lots of tents spread across a lawn."

"That doesn't sound very organized," I say.

He shrugs. "It's not. But they have to be ready to pack up and move in case there are problems along the river."

I pray they do not pack up and move before we've the chance to plead for my father. "How many people work there?"

"I'm not sure. Maybe twenty. Thirty at most?"

"Do soldiers live in the tents to guard them?"

Vogel sighs. "There may be a few. But they've likely increased their security since I escaped a year ago."

"You were young for a gladiator."

"Initiatum," he corrects.

"Young for an initiatum," I say. "And how is it you had to become one at all?" By taking a nonchalant spoonful of soup, I hope he'll divulge without thinking too much.

But Vogel is shrewd. He examines my face. "What did Casper tell you?" he asks.

"Only that you were in prison, and they decided you'd earn more coin as a fighter. He told me you had stolen food. Which is fine. I've stolen food before. I'm not proud of it, of course, but after Komran died and the rations and seeds and animals dried up, I think everyone has taken something to feed their families at some point."

I'm babbling—and Vogel knows it.

"I didn't steal food," he says.

And I feel the need to reassure him. "You really don't need to tell me why—"

"I tried to kill Prince Malthe."

I stop eating. "You tried to kill the prince?"

"I very nearly did," says Vogel with regret, although I wonder if he's more regretful that it didn't pan out how he would have liked. I survey the tavern, but no one's walked in. The owner is busy snapping dry twigs and feathering husks beneath his fish soup.

"What happened?"

Vogel narrows his eyes, but he wouldn't have brought it up unless he was planning to tell me the whole story. "I lived in Septown with my parents, my brothers, and my little sister, Hallie. One morning, Hallie saw a wild horse in the field beside our stonebrick. She was helping untangle its legs from brambles when Malthe and his soldiers rode into our street."

I can only imagine Malthe's reaction when he spied the trapped horse.

"He wanted to shoot it," Vogel says. "He's not a good shot. He didn't want a moving target." He studies the soup as it drips from his spoon. "But when Hallie screamed, he pushed her over. So I pushed Malthe. And naturally, it angered him and he got his soldier compatriots involved. They stabbed my parents and I was carted off to prison with my brothers."

"And your sister?" I ask.

Vogel swallows. "They killed her."

I'm speechless.

"When she was pushed to the ground, she knocked her head on the edge of the cobbles. She bled out next to that worthless wildock. In a matter of moments, everything capsized."

And suddenly, I understand it. Why he wanted to save the wild horse. Why he hates the Tyjans with so much passion. Why he wants more than anything to dethrone Ladislas and Malthe, even if he doesn't know where to begin. And most of all, why he doesn't think poorly of me when I cry about my dead mother.

"I'm sorry," I say.

He leans on his chin. "It's a horrible kingdom that needs to be fixed."

He's right. Only a horrible kingdom would allow a prince to murder a child.

"Your brothers?" I ask.

When he glances sideways, the enormity of what he has lost expands. All this time he has held this inside him. Little wonder he is angry and desperate for change. And maybe that's the reason he wants to help me. He knows what it's like to lose his whole world.

"How did you get through it?" I ask.

"I'm still trying," Vogel says. "Being in the ludela gave me time to reflect on what the Tyjans had taken from me. It made me realize that I wanted to set things right so that no more children were killed and no more families were broken apart." He finishes the last of his soup, then stares through the square in the wall. "I came to a point where I was prepared to make hard choices to avenge my family. Prepared to get my hands dirty in the worst way to stop their evil regime." He turns back to look at me, and sparks flicker where there used to be blankness.

My chest constricts. "What did you do?"

"Nothing yet. Just a bit of research."

"Is that what you did at Jove's cottage?"

"Jove's cottage?"

"I found scribblings in your quarters. Were you and Casper plotting something?"

"No," he says.

I don't believe him. I'm suddenly aware that he has a plan, and perhaps he's always had a plan for revenge. "And you're going to get *your hands dirty*?" I ask.

"I am," he says.

"What will you do?" I think of my father with the arrow in his torso, then push the image to the depths of my mind. I can see how his death could consume my existence, could set my own path for seeking vengeance.

But the fire diffuses from Vogel's eyes. He grips his shoulder, gouging fingers in his back. "It will require some sacrifice," he admits.

"Don't do something foolish," I beg.

An odd expression knots through his features, but I cannot interpret what it means. He bites down on his lower lip, his nails digging into his skin. I can feel him trying to pull away, but I do not want to lose him again.

"What about your sister?" I ask.

"What about her?"

"What was she like?"

Vogel pauses, cocking his head, as though the question hasn't come up before. "I don't want to talk about my sister," he says.

"Why not?"

He shifts. "Because I don't."

"She was caring, right?"

"Meadow, stop."

"She obviously loved animals since she tried to save the horse."

Vogel taps his spoon against the bowl, his pupils dark like polished coal. "She was a pain in the buttocks," he finally lets slip. "Always rescuing almost-smushed frogs and bringing them back to our tiny stonebrick. As if it wasn't crowded enough with four boys and two adults."

"A rescuer of those in need," I say.

"Yes," he agrees.

"And so are you."

"Not even close." Vogel dips his head. "Sadly, I'm not like her at all."

"But you're helping me save my father," I say. I reach across the sandbrick and our fingers touch in the middle of the table. I raise my eyes and he's looking at me like he wants to say something, but he doesn't know how.

"This plan you are researching," I say. "Is it dangerous?"

"Meadow—"

"Tell me, will people get hurt?"

When he doesn't answer, I grit my teeth, feeling my stomach drop to the cobbles.

"So not like my sister," Vogel says.

"But what is it that you're going to do?"

He shakes his head. "I just want justice. I just want a way to stop the Tyjans."

It sounds like he's still undecided. And I realize I should tell him of Ein. Perhaps if he joined a group of like minds, they could move toward a peaceful solution. After all, in the tent, Ein spoke of goodness. "I know someone who could help," I begin. "I met this boy at the Tournament. He approached me because he heard what I'd said at the Gathering. He's part of an organization that is working in secret to right the wrongs and to make a change."

"Really?" says Vogel, listening closely, resting a finger to his lip. "A group like that in Centriet?"

"Yes. I mean, we stole their horses that night though—"

"Oh. That was them?"

"Regardless, I'm sure they would forgive us for it."

I'm not so sure they would actually, but if I brought them Vogel, they might be thrilled with the bolstered numbers, especially if Casper was keen to join them, too.

"And you think this group is the answer to the Tyjan problem?" he asks.

I shrug. "I'm not certain, but it would be a start."

Vogel considers that. As he does, something catches his attention through the window, and he pulls away, rising from his seat.

"What is it?" I ask.

He ducks back down.

"Soldiers," he says. "We need to leave."

"Vogel, stop!"

We've wound our way through every street in Helliam, and I finally recognize where we are. We're outside the inn of the old man who told me he didn't have space to spare. Even when we left the tavern, I didn't spot soldiers roaming the lanes. But Vogel insists that he saw red uniforms, so we crouch behind the pile of logs, resting our spines against a shed.

We stay there, listening for footsteps, as the weak morning sun climbs higher in the sky. At one point, the old man emerges to empty filth from a tub in the gutter. The stink rises like heat in a stonebrick, and I squash my palm over my nose. It's almost middle day, and voices waft by as villagers meander from tavern to tavern.

"We have to go to the bridge," I say when I can abide the stench no more. I stand up, but Vogel jumps beside me.

"The soldiers, Meadow."

"We've done it before." I go to move, but he grabs my arm and I stop, feeling the strength of his grip.

"Sorry." He releases his hand at once.

"Is something the matter?"

He takes a breath. "What you said about the boy you met . . ."

I'm confused by his meaning. "The one from the group?"

Vogel nods. His cheeks have flushed, almost to the color that they were in the woodlands. He's fighting hard to keep his composure, but I sense the energy pulsing through him. I sense it better than most people would because I know what it's like to be caught by that feeling. By panic. He's panic-stricken. In a way I didn't think that he could. In the arena, his stance was utterly collected, even in the face of a terrifying death.

But now . . .

"His group has a plan?"

"What are you saying?" I ask.

"Do you know what his group intends to do?"

"Vogel, I . . . I don't know." I wish I could understand what has caused this, why he's suddenly become so fraught with alarm. "Let's go to the bridge," I tell him.

"Meadow. There's something I need to tell you first."

"Tell me." In the glare of the sun, his eyes are so light they scarcely look real. I watch them search every part of my face, like the words he seeks are lodged in my pores.

"We need to . . ." And then he stops. He gazes in the space above my shoulder. At first I think it's Farrow and his men, but I don't hear their telltale yells of excitement. Instead, it's a gentle tap on the ground, and a dazed gasp that is all too familiar. And Vogel steps aside as her voice rings out.

"I cannot believe we have found you!" she says.

CHAPTER TWENTY-FIVE

S PINNING ON MY HEELS, I ALMOST COLLIDE WITH ANAI'S ARMS. SHE wraps them around me with so much force that I very near faint from the squeeze.

"I was so worried!" she gushes.

I hug her back, hardly believing the familiarity I'm seeing within this foreign landscape. Casper is behind her. He clasps his hand with Vogel's, a relieved grin plastering his slender face.

"You survived!"

"How did you get here?" asks Anai. "Casper said you must have trekked through the Sparselands?"

"We did," I say.

"Oh my!" she exclaims. "Did you see . . . anything?"

"We saw too much."

Anai's eyes dart to my body to make sure I'm all intact. "What do you mean you saw too much? You're uninjured though?"

"Yes, we made it."

Casper exchanges looks with Vogel. He's possibly trying to gauge whether we truly are unharmed. Vogel shakes his head slightly, and I'm curious what he'd wanted to tell me. At least he appears to have calmed, but the cool disinterest has returned to his face.

"How about you?" I say to them both. "You followed the road and stayed clear of the soldiers?"

"The soldiers are here," says Casper. "We got in early

yesterday and saw them arrive late in the afternoon. They took a room in the southern quarters of the village. I don't know why. The chambers down there are far more costly, but there are women to entertain them, I believe."

He shifts between his feet, stretching his calves, and I notice the pack slung over his shoulder.

"How did you find us?" Vogel asks.

"I saw you running from the tavern," Anai chimes in. She's clearly pleased with her sharp eyes, turning to pop her brows at me. I wish I could be as relaxed as they are. "We should go to the bridge while it's busy," she says.

Casper nods in agreement. Vogel looks troubled all of a sudden and I wonder if he's feeling weary again from the remnants of the strangeness. But then he blinks, seeming to recover. His steely gaze focuses ahead, and I know it's time to find my father. The butterflies kick up in my stomach as Anai links her arm through mine. We lead the way between the fences, checking vigilantly for red uniforms as we enter the street, trying our best to blend in. The morning stalls have opened for business, the bank a commotion of haggling and baskets of headless trout. We bluster through the middle, winding between villagers, veering with the cobbled road until the smell of the fish grows softer behind us.

A few paces on, and we're at the bridge. It's unlocked, thank Obellis, the great spearlike gates flung wide and secured with greased bolts. I marvel at the throng of pedestrians hurrying over the ribbed footpath. Most are locals who descend on the far shore, eager to trawl their nets in less crowded waters. The soldiers of the Helliam army posting stand near the rail. They're not concerned by anyone in particular, but then, they do not wear the regal red of Malthe's personal guard; rather, they're dressed in gray and brown. Outlier soldiers. They would have trained in Fortian with the emperor's men, but some may have never stepped foot in Centriet. I'm thankful Malthe's soldiers are not patroling the bridge. I suspect they had a big night of drinking and feasting during the storm and briefly swept the streets before retreating to their rooms to doze away the headaches. And for the first time, I am glad of their vices. And I hope the liquor in Helliam is strong.

My sandals crunch the gravel on the bridge.

"I was terrified for you," says Anai, as we walk. "I wanted to go back and follow you through the woodlands. I fought and fought until Casper had to shout and was almost seized by a pair of soldiers."

"You did the right thing to keep going," I say.

Her relaxed demeanor threatens to crack.

"Did I?"

"Yes. We're here now, aren't we?" I elbow her ribcage to elicit a smile, but she unlinks our arms, a hand to her cheek.

"I remember what Casper said about those woods—how the magic from the Sparselands had seeped in. Were his assumptions accurate?"

"Yes," I say.

She grits her teeth. "What happened in there?"

Anai's feet have ground to a halt, so I take her hand, pulling her along. Again, it feels like a role reversal. In Maytown, Anai was always the dragger and I was the one who got tugged around. "We came across some people," I tell her. "I'm unsure if they were the ancestors of those who refused to live united under Erratide's rule or whether they were ghosts, but they were unnerving. They could manipulate the world to look like different things."

"Like what?" asks Casper, catching up, even though Vogel lingers behind.

I hadn't realized he was eavesdropping. Nevertheless, I don't mind. "Like one moment there was grass everywhere. The next there was swampland. Then the manicured lawns of noble gardens. It felt like staggering about in a dream."

We reach the midpoint of the bridge.

"How is that possible?" asks Anai.

"It was magic," I tell her. "There is no other explanation. The whole area had this strange glow. Pale yellow like when the sun hits your eyes. And these children chased after us through a cornfield. They were interested in Vogel. They took him and tried to sacrifice him, but in the end it didn't work."

"Why not?" asks Casper.

"I don't know."

"And they just let him go after that?"

I nod. "The only reason Vogel agreed to it in the first place was because he was trying to save my life." The memory of what we went through makes me feel for Vogel deeply. I swing around to see where he is. Our eyes connect, and my heart jolts. After knowing how he protected his sister, I realize he was protecting me, too. I smile at him, but he still looks pained, though he increases his pace to catch up to us.

"I hear you're a hero," says Casper. "Saving Meadow from those spooks in the Sparselands."

"She tried to save me also," he says. His voice comes out so sincere and loaded that I feel a lump rise in my throat.

Casper frowns, rubbing his forearm. "It seems that you two have been through a lot."

"We have," I agree. "But I'm now more than keen to free my father once and for all." My tone is steady. Confident, even. It sure doesn't match my trembling insides. But since we're here because of my actions, I have to pretend, so I square my shoulders.

"I have coin," says Casper.

"You do?"

"Yes." He opens his rucksack and pulls out a pouch. I can hear the gentle tinkle inside, but the purse seems heavy. "We can bribe our way in."

"Where did you get that?" I ask.

"The cottage. It's Jove's coin." Casper flushes. "It was probably wrong to take it from him, but since he's gone I thought we could use it. There's enough in here for the infirmary healers. We can show them half and then more if they're greedy."

I'm surprised he didn't share this before. "Is the infirmary very far from the bridge?"

"It's close," he says, "but it's hidden in the trees." He points in the distance where the land slopes with hills, the sunlight and shadows interspersed on the greenness.

"Is it part of the Sparselands?" I ask.

"No, it's called the Ellafay Forest," he replies. He glances at Vogel. "Do you mind if I steal her?"

"What for?" asks Vogel.

"It's all right." I tip his arm and Vogel bristles, but he doesn't object as Anai steps forward. He permits himself to be led to the rail as Casper gestures for me to keep walking.

"Is something the matter?" I ask.

"Oh no." Casper swats a fly from his collar. "I just wanted to talk about the plan. By the look of Vogel, he's not in the shape to negotiate on your behalf."

He's probably correct.

"What do you suggest?"

"Let me do it," Casper offers.

"Is that wise?" I hold up my palms. "The last thing I want is for you to be detained."

"The healers can be bribed, remember?" Casper pushes hair from his forehead, letting it flop beside his temple. "I'm a good talker. A people person. Vogel can sometimes come off a bit unfriendly if you know what I mean. And not to brag, but I was definitely the more popular one out of the two of us when we were there."

Now that I can believe.

"Well, if you're sure . . ."

"It would be my pleasure."

We've reached the end of the bridge. As we step from the sandbrick onto the grass, it dawns on me that not long ago, my father would have traveled this road in the wagon.

"Who'd have imagined that meeting you in Yahres would lead to us being here now?" I ask.

Casper shrugs.

"But thanks," I say. "I've said it to Vogel, but I want to say it to you, too. And thanks for looking after Anai on the road. We've never been out of Centriet before and the two of you have been so kind. People we can trust. Sometimes it seems there are so few people like that left in the kingdom."

We turn right and follow the road as it winds through the scrub. As Helliam fades, the familiar surge of panic rises in my stomach. Good or bad, I'm finally going to know what has happened to my father. Though I'm not sure I'm entirely ready to crawl out from the blissful unknown.

"Not going to faint, are you?" asks Casper.

"I hope not." I breathe out.

"Do you get panic spells often?" he asks.

"I get panic," I say. "I have never heard of panic spells before."

"They were common in my family," says Casper. "There's a saying my father used to tell me in the ancient language of Marasca called Evienne. My family was originally from Marasca, right near the Silvasca Lake, you see. Anyway, whenever someone needed to calm down, Marascans would say, *Vierre mon sur, plasir mes yeemas*. Then they'd inhale and exhale, making sure the belly rose and fell with each breath. Sounds most strange, I'm sure, but it's been used for centuries in the Marascan communities to compose people in times of high anxiety."

"I could use that a lot of the time."

He smiles again. "It works, I promise. I don't know why."

"What do I say again?"

"Vierre mon sur, plasir mes yeemas."

I try to say the words. They're not simple, but Casper keeps repeating them until they roll from my tongue with ease. By the time the words have indented in my memory, my nervousness has disappeared.

"See, it works," Casper says.

I chuckle, mostly because he's right, but also because of his jolly demeanor. I repeat the words and so does Casper until Vogel and Anai draw near to us.

"What are you saying?" asks Anai.

"Casper's teaching me Marascan," I tell her. *"Vierre mon sur, plasir mes yeemas."*

"Why are you teaching her that?" snaps Vogel.

"To calm me down," I interject, but Vogel looks visibly annoyed.

"Come with me," he murmurs in my ear.

"Where?"

"Vogel, stop being like that." Casper sighs, throwing up his hands, and I wonder why they're back to being at odds. Casper walks ahead with Anai. When they're far enough in front of us, Vogel dips his head to my cheek.

"You have to go," he says urgently.

"Go? Where?"

"Away from us."

"Away *where?*"

"Back to the city. Back through the Sparselands. Anywhere."

His insistence makes me falter. "Is that what you wanted to tell me when we were hiding? To run away?"

The query causes his eye to tic. His long lashes beat as he considers his answer, shaping and reshaping the words on his tongue.

"I can't—"

"No. Tell me, Vogel." I find myself glaring, simultaneously wanting to tug at his voice box while also praying this is nothing of consequence.

He takes a peek at Casper and Anai. "You need to abandon this journey now. You need to go back across the bridge. *And run.*"

"What are you talking about? My father, I can't—"

"Do not argue on this." He hisses the command, but the edges are rounded. If anything, it sounds a lot like a plea.

"I have to find my father," I tell him. "You know what will happen if we do not make it."

"And I'm telling *you*," Vogel says, "that you need to—"

"Vogel, it's so good to see you!"

I almost vault clean from my skin. I hadn't heard anyone creeping behind us. Neither had Vogel from the grimace on his lips. He swallows his warning and straightens up.

It's a man and a woman. They're tall and imposing, both the height of Vogel, maybe taller. They each have machetes strapped to their belts, dirt and sweat stains marring their faces. Ahead, Casper and Anai wheel around, and recognition flares in Casper's eyes.

"Casper, too!" the man snickers. "Well, follow us, then. This is fortunate, indeed."

CHAPTER TWENTY-SIX

I HUDDLE WITH ANAI AS WE LEAVE THE ROAD AND TRUDGE THROUGH the trees. I haven't yet determined if these two people work at the infirmary, although they do not resemble healers with their animal hide vests and scuffed boots. Perhaps they are security. The man has thick arms and powerful strides, his black-brown hair shorn below the ears, the strands marginally lighter than the whiskers on his chin. The woman is pale with tight yellow braids. They haven't made any comment about Casper and Vogel escaping, so I keep my mouth shut, keen to obtain my bearings before saying anything that may incriminate us before getting to my father.

"Will it be much longer?"

I cringe. Obviously Anai cannot bear the silence. The man wipes a finger under his nose, the grime shifting across his cheek. He peeks a bloodshot eye at the woman, whose full lips curl in quiet amusement.

"We're close," she says in monotone, clipping Anai's shoulder as she stomps by.

At least we're close. That's something. If the exchange goes poorly, we're near the road. We continue walking as the soft ground ruts and the clayed soil rises in blobby anthills. The air congests with humming crickets, the atmosphere heated, damp and heavy. The moisture gathers at the nape of my neck, the warm breeze coating my legs with dust. Beside me, Anai has slowed, her cheeks blotched scarlet, her skinny limbs dragging. The hulking man strolls next to Vogel, though Vogel says nothing, maintaining good pace. For some reason, Casper looks calm. He treads with purpose, which is kind of strange. Every few steps, his coin pouch jangles, and I hope he's concocting the right things to say, as my head has emptied and my throat is taut.

We keep moving. On and on. Dipping under rocks and pushing through scrub. The farther we trek, the more my chest aches. The more I'm convinced we'll get dreadfully lost. Was Vogel aware that this duo was coming? Was that why he'd advised me to run? It's too late now to pose the question, but he did seem shocked when they'd first appeared.

I squint the moisture out of my eyes. We cross a dry creek bed, then climb a small rise. The peak is laden with scattered stones and a tight ring of stumps that are singed from a fire. At the other side, the ground falls away, and the woman beckons for us to make haste. Without objection, we double our speed, reaching the edge to take in the view.

"Oh my!" Anai murmurs.

There's a sunken valley that winds between hills. The space is narrow, but terribly long, and filled with rows of improvised shelters. They're not the sterile tents I'd imagined when Vogel spoke of the infirmary camp. They're crooked poles hammered in the dirt with textile strips draped over as roofs. The material does not graze the ground. The ropes are loose and unraveling in the weather. And some of the fabric has become so worn that scraps have been used to plug the tears.

"Welcome home," says the woman.

Home?

We ascend from the hilltop into the valley. As we draw closer, all manner of people converge to welcome us into their camp. I scour the land for injured prisoners or a tent that might contain sanitized cots. But there's nothing like that, and it occurs to me that a wagon would never make it through the brush and carrying stretchers would be next to impossible.

Anai's nails dig into my arm.

"This cannot be the infirmary," she says.

In dismay, I realize it's definitely not. It's a base of some sort—perhaps for misfits, who like to roam the outer lands.

"Vogel," I say.

He stares straight ahead, looking worried that I might ask something I shouldn't.

"Casper," I call. "What is this place?"

"Our camp," he replies.

"You never mentioned that you had a camp."

Casper extends his arms out wide, gesturing to the surrounds with joy. "Yes, Meadow. This is our camp. Before I boarded with Jove in Yahres, right here is where I laid my head."

I'm confused as to where *here* is. Does he mean he dwelled in a tent in the middle of nowhere?

"You lived here, too?" I ask Vogel.

"Yes," he says, seemingly conscious that the man and woman are watching him closely.

"We didn't catch your names," says Anai.

"Jordus," says the man.

"Siella," says the woman.

"Why have you brought us here?" I demand. "Is this part of the infirmary?"

"*What* infirmary?" A smirk brushes Siella's lips that doesn't quite snake its way to her eyes.

"We do not have a working infirmary." Jordus leers. "Are you sick, city dwellers?" He and Siella laugh at that, and I'm not sure what the insult means. Clearly it's something beyond the fact that Anai and I are residents of Maytown.

We reach the bottom of the rise. A small crowd has gathered to greet us.

"Look what we found on the road," says Jordus, at the same time a whoop goes up from the spectators and Casper and Vogel are swallowed in embraces. Like with the magical beings in the woodlands, I'm confused by the array of people in the camp. Old and young. Strong and spindly. People of many different backgrounds. I cannot weave together an argument as to why they are hidden in the middle of a valley.

"And who are your friends?" asks an older man, his skin dark and his gray hair cropped short. He moseys serenely in front of the people, and they move aside in a sign of respect.

Casper removes himself from the welcoming hugs to answer. "This is Meadow and Anai," he says, pointing at each of us in turn. "They are from Centriet."

The older man nods. "Welcome," he says. "I am Knox. We are pleased to have you in our camp, even if you are only staying for a little while." He seems vaguely familiar, with his towering presence and gentle manner, if not a little intimidating. I'm about to ask for the infirmary again when Knox motions to Vogel and Casper and instructs them to get cleaned up, fed, and debriefed on what has been happening. I stare at Vogel as he's led away, wishing I could have talked to him more.

"What about us?" I say.

"Come along," says Knox.

Jordus and Siella stand on either side of Anai and me. We are herded into one of the closest tents. There are large barrels stacked on the grass, which provide some privacy from the people outside. Knox has told them to resume their duties, but I can't help feeling their eyes rolling over us as we settle on a splintered bench.

"I suppose you must be wondering why we live in the middle of a valley," says Knox, sitting opposite us, resting his fists on the wooden slatted surface.

"Among other things," I say.

Knox smiles. His teeth are beautifully straight. "Casper says you both hail from Centriet," he says.

"We're from Maytown," says Anai.

"Citizens," says Knox.

"Yes."

"Ah." Knox clears his throat. "Would you like some ale?" Before waiting for our answer, Jordus jumps up to open a brown bottle. He pours the liquid into wooden mugs and slides them in front of each of us.

"My father was injured in the Tournament," I tell Knox. "He is being transported via wagon to the infirmary in the Ellafay Forest. We are traveling there now. Vogel and Casper said it wasn't far from here. If it is all right with you, I would like us to be on our way."

Knox takes a long draft from his mug. "There's no infirmary in these parts. Not that I know of."

"What do you mean?"

"There's a sickbay in the Hellium village, but there's no army hospital."

"That can't be right," I say.

"Who told you there was?" asks Knox.

"Casper and Vogel," I repeat.

"I see." Knox shakes his head. "My apologies for being the bearer of bad news."

But if there's no infirmary . . . I stop and turn to Anai. Her eyes are wide as we ingest the information at the same time. If there's no infirmary, then we have been chasing a wagon that doesn't exist. And if the wagon doesn't exist, it means my father is not inside. It means my father could be anywhere. He could have died in the tunnels below the arena for all I know.

"But . . ."

"They wanted to bring you here," says Knox.

"Where is *here*?" asks Anai.

I'm glad she poses the question because my mind is whirling. All of a sudden, my father could be dead. All of a sudden, this travel and danger was in vain. But why? What was the point?

"You're in a camp of people who loathe the current regime."

My ears prick up. Revolutionaries? Was that why Vogel had so much hatred in his heart and a determination to change things?

"I don't understand," I say.

Knox nods, seemingly sympathetic. "If you agree to hear me out, perhaps I can enlighten you." When I don't object, he smiles sadly, wrinkles forming on the ridge of his cheekbones. One of his legs bounces on the ground and he reins it in with an unsteady hand. "I was from Centriet, too," he says. "I lived in a Tyjan villa since I was a child. Back then Emperor Samson was an elderly man who had ruled for almost seventy years. He had a son, Komran, and Komran had his own son—the current emperor, Ladislas."

Of course I know this already. The family tree of the Tyjan men. Samson, then Komran, then Ladislas, then Malthe.

"When Komran's first wife passed from the fever, he took a second named Ryell," says Knox.

This isn't news to me, either. After the tragedy of losing his first wife, he was entitled to marry another woman.

"I remember when he announced it to the kingdom," says Knox. "Everyone was shocked, especially Samson. Ryell was so young and so luminously beautiful. I recall wondering why she would choose to be with an old man like Komran when she could have had any young suitor she desired. Then again, Komran was next in line to the throne, so I suppose that helped."

Power does help.

"Not long after, Komran and Ryell had a daughter named Princess Astrid," says Knox, and I reflect on cleaning the wing in the Tyjan villa when Quinn spoke of the little girl. Astrid was Ladislas's half sister. The same age as the Princess Kalliope. And according to all the whispered stories, the absolute light of Komran's life.

"Astrid died in a ravine," I say.

"I took her to that ravine," says Knox. Behind him, Jordus and Siella stiffen. "It was just me and her," Knox reveals.

Just me and her.

Knox has paused, his raven-black eyes searching my face. It's like he wants me to ask him a question.

"You saw her die?" I ask.

He sighs. He swigs another mouthful of drink, but this time the liquid streams down his chin. "The reason I was with her at the ravine that morning was because Emperor Samson had asked me to kill her."

As he lets that truth sit before us, I feel the blood drain from my face. The admission brings forth so many more questions, but all I can manage is a spluttering "Why?"

"Why? Because he was Emperor Samson." Knox's shoulders rise and descend. "He was a tired old man with tired beliefs. He knew how much his son loved Astrid. He fretted that Komran would bypass Ladislas and name the princess as his successor instead."

"He could do that?" asks Anai.

"My word, he could've." Knox turns his head, glad to include her. "Although it was customary for heirs to be male, it was never a rule. Komran could choose."

"And Samson didn't want that."

"Of course he didn't. Samson desired an all-male line." Knox scoffs at the distant memory. "The possibility of a woman taking the throne—even in the future, even his *granddaughter*—consumed his thoughts, day after day, until he decided he must take action."

I do not possess clear memories of Samson, but my mother always spoke of the sweat on his brow. She called it the "sheen of insatiable appetite." *Men like Samson are seldom content with what they have*, she would muse on our walks. *They claw deeper, always stretching further, spreading their influence like disease to matters that shouldn't be theirs to control.*

"Emperor Samson decided that Astrid needed to be eliminated," says Knox, and I realize my mother had been right all along. "In his mind, it was the only way to safeguard the Tyjan crown. So he tasked me to take the princess on an outing and to make her passing look like an accident."

"And you did?" I ask.

Knox gulps. "I couldn't refuse the emperor. I had a young son and daughter of my own at the time, and I knew that if I upset Samson, he might do something terrible to my children. So I took Princess Astrid by carriage to the ravine. I took her to the edge of the cliff, fully intending to carry out my order. But when it came to the time to push her small body . . . she was so like a doll . . . that I just couldn't do it."

I let out a breath and relief courses through me that I do not need to hate this old man. But then I stop. "If you didn't do it, then what happened to Astrid? We mourned her in Centriet. They hung black banners in the streets. Her mother, Ryell, wore black and publicly mourned her passing. She . . . she . . ."

She ended her own life because she believed her daughter was dead.

"I took Princess Astrid to the Ellafay Forest," says Knox. "I took her where no one would know who she was. There was an elderly couple, who had desperately wanted their own offspring. I knew they would look after her well. So I left her with them and returned to the palace and told Emperor Samson that I had killed his granddaughter. Thus he announced to the kingdom that she had fallen into the ravine and everyone mourned her passing in the capital."

"But Ryell killed herself because of that lie," says Anai.

Knox looks far into the distance, his eyes misty. "I can never repent for a sin such as that. Emperor Samson died two years later and Komran assumed power afterward. I continued on in Komran's guard, never able to tell him the truth about his daughter and his wife. There were many times I wanted to come clean, but the one thing that kept me from doing so was my son and daughter. Again, I feared for their lives if anyone in the palace found out the truth. And then when Emperor Komran died two years ago, I hated myself even more because he went to his grave believing the lie about Astrid's death. I cannot make that right."

"No, you can't," I say.

Knox knuckles his eyes, but doesn't refute it. "After Komran's death, I imagined that I would be the advisor to Ladislas. After all, I had advised his grandfather and his father. But Ladislas was not like either of them. I knew this, of course. However, I was not prepared for just how different he would be when in power. He started spending more and more coin, most that we didn't have to begin with. He made an alliance with the King of Leeang that was ill-advised. And when I tried to speak to him about his mistakes, he became angry at me. He accused me of treason and I was shipped off to the Jasquek Mines in chains."

"Which is where he met us," says Casper, who has slipped into the tent with a jug of ale and a plate of dry bread. He slides onto the seat beside Anai, but any affection she held for him has flown away, and she scoots to the other end of the bench.

"Of course," I say. "There was no infirmary. Were you and Vogel even initiatums or was that falsehood, too?"

"No, we were initiatums," says Casper bitterly. "But when the ludela ran out of coin to house so many of us, Vogel and I were sent to the Jasquek Mines. We met Knox there, who told us about Princess Astrid living somewhere in the Ellafay Forest. When we escaped the mines, Knox went to look for her. And he found her—"

"Alive?" asks Anai.

"Alive."

At that moment, Vogel enters the tent with a girl about my age. She has bright blonde hair and seaweed-colored eyes, and skin as fair as a sandbrick sculpture.

"Astrid," I whisper.

She leans against a barrel, examining Anai and me in turn. She murmurs words under her breath that are lilting and fluid like leaves in a zephyr.

"Princess?" I ask.

She doesn't answer.

"It's an honor to meet you."

She chews on her lip. The surface is cracked and white from peeling. She touches a thumb against her chin.

"Princess?"

"She no longer speaks our tongue." Knox gouges at a dent in the table.

"Why not?" I ask.

"We do not know." He averts his gaze, although something seems wrong.

And then, Astrid falls to her haunches, holding her hands to her ears in pain.

"What's happening?" I ask.

Casper kneels beside her. He whispers the words from the Marascan language: *"Vierre mon sur, plasir mes yeemas."* At once, Astrid stills her lips and sits to attention, the calmness returning. She mutters the words back to him, over and over, clutching his wrists.

"What do you intend to do with her?" I ask.

"She must take power from Ladislas," says Knox.

"You cannot put her on the throne," I say.

"She's the only one who can dethrone the emperor."

"How can she dethrone him?" I ask. "If she cannot speak the language of the kingdom?" I turn to Vogel. "This was your plan all along? To put this poor girl on the throne?"

"Yes," he says.

"What about my father? Did you even see him get taken on the wagon?"

His voice wavers.

"No," he admits.

"Where is he then?"

"I don't know." Vogel's blue eyes burn into mine so bright and so strong that the world seems to blur.

"You don't know?" I'm on my feet. Tears streak my face, but I do not care.

"I'm sorry," he says.

"You're sorry?" I spit. "That I came all this way because you lied about my father? That you knew all this time that the infirmary was fake? You knew how much I needed to find him. He could be dead for all you know."

Vogel looks away, face red.

"You don't get to look away!" I shout. "How could you do this after all you have lost? Was it even true about your sister? Or just more lies to make me compliant?"

"It was true," he says.

"True? That word means nothing coming from you. And you'll never succeed." My eyes settle on Princess Astrid as she shakily stands, taking a piece of dry bread from Casper's plate. "This is your great, illustrious plan? How can you hope for her to rule?"

Anai rises and moves beside me. We stand together, hands woven tight.

"We're leaving," she says.

"Sit down," says Knox.

"No," I say, but Jordus and Siella are beside us in an instant, pressing palms to our shoulders.

"Which one is needed?" Knox asks Vogel.

He doesn't reply.

"Meadow," says Casper.

"You're sure?" he asks.

"Quite certain," says Casper. "We went through her history at the record keeper's cottage."

I can barely breathe. They were researching me? I cannot comprehend what they'd hope to find. "What do you need me for?" I ask.

"Wait," says Vogel. "There's another way. There are other groups like ours in the city, we could join with them—"

"Get him out of here."

Knox makes a signal to Jordus, and the big brute grabs for Vogel's collar. Vogel ducks and swings to the side, smashing a bottle on Jordus's boot.

"Go, Meadow!"

I blink, amazed. But Siella is fast and unclips her machete. She darts from behind one of the barrels, just as the noise of stamping begins.

"What in the kingdom?" She hesitates, dallying on the spot at the unnatural sound.

And then come the screams. Not from Astrid. Not from Anai or me. The screams come from outside the tent at the foot of the rise. Screams that soldiers from Centriet have breached the perimeter and are storming the camp.

Screams to run.

CHAPTER TWENTY-SEVEN

IT'S TOO MUCH TO TAKE IN ALL AT ONCE. THERE'S THE SCREAMING—the incessant screaming. Then there's the noise of blades clinking and tent poles falling and people's footsteps pounding against the compacted soil.

Before I can think to grab Anai and escape through the tail end of the structure, Astrid leaps to her feet and flees like she has wheels attached to her soles. Knox tears after her, yelling to the people to convene in their second location, wherever that may be, and not to let the soldiers take any of them alive. Jordus and Siella roll barrels across the entrance flap to keep the soldiers from getting inside. Casper dives for me, but I swerve out of the way and he stumbles on the edge of the table. I have no sympathy for him. Using the opportunity, Anai and I pursue Astrid and Knox out the back of the shelter, but Vogel is on our heels.

"Over there!" pants Anai.

We side-dodge through the alley of a rear tent and head into the forest. Vogel is still behind us, but he struggles to give chase.

"Up here," I say to Anai. I figure if we hike up the hill, there is no way Vogel will be able to catch us. "Maybe we can circle around and get back to the road."

But when Anai doesn't answer, I spin around. She's nowhere to be seen.

"Anai!" I shout. Where did she go? I skid back down the rise to find her. She isn't in the tents and the soldiers are coming. They scatter through the camp like fire ants, swords poised for the moment they spy us. Backing away, I skirt the border and duck behind a water tank. It's thin and made from grooved metal. As far as I dare, I peer around it.

And stop.

There's a band of soldiers lurking in front of Knox's tent.

"Get on the ground!" a soldier yells, his weapon pointed at a group of women.

They cluster in a unified bunch and lower themselves onto the dirt.

"In a line!"

They shuffle apart and sit, holding hands, in a long row. I can hear some of the women sobbing, calling to Obellis, pleading for forgiveness.

"Hold your tongues!" the soldier bellows. "Unless you can tell us the location of the girl."

I freeze. They mean me, of course. They have no idea that this camp houses the half sister of the current emperor. Not that I suspect Ladislas would be worried about Astrid stealing the crown from him. Nevertheless . . .

"What girl?" asks a woman. I recognize her voice to be hard and confident. Defiant, even. She sounds like she could be Siella's twin.

"A girl with long black hair. She came from the road just now."

"There is no one who fits that description," says the woman.

"If we find her, peasant, I will take out your eyes."

Farrow.

My insides squeeze. No doubt he would do such a dreadful thing, knowing it would impress Prince Malthe.

"Sylvan and Wyren, head back to Helliam," he commands. "Alert the army posting that we have a treasonous camp hidden in the forest that needs to be taken care of."

The soldiers speed through the wilderness. I hope they do not make it to the bridge, and instead get lost in the maze of trees.

Someone rests their hand on my back. I swing around and almost scream.

It's Vogel.

I wriggle away. I don't want his treachery anywhere near me. But given the soldiers are roving about, I cannot retreat without making a sound. He lifts his hand as if he knows this.

All of a sudden, there's a shouting noise. A soldier tosses Knox in the middle of the women. He lands heavily, square on his tailbone, but he doesn't cry out or beg for mercy or hide his face with a cupped hand.

"By the wrath of Obellis," Farrow says, his voice changing with shocked recognition. "Old man, you are quite the sly dog. Last I heard, you were near death in the mines. The emperor will be most pleased to learn of your new whereabouts."

Knox pretends not to hear.

"Your daughter is well," Farrow continues. "Though most unfortunately, the same cannot be said for her husband. Pompous fool kept speaking out on your behalf. He was sliced and diced in the gladiator ring. The poor sod didn't even try to fight back." A slow rasp puffs from his lips and he clucks his tongue as if he cares.

"And my son?" asks Knox.

"As loyal as ever."

"He will not be harmed because of me?"

There's a pause. I sense Knox's fear—and if I can sense it, then Farrow can, too. And even before his name is revealed, it dawns on me who Knox resembles.

Gyzen.

"He thinks you're dead—and he's glad of it," says Farrow cruelly. "Everyone knows what scum you are to speak out of turn about the emperor. And now it all makes sense," he scoffs. "This camp is yours and these people are your followers. They all wish harm to Emperor Ladislas, I presume? Is that correct, girls? You would hurt your ruler simply because this tired old fool told you lies about his superior?"

"No," the women answer.

"I wish I could believe it," Farrow says. "I want to believe that this old man could change, but I've seen his deception play out before."

It is then I see movement behind a tree trunk, a few steps from my spot near the tank. At first I think it must be Anai, but the figure drops quickly, breathing hard. She tentatively grabs at her yellow hair, detaching the strands from the cobwebbed bark. She surveys the landscape—the hill, the shrubs—and braces her weight, palm to the soil.

"Astrid!" I try to hiss her name without actually alerting her to me.

Carefully Astrid clambers to her feet and wanders nearer to Knox's tent. If she goes much closer, the soldiers will see her, never mind hear her boots on the twigs. And I don't know what I'm thinking—because I don't even know for certain that this *is* Astrid—but I jump up and grab her hand, pulling her behind a second tank.

It's a little way from where Vogel hides, and my ankle rolls as we bend low. Astrid lets out a tiny whimper, her fingers tangling in knots in my hair. The tugs feel like fire and stars, but I bite my tongue and blink through the pain. Farrow continues to threaten the women, asking them more about Knox's plans.

They refuse to answer. Again and again.

At my side, Astrid burbles once more. It's louder this time like she wants me to speak. She juts her forehead at the gap above my scalp, as if there is something I cannot see. I try to shush her with a finger to my lips—and then to hers—but it doesn't make a difference. Finally, I resort to a hand across her mouth, but she pulls backward and shakes her head. She begins to talk with heightened indignance, still pointing at me, her green eyes ablaze. *"Vierre mon sur, plasir mes yeemas!"* She's forgetting the soldiers are footsteps away.

I clench my teeth. "Please be quiet!" I try to smile, but it makes her more frantic.

She tugs on my hem, her forearms rigid. *"Vierre mon sur, plasir mes yeemas!"*

And I remember when Casper echoed the words and she calmed right down, so I look at her. I brush the blonde strands out of her eyes and catch Vogel's stare from across the space.

"It's all right," I mouth to him.

Astrid repeats the Marascan phrase.

So I whisper in her ear: *"Vierre mon sur . . ."*

"No!" hollers Vogel.

". . . plasir mes yeemas."

"NO!"

I finish the words and I can't understand why Vogel screamed. His voice alerts Farrow and the other soldiers, who stream toward us, their pupils alight. They surround the tanks in a matter of moments, small wicked simpers smearing their faces. And all that spins through my head is: *Why, Vogel? Why did you scream and give us away?*

I don't know.

And then, something strange. I feel like something wants out of me, as though I'm going to be sick on the lawn. But the feeling strikes in unremitting waves and I fall on my back with my head to the trees.

And then . . .

And then . . .

I close my eyes and the world goes black and my ears go quiet. And in my dreams I'm twisting and floating and breaking free.

And then it's silent.

CHAPTER TWENTY-EIGHT

MY HEAD HURTS SO MUCH, YET MY BODY FEELS STRANGELY relaxed. As I rock my neck from side to side, I feel my senses slowly return. Spreading my arms beside me, the material glides between the folds of my skin. And then I realize I am sandwiched between two sets of silken sheets and there's a soft cloudlike mound beneath the back of my head, and my eyes jolt open at the understanding that I'm lying in an actual bed. And I've never been in an actual bed with feathers cushioning my spine.

A luxurious dark blue canopy glares down at me. My attention slides over its stitching and the shiny material that is bunched together in intentional drapes. I balance on my elbows, sweeping the room, a trepidation settling in the depths of my stomach. I'm in a large chamber like the one I spent a whole morning cleaning with Quinn. However, this chamber is furnished with brass fittings and thick white carpet. There are rows of candles along the mantelpieces, a huge dressing screen tipped with gold and an assortment of elaborate tables with ornaments of women in ball gowns perched on lace cloths.

I rest a hand to my forehead, trying to coax my memory back. I remember fragments here and there. Little pieces of a grander picture. I remember being in the camp in the forest and hearing Knox tell me the truth about Astrid. I remember hiding behind the tanks and being discovered when Vogel screamed.

But then what?

Nothing.

It's blank.

The walls of darkness fenced me in.

I struggle for anything—images, sounds, aromas of the journey as we left the valley. But my very next memory is right here, swathed in extravagance, though I surely don't deserve it. And it frightens me, those missing moments. What has occurred since I've been asleep?

Tugging the sheets off my body, I glance down. I stare at my legs. They are stretched out across the padding, but something is wrong. They are not *my* legs. And yet these legs are attached to me, there's no question about that. I touch my hips, where they join to my torso. I squeeze my thighs, but the surface is different. The flesh is pale like churned cream. The calves are slender, whereas mine should be muscled. And then another thought takes root, expanding out with disturbing haste. Had I imagined traveling to the camp? Had I dreamed my meeting with Knox? Was I actually passed out in Malthe's tower? Has he sawn off my legs and replaced them with others?

I fling the legs onto the floor. I can feel my weight, so the legs must be mine. There isn't a winding red scar around my joints. There are no stitches and there is no pain when I scuff my heels across the wool. But when I straighten, something is off. I'm clearly farther from the ground than usual. It's at that point I notice my arms. I have less freckles. My fingers are slimmer. And when I turn, my hair sweeps my elbow—hair that is yellow like the color of straw.

And that is not right.

I run to the mirror. I linger before it, my eyes to the ground. Although I try, I cannot look up. Rather, I gaze at my legs in the glass, trying to understand how it is possible that legs of mine are so thin and long. I count backward under my breath, but when I reach zero, I do not peek. It's only when I think of Anai and my father that I tell myself if I hurry through this, then perhaps I can start unraveling where they are and how in the kingdom we'll return to Maytown.

I raise my eyes.

My mouth falls ajar. A mouth that is not mine. I crane my swanlike neck at an angle so my new pert nose almost touches the glass. My clear green eyes stare back in horror. Eyes as green as the weed beneath the Geynes. A torrent of emotions rush through my veins.

I am no longer me.

I am Princess Astrid.

I do not scream. Instead I fear I might fall to the carpet and never wake up. Either that or the contents of my stomach may burst from my throat. I touch my rounded cheeks, my full lips, and my absurdly long eyelashes. I pull at my mountains of blonde hair. I raise and lower my soft eyebrows and suck in my cheeks to fully take in the new shape of my face and chin. How is it that I am in her body and yet I am me in her head?

And worse still . . . does that mean she resides in *my* body?

I race across the chamber to the window and peer outside. I must be in the Tyjan wing, because I am up high and the outdoor square in the middle of the palace glistens below. How long have I been asleep? Where are the others from the camp? Are they safe? For the first time I glance down at my clothing and realize I am wearing a long-sleeved gown embroidered with roses and swirling leaves. The collar is frilly and knotted at my neck as if I am some sort of Tyjan princess. Which is absurd. But it also means I'm free to do whatever I like in Kalliope's villa, so I gallop to the big double doors and throw them open, even though I'm sure it's not proper to be running from my quarters in sleep garments.

"Your Highness!" Standing on the other side of the doors is Tallesa. With my new body, I am the same height as her, except that she bows her head immediately, which renders me taller. She must have been waiting for me to wake up. "I do apologize," she says. "I did not mean to startle you. I just came up to inquire as to whether you need anything."

"What day is it?" I ask.

If my question surprises her, she does not give any indication that it is abnormal. "It is Fortieth Day," she says, indicating the number of days since the beginning of the season.

"And how long have I been asleep?"

"Just a night since your return." She walks to a large dresser and opens the doors. "May I help you with your dressing, Your Highness? It is a lovely day out."

"No," I say.

"Then some food, perhaps?" Tallesa lifts a tray from a side table and carries it into the chamber, placing it on a half-moon stand that rests against the wall.

"Tallesa," I say. "I need your help."

Her eyes bulge that I know her name, but she recovers swiftly. "What would you have me do for you?" she asks.

"How did I get here?"

"I beg your pardon, Your Highness?"

"How did I get into the palace?"

"The soldiers," she begins, then stops talking and steps backward, her head lowered again. Kalliope sweeps into the chamber in a long green robe, tied at the waist with a thin, silver tassel.

"Leave us, Midla," she says to Tallesa.

"Yes, Your Highness," says Tallesa. She steps into the hall and closes the doors behind her, and I'm so overwhelmed by so many things that I shrink back from Kalliope and dip into a low curtsy.

"You do not need to do that to me," Kalliope exclaims, giggling at my lack of knowledge when it comes to Tyjan customs. Her laugh is as irritating as squeaky shoes on freshly buffed timber. She picks at the tray that Tallesa left, selecting a pouch of sunbaked tomato and popping it onto her tongue with a broad grin. "I am just so delighted that you have been found alive and well!" She hugs me with so much force that I am nearly relinquished of all my breath. "Do you remember when we played together as children?" Her eyes shine at another memory I'll never be able to recover. "You would tell me to hide while you counted and then you would forget to come and find me!" She laughs again, high-pitched and ridiculous, although she clearly believes the sound becomes her. "I cried for days when I heard you died. We all did. It was a harrowing time. I know your father never got over your absence. We would catch him staring into the distance as though he was trying to figure out how to bring you back to life."

"How did I get here?" I ask.

"My brother's guard found you hidden in the forest near the Helliam army posting," she says in a gushing voice. "I believe they were returning from official business and happened upon your camp. You were being kept there by traitors to the crown."

"What happened to them?" I ask.

"Who?"

"The traitors."

"They are in the cells," says Kalliope.

"How did you know I was not one of them?"

"We didn't," she says. "You were to be condemned just like the others, but then my father's disloyal former advisor, Knox, revealed your true identity to us. My father is most pleased to get his half sister back."

"He is?"

"Of course he is! Your blood is the same as ours, Astrid!" Kalliope rushes forward and hugs me again.

"There was a girl in the camp with long dark hair," I say. "Did you see if she was captured?"

"I did not see all of the people," says Kalliope. "But you must get dressed, as we are about to go out and see them now."

"Now?"

"Yes!" Kalliope spins toward the dressing screen. She tugs on a cord that hangs from the ceiling and a bell rings. The double doors open at once.

"Your Highness?" It's Tallesa again.

"Where is Princess Astrid's dress?" she asks.

"I will get it immediately, Your Highness," says Tallesa, bowing even lower than before and taking off across the landing at a trot.

I blink as I look at Kalliope.

"What is it?" she asks.

"Nothing," I say.

As she turns, she regards me closely. I try to look back without staring too much, but there's something strange above her head. It appears like a whirl of intense color—a whole stripe that curves with her head shape as if she wears a glittering crown. The color is pale orange with pieces of yellow woven inside. But there's more to it than the various shades of warmth. There's a texture to it as well, which makes me squint to be sure that I am not seeing things that are not there. But the more I try not to see, the clearer the image becomes. It's soft and wispy at the edges. As she moves to the table to collect another handful of food, the colors move with her, as if they are attached to her body with invisible strings.

Tallesa reenters the chamber with a dress in her arms. Even at a distance, a similar halo flutters around her scalp. Although it is a close shade to Kalliope's—Tallesa's is a burnt orange color—I instinctively know that the two shades do not match. Which is strange that I know this with such certainty, but I do. And it's strange that they cannot feel them. But there are many more things that are strange today and this does not top the list.

Tallesa gestures for me to walk behind the screen with her. She is so overtly pleasant and keen to assist that it makes me feel ill.

"I can dress myself," I say.

Tallesa looks to Kalliope.

"Let her do as she wishes, she is your superior," Kalliope says, waving Tallesa out of the chamber for a second time.

I walk behind the screen and tug off my night clothing, still amazed that my hands and feet and body size are not my own. The dress that Tallesa brought for me is beige and silky, and I unhook the clasps at the side and step into the expensive material. As I pull it around me and fasten the midsection, I can barely breathe. It makes me feel even more trapped. What am I supposed to do now? How do I get back in my old body when I don't even know how the swap happened? All I remember is being beside Astrid, hunkered on the dirt in the forest, trying to make her fall silent. No one bustled near or interfered with us while we were concealed. The only thing that happened in those last few moments was that Vogel yelled "No!"

I stop. But why? Why did he yell that word? I recall thinking it was odd at the time. After all, it alerted the soldiers to our hiding place when we had not yet been discovered. Since he yelled it so loudly, it must have been important for him to deliver the message to me. But what was he telling me not to do? What was he telling me not to say?

The words.

Of course! I shake my head at the truth of it. I said the Marascan words that Casper had taught me on our walk. Astrid had whispered the same words before I uttered them. Was that the reason we swapped our bodies? And did Casper know it would happen? It doesn't make sense. Casper had said those words to Astrid before to calm her in the tent and nothing had happened to him.

"Are you dressed?" calls Kalliope, but then she stops. There's the creak of doors opening again and someone with heavier footsteps walks in.

I peer through the crack between the two paneled screens. Freya is standing on the landing outside the room. She's pale in the face, and she dips her voice low.

"Your Highness, I had hoped—"

Kalliope shakes her head.

"But . . ." says Freya.

"I'm sorry," says Kalliope. "My father has already made his decision."

Freya nods, her face growing whiter, placing a palm to her lips in distress. She backs out and shuts the door.

"Are you ready, Astrid?" Kalliope repeats.

I step out from behind the screen, feeling so out of place that my knees are shaking. In response, Kalliope grabs my hands and even the sensation of her fingers brushing mine feels different from within this foreign casing.

"Is it grand to be back in your home?" asks Kalliope.

"Yes," I say.

She kisses my cheek.

"Come now," she says.

"Where are we going?"

Kalliope smiles. "To gain justice for you."

CHAPTER TWENTY-NINE

As KALLIOPE AND I FLOAT ALONG THE CORRIDORS FILLED WITH urns and tapestries that I had polished and dusted in my life as Mollie, the servants curtsy and drop their heads, trying not to gape when it's clear they want to. They know the story about tiny Princess Astrid who died in the ravine in a terrible accident. They know the story of her grief-stricken mother, Ryell, who sliced her own throat in the middle of the night. They know that Emperor Komran mourned his daughter until the day he died, filling the halls with portraits of her face.

To have Astrid back is a miracle.

I am a miracle.

I try to rein in my stare. The servants have colorful halos, too. Pinks and greens and purples and oranges. All different textures and lively with movement. I notice that old Victoria looks particularly moved by Astrid's arrival, as does Quinn, who smiles sweetly, at the same time keeping her little chest puffed out at being able to witness such an important person's return. But when Kalliope and I descend the staircase, I catch a glimpse of Carliss in the wings. Her face is flushed and her eyes are red. She darts from the foyer to the courtyard outside.

I wish I could chase her.

"Come this way," says Freya, and my skin twinges at the sound of her voice. Part of me wants to pull her aside and spill the whole story, but then I remember how I left things by running off to Maytown instead of going to the safe house with the woman named Portia. If she ever believed that I had been swapped into Astrid's body, I doubt she would be happy to help me out of this mess.

At the front of the palace, an elaborate Tyjan carriage waits near the stairs. It's by far the most ornamental I've seen, with its blue and white gemstones notched to the wheel's spokes. A coachman opens the door for Kalliope and me, helping us inside with a gilded step. I settle on the slippery seat and Kalliope sits opposite with her elbow resting on the window frame. As the door shuts behind her, I stare outside at the flotilla of carriages parading across the bridge. Obviously the nobles who were visiting for the Tournament are still in Centriet—and they appear to be welcome at this event.

"Where are we going?" I ask.

"To the square," says Kalliope.

To the rest of Centriet, the "square" would describe many quarters in many different districts of the city, but to Kalliope, there is only one location worthy of the name in her small insular world. The square is the Emperor's Quadrant. It's a large private area used by the Tyjans for fairs and jousts and luscious outdoor theater productions. It takes us mere moments of bumping through the streets before we pass through its whorled iron gates. Once inside, the ground shimmers with pigment, forming intricate patterns in umber and crimson. Granite fountains spray crystalline water, offset by the backing of ivy-snarled fences.

The coachman slows the horses to a clop, steering us beneath a bright rouge awning. We join the carriages that have already halted, their outlines creating an arc on the cobbles.

At once I understand why we are here.

A trial. It must be a trial.

"The prisoners have been summoned?" I ask.

"Indeed they have," Kalliope replies.

None of the carriages open their doors.

"We stay inside," Kalliope explains.

"Why?" I ask.

"To keep us safe."

"How will we listen to what they say?"

Kalliope sighs and knits her brows as though I ask the silliest questions. She turns her attention to the shining glass as the remaining carriages choose their positions. Squinting into the dazzling sun, I'm able to distinguish a handful of nobles. Their hues dance. Even from this distance. As if their auras are eager to be noticed.

"This is so thrilling, is it not?" says Kalliope, and although I admit I was fortunate to board in her villa as opposed to that of her brother's, I cannot comprehend how she could be this elated about what is coming.

"I am nervous about it," I say. The instant the words leave my lips, I frown. I *am* nervous, but my stomach does not fold over on itself and my pulse does not race like a sailboat in the wind. It's a strange, empty feeling to know that I am anxious, but the emotion does not materialize physically. I'm unsure what to make of it, except that it must be something to do with being in a different body.

A moment later, a crowd of citizens enters the gates. Surrounded by soldiers on horseback, their bodies and clothing squeeze together, no air between as they shuffle and chatter. Gyzen jostles at the rim of the group, making certain none dawdle before reaching the middle of the square. They're not in any trouble as far as I can discern. More likely they've volunteered to take news of what happens here back to their families in the outer villages.

Once they're assembled, fresh motion erupts as a plain horse and wagon emerges from the street. As it draws nearer, silhouettes take shape, their features sharpening in the morning light, their figures shaking as they balance on the cart.

My palms grow damp.

These are the people from Knox's camp. I recognize Jordus and some of his comrades. Not all the people are present, I note as I try to count how many there are. Seven in total. The wagon stops in front of the crowd, just beside a stone wall. There are stains on the mortar that must have been scrubbed, though the telltale signs of redness remain.

"They were the ones who kept you from returning home to us," says Kalliope. "Why they believed they had the right, I do not know."

Another wagon appears in the Quadrant. This one houses six more people, shackled to the bars at the rear of the vehicle.

A small cry escapes my lips. Knox, the sole man, is cuffed among a gaggle of women. Sifting through the faces, I can't see Anai, but there is one girl I do recognize with long black hair and dark, scared eyes.

It's me.

Meadow.

Standing alone.

It's a nightmare come to life to witness myself so helpless and fraught. Instinctively, I stare at my new slender hands. I claw at the knuckles that will never be mine.

"What are they doing?" I choke to Kalliope as I'm unbuckled from the bar and led with the prisoners to the cobbles in front of the blood-splattered wall.

"They have to bear their punishments," she says. "It was a treacherous act that they were committing, keeping you a hostage in their filthy camp."

"But they didn't," I say.

Kalliope grunts, choosing not to acknowledge my words.

"Is this not a trial?"

"There was no need. My father decreed that the act was treason and sentenced all from the camp to death."

Everything spins. "He can't do that."

"What nonsense you speak. Of course he can."

"If I could talk to the emperor—"

"And what would you say? Would you really think to defy your sovereign?" There's a deep twang in Kalliope's tone. It does not match her usual pitch. But the longer we linger, the less chance there is that Ladislas could be offered the truth.

I rattle the door, but the metal holds. "He's going to murder those innocent people!"

"Do not say they are innocent," says Kalliope. "They are condemned because of their crimes."

"How do you know they are guilty?" I ask.

Her nostrils flare. "I just do."

"So you have no proof—"

"I don't need proof. My father has made his ruling already."

My blood simmers as I glare at her. How can she sit there and not understand? Knox and his followers are people above all. And people should at least get a trial. I bang my fists against the window, hoping the coachman will hear my call. But as with the time I was taken to the palace, the effort is futile, and he does not respond. Not only am I trapped in a foreign body, I'm also imprisoned in metal and glass. It's made more apparent when the noise outside swells as the citizens are driven to taunt the prisoners.

Knox is led to the sandbrick cube. It reminds me of the platform in Jove's cottage. The old man is roughly pushed. He sits with a jolt, his feet to the ground, shouting something I can't comprehend. His face twists as he combs the carriages, and then the prisoners, and the crowd before him. I wonder if he is searching for his son. I scan the periphery to find the soldier, and it is only by chance that I spot Gyzen—standing by an arch, his chest heaving.

"He used to work for your father," I say, and Kalliope pales. She must know I speak true.

"Did he tell you that?" she asks.

"Yes."

She swallows, preoccupied with Knox, too. No doubt she

knew of the old man when he worked in the palace advising her grandfather.

"Can you not do anything?" I ask.

"I cannot. He is the emperor and I am his daughter." Kalliope shifts, ruffling her skirts, unable to wrestle her gaze from the window. But then she says brightly, "And why would I want to? Knox is nothing but a ghastly traitor."

As she says the final reproachful word, a masked soldier strides behind Knox. Raising his sword, he strikes Knox's back. The point rips out the front of his chest, and the soldier shears it up and out through his shoulder. Knox slumps forward. As his forehead hits the cobbles, I press my face into the glass. The crowd cheers, but Gyzen turns—his shoulders quaking, his legs almost buckled.

Kalliope's silent as the corpse is lifted and heaved carelessly onto the wagon.

"Your father must be here," I plead. "In one of the carriages . . . We could implore him—"

"No." Her posture is flawless and she tosses her hair, her aura flashing like honeyed wine.

"You would let these people die?" I yell.

"It's not my place to interfere. The men—"

"You'd let the men decide?"

"Have you failed to notice that a man is our emperor?"

I'm about to shout back at her, but then Astrid is dragged forward. My vision distorts. I hammer the glass, the panic ignited, pouring out of my throat.

"Kalliope, please! This is wrong! Please! We have to stop this brutality now!"

"It is justice for you," she says.

"It's *not!*"

"In time it shall feel better," she vows.

Astrid plonks on the brick without fight, as though she's already gone from the world. She does not acknowledge the crowd or the soldiers. She might as well be swimming in the river or sleeping in a reed bed or drinking a mug of lukewarm broth. The color dancing around her head is light blue with rippling edges. It's streaked with patches of white and sea green. Foam and kelp. Clouds and forest. The perfect match for the hue of my own.

I yell the words that Casper taught me, even though if they worked, it would be me who would feel the pain. But I feel so much pain already. It's *me*. *Mine*. That body belongs to no one else. If it is going to be executed, then it should be me in it. It should be me to feel the triumphant agony. But Astrid's lips are closed. She does not speak, so it does not matter how much I shriek or how much Kalliope lunges at me and tries to make me fall into line.

"Good-bye," I whisper.

And the blade goes through her. I expect to feel just a little identical pain. But I feel nothing, despite pressing into my current chest. I howl as Astrid falls sideways on the stonebrick. I howl as my body is thrown in the wagon. I continue to howl as the others from the camp are delivered a similar fate before us.

And then there's a wagon full of lifeless bodies, and the crowd in the square is told to remain. They wait for the carriages to begin their departure. We move first.

Always the Tyjans.

"We're monsters," I say.

"Stop it," says Kalliope.

I shake my head. "Do you know what you've done?"

"Nothing," she says through gritted teeth.

"Exactly," I say. "You have done nothing."

Even through my curtain of tears, I catch the hollow look she gives me.

"You will pull yourself together," she says.

"How can you think what you saw here was just?"

Kalliope flops against the seat and ignores my presence for the rest of the journey. And as we roll past the noble houses, I wonder what the point of any of this is anymore.

When I am dead.

CHAPTER THIRTY

I REFUSE TO LEAVE MY ROOM FOR THE REST OF THE DAY. IT FEELS indulgent to barricade myself in such an opulent space when I am a girl from Maytown who lives, but whenever I inadvertently see my hands or catch a glimpse of the reflection that is not a reflection of me, I'm reminded over again of what happened in the noble district and that by all accounts, I could be viewed like this—as Astrid—for the rest of my natural life. And then I remember what my real body looked like as the sword split my chest in two. And I tumble to my knees, gagging, the tears streaking my unfamiliar face. No matter what I do, I cannot push the image from my head. Nor can my heart settle when I do not know what has become of Anai and my father.

It is well into the evening by the time I'm roused by a knock on the door. I'm inclined to feign a serious ailment, although it wouldn't be much of a lie. My eyes are sore and swollen from crying. Every limb is devoid of energy. Yes, my soul shattered when Vogel killed the tortured people in the tower, but at least I was able to function. This feels entirely different. It feels like an ache that no amount of sleep will be able to erase. And I scold myself for not having the strength to breathe in and strategize, but so many issues feel secondary to what happened to my old body— and the selfishness makes me weep anew.

It is only when the knock sounds again that I realize I am still trapped in my head.

"Come in," I force myself to say.

The doors open, and Carliss tiptoes in. She holds a bowl of broth from the kitchens, but she places it at the rear of the chamber. She does not bother carrying a spoon, so it seems unlikely she has come to feed me. Knotting her fingers, she scampers to my side and collapses to her knees on the carpet by my feet. Before I can tell her to get up, she lifts her chin and her eyes twitch in pain.

"Princess," she says. "I'm Carliss, a Midla. I am grateful beyond measure that you have returned to us."

I don't say anything.

"May I ask for your assistance?" When I still hesitate, she takes it as a sign to continue, and I should have known better, but I guess I am curious. "There was a boy who was arrested at the camp they found you in," she says. "I know I am not supposed to know these things, but I saw him outside. He is a friend of my family's and I would dearly love to visit him if you'll permit it."

The fib is a good one. She is talking about Vogel. And, of course, he is not a friend of her family's, but she cannot tell me the truth of their relations, even if I know more about the truth of their relations than she is aware.

"When did you see the boy? What is his name?"

"Vogel," she answers instantly. "I saw him being led to the holding cells by a pair of soldiers. It was after you had left with Princess Kalliope. I watched the passageway faithfully all afternoon, and he has not been removed from the dungeon. I am scared, Princess Astrid. I heard what happened to the other prisoners. I fear that they will do the same to Vogel now that he has been caught."

"What do you think I can do?" I ask.

"Allow me to visit him," she repeats.

"How?"

"Her Highness won't let me," she says. "But the soldiers must obey your orders." The way she speaks with a rising pitch change discloses that she isn't sure. But I have some questions of my own for Vogel. He might be the only one left who can help me—or fill me in on what happened to Anai.

"Did they arrest anyone else?" I ask.

"No one," Carliss replies, her eyes shining with hope that I'm considering her request. Her hue flares a bold red and copper. It possesses barbed edges that tumble and thrash.

But something doesn't quite make sense.

"You said you saw Vogel *after* we left?"

She nods.

"Then why did you look so upset? I saw you crying before we departed."

Redness crawls up Carliss's throat, splaying in patches across her cheeks. She cannot understand why a Tyjan princess would have paid so much heed to a lowly servant. It makes me curious what else she is hiding, but then her large eyes brim with water. These tears are different from the ones shed for Vogel, and yet they seem equally as genuine.

"I heard about one of the prisoners," she says. "I knew her. She was my friend."

I freeze, praying she won't say my name.

"Mollie," she sobs, and I breathe out.

Of course. Carliss had never known my true identity. She'd only known the reluctant servant who'd told her not to pursue the boy. I wonder what she would think of me now—if she knew that *I* had traveled with Vogel. That we'd slept in the cave. That we'd journeyed through the Sparselands. That we'd sheltered from the storm in a nook beneath a bridge.

"So will you help me, Princess?" Carliss asks.

I try to shove Vogel out of my mind. "I'll attempt to take you tonight," I say.

She stares. "Really?"

"I can only try."

"Thank you!" Carliss backs to the doors. "I will leave you to get cleaned up." She motions to the broth bowl. "Please eat something. The Grande says you must be famished."

And with that, she slips into the hall before I can stop her or change my mind. I'm suddenly plagued with a barrage of doubts. Would visiting a prisoner really be simple? Would everyone truly believe I'm a Tyjan? I do not know, but if I look the part, then perhaps the odds would be tipped in my favor. As I murmur and pace, I'm distinctly aware that her request has granted me a second wind.

I leap up and creak open the closet, searching for the most regal dress I can find. I finally locate one that's studded with embellishments, slipping on leather sandals to match. Astrid's feet are slimmer than mine. Her ankles, too, are particularly narrow. And I wonder for how long I will think of my old body. Will I eventually forget what it felt like being me? Will my memories fade a little more each night until Meadow Sircha dissolves in the wind?

When I venture onto the landing, Tallesa rushes over to greet me with a bow. "What can I do for you, Your Highness?" she asks.

"Clean my quarters," I say.

"As you wish." She disappears inside without asking any questions, and I almost feel sad that the girl who butted heads with me has been reduced to fawning obedience. Either she believes wholeheartedly in her role as Midla, or she has witnessed too often the consequences when Midlas do not conform.

Nevertheless, with Tallesa occupied, I descend the staircase into the foyer. No longer empty of all but servants, tonight there are noble women lounging on chaises, dipping their feet in the petal-drenched bathing pool. The servants are still present, of course, but they hang back, holding silver platters of raisins and sliced plums. Candles smoke in the four corners, and a persistent haze settles by the rafters, the dizzying fragrance misting my sight.

Kalliope flits over as I step onto the tiles. She's recovered well from our carriage ride, her yellow hair newly washed and styled, sweet white blossoms threaded through her curls. She leaves behind three red-haired women whose eyes bore into my profile. When it's apparent I shall not be introduced, one of them calls for a fresh jug of wine.

"I have told them you are one of the noble's daughters," Kalliope says softly, guiding me clear of the bathing pool and out the back exit I know so well from being a servant. "The Midlas and Lissettes are aware of your identity, but the emperor wishes to officially announce you tomorrow night at the royal banquet."

"The royal banquet?"

Kalliope nods. "It is a celebration of the Tournament's conclusion. The king of Leeang will be in attendance."

I make a face. "He will? *Why?*"

"Why? Because it was one of his gladiators who prevailed." Kalliope squeezes my arm in camaraderie, as if my shouting in the carriage never happened and we are now—and always will be—the firmest of friends. "He is an important ally to our kingdom," she explains. "My father will go above and beyond to show him the prosperity of our city. He is even preparing the famed Victoreglia for King Rolyo's viewing pleasure. It will take place the morning after the banquet and you and I shall be part of the audience."

I vaguely associate the term Victoreglia with an ancient custom used to honor the winning kingdom of the Tournament. From what I know, it is bloody and cruel, but my thoughts are elsewhere and Kalliope notices.

"Where is your mind?" she asks.

"Nowhere."

"It does not seem like nowhere," she says. "Fear not, dear Astrid. The banquet is mainly for show. I promise it is not solely to rejoice in your return. No eyes shall be looking upon you. At least not until your true identity is revealed."

My true identity.

I suppress a cough, realizing that I need some air. I begin to walk toward the foyer, but Kalliope steps in front of me.

"Where are you going?"

"Outside," I say. "The scent from the candles is terribly potent."

"You may not remember the palace," she says, "since so many years have passed since you've been here."

As if on command, Carliss steps into the passage and bows low to both of us.

A frown crosses Kalliope's face. "Go back into the kitchens, Midla."

I wait for Carliss to protest—but she doesn't—although she throws a look my way. I recall how she said that the soldiers would obey me.

"Couldn't she show me about the grounds?"

Kalliope seems offended by my question, but she bites back her distaste with a casual smile. "She's needed in the kitchens, Astrid. Banquet preparation takes a lot of hands."

"But . . ." says Carliss, and Kalliope glares with so much venom that the Midla retreats.

"Excuse me for a moment," says the princess. "I must make certain she returns to her duties."

She disappears with a whip of her hair, abandoning me in the hall. I hope Carliss avoids reprimanding; but then, she'd be reckless to forget her place.

But I don't linger. With the path unhindered, I retreat toward the middle square. Carliss will be terribly upset when she learns I've visited Vogel alone. And yet I'm filled with a sense of relief. Speaking to Vogel about Anai would be awfully difficult if she were present. And besides, if Vogel had only used Carliss, I cannot imagine their reunion would be pleasant.

Unsurprisingly, it is a lot easier to make my way to the dungeon when I am wrapped in a Tyjan body. True, none of the soldiers know that I am supposedly Princess Astrid, but with my gown and sleek appearance, they know that I am at least of noble blood. The soldiers nod or stand to attention as I saunter past, not looking at them. One word from me and they could be dismissed. The inner power is strangely thrilling.

Even so, when I arrive at the basement, a soldier asks me why I am here. Instinctively I hide my face, before realizing my face is actually the key.

"There is a prisoner I wish to speak with," I say, using my most commanding voice. "Lead me to the boy who was brought from the camp. His name is Vogel, I understand."

"Does the emperor know about this?" asks the soldier.

"He will know soon enough if you dare question one of his noble guests." I keep my tone level and assured, and after a moment, the soldier relents.

If only everything in life was that easy, but maybe it is if you are born into the right family in Centriet. I begin my descent into the torchlit darkness, following the soldier down the ramp, curving swiftly around the bend. We pass two more soldiers, who are guarding from within. When they see me, they allow me to pass without comment. In fact, they move out of the way so I can stroll through without having to break my stride. It is galling that I command so much respect from these men who would have so easily clapped and cheered while a sword punctured my heart if I were in my real body.

The soldier unlocks a door for me and pulls it open. It is dark inside.

"Give me that torch." I point to the hallway light.

The soldier lifts it off the bracket and passes it to me. I step inside the enclosed space and the soldier roots his feet in the stones.

"Leave me," I say.

"It could be dangerous," he objects.

"Did you not hear what I requested?" I ask. "Leave me and I will knock on the door when I am ready for you to escort me back."

"As you wish."

I inch inside and the soldier closes the door. As the wood

clunks in place, I contemplate whether I've made a grievous error. But then I see Vogel crouched on the floor. He is wide-awake and whole, the flicker of the flames beating against his cheek. He regards me warily, an ethereal turquoise and silver flitting above his crown. When he registers who I am, his eyes swell. He rises from his sitting position and drops to one knee, his shoulders shaking as he bows his head.

"Your Highness," he says.

"Do not start with that nonsense." I attach the torch to a brace on the wall and sit on the stones beside him.

He glances up, surprised. "Princess, your language has been restored." When I look at him closely, his eyes are wide, but distress is clearly wound through his features.

"It has been." I cross my legs, the coldness seeping through the fabric of my skirt. It's peculiar. It's almost as if Vogel is not aware what has happened. But shouldn't he know that I'm Meadow inside? After all, he was the one who shouted at me not to say the Marascan words. I gesture with a palm for him to rise, and the shock trickles from his face. He pushes himself into a corner, scrunching his fists, his hue bouncing.

"What do you remember?" he asks.

"Only darkness."

"And before that?"

"Nothing clear. Would you tell me what happened? How did I come to be here now?"

He winces—I'm sure of it. Astrid wasn't meant to return to the palace. She was meant to remain in the hidden valley, plotting revolution with Knox and his followers. Vogel is silent, staring at the brickwork, wiping his face with the backs of his hands. "You really don't remember?" He's likely concerned that if she's forgotten everything, then their plan has failed.

And I don't want that, so I lie—and tell him I remember parts of the camp. If he thinks my memory needs only a prod, he may reveal more secrets to me. I speak of the shelters and the barrels of ale and the day the soldiers poured down the hill. "There was one girl I recall in particular. She was sad because she'd lost her father."

Vogel exhales. "Her name was Meadow." The way he speaks my name with such care makes me wonder how he could have deceived me.

"How did you know her?" I ask, and he tenses.

"I do not wish to speak of her now."

"Why not?"

"Because . . ." And he turns away. "I heard about what happened in the square." There's pain in his face. So much pain. Like he's actually distraught that he sent me to my doom.

"Why her?" I ask.

"What do you mean?"

"Why did you need to bring *Meadow* to the camp?"

He glances at the torchlight, tussling with himself, and I'm afraid he'll close off altogether.

"Tell me," I whisper. "I need to know."

Vogel sighs, his eyes growing distant. I long to reach inside his head and pull him back, but then he shrugs. "Knox believed you were under a spell. After escaping the mines, he visited you twice. He said that the first time you spoke at length. On his second visit, your language had gone." He rubs his forearm. "Knox knew it was magic. How it happened though, he wasn't sure. But in the following days, he entered the Sparselands. And he found out how we could break the spell."

"With Meadow?" I ask.

Vogel nods—but slowly, as if my name hurts to hear. "It had to be someone with the same day of birth, so Knox sent scouts to every main city."

This is not what I'd expected. "And you found Meadow."

"By accident," he says. "We had her name, but we couldn't locate her. We were readying to leave when she came to our cottage." His attention drifts from the cell again, the memory tugging him back to that night. "When Prince Malthe took her, she called out her name, and we knew from that moment we had to trail her."

Tightness pulls my chest inward. They had planned this. They'd been searching for me. I don't know whether to cry or to scream, but I want to know more, which means I do neither. I wriggle closer to where he sits. "And they had to say the Marascan words."

Vogel blinks. "The Marascan words?"

"Vierre mon sur, plasir mes yeemas."

"You remember that," he says with surprise, his eyes flitting back to my face. "They were the words to break the enchantment, but I'm fairly certain they're not Marascan."

So Casper lied. I almost laugh at how naïve I was. How trusting. How obtuse. "And after the words were spoken," I say, "what was supposed to happen to Meadow?"

"We didn't know." Vogel pauses, looking even more troubled than he had at the start. "Knox promised the words would bring back your language. As for Meadow . . . we weren't sure."

And there it is. The horrible truth. Princess Astrid would be healed, my life be damned.

"You believed that the Tyjans were more important?"

"Of course not, Princess."

"I am not the princess."

He stares at me for the longest time as the meaning of my words spool in his head. "You're not Princess Astrid?" he asks.

"I'm not. So you see, your revolting plan didn't work."

Vogel's eye grow rounder. "Meadow?"

I nod. "Look what you've done to me."

Water gleams between his lashes, and he drags himself closer, grabbing my hands. "You're *Meadow*?"

"Yes, of course, I'm Meadow!" I pull away. He has no right to touch me.

"How did this happen?"

"How do you think? It was you and Casper and Knox that did this!"

Whatever he was going to say, he stops. He stops as though all words elude him. It's like the basement has filled with ocean and we're both underwater and can't make a sound.

"I'm so sorry," he says, at last.

"You're sorry?"

"I am. Beyond all words."

"I'm trapped in her body forever," I tell him. "Sorry means nothing. Not anymore."

"You're right." And he lowers his head again, and I hate that I feel his pain in my chest. "I didn't know this would happen," he whispers.

"But you must have known it was something bad!" Fire blazes inside my belly, so I stare at the wall to focus my thoughts. The last thing I need is for the soldiers to come upon hearing me shouting at one of their prisoners. I inspect the patterns and steady my breathing, even though my arms still tremble by my sides. "You told me you got close to Carliss in the palace because you wanted to save Jove. But it wasn't Jove you came for, was it? It was me. You found out that I was born on the same day as Astrid and you wanted to get into the palace for *me*."

By the look on his face, I have discovered the truth. He doesn't try to defend himself.

"I wondered why you were so much nicer. Why you'd changed from that boy that I met at the Gathering." He'd needed me to trust him, I realize. To believe that he cared about my father. And I, like a fool, had fallen for his lies.

"I'm sorry, Meadow."

"Stop saying you're sorry!"

Tipping his head against his shoulder, he closes his eyes as if I've slapped him. "I did try to tell you," he says.

"In Helliam?" I scoff. "That was a little too late."

"I know that." His mouth has set, and a line ridges from

his jaw to his collar. "You have to understand, I didn't know if I should. I didn't know—"

"If you could trust me?" I ask.

"It wasn't that." He wrings his sleeve, and I notice the patches of dried red stains. There are more on his cuffs, some near his stomach. Remembering the boy who was kicked in the village, I'm sure Farrow didn't hold back with Vogel. "We'd been working on this plan for so long," he says. "For the past year, it was our sole focus. I didn't know if my mind was just clouded. I needed to get myself together before I thought about setting you free."

"And what do you think now?" I ask.

"I wish I could have saved you," he says. "When I thought you'd died in the Emperor's Quadrant, I hated myself for doing that to you." His pain is real. It's horribly real. It's a bone-deep sadness like when he spoke of his sister. It pierces my heart, but I cannot forgive him. Not when I think of how much has been taken.

"I watched myself get executed," I say. "And I'm stuck like this. Trapped in the body of the ruling family that I hate. They killed my mother through their selfishness and now I'm just supposed to live as one of them? I don't want to be this person. Princess or not. I'm not *me*."

"Perhaps there's a way . . ." Vogel shakes his head, as if suddenly recalling my body has gone. My breath hitches as I think of it, too. I won't be given a committal to sea. I'll be buried or burned or tossed away without a marker to profess I existed.

I stand up on Astrid's legs. Despite it all, they're firm and strong. "Do you know what happened to Anai or my father? The truth this time."

He shakes his head. "I do not know where your father is, but I was telling the truth when I said he was alive. As for Anai, I have no way of knowing. I didn't see her after the soldiers arrived."

She wasn't executed in the square, but that does not make me any less anxious. I turn swiftly and walk to the wall, grabbing the torch.

"Meadow," he calls.

I pause, poised to knock for the soldier.

"Please let me say just one last thing."

I don't want to listen anymore, but I drop my fist. "You must speak quickly."

He nods. "You should know that in the end I realized what we were doing was wrong. I thought I was doing it for my family—to avenge their deaths at any cost. That was the mission. Or I thought it was. But I couldn't have been more misguided. And when you told me in the tavern that my sister was a saver of people, it dawned on me that this is not what she would have wanted me to do. She would have hated it. She would have looked at me, not as her big brother, but as one of them."

"One of who?"

"She would have told me not to be like the Tyjans."

"A Tyjan like me." The thought stings. I take a step closer to the door. And whatever he says next—it could be apologies, it could be protests that it's not what he meant—I shut it out.

I shut him out.

And I knock.

CHAPTER THIRTY-ONE

I DON'T KNOW WHAT TO THINK ABOUT VOGEL. MY INSIDES ARE ALL cramped up. When I burst from the entrance and am wrapped in the cool night air, I can't help feeling deep inside that I should hate him more.

But I don't.

I can't help it.

Needing a place to dwell on this longer, I head toward Kalliope's villa. I'm just about to squeeze through the pillars when a willowy shadow skitters from a column.

It's Kalliope herself.

She merges with the evening, a brown shawl draped across her shoulders. She turns and barrels through a series of arches that, up until this point, I had not noticed. A red-haired woman pops from the villa, scouring the square to locate the princess. She treads on the lawn and follows a pathway, heading for the foot of Malthe's tower.

It's then another shadow zags by and Kalliope enters her villa again. I pursue her footsteps through a side conservatorium, stopping at the doorway to the servants' rear courtyard.

Kalliope unlocks the gate. She heaves it open and patters outside. The wood sits ajar, so I dart past the cauldrons and wedge behind it, my ear to the gap.

"What have you got in the bag this time?" an unrecognizable male voice asks with impatience.

"Jewels," says Kalliope.

"It's difficult," he says.

"They do not have any markings," she tells him.

"It doesn't matter," the man begins, but Kalliope cuts him off with a hiss.

"I understand the position this may put you in, but I have made certain not to wear them in public."

I'm entranced by her responsible timbre, so different to the flighty indifference I'm used to. Perhaps she's more than her outward projection.

"We still have our buyers in the north," says the man.

"Good," says Kalliope. "That should tide us over until the end of the season at least. After that, we can try the merchants in the west."

"Yes, Your Highness," the man replies.

There's a soft sound of tinkles and ribbons as the princess passes her wares to his hands. He unbuckles and buckles something with a flap.

"And how is Portia?" Kalliope asks.

My ears prick at the name. *Portia?* The woman with whom Freya had wanted me to stay?

"She's well," says the man. "She misses her home, but I guess that is natural, given the circumstances."

"It is," says the princess, "but do send word if the workload become too much to bear. It's demanding at present with the guests for the Tournament, but when it is over, we can reassess."

"Thank you," he says. "Go in safety."

"And you."

His footsteps ebb into the night. Kalliope lingers a little longer on the grass. Through the gap, I see her watching Lake Lirye, as the moonbeams wisp the surface with white. If the princess knows Portia, then she must work with Freya. And Errol. And Pelletier. And perhaps even Gyzen. When I caught her entering the palace through the servant door, she may have been meeting with someone in secret. But then I remember when I met Ladislas—and how she'd allowed him to give me to Malthe. She'd been bored that evening. Bored and erratic. And she wouldn't have saved me, just like in the Quadrant.

Kalliope strides toward the courtyard, and I dive behind a lopsided cauldron. The rusted metal is rough on my cheek, and the smell of soap and linen is pungent. She swishes past, breathing hard, checking that no one observes from the kitchens. If there was ever a good time to confront her about this, it would be now.

"Princess, wait!"

I rise from the cauldron, but she's already gone. Her footsteps click through the villa like raindrops. I stick to the walls, my gait unsteady, as she winds like a thief through the adjacent chambers. She vanishes into the center of the palace. The noble women are still in the foyer. Their laughter and clapping and conversational tones keep the interior humming with life.

But I keep following. I need to know—if I can trust her, if we can be allies. Kalliope's outline darts through the pillars, veering outside to the square once more. I tail her figure under the arches. The shadows paint wobbly black crescents on the bricks. They split and reform as she runs through the torchlight, scattering the stones of the path in her midst.

She makes it to the end of the track, where pine trees grow in a secluded circle. Their tops point up like bloated spears that sway beneath the wide dark sky. It must be a place for quiet reflection, away from the hounding and gossip of nobles. She steals inside, and I'm left on the track with the rustle of the breeze nipping my shoulders.

I walk on.

There's a noise up ahead. Quiet at first, like crackling leaves. It isn't loud, but the closer I get, the more it sounds like somebody struggling.

I creep along faster, my heart in my mouth. The fracas is coming from inside the trees. Does someone know of Kalliope's secret? Did they hear her outside when she passed on her jewels? I skid over the last bit of path, pushing the pine needles back with my hands. As I plunge through, the noise increases. Then the air shifts and everything sharpens.

And there, framed in the middle of the foliage, are Princess Kalliope and the soldier, Gyzen. His arms are clasped around her waist. She stands on her toes, her face pressed to his. My intake of breath makes them jump. They stare at me and I stare at them.

"I'm sorry," I mumble, tripping back. "I didn't realize . . . I'm really sorry."

Before they react, I take my leave, stumbling out, my face glowing red. The loose stones slide beneath my sandals as I hasten to make it back to the villa. I do not hear their footsteps behind me, so I slow to a jog to reset my bearings.

Kalliope and Gyzen.

A covert couple.

What do I do with this information?

I haven't a clue and I'm still startled, but obviously, I will keep it to myself. If the emperor found out—if *Malthe* found out—the consequences would be terribly grim.

I'm finally nearing the edge of the square when a figure lunges in front of me. I pull up quickly and throw out my palms. They land in the middle of Farrow's shirt. His stink is the same as it was on the road. Sweaty and horse-haired.

"Princess?" he says.

"Soldier," I say, hiding my alarm.

"What are you doing out here by yourself?" He doesn't speak with any suspicion. If anything, he uses a fatherly tone.

I clear my throat, raising my voice. "I do not need your permission for a stroll."

"I was not suggesting such a thing," says Farrow. "I was simply looking for a soldier named Gyzen. By any chance, have you seen him out here?"

"Yes," I tell him.

"You have? Where?"

"Near South and East Gates."

"Thank you, Princess." Farrow bows, slinking back the way he came. Behind me, I hear a sigh of relief. Kalliope emerges, and she is alone.

"What are you doing out here?" she snaps coldly.

"I just—"

"You just what? Go back into the villa."

"You can trust me," I tell her.

She narrows her eyes. "I have nothing to say that requires your trust."

"But you and the soldier, I would never tell—"

"I would deny it unequivocally," Kalliope says. She sweeps past, leaving me on the path. But I don't follow. "Come on," she says.

I turn my body back to the arches, and she must realize that I could approach Gyzen. "Don't," she says. "Please come along." She marches toward me and takes my hands.

I hesitate.

"If my father found out . . . I do not know what he would do."

Neither do I, but I could make a fine guess. Soldiers and Tyjans are not supposed to mix. I do not believe that the princess would suffer, but Gyzen would be slaughtered—perhaps in the ring.

I nod.

"Come on," she says again.

"Your secret is safe with me," I say.

"Thank you, Astrid."

"But can I ask you something?"

"Not tonight."

And she walks away.

CHAPTER THIRTY-TWO

THE NEXT MORNING I HAD HOPED TO SPEAK TO KALLIOPE about the jewels and Portia and now this new development with Gyzen, but she is absent from the villa when I try to find her. Freya informs me she is touring the countryside with the king of Leeang. Apparently it is a normal occurrence for the princess to act as Centriet's guide. I inwardly hope that she is all right, although Freya doesn't seem the slightest bit worried. In response to my pinched look, she promises no harm will come to Kalliope. Still, I hope there's an escort with her. Just in case. Then I think about Gyzen being her escort and I feel worse.

After morning meal, I head to the kitchens to find Carliss. She is kneading dough on a wooden board, her face smothered with flour and paste. When the rest of the kitchen servants notice my arrival, they offer me cherries and roasted nuts.

"I wish to speak to this Midla," I say.

Welsha nods and pushes Carliss in the small of her back. "Wash your hands before you go to her, you filthy child."

Carliss dunks her hands in a basin and scrubs under her fingernails. Then, to the awe of the Midlas and Midlons, she silently trails me into the foyer. We climb the staircase en route to my chamber, and Tallesa rushes to intercept us. Instead, I tell her to proceed downstairs and clean the tiles in the bathing pool.

Tallesa's eyes are daggers at Carliss, but her voice rings

pleasant. "Of course, Your Highness." Her feet patter along the corridor as she rushes to retrieve a pail and cloth.

"She will loathe me forever," Carliss says, the moment we're safely inside my room. She buries her toe in the plush carpet as I latch the handles with a gold hook and ring.

Once it's in place, I spin around. Carliss's hands are pressed at the palms. She knocks her thumbs against her chest, her attention turning to Vogel again. "Did you speak to him? Was he in the dungeon?"

"He was in the basement cells," I confirm.

"Are they feeding him?"

"I do not know."

"And did you find out what they're planning to do?"

I shrug because I don't know that, either. In fact I realize I discovered almost nothing. Nothing about Vogel's wellbeing, at least. And suddenly I feel disgustingly selfish.

"Could you talk to the emperor?" Carliss asks.

I'm shocked by the way she speaks so boldly.

"Perhaps he could be pardoned," she says.

Her optimism is sweet, but faulty. If Ladislas were to do anything of note, it would be to push for a swift execution.

"I just wanted to let you know he's alive."

"But for how long?" Carliss asks. "They arrested someone else, you know. She was brought from the Nothrick Prison this morning."

My heart ticks faster. Could it be Anai?

"Who brought her in?"

"Prince Malthe's patrol."

"Where did they take her?"

"To the prince's villa." Carliss's interest begins to wane.

But mine picks up. It *might* be Anai. Vogel surmised she'd escaped in the forest. The soldiers could have scooped her up later and taken her straight to a Nothrick cell. And since she's now been brought to the tower, then Malthe must have plans for her.

Plans that may involve benches and blood. Plans I cannot bear to consider.

"What did the girl look like?" I ask.

"Brawny. Blonde, I think."

Perhaps it isn't Anai after all, but no one deserves to be tortured by Malthe. Up until now, I've tried to avoid him. Even contained in Astrid's body. But if there's a chance I can use this face to save someone's life, then I need to be brave.

"You should go back to the kitchens," I say.

"What will you do about Vogel?" asks Carliss.

"I'm not sure." She begins to protest, but I shake my head and she falls silent. I feel bad. I really do. I know what it's like to feel helpless and afraid. "I will do what I can," I reassure her. "I know he means a lot to you."

Her eyes flash but she leaves without comment, and I wait until her steps disappear. In her absence, I attempt to muster my courage, but the more I search, the harder it hides. In the end, I drag myself to the hallway, sweat slicking my warm skin. I tell myself to act without thinking, which is not ideal, but it gets my feet moving.

And then I'm on my way to Malthe's villa to find out more about the girl. I avert my gaze as I pass through the foyer, though no one tries to gain my attention. The smell of blossoms swirls outside as I triple my speed across the square. But my nerves spring forth as the tower looms. I spy the willow where I hid with Vogel, the track by the storehouse, and the door to the storeroom. I trace the grass where I bolted from the tunnel. Indents from the chairs remain in the lawn.

Move. Just move.

I shuffle on, and then I'm standing at the mouth of the tower. I repeat to myself that I'm in no danger. That no one would tie Princess Astrid to a table.

A soldier strides through the entrance hall. When his eyes snag mine, his features tense.

"Gyzen," I say.

"Princess," he whispers.

"Would I be permitted to come inside?"

There's fear in his eyes like I have never seen as he tries to bring his emotions in line. "What do you need in Prince Malthe's quarters?"

He thinks I am going to turn him in.

"Nothing to do with last night," I say.

Gyzen's shoulders do not relax. Threadlike redness mars his eyeballs as if he's had not a wink of sleep. "Thank you," he says.

"But I need your help."

He nods, almost mystified that I should ask for his assistance.

"A prisoner was brought from the Nothrick Prison. Do you know her name?"

"Siella," he says.

I'm quite surprised that he knows her name—and moreso by his hasty reply. Perhaps the fatigue has loosened his tongue.

"Why has she been brought to the tower?"

Gyzen thins his eyes at me. He must be wondering how I know so much—or why I am so suspicious of Malthe. He tightens his arms in front of his chest. "The activities of the prince are his alone."

"If she's in trouble in there," I say, "I would ask that you help her. To get her out."

"I cannot," says Gyzen. "It is never wise for a soldier to disobey his prince." His lips twitch, yet he cannot conceal it, and I know he's thinking about his father.

"Let me speak to Prince Malthe," I say.

"He does not wish to be disturbed," says Gyzen.

I move to push past because I am a Tyjan, but Gyzen throws his arm across the doorway.

"You have no authority in here," he says. "You need to go back to your current residences."

I contemplate threatening to spill his secret about his kiss with

Kalliope last night. But what would that prove? If I entered the villa, I could hardly get Siella out. And I want Gyzen on my side. There are very few soldiers who display any kindness. But his loyalty to Malthe is truly vexing, no matter what he believes inside.

"The prince is not here," Gyzen whispers. "He is with his sister entertaining King Rolyo. The prisoner will be quite safe for now. She will not be harmed if that's what concerns you."

"Why won't you help her?" I ask.

Gyzen sighs. "I am sorry. Really. But I have my orders." Noises echo in the chamber behind him, and he turns side-on. "Is there anything else?"

He says it like he thinks there is not, like he's managed to dissuade me from asking too much. But there is something I need from him.

"A spare from the Training Rounds didn't die."

"A spare?"

"Yes." And I see the memory rise and fall in his onyx stare. He must remember my father in the ring. The one he shot in the flank with his arrow. "I want to know what happened to that man. Where is he now?"

"I have no idea."

I cannot tell if he's lying or not.

"You need to find out."

"Why?"

"Because." I do not remind him again of Kalliope, but my glare alone is enough to persuade him.

"Very well. I will do what I can and I'll let you know if I discover anything." He nods past my shoulder, and I pivot on the spot. A soldier stands on the grass behind me.

"Excuse me," he says, bowing low. "But Emperor Ladislas requests that you join him."

✦

Emperor Ladislas is waiting for me in the throne room. The moment the doors close behind me, he lifts his arm and waves me forward. When I reach the foot of the stairs, I realize we're alone. Not even his turtle-nosed advisor is here to witness our meeting.

"Astrid," says the emperor. "Welcome home." He speaks without smiling, Astrid's royal title eluding him, it seems.

I curtsy to give him a semblance of respect, but my palms and the back of my neck grow damp.

"You have been treated well?" he asks.

"Yes, Your Majesty."

"Most pleasing to hear." As he squints at me, he wriggles on his cushion. "I was told you were kept as a prisoner in the forest?"

I swallow, wondering the specifics he craves. "I was, yes."

"And before?" he asks. His voice is sharp. "You'll understand my confusion . . . not knowing where you've been for all these years."

He certainly doesn't mince his words—and I'm worried how much is safe to reveal. So I tell him the truth. "My memory escapes me. Before being kidnapped is just a blur."

When I do not elaborate, he paws at his sleeve, pulling out a silken cloth. As he blows his nose, I avert my eyes. He takes his time, as if I'm a servant.

"No memory?" he says, when he's finally finished. Sniffing, he wipes his upper lip.

"Perhaps it will never come back," I say.

Ladislas folds his hands. "Perhaps."

There's a long pause. The emperor slumps back, and it dawns on me the reason I'm here. Ladislas knows that Astrid is a Tyjan. His half sister with a tragic history. And although she has less claim to the throne, of course, her presence would make him concerned.

So I need to give him cause to relax.

Cause for him to leave me alone.

"Your soldiers saved my life," I say. "Without them . . . I can't bear to think it." I watch his eyes narrow and widen. "I'll forever be in their debt. And yours."

He runs a finger over his whiskers.

"Do you mean to keep me here?" I ask.

"Do you wish to stay?"

"If you allow it, Your Grace. I understand that I may not deserve it."

He scrutinizes my face and my body, as if he is searching for something within. My head roars. Does he believe what I'm saying? Or does he think I'm a danger to his crown? But I cannot draw the thoughts from his skull, and after a moment, he lets out a sigh.

"It's pleasing to have you back, little sister. I look forward to your presence at the banquet this evening."

I curtsy again because he smiles. A smile that's easy to recognize. It's a smile of relief. I am just a girl. No threat to him. No threat to his rule.

"Thank you, Your Majesty."

He motions me to leave, and I turn to the follow the aisle to the doors. And it's only when I emerge in the sunshine that I realize what I may have avoided.

CHAPTER THIRTY-THREE

THE BANQUET HALL IS ADORNED WITH FRESH FLOWERS, hanging garlands, and long tables with white-cushioned benches. The cushions are edged with scarlet tassels and are finely stitched with golden thread. I didn't know golden thread existed. Well, not to be used for the material attached to a chair. Then again, I didn't know candles could be made with luminous blue wax or that anyone—emperor or otherwise—could afford over one hundred silver bowls, simply for guests to wash their fingers.

I take my allocated seat next to two noble women, who appear to only speak Leeangi. I wonder whether Kalliope had a hand in placing me between people who would not ask me any questions. If she had, I am thankful for it, although she may have done so out of fear that I would reveal her secret. Not that I blame her. After what happened to Gyzen's father, even I'm apprehensive that word will get out.

Smoothing the emerald silk of my dress, I focus on the dinner spread. Patterned bowls are filled with boiled vegetables and cuts of meat are served on bronze trays. I spoon some food onto my meal board, then fork the delicacies into my mouth. Though I'm grateful for each bite, I can't help reflecting on the unfairness of it all. I imagine the difference among my father's, Anai's, and Vogel's experiences right now, and it makes the salted beef and peppered carrot taste like guilt between my teeth.

Angling my body to the front of the room, I observe the emperor at his raised table. On his left are Kalliope and Malthe. On his right is the king of Leeang. I scrutinize Rolyo with his long dark hair and his clear complexion, almost like marble. He passes his meal board to a rotund servant, who shaves the meat into thin slices. The king does not look at anyone in particular, though he seems relaxed with his elbows on the linen. Quite the opposite to Emperor Ladislas, whose forehead and jugular shine with sweat. Kalliope pats her father on the arm. She is smiling and sunny like she always is, as if nothing around her is worthy of a frown. Malthe feasts on beans and roast sprouts. He must have had a good day with Rolyo, for his shoulders have dropped and he's positively beaming.

The bald man I'd seen at the arena rings a bell that's attached to the wall. The sound makes everyone lay down their cutlery, and Ladislas rises, brushing crumbs from his tunic. He gestures to the king beside him.

"I would like to congratulate King Rolyo of Leeang. We welcome him as the victor of the Tournament. His sensational gladiator, Elyor Vass, has become the newest, unvanquished champion."

Elyor Vass, the man I had seen destroy one of the spares on the opening day of the Tournament, is sitting on the end of a row of tables, stuffing spiced pork into his mouth. He holds up a goblet of ale as the nobles clap civilly at his vulgar presence.

"As the winning kingdom of the Tournament, King Rolyo is entitled to a Victoreglia," Ladislas continues. "For those who do not know of this ancient custom, it dates back to the early contests held by our forefathers. The Victoreglia is a show of respect. The winning kingdom is permitted to bring two animals of their choice to face a gladiator from each of the losing kingdoms. As the winner, Leeang will provide the animals and Erraforge and Torquella will provide the gladiators to die for the king's enjoyment."

"Our animals are fearsome beasts," boasts King Rolyo. "I hope your gladiators are prepared to be ripped to pieces." He chuckles loudly, and Ladislas joins him, making everyone else in the room follow suit.

Not me.

"Do you have a gladiator remaining?" Emperor Ladislas asks a man who sits farther to his right than King Rolyo. I recognize the man as High Sovereign Zementa of Torquella.

"We have Pollard Reynes," says the High Sovereign.

"No, no!" King Rolyo interjects. "Pollard Reynes lost an arm in his match, did he not? We require a whole gladiator. Those are the rules."

The High Sovereign relents. "It will be done."

King Rolyo nods deftly, as though it never should have been something up for discussion in the first place. He slides his golden eyes toward Ladislas.

"And yourself, Emperor? Do you have a gladiator to meet my chosen beast?"

"We do," Ladislas answers at once, as though he had been waiting for the question and has carefully prepared a measured response. "Our rogue gladiator who escaped the Tournament was recently apprehended. His participation will be a fine way to pay us back for his cowardly sins."

I can't believe Emperor Ladislas means to enter Vogel in the Victoreglia. No wonder Malthe looks so pleased with himself. And no wonder Vogel was not executed with the other people from the camp.

"I look forward to it immensely," says King Rolyo, combing his glossy black hair with his fingers.

"But of course," says Ladislas with a simpering smile. "And now for my next announcement!"

I swallow thickly and reach for more water, knowing the attention will soon be on me.

"Stand, my daughter," says Ladislas.

Kalliope keeps her smile pasted on, but she's clearly shocked by the sudden request. Nevertheless, she obeys her father. She stands and displays her orchid-white teeth.

"Allow me," says King Rolyo.

"By all means," says Ladislas.

The way he defers so quickly to the king reminds me of what Knox had mentioned.

"Princess Kalliope shall be joining me on my voyage back to Leeang," says Rolyo.

Her smile slips at the edges. "I shall?"

"*You shall.*" Emperor Ladislas makes no mistake. "You, my dearest and loveliest daughter, are to wed King Rolyo's eldest son."

It's horrific news. His eldest son is the crown prince of the Island of Leeang. And that would mean that Princess Kalliope would be forced to live away from her home.

But she smiles, ever the respectful daughter, and stretches her lips even wider than before. I'm sure the rest of the room is astounded, but they break into heartfelt applause and stamp their boots and sandals on the floor. Kalliope sits on the bench, her cheeks burning. She keeps her gaze on the meal board and fork. It wasn't the plan. I can tell by her eyes that die a little as the light in them dims. I can almost see the cogs of her mind, writhing and flailing, as she tries to stay calm. But a few moments later, she stands up again. "Excuse me, Father. I am feeling unwell."

She slides her legs over the bench, ignoring the host of disapproving murmurs. Then her heels tap an off-key medley and she vanishes swiftly through a side door.

The hall fills with terrible silence. King Rolyo's fists clench and release. The whites of his eyes bulge with veins at being dismissed by the emperor's daughter. I want to follow the princess outside, but I do not dare to lift my feet. No one does. In fact, no one moves. Frightened that the king will unleash his fury.

And it's in the midst of this awkward stalemate that Prince

Malthe vaults from his seat. "I have an announcement," he says with a grin, stealing the floor before Rolyo can speak.

The interjection throws the king, who reaches for his goblet and takes a quick draft. The liquid seems to quell his anger, and renders him noiseless. At least for now. I hope Malthe's speech is something enthralling. Something clever and perhaps sycophantic. By the look on Ladislas's face, we are doomed, but Malthe clears his throat and barrels on.

"King Rolyo," he says. "My father and I have some pleasing information to share with you."

Ladislas looks stunned, clearly unaware of his son's impromptu sharing of news. Rolyo raises an eyebrow in annoyance, slamming his goblet, sloshing its contents. The High Sovereign Zementa curls his lips at being excluded from the conversation.

"We all know the devastation of the wilting sickness." Malthe rests a palm to his heart. "It's a ghastly path to the Afterworld, and few who contract the illness survive."

I feel on edge at his theatrical display. Is he planning to ask the king for zyphene? Is he going to say that finally the Tyjans have sufficient coin to afford the medicine? The thought that he is makes me want to scream. I want to yell that it's much too late. It should have been paid for years ago and then my mother might have been saved.

"Yes, I know of the wilting sickness." King Rolyo sticks a fork in some mutton. "It swept our ports the last two winters. Many were killed."

The High Sovereign nods.

"Well, I have been working with a healer," says Malthe. "It has taken time and a lot of coin. But we are proud to announce—in front of this room—that we have found a cure at last."

The air goes out of my body. What is he talking about? I wait for King Rolyo to tell him that *No, we already have an herb called zyphene to cure the wilting sickness for the correct price*, but he doesn't. In fact, he looks staggered that Malthe is even suggesting that such an elixir exists.

"A cure?" he says.

Malthe smiles, looking sideways at his father. "Indeed, King Rolyo. I have been working on this steadily and we have found a way to wipe it out." He seems more interested in the reaction of his father, but Ladislas looks like he's been belted in the face.

"Why did you not tell me of this?" he hisses.

"I did not think—"

"No, son. You never do. Proclaiming fantasies when they are untested!"

"I wish to see it," King Rolyo interrupts, and High Sovereign Zementa agrees. Ladislas's head looks like it will pop off. He obviously does not trust his son, and if this fails . . . the kings will be furious.

But I don't understand. There's already a cure. How are they not familiar with zyphene? I scan people's faces, and they're all in shock.

But it's shock that a cure has finally been found.

Not that one already exists.

I swallow as Malthe natters on, his voice distorting like an echo in a tunnel. He speaks of the trials he conducted in his tower. He speaks of how this will save many lives.

And I reach inside my head for answers. How had I first learned of zyphene? I need to project myself back past a year, back to the dark days when I was sixteen.

To the afternoon when my mother fell ill. We were outdoors, collecting dry twigs. I was telling her stories of Anai and me when she clutched at her throat, blinking into the sunlight. It was almost like a slicing of time—one moment full of life, the next she was not. I'd dragged her back to our stonebrick at once. Dabbed water on her brow. Brewed herbs from the forest. Over the days, her condition worsened. The village healer had bowed his head. He'd told us we must prepare for her ending. That he didn't know when it would come. But soon.

And I'd cried. So much. So so much. With the ferocity that belonged to a daughter in despair. I'd trawled the markets along the Geynes, desperate for something that wasn't there. It was only after her death that I found it—when a storekeeper showed me her plant called zyphene. She said it grew wild in the fields of Quizzano, a far-off kingdom to the north of the world. And she told me through my tears and my numbness that most other kingdoms had purchased this cure. It was only that our new Tyjan emperor preferred to spend his coin elsewhere.

And I'd taken her word as fact right then. I'd squeezed it inside me and let it bloom. I'd stumbled back to my stonebrick, weeping, wishing the Tyjans had never been born.

And why? Perhaps it lessened the pain. I don't know, but I'm numb again. Numb and dazed by the truth of it all, as it slowly sinks in that I was wrong. There wasn't a cure. Not back then. The storekeeper lied to sell her wares. I pick up a cloth and press it to my lips, hiding the fact I can barely breathe. Although the Tyjans are awful rulers, it wasn't their fault that my mother is dead. No matter their spending, it wouldn't have mattered. They couldn't import what didn't exist.

Tears gather, blurring my vision, as Malthe finishes talking of his cure. Something about using human blood and mixing it with a kind of bacteria. Ladislas jabs his son in the ribs. He commands us all to retire for the evening.

Which means the announcement that I am Princess Astrid is cast aside for a future engagement.

I cannot visit Kalliope right away because so many of the other noble women have the same idea, although they seem to come back down the staircase swiftly, so their conversations must be painfully short. Instead I contemplate slipping to the cells to let Vogel know what they have planned for him. But then I see Emperor

Ladislas leading the king of Leeang to the far end of the square. He must be keen to present the gladiator who will take on Rolyo's Victoreglia beast.

Not knowing what else to do, I climb the stairs to my chamber. I sift through what happened at the banquet, trying to understand what it means. I end up pacing the soft carpet, mad at myself for believing the storekeeper. Mad at myself for getting so stuck that I permitted falsehoods to harden as truth.

Zyphene. It had never been real. How could I have been so foolish? Letting myself get carried away was not something *I* was supposed to do.

I miss my father so much at that moment. I need to hold him. For him to hold me. But what if Gyzen cannot find him? What if I have lost him, too?

It's much later when I walk to the door. The hallway outside is silent and still. I haven't heard footsteps for quite some time, so I pull back the boards and pass through. I hurry toward Kalliope's chamber. It's the last on the left, shrouded in dusk. Steeling myself, I knock on the panels, praying to Obellis that I'll find her alone.

"Leave me," comes the request from inside.

"It's Astrid," I say as quietly as I can. By her tone, I expect that it will not matter and she'll demand I depart all the same.

But she doesn't. She opens the doors herself, so she must have sent her servants downstairs. Checking the landing, she pulls me inside with surprising strength for one so slight. Her chambers are painted in dark green and gold. Natural colors—leaves and pollen. She shuts the door and latches it tight so no one will be able to follow me in.

"Take a seat, Astrid," she says. "Please."

I gaze about for a space to recline. A warm fire burns in a hearth, its mantel piled with sodden kerchiefs. Kalliope drifts over with me. She plops on a chaise and pats beside her. Gone is the flighty girl from the hall who twirls and giggles and agrees with her father.

"I'm glad you came," she says, as I sit.

"You are?"

"Yes." She leans back. Spirals are carved in the darkened wood, the etchings reminiscent of crashing waves. "So many nobles came to see me. It's bothersome because they don't care at all. They're delighted that I'm to be shipped to an island. They do not know who I really am."

"Who are you?" I ask.

Kalliope exhales. "My outsides and insides are very different. They always have been out of necessity. I suppose it sounds like a strange thing to say."

But it isn't strange to me at all when I think of how I'm Astrid and Meadow. It's probably the only thing she could tell me that would make me understand her the most.

"Though it doesn't matter now," she says with a sigh. "All this pretending about who I am to keep myself safe has amounted to nothing. What is the point when I'm now going to be sent to Leeang in a few days? Without ever being consulted? To be married to a son of that brute? And the worst part about it is that it's probably my fault."

"How so?" I ask.

"Because of who I told everyone I was," says Kalliope. "How I showed myself to the world. Because I pretended so well that I was in love with the idea of being Tyjan and that I believed my father's ideas and decisions were the right ones. I sold it to him beautifully. So, of course, why would he ever think to ask me about what I wanted in a decision such as this?"

Now I understand.

Kalliope wipes her eyes. "I'm sorry you have to see to this," she says. "But I realize now that I should have spoken to you openly last night after you protected Gyzen and me from that vile creature, Farrow. I love Gyzen, you see. I've loved him for a long time, probably ever since we were children. It was only recently that I let him know it though because . . . again . . . I am two people, Astrid. And if you separate yourself into two different people for long enough, sometimes it starts to feel like the most normal thing in the kingdom. Does that make any sense?"

"Yes, it does actually." And it's difficult not to reveal my secret. I realize now that we do have our differences. Kalliope splits in two to survive, while I am split, yet I long to be one. "You had no other choice than to do that," I say.

Kalliope breaks into a wet smile, but then shakes it away, almost as if she realizes that she is pretending again. "My father should not be on the throne," she says. "If I am myself speaking freely, then that is the absolute truth. But there isn't much to be done about it, short of something dreadfully unlawful."

I'm astonished that she speaks this way.

"But when his time comes, it should be you who takes over from him," she says.

"Me?"

"Yes. You should be the one to take the crown. You are the daughter of Komran. I always worried what would happen when my father died and Malthe succeeded him. You don't know much about my brother, Astrid, but he is cruel and sadistic and he would bring the kingdom to its knees."

She doesn't need to convince me of that.

"What about you?" I ask.

"I am lost now," she says.

"The kingdom needs you here," I say.

"I cannot disobey," she replies.

"But your father would listen to you," I protest. "If you went to him with your objections—"

"No. He's put our kingdom in a great deal of debt. He needs King Rolyo to assist with the finances. That is why—for too long—he's had to bend to him like a convict." She pauses for a moment to gather her thoughts. "There is something that I need you to do for me. When I leave with the king, you will inherit this villa and all the servants inside it, too."

I had not thought of that, and the responsibility of it is heavy and frightening. Kalliope must see my shoulders go rigid.

"No, no," she says. "These servants are fine. But"—and she drops her voice—"I would ask that you do something extra." She swallows, as if she does not want to part with this information and yet she knows she has no other choice due to her limited time in Centriet. "You said I could trust you," she says.

"You can."

Kalliope nods. "There's much violence in this kingdom. My brother is perhaps the worst perpetrator of them all, and I fear with time he will only get worse."

She's stalling. I don't blame her, but I'm suddenly aware what she's going to say.

"I help women whom he captures," she tells me. "Not all of them, but those that I can. I would ask in my absence that you would continue this work. I have others who help, but they need someone with influence in the palace in order to carry out their roles." She goes on to explain part of what I already know. Freya, Errol, and Pelletier assist her. So does Gyzen. However, it is getting tricky to conceal her part in the operation.

"I heard you giving jewels to someone outside the palace," I say.

"Yes," says Kalliope. "We have people working on the outside. There is a safe house in the eastern part of the city. I give them coin or jewels when I can so they can buy food and medical supplies."

"And that is it?" I ask. "You will go with the king?"

"I have to go with the king," she says. "But the Island of Leeang is a wealthy realm. If I can help from across the sea, then I shall, Astrid. I promise you that."

"Your father did not announce my identity at the banquet," I say.

"He probably knows that if he did so, King Rolyo would want to wed you to one of his other seven sons," she says. "He may be a poor ruler, but he is not senseless. He will not want to lose two of his kin in one night."

"What about you and Gyzen?" I ask.

Kalliope breathes out, reaching for a handkerchief to dab her eyes. "We will say our good-byes before I leave," she says. "But if I know anything, I know that he feels the same way as I do. That we have a duty to our kingdom and we must fulfil it."

"You really believe that?" I ask in awe.

Kalliope shrugs. "I suppose that I'll have to."

We sit in silence for a little while. I listen to the gentle sound of the logs crackling to ash in the fireplace.

"The ladies told me of the Victoreglia," says Kalliope, "and that the gladiator, Vogel, has been put forward by my father and brother."

I nod.

"And you know him?" she asks. "You lived with him when you were at the camp?"

"Yes," I lie.

"What was he like? Violent and cocky like so many men?"

"No," I say a little too fast, so fast in fact that Kalliope stares at me closely and tips her head to one side.

"What does that mean?" she asks.

"Nothing."

"He was the one who refused to fight." Kalliope nods to herself, obviously remembering his part in the Tournament. "He was handsome from memory," she says. "And kind. With principles not to injure those weaker."

I feel a blush come to my face, but I don't know why after all he has done.

"There was nothing between you?" Kalliope presses.

"No," I say.

"Probably for the best." Kalliope sighs and stands up, strolling to the window to glance outside. "He will not survive the Victoreglia," she says. "They're not meant to. So it's good you don't care."

"Yes," I say, rising beside her, but suddenly the urge to see Vogel is strong. Kalliope is correct. He is going to die, and I do not want him to be all alone after his visit with the emperor and the king. And I suppose also—like the princess with Gyzen—I want to say good-bye to him. "I have to leave now because—"

"I know." Kalliope smiles and waves me on.

CHAPTER THIRTY-FOUR

SINCE THE SOLDIERS ARE AWARE OF MY PRESENCE IN THE PALACE, I descend to the basement without being questioned. The emperor and the king of Leeang are long gone, and the moon peeks out from a swirl of dark sky.

When I reach the row of secured cells, a soldier unlocks the door for me. After I enter, he bolts me inside. No words exchanged. No warning this time. A roaring torch burns on the wall, splashing the stones with a copper glow. I feel the warmth against my cheek as Vogel stirs, glancing up from a corner. Recognition bathes his face, and when it does, my throat catches.

"Have you come to tell me good news?" he asks.

"No," I say.

"That's a shame."

I hover by the closed door. For some reason, I'm more nervous this time. "Is it all right if I sit down?" I ask.

He nods at that. "Of course it is."

I sit gingerly on the floor, leaving a gaping space between us. I rest my spine against the hinges and stretch my legs in front of me. I fiddle with my hands, pressing them together, not sure where my words will lead.

"I'm sorry," I say.

"For what?" he asks.

"All that yelling when I saw you before."

Vogel manages a smile, and it makes me wonder what his

life was like before Malthe and the Tyjans destroyed his family. I'm curious what he did for fun. Was he was a rascal who spent his days stealing breadsticks, or was he was the perfect son who helped his mother clean garments on washboards? I suppose I'll never know.

"You had every right to yell at me," he says. "I deserved it—and so much more. Afterward, I had time to reflect on what you said. It shocked me a bit when I realized all the things I had done and all the things I was prepared to do to get Ladislas off the throne."

"But your family . . ." I say.

"I can never apologize enough," he interjects.

"You did try to warn me," I say. "I had time to think on it, too. And you're not all bad, you know. I mean it." Strangely, as the words come out, I realize I deeply believe what I'm saying. He's not bad. Not at all. And I'm not just spewing compliments because I know that Vogel is destined to die in the morning. I think of what I would do if my whole family had been slaughtered—and I do not know the answer. Certainly, my mother's death turned me inside out, but she died slowly, and I had time to say farewell. I cannot imagine what having your sister, father, mother, and brothers killed in front of you in an instant would feel like. No chance to say any last words. No chance to think over what it will all mean.

"Why are you here?" he asks.

"I learned more about the Victoreglia," I say.

"Ah." He nods, frowning. So clearly he knows about the barbaric tradition, too. "I was blessed with a visit from the emperor and the king of Leeang himself," he says.

"What did they want?"

"To lie through their teeth. To tell me what an honor it is." He runs his fingernails along the stones, the rough noise making my innards flinch.

"I want to help you," I say.

"You mustn't," he says, and the truth is—I do not know how I could intervene. "You have to keep your secret," he tells me. He looks pained to acknowledge that I am Astrid, since he had a hand in it, but he presses on. "Whatever happens to me tomorrow, you must not let any of them know what occured between you and the princess. With your position, you have a chance to change things from within. That way, at least I can go to my grave knowing that all is not lost."

So he knows he is going to die.

"What did they tell you?" I ask.

"Nothing. They would not reveal the creature that will kill me."

"What happens if you kill it?"

"It will not happen."

But I'm optimistic. "It may, Vogel. You were trained in the ludela, and they'll give you a weapon."

"The reason it will not happen," says Vogel, "is because I will not fight tomorrow."

I understand why he'd not fight a human, but to let an animal kill him pains me. It conjures up Knox's son-in-law who died in the arena when he wouldn't bear arms. It hurts to think that Vogel would stand there and let an animal shear through his body.

"Why not?" I ask.

"Because," he says, "they will not get that satisfaction from me." He rubs a palm across his collar, where dirt has lodged in the crease of his neck. "The king of Leeang is a bloodthirsty ogre. He's worse than the emperor. I can't let them win."

"But there's a chance that if you fight—and prevail—you'll survive," I say, though my doubts are immense.

"I know about the Victoreglia," says Vogel. "And there's no chance I'm coming out of it breathing. Even if it was possible to slaughter their wild animal—and I somehow achieved it—it would be perfectly acceptable for the Leeangi king to murder me where I stood. It would be poor form in the kingdom's eyes if he did not follow through."

"You don't seem scared," I say.

"I am," he assures me, which I realize does little to assure me at all.

"Malthe has Siella in his tower," I say.

Vogel rests a hand to his forehead. "That brute will go on torturing people if his father does not bring him in line. It's senseless."

"He thinks it's not." I tell him about Malthe's experiments.

"So the fool thinks he's helping the kingdom?" spits Vogel. "By torturing live subjects in the name of healing?"

I swallow. "You remember my mother? How she died from the wilting sickness?"

"Yes."

"Well." I breathe out. "Turns out I was wrong about the cure. There was never a cure last year when she died. Malthe claims he's only just discovered one now."

Vogel stares at me. "Are you sure?"

"Very sure."

"I . . . That's awful."

"I can't help thinking that this . . . all this . . ." I gesture to me, to him, to the cell around us. "It never would have come to pass if I'd known that zyphene did not exist. I've been fighting something that is not real—this need to make the Tyjans pay."

"They do need to pay," says Vogel.

"They do, but not for the reasons I thought." I sigh. How can I tell him such things when he's the one sitting on death row? The truth is that, yes, I am Astrid. But I don't want to be. I'm not sure I'm strong enough to make change after he is gone. And what kind of impact am I supposed to make? Be wed to a distant son of the king and ferried away on a ship like Kalliope? It all feels so futile now, but I cannot let him know I'm afraid.

"Did they execute Casper?" asks Vogel.

"I didn't see him among the prisoners," I say. Vogel doesn't ask me to look for him. He probably knows that I will forever feel betrayed.

We sit in silence. I wring my hands. Vogel doesn't, though he seems uncertain.

"Why did you really come here?" he asks.

"To tell you what I know," I say.

"No, really." Vogel inhales. "You hated me before with every piece of your being. And you should still. So why did you come?"

"I don't know," I say.

"Meadow."

A tear glasses my eye. Will anyone ever call me that again once Vogel has gone to the Afterworld?

"I didn't want you to be alone," I say. "Knowing what will happen tomorrow."

"Thank you." He tilts his head at me. "I hoped you would come."

"You did?"

"Yes."

"Why?"

"Because." Vogel stretches his arms. "It was nice," he says. "To travel with you on the road. To talk to you. To become your friend. It reminded me of how I used to be before all of this clouded my life."

And suddenly I feel something inside me that I don't think I've felt until this moment. It feels like my heart is breaking. But it's not like the grief for my mother or the desperation that I cannot locate my father and Anai. This is something else. Like my insides are being pulled and stretched, but I don't know how to make them stop.

And I realize—with startling awareness—that no fiber in me wants Vogel to die. It feels like what we are to each other is incomplete, it's unfinished, it's wrong. Like we could be something more with time, but he slips through my fingers and I cannot hold on. He's adrift to me and I to him, and I haven't the answers to make this right.

"Meadow?" he asks, his face concerned.

"I don't want you to die," I say.

He smiles at that, which makes me annoyed, until I see the ache in his eyes.

"You'll be all right," he says. "You know that."

I shake my head.

"Well, even if you're not." Vogel sniffs, his facade slipping. "At least I'll know that someone will miss me."

It makes me think of Mistress Howella, who used to tell stories to the village children. She said that she had once been young, and when she was young she met a boy. She said that he rode to the village on a pony. He only spoke to her once. Mistress Howella picked strawberries from the fields, but when she returned, the boy was gone. She said she never got over it. No one knew his name. No one knew where he went. And the moral to the story that Mistress Howella liked to impress upon the young was that sometimes important people come into your life and you need to pay attention. For if you don't, they will leave without warning, a huge hole left in their place. And the hole cannot be filled with another. And since they're not there, you will live a half-life, always wondering what could have been.

It seems so unfair that I will never know Vogel.

"You should probably go," he says. "If you can help it, don't come tomorrow. After all, I will just be sitting in wait."

"Vogel," I say.

"I'm sorry," he says.

"It's me who should be sorry," I say.

"You apologize too much," he says, standing and walking over to me.

"I've always been like that," I tell him as he takes my hands and helps me stand. His eyes scorch me with their blueness, his arms closing around my shoulders.

"I know it's you inside," he says. "But I wish I could see the old you." He's so close, I can hear his heartbeat. Or perhaps it's mine. I cannot tell. All I know is that I want him to live. This should be the start and not the conclusion. I want to know what it's like when he laughs. When we laugh together. And nothing is wrong.

"I want to save you," I say.

"You have." Vogel's voice is quiet, but sure. I pull away and lift my chin. He's gazing at me, but it's different this time. The air shifts and his hue settles, lighting his head from behind like a torch. His hand touches the side of my face. "Live a long life, Meadow," he whispers.

There's a knock.

"My lady, you must go back to your villa. By order of the emperor," says a soldier's voice.

I step back from Vogel at once as a metallic instrument thuds in the lock. "I will try to make them free you," I say, the tears filling my eyes again.

"No, Meadow," he says. "I don't want that. You have to live here without suspicion." He reaches over to wipe my tears, and despite the soldier, I embrace him tight.

And I know I'll forever exist with a puncture that cannot be mended because he is gone.

CHAPTER THIRTY-FIVE

I DRIFT IN AND OUT OF SLEEP, PLAGUED BY THOUGHTS OF VOGEL dying. It combines with visions of my parents and Anai trapped together in sinking sand. I roll over, staring at the canopy, listening to the whip of the wind through the trees. I think of Vogel hunched in his cell about to greet sunrise for the final time.

I don't know what to do.

Although it's still dark, I get out of bed and dress. Perhaps I can steal to the emperor's quarters and beg for clemency once and for all. I'm almost to the double doors when I stop. The sun is rising above the lake, coating the land with yellow-gold. And the light makes me pause and understand that my desperate pleas would not make a difference. The emperor needs King Rolyo's coin in order to keep our kingdom afloat. If he so freely gives his daughter to an unknown son of the king, then there is no possible way that he is going to stop the Victoreglia from happening.

And beyond all that, perhaps most importantly, Vogel doesn't wish me to interfere.

The palace wakes as the light grows stronger, and the rest of the morning passes around me. There are blurs of people and movement and sounds as Tallesa fixes my hair and gown. Since I'm too wound up to speak, she tries to make polite conversation. Food. Dresses. The splendor of the palace. How the weather is perfect for a stroll. Her persistence is admirable, but my eyes glaze over, stopping on nothing but the sun in the sky. The closer it inches into the middle of the blueness, the faster my heart skips out of my chest.

You don't need to watch, Vogel told me last night.

But I do. I have to. He deserves that much. I can still feel the warmth of his skin and the brush of his fingers, swabbing my tears.

When middle day sweeps across the square, I take my leave to the carriages downstairs. My only comfort is riding with Kalliope.

"You know you don't have to do this," she says.

"I should," I tell her.

She nods. She sits back with her arm trailing along the bottom of the fitted glass. She doesn't press the issue, and I presume her mind is elsewhere. So much has changed for her since the banquet. So much, it seems, that can't be undone.

"Did you manage to speak with Gyzen?" I ask.

She shakes her head, though she doesn't tear her eyes from the window. "I don't think he wants to talk at the moment."

"What gives you that impression?"

She sighs. "It is just a sense I got when I saw him from a distance. It was like he bristled because of me. I don't know. With any luck I will get a chance to speak to him after this dreadful display." She stops abruptly, realizing what she has said. "Honestly, Astrid. It isn't worth the pain of watching the Victoreglia if you care for the boy. Did you speak with him last night?"

"Yes."

"Did you say your farewells?"

I nod.

"But?"

"But I have to. If it was me, I would want at least one person in the crowd who knew me well as I took my last breath."

We pull up—not in a square in the noble district, but at the arena. It looks so different without the crowd jostling for meat and mugs of ale. Nevertheless, our great trail of carriages garner the attention of watching villagers. Many begin to follow us, curious why we're in their streets. The Tyjan soldiers push them back, clearing a path to the arena steps. The coachman opens the carriage door and ushers us quickly onto the cobbles.

Kalliope threads her arm through mine. We follow the emperor, King Rolyo, and Zementa. Prince Malthe appears from an adjacent carriage. I feel his eyes as we climb the staircase.

"You could still feign illness," Kalliope whispers. "Or I could do it."

"No," I say.

At the top of the steps, we pause on the landing, the shock of sunlight brighter than flames. Without the stamping and shouting of people, the arena stands are hauntingly silent. Ladislas gestures to an empty row, where Midlons have set up cushioned chairs. The rulers claim their seats before us, their servants on hand with refreshments and parasols.

As Kalliope and I take our place with the nobles, a black-clad figure slides beside me.

"Astrid." It's Malthe. He practically purrs it.

"Yes?" I say.

"You look most pleasing." The corners of his mouth rise in a question that I dare not give the answer to. He leans closer. He smells like bathwater.

"She is your aunt," Kalliope snaps.

I edge away from Malthe's arm, but then I remember about Siella. "Did you find more people from the camp?" I ask.

"We did," he says. "How did you know that?"

"I didn't," I lie.

He regards me with interest. "Well, two more girls have since been secured."

"*Two* girls?" I blink in haste, trying to suppress the blow from the news. "What were their names?"

"What does it matter?" His fiery pupils drill into mine. He nudges himself against my shoulder, and I bite my tongue to appear nonchalant.

"You're probably right."

"Siella," he blurts. "And the second one was a girl called Annie."

Annie?

It's Anai. I want to slap him for being so careless with my best friend's name.

"She knew a girl who was executed." Malthe rolls his eyes to the clouds, almost laughing. "I think she was trying to scope out the palace to launch an escape or something like that. Anyway, you needn't worry. We have sent more patrols to hunt down the stragglers."

"Thank the Lord Obellis," I say.

"You are safe," says Malthe with a preposterous smile. He pushes his sleeves past his elbows in a flagrant attempt to showcase his arms.

"Where are the prisoners now?" I ask.

I know, of course, where Siella resides.

"I have them both detained," says Malthe. "There is no need for your concern."

"But what will become of them after today? Will they both be sent to the Emperor's Quadrant?"

Malthe looks most surprised that I care, but the wonder quickly fades from his skin. "I assume you heard the good news?" he asks.

"Good news?"

"That I announced at the banquet?"

My spirits plunge. Of course I remember him finding a cure for the wilting sickness. "It was quite an accomplishment," I say, trying—like Kalliope—to be good at pretending.

Delighted to think I'm applauding his efforts, Malthe relaxes and spreads his legs wider. "My healers and I toiled day and night, as we knew how much this cure was needed." I loathe how smug this seems to make him, as though he's a martyr for torturing live subjects. "So to answer your question, the prisoners we spoke of will assist me in some of my upcoming studies."

I'm nauseated at what that could mean.

He taps a finger beneath his eye. "I wish to cure the ailing sight that seems to occur when a person gets older. I haven't yet started the trials, mind you, but the emperor is keen to get underway."

Of course he is. He could sell the treatments and perchance pay off the kingdom's debts.

"Maybe you could give me a tour," I say.

"Perhaps," says Malthe.

"Before you start, I mean." I do not wish to push the issue, else he may suspect my motives. But Gyzen couldn't stop me from entering the tower with the seal of approval from the prince himself. I'm not sure how I'd release the prisoners, but getting inside is the very first step.

Kalliope taps my forearm. "Astrid? The Victoreglia is about to begin."

She's right. A young Rigorate appears, standing alone on a lower bench. He scans the rows, lips moving as he counts. When he gets to the end, he checks again. Finally deducing that all guests are present, he makes a sign to High Sovereign Zementa.

"The High Sovereign has the floor," he announces as Zementa stands to address King Rolyo.

"My gratitude." Zementa turns. He seems thinner and frailer than the first time I saw him. "Torquella offers you one of its gladiators as a congratulations for your win in the Tournament. May his spilled blood be a sign of respect and forge a deeper bond between us. Torquella honors Leeang on this day. The sacrifice is given freely." He looks across at the waiting Rigorate and gives two nods in his direction. In response to the gesture, servants are summoned who heave the strawberry doors apart. Like in the Tournament, a man emerges wearing a loincloth and carrying a dagger. But his face betrays a range of emotions that prominent gladiators are meant to conceal.

It is easy to feel sorry for him. He's gangly and nervous and so out of place. His hair is shaved so his scalp shines through, and his naked trunk is covered in pustules. He has a fast-paced, yellow aura that spins and hurtles around his ears. As he watches the servants vacate the arena, a lone tear carves a trail down his cheek.

"Who is this buffoon?" Rolyo chortles. "A representation of men from Torquella?"

To my left, Kalliope tenses.

"The king is a pig," she murmurs to me.

The gladiator runs at the strawberry doors and tries to prize them open with his fingers. The wood is sharp and bites his skin, and soon his hands are awash with red.

He begins to wail, and the sound is piercing. The doors fly open, smacking his head. He falls backward, jolting his tailbone, blood gushing from a wound at his temple. He groans and tries to suck in air, but he must be winded from the impact of the fall. He blinks furiously, his head lolling sideways, as if he's lost all sense of control.

And then through the darkness of the strawberry-colored doors pokes the rounded head of something startling. Two jeweled eyes fix on the gladiator as he rolls backward, clutching his skull. The scaled body slithers forward, creating swirls in the soft sand. It's dotted with black and white and green, with shots of yellow patterned in diamonds. It slides nearer the fallen gladiator, coiling around to encircle his waist. The body just keeps coming and coming until I think that this cannot be real. I have never encountered a snake so huge. When the tail ends, the doors close. The Torquellan tries to wrench it from his middle, but the length of it tightens like a knot of rope.

The gladiator screams.

The snake loops in front, rearing up, its jaw stretched wide. A liquid shoots out and splashes the man, coating his face from his brows to chin.

I brace myself for a horrendous slow death, but all of a sudden, the screaming stops. The gladiator drops to the ground. Dead. No shaking of limbs. No wild scared eyes. Exhalations happen in unison, though Rolyo lets out a dissatisfied grunt.

"Disrespectful to Leeang," he says. "I wanted to see the Torquellan fight."

The snake lets its jaw go slack, positioning the opening at the dead man's head. It adjusts and readjusts its grip, then clamps its mouth around his scalp. Its coiled body twists the Torquellan, forcing him deeper, making swallowing efficient. The long, thin body expands like a stocking as the lifeless gladiator is shoveled in.

Turning away, I push down the sick, though it burns, unrelenting, at the back of my throat. If the scene in front of me now is brutal, then the next with Vogel will razor my heart. I don't think I am strong enough to sit through what's coming and not fall apart.

Kalliope's hand finds its way to my wrist. "Are you sure you can do this?"

"I can do this," I whisper.

After the snake devours its meal, King Rolyo seems neither enthralled nor disgusted. Perhaps there are many large snakes on his island. "Your gladiator best be more entertaining." He winks at Ladislas pointedly, and the emperor flushes beneath his beard. He knows if Rolyo leaves in anger, he will not be obliging in future dealings. I don't hear his precise response, but he does give the king a cajoling thump. Though remembering how Vogel vowed not to fight, I wonder how long the humor will last.

The snake slithers to the edge of the arena, bulging in a horribly familiar shape. The Rigorate looks to the emperor this time, and Ladislas wastes no time standing up.

"Erraforge offers you one of its gladiators as a congratulations for your win in the Tournament," he says. "May his spilled blood be a sign of respect and forge a deeper bond between us. Erraforge honors Leeang on this day. The sacrifice is given freely."

He offers two nods to the Rigorate, despite King Rolyo openly yawning.

It's about to happen—and I'm not ready. How could I ever be ready for this? As the servants return and open the doors, Vogel walks slowly out of the darkness. His handsome blue aura dances above him, almost the color of his beautiful eyes. My breath halts as he studies the ring. He's ready for it—and I hate that so much. He does not wail or dash to the exit like the Torquellan gladiator when the servants depart. There's defeat and calmness. Weariness, too. Relief, perhaps, that he'll soon see his family. And as much as I dearly wish he would try, I realize now that I have to accept this. He's going to die on the sand today—and I must sit here and say not a word.

Perspiration beads on my palms as King Rolyo glances at Ladislas. "He does not look like he will fight," he says.

"He will," says the emperor.

"Are you certain of that?" No doubt Vogel's stance in the Training Rounds has left a scar in Rolyo's memory.

"He will fight for *you*," Ladislas corrects.

"Ask him then," the king demands.

Although he looks pained to indulge this request, Ladislas turns to address Prince Malthe. "This is the one that you chose?" he asks.

"Yes, Father."

"Then tell him to fight."

Malthe's jaw trembles slightly, but he battles hard to keep it in line. Knitting his brows, he rises from his cushion, meeting Vogel with a glare of his own.

"You will fight, gladiator," he says.

"I will not."

"Make him obey you," says Ladislas sharply. Trying to hide the edge to his tone, his features twist to a stiffened scowl.

Vogel looks at me ever so quickly, then flashes his attention back to the king. "King Rolyo," he says. "I will fight for you if you make the emperor do something in return."

Ladislas slaps his fist against the rail, but Rolyo holds up a hand for quiet. The power over Ladislas appeals to him greatly, and his lips take the form of an arrogant smirk. "Speak, gladiator," he says. "Speak true. What would you have me demand of the emperor?"

"That he frees two prisoners," Vogel says, and my eyes widen. *He knows of Anai.*

"Whom?" asks the king.

"Two women," says Vogel. "They were captured by the prince and locked in his tower."

King Rolyo slides his attention to Malthe.

"Is it true?" he demands.

"They were plotting against us!"

"Women?" laughs Rolyo. "Plotting against men? They do not have the capacity for such thoughts!"

And I've never been happier that a bigoted old fool would carry ludicrous beliefs such as those.

"So you will fight if these women are released?" asks the king.

"To the death," says Vogel.

"Very well." King Rolyo flicks between Ladislas and Malthe. "You will release these women when we return to the palace."

"But—" Malthe begins.

"Show some manners," says the king.

"It will be done," says Ladislas swiftly. He turns to Vogel. "You have your wish. Does this mean you will put on a good show?"

Vogel nods, and I lean forward, placing my hands beneath my thighs. This isn't what he'd wanted to do. This isn't how he'd desired to die. I wish I could tell him how much this means. That this sacrifice is beyond astounding. That my best friend might be saved on this day because of his gift. This final giving-in.

"Give him a blade," says King Rolyo.

The Rigorate clicks his fingers, and a servant hurls a sword at Vogel's feet. The weapon bounces against the sand, coming to rest a few paces from the snake. Sunbeams hit the steel point and send a streak of light into the stands. The snake doesn't stir, and I hold my breath, unable to keep my toes from shaking.

True to his word, Vogel picks up the weapon. He grips it easily, testing the weight. If he was a stranger, I'd truly believe he was eager to entertain the king.

The doors open.

Vogel turns, ready to run or attack at will. I wait for a second snake to appear, but rather than a pair of wicked eyes, a pointed snout nudges into the ring. It's long and layered with irregular bumps, and sharp white teeth protrude from its lips. The beast creeps forward on its four short legs, its skin the color of river stalks.

A crocodile.

I've heard tales about them. Some people in Maytown have sketches on scrolls. But I never imagined they were anything more than fictional villains to frighten children. This beast is three times the length of a human, green eyes slashed in the center with black. Its solid physique enters the arena, its belly scraping a curve in the sand.

"We breed many in our farms," says King Rolyo. "This is one of our females called Saxa. She grew much faster than her brothers and sisters, so we butchered the rest and fed them to her."

To quell my disgust, I focus on the beast. She should be clumsy on land, at least. If the pictures are true, then these creatures crave water. They swim near the surface, ridged with mud.

Vogel obviously thinks so, too. The crocodile sizes him up without blinking. She opens and closes her mouth like a beak, her jagged teeth glistening with rotten meat. Vogel jogs backward and darts to the side, trying to shelter behind the tail. He holds the sword like it weighs almost nothing, urging the creature to react to his movements.

He waits.

And waits some more.

At first, the crocodile watches him. For a while, it seems she may have lost interest in the strange boy wielding the silver weapon. Perhaps she's already eaten her fill, this gladiator before her a mere disturbance. However, I doubt that the king would have brought a well-fed crocodile to the Victoreglia.

And I am right.

All of a sudden, the crocodile rotates, snapping her jaws. The distance is sufficient that Vogel is safe, but the crocodile's feet punch marks in the sand. I let out a yelp as the beast propels, the gnarled body sprinting at a terrifying pace. Vogel swerves to the left and runs, weaving his footsteps, keeping out of its path.

"Intriguing behavior," says Malthe in amusement.

The crocodile lunges, and Vogel dives. He hits his arm, but rolls briskly, sending sand grains flying like sheets of rain. The crocodile spins and scuttles toward him. Vogel scrambles, still gripping the sword. He gallops as fast as he can to the fence, wheeling around, his breath coming fast.

It's a horrible display to witness. It's awful knowing what the end will be and not being able to prevent it. The crocodile charges at Vogel again. With her huge tail thrashing, she severs his escape route, first one way and then the other. She's smart. She knows how best to linger until Vogel has committed to a choice of direction. But thankfully Vogel feints to the right, and the crocodile lurches, letting him pass.

It continues like this for many more moments—so many that time means nothing to me. Vogel ducks and veers like a fighter, always seeming one step ahead. His skin glistens with the dark sheen of effort, the sunbeams tanning his muscled limbs. His yellow hair dampens and he pushes it back, squinting the sweat from between his lashes.

And still she keeps coming.

Vogel sprints, but the toll from the falls is wearing him down. On his next jump, his ankle twists, and when he pulls up, he curses in pain. He recovers quickly, though he's slower this time. The crocodile inches closer once more. He cannot keep running. Not like this. He needs to change tactics and brandish the sword.

King Rolyo claps his hands in glee. "This is what the Victoreglia is about!" he shouts.

As if on cue, Vogel steels himself. He pulls back swiftly, then darts forward, slashing the blade at the crocodile's flank.

It nicks her, and she jolts in outrage. A little blood seeps from a wound near her tummy. Her jaws clap in quicker succession, inhibiting Vogel from a second attempt.

My lips part as Vogel hangs back, calculating his next maneuver. He slashes the sword in a few practice air strikes, but his ankle catches as he swings between feet. He retreats slowly—one step, then two—inspecting the curve of stonebrick wall. It's smooth and gray and the plants remain present, streaming wildly from their pots to the rail.

Perhaps an escape. Is that what he's thinking? He could climb the vines and race for an exit? But he tears his eyes from the plants and I know that he wouldn't try it. That he's made up his mind.

Behind him, the snake shifts. It stretches and slithers like a moving log. Its oversize body acts like a barrier—a barrier that Vogel doesn't notice.

Angered by the gash, the crocodile regroups. She lifts her head, swallowing, watching. Something about her expression is different. Like she's lost her patience and this is the moment. She surges at Vogel, her tail swishing, her four legs slamming as she drives toward him. Taken off guard by the sudden advance, he steps back swiftly, tripping over the snake.

I cannot help it. I stand. As he falls, she pounces, grabbing hold of one leg. She tightens her grip as blood explodes, coloring her teeth in a gruesome red. Vogel whacks her with the blade, causing her jaw to dislodge from his flesh. He tries to wrench his leg to freedom, but the crocodile must have punctured an artery or sheared through sinew, as he can't make it move. Instead, all he can do is rest with his back to the snake, his eyes wild with fear.

He slashes the sword in front of him, trying to keep the creature at bay.

My mind races at what to do. I cannot sit by and let this unfold. "Prince Malthe," I whimper.

"Watch," he urges me, nodding toward the bloodied sand.

"I can't."

Vogel lets out a cry as he swivels his leg and it scrapes the ground. The crocodile seizes the sword with her mouth, hurling it out of reach of his hands. With a thrust, she grabs his uninjured thigh. This time the cut is ragged and deep. His whole leg disappears inside her, the teeth overlapping around his hip. I wait for the sickening pop of bones, but it does not come. At least not yet. With some kind of strength, Vogel raises his fist and punches the crocodile square in the snout.

She lets go and crawls back, but I don't even know if the leg is connected. Fluid gushes from multiple tears, and Vogel's face is ashen with blood loss. I know in my heart that it won't be long. He'll close those beautiful eyes and be gone. His arms go limp, though his throat still flexes, the last of the life draining out of him.

In awe, Malthe stands beside me to absorb the view of Vogel's state. He takes my hand as if we are lovers, squeezing my palm firmly in his.

I pull away and glare at him, but he doesn't notice my mood, of course. I see the blueness whizzing around him. There's something about it. Something strange.

I pause, squinting.

It's ice-blue.

I look back to Vogel, although it is painful. I shut out the image of the blood and the carnage and focus on the aura above his head.

Ice-blue.

It's the same color.

Vogel and Malthe have the very same hue. A surge of amazement courses through me. But now that I know this, what can I do?

The crocodile creeps forward again. I have to do this before Vogel dies. But what about Malthe? How will I make him . . . ?

I breathe out.

"Listen," I say.

Malthe's boots drum against the stones. "Shut up," he says. "He's about to lose a limb!"

"Can you say something for me?" I ask.

"What?"

"Vierre mon sur, plasir mes yeemas."

He's distracted still, but he snorts at my question. "What in the name of Obellis does that mean?"

"It's a curse," I say, wringing my hands. "To make sure that when this fool dies, he will never be granted any favors in the Afterworld."

Malthe blinks and looks at me, and it takes all my grit to smile at him. To smile at this monster who carved up women. Who killed Vogel's sister. Who tried to kill me. Who cannot wait to see Vogel die in the cruelest way, dismembered for his pleasure.

"What are the words?" he says again.

"Vierre mon sur, plasir mes yeemas."

Malthe nods. *"Vierre mon sur, plasir mes yeemas."*

I drop his hand. I run to the rail. "The words Casper taught me!" I yell to Vogel. "Say them now!"

Vogel looks woozily up at me. His eyes connect, but I'm not sure he sees.

"Vierre mon sur, plasir mes yeemas!" I scream it again, but it's lost in the breeze.

The crocodile chooses that time to strike. It grips Vogel's stomach, dragging him sideways. As more blood pools in the sand from the wound, his eyes droop, and I turn away.

I cannot breathe. I cannot cry. All I can do is run from the ring. And my heart may be ripped, but I cannot feel it. And I doubt I will ever feel it again.

CHAPTER THIRTY-SIX

BY THE TIME KALLIOPE APPEARS BY THE CARRIAGE, MY FACE IS puffy, but my breathing has returned. I'm frightened I may be in trouble for my outburst, which isn't something that Vogel wanted.

Vogel.

He's dead.

It doesn't seem real, and yet it feels beyond real all the same. Which I don't understand, and I can't understand. I stare at the fingers that are not mine, watching them shake through the film of my tears.

Will Anai ever be saved? I don't know. I don't even know if they've harmed her already. And now that I've hollered in front of the rulers, they may be suspicious of who I am. Will they conclude that Vogel and I were in league together? Perhaps they will. But worst of all, I do not care and part of me worries that I never shall. I want to go back to my old life in Maytown. Where I am Meadow, who's finished her tutelage. Where I am Meadow, who works at the markets, side by side with her best friend, Anai. At least there, in that imagined place, I might have discovered a semblance of happy. But here and now, trapped as a Tyjan, the path ahead has been shrouded by darkness.

"Astrid, I am so sorry you saw that." Kalliope climbs into the carriage beside me. "If there is a way I can make things better . . ."

I open my mouth, then close it again.

"I think he went quickly in the end," she continues. "I pray that his pain was not too great."

But for all her words, I cannot take comfort when I witnessed the agony etched on his face.

"Is your father angry at me?" I manage. I'm surprised my voice isn't skewed with hysteria.

"I do not know," she says with a sigh. "He could not say much in front of the king. But my brother told him you were cursing the rebel, so how you acted should not cause concern. I believe they thought you deserved your fury. After all, as they see it, you were taken as a hostage."

I feel so alone. So separate. Even though Kalliope knows fragments of my feelings for Vogel and I know fragments of her feelings for Gyzen, we do not know the deepest or the truest parts of each other.

"The promise about releasing the prisoners," I say. "Will your father honor that request?"

"Maybe," she says. "It depends on the amount of pressure King Rolyo puts on him—and I'm not so sure that King Rolyo will care since he got his fill from the entertainment." She halts. "I'm sorry, I should not say it like that. But I will speak to my father on your behalf. I do not know if he will listen to me, but maybe he will since I'm soon to be married."

We lapse into silence for the rest of the ride, the air crammed with too much sadness. But it's not only me. I feel for her, too. To be sent to an island—solo and afraid—to be wed to a stranger is a terrifying prospect. I don't know a lot about the Island of Leeang. The culture. The people. I regret that now. For perhaps if I did, I could help Kalliope. I could tell her something that was beautiful about it.

Glancing out the polished window, I realize we have arrived at the palace. The coachman steers us past the stables and around the rear to the private entrance.

When we disembark, my face is still red, but we head for the gate and stride through the courtyard. None of the servants stare directly, though Kalliope orders them back to the kitchens. I notice the void of Carliss's absence. I'm sad that she could not say good-bye. No doubt she will hear of Vogel's death, but at least she did not see it up close, so the horror of it will forever stay masked.

I follow Kalliope through the foyer. At the top of the stairs, she looks at me.

"Do you wish to be alone?" she asks.

I nod.

"Then the Grande will pass on the message."

"Thank you." And I walk on without her. One heavy foot in front of the other. The corridor unfolds like a field of quagmire, sapping effort I do not possess to cross it.

I'm still far from the entrance to my chambers when a figure darts from one of the rooms. She collapses at my feet and I feel the wetness dripping from her eyes onto my toes.

"Carliss?"

Her sobs grow louder. "Is it true?"

"It is."

"I lied," she says. "I loved him."

I don't know why, but her pain seeps inside me. It hits my own and merges as one.

"I know," I say, because she did not hide it. Not even when she said that he was her friend.

"But he didn't love me," she says, looking up. "I always knew it, Princess Astrid. I told people that we were in love because that's what I wanted. What I'd hoped to be real."

I close my eyes, then reach down. I pull her up so we're face-to-face. "He may have loved you," I say to calm her, even though I remember what he'd said in the forest.

"No," she says. "He never did. And that's all right. I will be fine." Her words don't match her crestfallen face, nor the heartbreak that's making her tremor. She's trying to hold herself together, and the more she tries, the more she cannot.

"Do you wish to know what happened?" I ask.

"I do," she says. "But not right now."

I nod, feeling suddenly protective of this girl who wears her heart on her cuff. She presses her fingers into her brow bones, drawing circles to loosen the muscles.

"I have kept you too long, Your Highness," she says. "And talking of love. I apologize." She wipes her face and curtseys swiftly.

"It is no bother," I tell her.

She smiles. "Have you been in love yourself, Princess?" Her features are wide. Hopeful, it seems.

"I'm not sure," I say with a frown. "But I've heard it is worth all of the gold in the kingdom."

"I beg your pardon?" She looks at me strangely.

"Love," I say.

"I know what you mean." She shakes her head. "It's just that I thought . . ." She reconsiders. "Never mind."

When I arrive outside my chambers, I take a deep breath and unlatch the doors. Only when they are shut behind me do I let it free in the vast waste of space. I close my eyes. I take more gasps. But none are sufficient to fill me up. How can anything bring me to life after what happened—now that he is gone?

I haven't the answer, but I open my eyes—and immediately freeze, for I'm not alone. Standing by the casement in his royal attire is the horrifying outline of Prince Malthe. My heart thunders and I rally myself to lunge backward and escape through the villa. But before I can, he turns on the spot and fixes his dark brown eyes on me.

"Meadow?"

I blink.

"Meadow, it's me."

It's too much information at once. How does Prince Malthe know my real name? How does he know I've been swapped with a princess? But then it comes to me in a rush—this isn't Prince Malthe. It can't be. It's not. And yet if he knows who I truly am, then he must be . . . *He has to* . . . He can only be . . .

"Vogel?"

He moves from the casement, slow and precise. He halts, unsure, in the middle of the room. There's a thick red rug under his boots and a lantern of glass above his head.

"Yes," he says.

"But you died," I say. "I watched you die. The crocodile . . ." My breathing is coming too fast for my chest now the reality is slotting together. The body in the arena that was bitten in two was not Vogel. He felt no pain. The screams of death. The wailing. The blood. It wasn't him. It belonged to Prince Malthe.

Prince Malthe is dead.

My mouth drops.

"I thought you didn't hear what I said," I murmur.

"Everyone heard you," he says with a scoff. "You screamed it so loud that the atmosphere shook."

A chuckle gurgles out of my throat, even though I'm half crying that it's really him. That he isn't dead. That he still exists. "So you said the words?"

"I did," he says.

I slide my eyes over his face from his long lashes to his tightly wrought lips. I gather all the pieces between. The dusting of freckles. The scar on his cheek.

"How did you know what would happen?" he asks in a voice that sounds like Malthe, but isn't.

"I see people's auras," I tell him.

"Their auras?"

"These colors that seem to attach to their crowns."

He runs a fingernail over his hands, then trails a palm through the dark wavy hair. "I'm Malthe?" he says.

"You're Vogel," I correct, the reminder jolting him back to the present.

"Anai will be safe," he says, nodding, as if suddenly realizing the extent of his power. "Siella, too. I will tell the soldiers to release them both without alerting the emperor."

"How did you know that Anai was captured?"

"I heard some of the soldiers talking."

"Thank you," I say.

"For what?"

"What you did. The last thing you wanted was to fight for King Rolyo." I chance a step away from the door. "I remember what you said in the basement. You promised me that you would not fight, yet you did for the chance to save those girls." As the prince, Vogel is still tall, but he brings a softness to Malthe's hard eyes. "See, Vogel? I told you before that you were a good person. And I was right."

"You won't let that go," he says with a smile.

"I won't."

"Why?"

"Because," I say. "I have to remind you that I am still me. *Meadow*. The girl from the Gathering that night."

He shakes his head. "I would never forget. I could not forget." He glances away.

I want to feel his arms around me—like in the cell—but I hesitate. I know it's him. There is no question. Of all people, I don't need convincing. And that he's alive when I'd thought he was gone, the happiness of that shreds my resistance.

"Does it seem normal after a while? To exist in a foreign shell?" he asks.

"No," I say. "But it feels more bearable. And when there is someone who remembers your name—your true name—it helps immensely."

I reach him in the middle of the rug. The space between us is barely a space. There's nothing of Malthe in him at all, save for the outside, but Vogel shines through. I wonder if he can see the real me burning brightly from within Astrid's skin.

"Meadow?" he asks.

"Yes?" I whisper.

He takes a step and the space disappears.

"I really thought I was dead," he tells me. "I thought it was my time to go. But when I saw you in the stands, something changed and my mind rebelled." His eyes soften, as he looks at me, confused somehow by what it means. That he wanted to live, despite the grief of watching his family slaughtered before him.

Gently, he laces his fingers through mine, and I glance down at our entwined hands. My heart hammers against my breast-bone as he lifts my palm, touching it to his mouth. And when I gaze at his dark eyes, I don't see brown, I see ice-blue. I don't see Malthe, I see only the boy with the yellow hair who carried a bow. And the way he's looking back at me, he does not see the long-lost princess. He sees the sad young girl from Maytown who ran through the slums with a piece of parchment.

The vibrant blueness whirls around him, showering his shoulders with glittering light. His fingers cradle the side of my face, and I cannot stand it. Not anymore. I stand on my tiptoes, feeling his breath, as his hue brightens, eclipsing his features. In the shadow, he looks like Vogel again. He leans down, pulling me closer, and this time—I can no longer wait.

I crash into him. His lips meet mine. They're warm and soft and my body quakes. He lets his hands glide into my hair as I press against the strength of his chest. I'm lost in him, and he in me. The chamber, the kingdom, it vanishes around us. And all of a sudden, the world makes sense. When it shouldn't at all.

And I'm brought back to life.

My heartbeat thrumming, we pull away, our cheeks flushed as we drag in air. I touch my lip, my shoulders heaving.

"I have to go," he whispers.

"Yes."

His presence here would draw suspicion, and I know he wants to release Anai. I'm unsure what we'll do from here, but I'm no longer scared to search for a way.

He walks to the door with the posture of a Tyjan, but with the gait of Vogel, and gives a shy smile.

"This is not good-bye," he says.

"I sure hope not."

And I know Mistress Howella would be proud.

CHAPTER THIRTY-SEVEN

I T'S LONG AFTER THE SUN HAS DESCENDED WHEN KALLIOPE SNEAKS to my chamber with Freya. I am in bed, but wide-awake, a candle burning on the edge of the mantel.

"Get dressed," Kalliope hisses at me as Freya shuffles to the cabinet for a frock. "I need to show you where the safe house resides so you'll know what to do when I have gone." Her pitch betrays no fear for her future. Only mine. So she's pretending again.

"I'll wear what I'm in," I say.

"Your night garments?"

"At least with a cloak," says Freya with a huff. She detangles one from the other robes and passes the bulky apparel to me. I dare not argue, slipping it on.

"Come quietly along now," Kalliope whispers.

Like forgotten spirits who are trapped between worlds, we waft through the empty halls. I'm surprised we do not pass any servants as we maneuver the courtyard that had once been my prison. Outside a carriage is waiting for us, helmed at the reins by Pelletier and Errol. Kalliope and I climb inside, leaving Freya on the grass to fasten the door.

Torches blaze along the bridge, their orange flames reflected in the reed-strewn lake. I expect the soldiers to ask of our business, but they let us pass without any questions. I wonder if Gyzen is the cause of our ease as he stands with his comrades, not the least bit concerned. I do notice him glance at Kalliope, though I would have missed it had I not known to look.

The journey is a long one. Kalliope narrates a little, imparting the names of various villages that I have no hope of remembering.

"Freya and Gyzen have documents," she tells me. "They are coded, of course, but they can assist you with your organization."

"Is that not a tiny bit dangerous?" I ask.

"The whole thing is dangerous," she says. "But without the documents, we have no way of recalling the people we saved, where they have been resettled, and what story we have fabricated to keep them safe. In the end, the documents serve as our own protection." A sharpness has crept into her tone. "We know what we are doing, Astrid. I promise you that."

I do not doubt it.

"This safe house," I say. "How many does it harbor in total?"

"As many as we require at any given time," says Kalliope. "Hopefully my father will curb my brother's nightly activities with his patrolmen, especially if Gyzen has a say in it, but it could get worse after he lost face at the Victoreglia. There may be more innocents that he locks in the Nothrick Prison. And the two girls he has in his tower . . . I do not believe King Rolyo will save them."

I wish I could ease her mind about Malthe and tell her he's inhabited by a kinder soul. But explaining what happened would be far too risky, however much I have come to trust her.

As the city whips by, we sink into silence. We've covered a mammoth distance already. Nudging my back into the cushions, I stare at the shadows engulfing the stonework. Perhaps we've ventured to the city's far east. I'm unfamiliar with these surroundings. There are plenty of homes, and outdoor latrine pits, and muddy pathways plugged up with thistles.

We bump around another bend, dipping under a bridge that is crumbling with age. A quaint little village spans before us with stonebricks built in well-ordered rows. Our carriage rolls into a ditch—and stops. We're hidden behind a thicket of trees. Pelletier opens the door for us, and the princess motions for me to move.

I oblige, stepping down from the carriage, pulling the cloak tight to my shoulders. The servants remain to guard the horses as I follow Kalliope across the grass.

She's made this journey before. Perchance on a regular basis. It's easy to tell by the way she corkscrews, keeping the pace like a seasoned explorer. We wind past taverns and through old chicken yards, which contain the remnants of half-formed turnips. We duck below a jungle of branches, marching briskly along deserted lanes. The cover of darkness conceals us well. No one stops to gape at our presence. Finally, we arrive in front of a stonebrick that looks no different from the thousand others. Tall panels screen the windows and the entrance board is hidden by pots.

Kalliope taps quietly on the door. Twice to show me the secret knock.

Bang. Bang-bang-bang. Bang-bang.

The large board shifts and an eye peeks out.

Kalliope presses her face to the crack and, a moment later, the door creaks ajar. She beckons me to follow her in, so I squeeze through the entrance and halt in the hallway. It's dim and dusty and terribly enclosed with the faintest scent of log ash and cabbage. As we turn and enter a second room, four solid walls and stale air greet us. I feel like a moth inside a cupboard, forgotten among the cups and dishes.

With a thud, the hefty door slams shut. A girl lights a candle and sets it down. There's nothing in here but a stark wooden table that's scratched and neglected upon the stones.

"Lilly," Kalliope says to the girl, spreading her arms to embrace her close. "This is the one we told you about. Her Royal Highness, Princess Astrid."

As Lilly absorbs my name and my face, I do the same. She's stocky and short. Her dark hair falls in waves to her shoulders.

But I've heard that name mentioned before . . .

Lilly.

"She used to be my Grande Personale." Kalliope pats the girl on the arm. "I brought her here in absolute secret. She is one of the only people I trust."

Lilly seems awed by the company of Astrid.

"I am honored," she says. "I'd heard you returned."

"Lilly is known as Portia," says Kalliope. "It is one of the ways we protect her identity, since she is a former servant."

Lilly curtseys to show her respect. She wears the plain clothes of the village folk. I wonder how she has taken the news that Kalliope is leaving and I will take over.

"How is Tallesa?" she asks the princess. "Does she ask of me often?"

"She does," says Kalliope.

Lilly touches a hand to her throat. "I shouldn't have left without saying I loved her."

So Lilly left at Kalliope's request to live in the safe house and manage affairs? No wonder Tallesa was suspicious of "Mollie" and was loathe to welcome her into the villa.

There's a frantic knock on the door behind us, and Lilly leaves to answer the summons.

"Why can't Tallesa know?" I ask.

"She cannot keep secrets," Kalliope says. As Lilly vanishes into the hall, the princess lowers her voice to a whisper. "It's been hard for Lilly. She's in love with Tallesa—more so now than she was in the palace. Absence has made her heart grow fonder, and she may beg you to bring in Tallesa. But although Lilly is very dependable, I would caution you not to tell many others. If the emperor suspects anything at all, you will be watched—and that helps no one."

At that instant, Lilly returns. Her eyes are wide, and her face is pale.

"I'm sorry. Could you excuse me a moment?"

"What has happened?" Kalliope asks.

"A man has bolted," Lilly says. "It's the same one who ran this morning. Since the executions, he's been trying to escape, though he can't roam far in his current condition."

"We can help you locate him," Kalliope says. She turns to me. "Sometimes they run. They try to leave because they think it is safer."

"I do apologize for this," says Lilly.

We depart the tiny cramped room and slip back out the entrance door. I ponder how long the man's been hiding, shut away from the sunshine and fresh air. Naturally, people would try to flee, desperate to return to their old lives.

"We normally don't house men," says Kalliope. "But sometimes, things happen, and it can't be avoided."

One by one, we enter the street, trying to playact that we are not searching. A few people from nearby stonebricks peek from their cloth-covered windows with interest. We obscure our heads, our footsteps measured, meandering wisely in different directions. I tug to the left and the right and the side, gradually losing myself in the dimness.

I keep walking.

The shadows heighten and the tapered passages curl like warrens. The stench of waste grows ever stronger, the cobblestones shining with liquid and sludge. I lift my hem clear of the surface, though it's already covered in moisture and muck. I wonder how I will ever do this, especially when the princess is gone.

But I keep walking.

Before long, I hear the panting of someone ahead. It sounds like the deep inflections of pain, of a wretched soul who can barely move. I continue to follow the ragged noise, turning corners here and there, jogging up and down laneways. I come upon a man by a wall, his hand resting against a fissure.

"Are you all right?"

He wheezes softly, his upper body bent as he drags in air. As he clutches his side, glancing up in defeat, a sliver of moonlight catches his face.

I freeze. It cannot be. It *can't*. He's like an oasis in the middle of a drought. Why is he here in this darkened alley? How is he here after all this time? And I race before I can stop myself. I plunge to my knees, my chest shaking. Extending my arms around his body, I sob like a child who has finally been found.

The man hasn't the energy to run and he stands still. What must he see? An odd girl with bright blonde hair sitting in the dirt, tears coating her face. He lets out a grunt. "What is wrong?" he asks in a voice so familiar that my heart smithereens.

"Father," I whisper.

"My dear," he says. "I do not know whom your father may be—"

"It's me. Meadow." I hold him tighter.

"Meadow?" he asks.

"Yes, it is me."

"Are you a ghost?" he asks.

"No."

"You must be," he says, detaching my arms. "My daughter was killed in the Emperor's Quadrant."

I shake my head. "I did not die."

"Stop this," he says, turning away. His features crumple, and I hate it so much. But he's here. Alive. With me at last. And I know if I push, he will understand.

"You live in Maytown," I say. "In a stonebrick. You had a wife from Leeang called Pearl. After she passed from the wilting sickness, you set her afloat on the waves of the Geynes."

I can see from my father's rigid expression that he does not like that I know these things. I watch him struggle for an explanation.

"We tried to save her," I say.

"Stop." He holds out a shaky hand to shush me. "This does not mean that you are my daughter. Who are you? One that works for Portia?"

"No," I say.

"Do not speak of my family."

But despite his anger, I don't give up. "We fed my mother yarrow from the river. We crushed it in bowls and dissolved it in water. She drank it to stop the incessant coughing." I press my lips, the next part hard. "When she died, my heart filled up with hate. I truly believed that she could have been saved if the Tyjans imported an herb called zyphene."

My father jaw twitches at that. "What do you know about zyphene?"

"That it was a cure for the wilting sickness. Or I thought it was."

He breathes out. "I do not know how you know so much. I really don't. But the truth is this: my daughter, Meadow, believed in zyphene—even though zyphene did not exist."

"You knew it didn't exist?" I ask.

"I knew the wilting sickness was fatal."

"But you let her believe that her mother could be saved?"

"I let her deal with what happened to her mother in any way she chose," he says. He pauses, as if he's suddenly aware that he's said too much to a stranger in a lane. But then, he continues. "Deep down she knew the truth, but I think she just needed someone to blame."

Tears well in my eyes, and I nod. He's right, of course. I know that now. I wouldn't have listened to a word against zyphene. I was so sad and angry and confused that she died so quickly, that nothing could be done. So he let me have it. He stood well back, waiting for me to emerge from the fog. I don't know how he managed to be patient—or how he knew it was what I'd needed.

"Thank you," I say, straightening up, letting his words soak through my skin. As painful as it is to reflect on the past, hearing his voice makes me feel less alone.

We stand together, wrapped in the quiet, the gloom of the buildings preserving the moment. My father's eyes regard me again, and I sense that something has altered within him.

"There is something about you," he says. "May I ask you some questions?"

"Of course," I say.

"What is the nickname that I gave to my daughter?"

"Paddock," I say.

He quietly laughs. The sound of it makes my tears spill over. It reminds me of strolling with him at the wharves.

"Who was my daughter's best friend?"

"Anai."

"And what did my daughter aspire to be?"

I'm taken aback. My aspirations? They liquefied when my mother died. But before that, what did I live for? Working at the markets? Falling in love?

No.

I touch my cheek. I was lost.

"I didn't know. I couldn't decide."

"What did she save of her mother's possessions?"

"A tapestry of a blossoming rose. She sewed it when you and I went fishing. She didn't like the water, so she'd sit on the grass. She'd bury her feet to her ankles in the sand to hinder the burn from the middle day sun."

His eyebrows furrow, and I know I've got him. We never told anyone about that rose. He tentatively glides a hand to my shoulder. "Am I asleep? This cannot be real."

I tell him about the swapping of bodies. How I journeyed through the kingdom to the camp in the valley. I watch his face change from sadness, to wonder, and all the shades that lie in between.

"But . . ." He shakes his head. "Is it magic?"

"I have to believe it is," I say.

"And you're happy," he asks, "in this new body?"

"I do not know how else to be." It shocks me a bit that I say that to him, as though losing myself isn't so bad. "So you believe what I'm saying?"

"I don't know fully. But for some reason, it does feel like you." Pain crosses my father's face, but he reels it in. "Do others know?"

"Only one."

"And are you safe?"

"I think I am at the moment," I tell him.

He relaxes at that, but then he shifts, and the bandage circling his hip peels away. The gash has been mended with neat little stitches, but it pouches apart when he rests on his foot.

"You're the one who's unsafe," I scold. "Running out here when you're not fully healed? Terribly reckless if you want my opinion."

"What would you have me do?" he asks.

My heart zips that he wants my advice, though I try to keep my expression neutral. I sigh. "Don't run. Recover in the safe house. Which reminds me, how did you manage to get here?"

"I was brought here straight from the Tournament," he says. He looks at me, suddenly realizing that perhaps I don't know that he was a spare. But before he can tell me what I already know, the voice of Lilly carries through the streets, so I shake my head and take his hand.

"You can tell me about it later." I drape his arm across my shoulder. We trudge back along the laneways, popping out at the cobbled road near the safe house. Kalliope and Lilly see us at once and swoop on my father at a dignified pace. Fortunately for him, they cannot start yelling, due to the villagers roaming the street.

After curt whispers have been exchanged, Princess Kalliope turns to me.

"We should be heading back now," she says.

I look at my father, and he nods in agreement. He's aware I'll return, so I give him a smile, not wanting to go, but knowing I need to. It's the hardest thing to abandon him here, but he squeezes my hand to give me the courage.

So I go.

"This work will suit you," says Kalliope as we hurry through the fields beneath the shimmer of moonlight. An owl hoots in the distance somewhere, and strangely, I think that it could be the truth. "But you may need others to help in the future, so you must make certain you can trust them first."

"How?" I ask, still thinking of my father.

"Usually with time," Kalliope says. She winds between trees. "There was a girl at the villa. We brought her to stay from the Nothrick Prison."

My ears prick up at that. "A girl?"

"Yes. We thought she might assist us. Gyzen believed she displayed the qualities of someone fearless in the face of peril."

In awe, I realize she's talking of me.

Me.

Meadow.

"What happened?" I ask.

"We failed to save her." The princess frowns, wringing her hands beside her skirt. "It's hard. Sometimes bad things happen. Such awful things we cannot prevent." She looks at me closely. "But I'll push on, and so must you—and we'll find the cracks. And one day, Astrid, things will change. I feel it here." She taps her heart.

And as we reach the carriage, I finally understand that this journey has not all been in vain. Yes, it may be true that my mother could never have been saved. And yes, it may be true that I am stuck in a strange body and can never reclaim my old one. But without me going to the Gathering that night as a reaction to my grief for someone I had loved and lost, so many things would not have transpired to get me here now. To set me on this course.

And I know that I would have loved to have wandered a different path. A path where both my mother and my father lived to old age in our stonebrick in Maytown. But I also know that my mother's death has forced me to rise when I otherwise would have cowered—and she would be proud.

Her stars have shifted to a new, unchartered universe.

And so have mine.

Acknowledgements

Enormous gratitude to the following people . . .

To my husband, Matt: Thank you for reading my chapters, gently reminding me to back up my documents and always believing that I could do this. Your confidence in me is astounding. I love you.

To my parents, Colin and Helen: Thank you for being the greatest parents anyone could ask for. You have always encouraged me to choose the path that makes me happy, which is why I never gave up the dream to be a writer. Thank you for everything.

To my sister, Nat: Thank you for being someone I have always been able to look up to.

To Ivone, Jo and Elly: Thanks for being my biggest supporters and the absolute best friends in the world.

To my writer pals Kara Thomas, Kate Boorman, Jennifer Walkup and Dana Alison Levy: Thanks for the tough love and reassuring words as I worked on this book. (Especially to Kara, who read the first chapter so many times I'm surprised she still speaks to me!)

To the LBs: Thanks for being my writerly corner of the universe. Special shout outs to Sarah, Janine, Shari, Jenn (again!) and Dawn, who read early chapters and were super encouraging.

To Marinda Valenti: Thanks for being an extraordinary editor. Your guidance during this process was invaluable, and I know we'll work together again!

Huge thanks to Jenny Zemanek, Stacey Blake, Jessica Khoury and Brittany Wang for all your help along the way!

And finally to you, the reader: Thank you for taking a chance and picking up *A Shifting of Stars*. Telling stories is something I love to do, and I'm so grateful that I was able to share this book with you!

DID YOU ENJOY THIS BOOK?

You can help!

Reviews help authors spread word about their books to new readers.

If you enjoyed reading *A Shifting of Stars*,
please consider leaving a review on the book's Amazon page.

Thank you!

BECOME A MEMBER

Want to be first in line to hear about Kathy's book news?

Want the chance to read Kathy's upcoming novels
before their release dates?

Want to grab some Of Stars freebies?

Become a Member on Kathy Kimbray's website:
www.kathykimbray.com

About the Author

Kathy Kimbray is a YA author from Australia.

After graduating from the University of Technology, Sydney, with a degree in Media Arts and Production, she went on to complete postgraduate studies in education and spent many years as a primary school teacher.

Now a full-time novelist, Kathy is lucky to be able to tell stories every day.

Aside from writing, Kathy is an avid reader, dancer, language learner, musical theater enthusiast and fan of terrible reality TV. She lives with her husband in Sydney, and dreams of one day owning that elusive chateau in France.

Visit her at: www.kathykimbray.com

Made in the USA
Monee, IL
04 January 2020

19820332R00224